Mystical Consequences

by

M. Flagg

The Champion Chronicles, Book 2

Mystical Consequences

COPYRIGHT © 2023 by M. Flagg

Cover Art by *Rae Monet, Inc.*

The Wild Rose Press, Inc.
PO Box 708
Adams Basin, NY 14410-0708
Visit us at www.thewildrosepress.com

Publishing History
First Edition, 2023
Trade Paperback ISBN 978-1-5092-5128-5
Digital ISBN 978-1-5092-5129-2

The Champion Chronicles, Book 2
Published in the United States of America

Knots curdling in her stomach didn't go away. They tightened like a vise to choke her soul.

Holding on to the wooden footboard, Alana just stood there. She had memorized everything about tonight including his screams. Like flaming arrows arching through the sky, they had pierced her aching heart. Only one other night, when a different terror changed her life, had she felt paralyzed like this...

Just like thousands of times before, she relived the pleasure and the pain. What started with a kiss quickly surged to synchronized desire. That night, raw need had her heart racing with anticipation... Michael's touch had been too enticing. Forbidden love led to an ecstasy never dreamed possible, before or since.

"Every detail still haunts me, my love." Drawn to him, she moved closer. She wanted to soothe him. She wanted to scream at him. A crooked finger brushed his cheek, not knowing which 'want' would win.

"Why did you do this? Look at you...pasty skin, eyelids sunken and black. High cheekbones so bruised and hollow...sword wounds, broken ribs, clawed crevices and a shoulder bite so raw and...Oh, God. You wanted to destroy yourself. You wanted to leave me forever." His thin lips, so sensual, so kissable and cool, had no color.

She backed away even though outraged at what had been done to him. Leave him now, she thought, don't give in to this crushing need. And how you still tug at my soul...

Her resolve crumbled like a house made of cards.

Praise for M. Flagg

"A fresh voice in paranormal has arrived."~N.N. Light's Book Heaven

"Flagg's writing style varies from exquisite word choice and imagery in many descriptions to the simplistic in other situations." ~ *Bitten by Books*

[His Soul to Keep] - "This novel makes you want more and more. I highly recommend it if you love a wonderful sci-fi plot along with your romance!"~ *All Romance E-Books (5 of 5)*

[Night of the Crescent Moon] - "I couldn't stop turning the page. I love vampires and M. Flagg delivered. Martine carried the story and never let go. Unrequited love buried so deep as to become unrecognizable and all too human emotions in this paranormal world make Night of the Crescent Moon a must read!" ~ *Linda J. Parisi, Author of the Blood Rogue Series, 2022 HOLT Medallion Winner for Honorable Rogue*

Dedication

This book is dedicated to my family and friends who encouraged me to write my stories about redemption and love. I'd be nothing without all of you.

Prologue

One vain-glorious battle with one sole purpose: Retribution.

Eight days in a poisoned state. Eight days of a fantasy that forced a vampire to survive. His mind had twisted on the precipice of insanity. He did what he had to do for the love of his Guardian, for the love of his human son. Anguish beyond endurance shattered his soul into tiny fractals. None of which insured his rescue.

Yet the angel had found him, had guided his mind in a melodrama of comfort and hope. *Mystically enhanced, one of kind...* The vampire knew these descriptions to be truth. With loss of comfort and hope, an opaque darkness had descended. His body bled dry, yet he survived. This was another truth. And through the eyes of the angel, Michael Malone sensed many more truths would follow if he could only find the courage to face what he had done.

Broken in spirit, his mind had forced reality farther away. Too unnerved to accept his destiny, he had told the heavenly entity, *"Let me die."* There would be no healing. There would be no sense of stillness in his guilty soul. He would never face the consequences of his undead deeds. His preference? An end to his existence. An eternity in the fires of Hell.

Part One – Healing

Chapter 1

Alana Ciminio sensed true terror in Michael Malone's soul, as well as unrelenting agony. No ability to smell, hear, or speak. Total paralysis. She prayed he would recognize *his* Guardian's heartbeat, the slow, steady rhythm a reassurance of his rescue from evil unleashed. Her warm breath bathed his brow, and she kept him wrapped in a fierce embrace.

On this necessary flight away from Manhattan to Portofino, her eyes had not closed. She clung to the battered body of the vampire she would always love. The mind can race out of worry—out of fury. In flight for hours, she hadn't ventured out of Michael's makeshift shelter. Staring past the two demon specialists, the private jet's bedroom didn't appear all that luxurious with bags of blood, computer screens beeping, and a hazmat bag filled with the vampire's bloody clothes.

Soon he'll be safe, safe from NWT, safe *from Clayton Mails, the sorcerers' sniveling liaison who dared to do this to the creature that still has my heart.* After the specialists had cleaned and sutured every wound to encourage self-healing, she still refused to let him go. *Michael has to know he's in my arms and finally safe.*

****

A comfortable living room took up the wide midsection of the remodeled private jet, but Miles Bookman sat uneasy, mumbling under his breath, "Turbulence. Good Lord, just what I need." The Researcher for the Georgian Circle didn't like to fly. He stared at the new blank document on his laptop, which should be his latest journal entry as the Medico Research Labs private transport started its descent over the Amalfi Coast. He stared at the date: May 30, 2005. Other than that? *Nothing... I bloody well don't even know where to start with this event. And blasted turbulence!*

From the couch, his daughter Celia gave an understanding smile. "We're going to be safely landing soon, Dad."

Acutely aware of her immense psychic ability, nothing eased Miles's fear of flying, even though he appreciated the attempt. He searched her bright-green eyes. "Is that a wish or a vision, honey?" Like all aboard this secret flight, Celia looked exhausted snuggling closer to Thorn, the burly empath who had been Michael's loyal companion for the past seven years.

"Come on, Daddy B, Cesar's home-in-the-sky is state-of-the-art. I don't foresee a fireball in our future. Michael's safe, and so are we all. And we now know how Thorn had some heavenly help to stay in his mind for eight days—until Michael couldn't fight the poison in his system anymore and shut down. We have loads of info that will—"

"You realize this is a mystical intervention of colossal proportions, honey." Days would pass before Miles could even begin to piece it all together. But as for his initial report, he simply didn't know where to start.

Leaning his head back against the leather chair, Miles took a steady breath as he repositioned his reading glasses on the bridge of his nose. *Thorn will hand over a detailed description of what occurred in Manhattan. Almost seven uneventful years and now this… one night of chaos and eight days of a poisoned mind's rants and raves. Michael has many issues to answer for.*

Over thirty years of experience dissecting and cataloging paranormal events, and for once, his fingers remained frozen over the laptop's keyboard. Impatience had him as uncomfortable as being strapped into a seat thousands of feet in the air.

Fortunately, the rescue had been a complete success. Miles had spent only minutes with Alana, his adopted daughter, during the flight from a private airport in New Jersey. Since his rescue, she had not left the vampire's side. Later, he'd document how it was Alana's precise strategy that had made Michael's rescue from the bowels of the New World Technologies building in Manhattan a complete win. But the mystically-enhanced vampire? He was exsanguinated, close to unrecognizable, his injuries extensive. In addition, an unknown poison had utterly destroyed Michael's nervous system making a full recovery doubtful. After another sharp exhale, his gaze slid to Lukas Malone. Another mystery—the vampire's human son, he thought, a truly troubled boy.

Little if any documentation existed to explain how a vampire could father a human child. For the past year, Lukas, who turned fifteen on the night of the mayhem in the city, had been missing. Appearing asleep in a plush recliner, he was well aware that the slender teen's relaxed pose hid edginess as well as a very anxious mind. That this boy had the same mystical abilities as his unnatural father made him all the more dangerous. That this child had the face of an angel and the rage of a demon made him all the more unpredictable.

"So what's the first thing you tell the Council when we land, Miles?" Thorn asked, which pulled him out of his thoughts.

Hesitating before being utterly candid, he replied, "I have absolutely no idea. Feel free to jump in with a brilliant thought any time."

Sitting across from him, the burly man gave a gentle shrug. "You might want to start with the obvious. The Georgians have monitored Michael ever since he was sired. Skip two centuries of the drink and drain and begin where he gets reacquainted with his conscience in 1890, which tagged him mystically enhanced and put him on your Sovereign Council's radar. He should be their Number One with a bullet. Does that help?"

"All relevant issues, which the Council already knows." He stared at the blank page, an uncharacteristic issue, which couldn't be blamed on his fear of flying.

"Well, at least we now know why he did it, Dad. This is a psychic's field day," Celia stated with a quick glance at Lukas, the apparent reason for Michael's unfettered revenge ten nights ago.

"I agree, and there's much, much more, Miles." Thorn added in a hushed tone, "When Celia and I finish documenting the eight days of dream scenes, you'll have it all."

He typed *"proof of manipulation"* and then

"Michael Malone did not expect to survive."

Thorn gave a serious nod, which matched his serious expression. "Now you're cookin'. Tell me again how this sanctuary thing works? What happens first?"

Curled in the plush chair next to him, Lukas's deep-blue eyes remained closed, but his curious ears had to be wide open, the researcher assumed. "Mystical healers have been summoned." That's all he gave—verbally. The rest? The empath could glean from his mind. *Their involvement is another rarity for examination. The good sisters aren't usually so hands-on, but what Michael did in Manhattan to disrupt evil could be classified as close to miraculous.*

"Nothing surprises me anymore," Thorn replied, the weary edge to his voice duly noted.

Eight days in Michael's mind had taken a toll on the empath. Miles was positive. Thorn appeared haggard and tense. He'd lost weight and his paunch was gone… mysteriously replaced with muscle. His broad face was thinner as well. As Thorn and Celia fastened their seat belts, he wondered how much more gray would soon grace his aching temples because of Michael's selfish revenge. Before this was over, he saw his thinning hair more salt than pepper.

The laptop closed, although he still held it tight in a white-knuckled grip. He tried to swallow, hoping to squelch his anxiety as the engines roared and the wheels hit the ground on a private airstrip outside of La Spezia, Italy. Only after the plane taxied into the last hangar of the small airport did his grip finally loosen.

****

A roll-away ramp was set in place as soon as the door opened. Miles exited first to greet Cesar Gonzalez, the owner of Medico Research Labs in Florence. The Georgian Sovereign Council member had once been a Guardian of Souls who served his mystical ten-year mission in 1970s Spain. Cesar's mentor, a local doctor, taught the mystical warrior how to fight demons of the night and how to stitch a wound with precision. When released from his mystical mission at age twenty-six, Cesar had breezed through med school, eventually founding the internationally acclaimed company, a forerunner in the study of infectious diseases.

But Cesar also employed scientists of another kind. The kind that knew the reality of vampire attacks, of demons conjured by sorcerers—many unnatural things the typical human didn't know existed.

In one corner of the hangar, a white truck idled. Ground crew, all of them Georgians, locked the private hangar's reinforced metal doors. The engines whirred down as Cesar approached, placing an American passport in his hand. Miles studied the photo inside. "This is perfect."

Cesar gave a nod. "The Georgian network is indeed vast and talented."

Then Miles motioned Lukas over. Although the boy looked years younger than his age, every council member was well aware of Lukas's dangerously unpredictable nature, Cesar included. The way the boy eyed Thorn again wasn't kind, and the way Lukas kept a discreet distance from everyone was unsettling. Right after take-off, the boy had cringed and cursed while Celia turned his unruly sandy-blond curls a soft-brunette. It took two cans of sable-brown highlight spray, which smelled awful, but the superficial disguise would get Michael's son through customs and to

Alana's home without raising suspicion—in the event they were being watched.

Cesar handed Lukas the forged passport. "Do you remember what Mister Bookman discussed with you before you left Manhattan? It's necessary to keep your true identity hidden."

Lukas eyed the doctored photo. "I know—I mean I understand."

"Security is tight even in this private airport. As far as Italian officials are concerned, Evan Bookman is your nephew, Miles, on holiday with you in Portofino."

He nodded as Lukas shrugged before tucking the passport into the back pocket of his khaki pants. Now on solid ground, the researcher's anxiety level reduced significantly. But full-blown concern remained as Miles's focus shifted back to the open door of the plane.

****

Alana came down the ramp not at all sure she was really ready for this. Her lips were drawn tight and every muscle in her body tense. Highly trained demon specialists had cared for Michael during the flight—in any way they could. Now Doctor Chamberlain's assistant guided the stretcher down the ramp which was locked to the jet's open door. Strapped to it was a thick body bag containing Michael. She scrutinized the placement of the body bag into a bio-hazard locker, the length of the white truck. A flashy metallic sign *Hot Tubs of Rome* lined the truck's sides.

"It takes a different route to Portofino, Alana, just in case," Cesar stated.

"I'm sure my aunt has a-a story ready if questioned." The truck's sign would satisfy any nosey neighbors who might see it pull into her garage. *Lord only knows just how many old Italian ladies are sitting outside chattering away and enjoying the beautiful May day.*

Although reluctant to leave Michael, Alana followed Cesar to a dark-blue stretch limousine with everyone else already seated inside. Celia, Thorn, and Michael's son sat facing them. Miles, her adopted father, made room for her next to him. Then Cesar settled in and closed the door. "God, just let him get there without anything happening," she whispered.

When they pulled past airport security without incident, Cesar leaned in to her. "All will continue to go smoothly. Michael's out of danger, and you should know that Philip is safe as well."

She turned to him. "The car accident? Did NWT buy it?"

"A good friend in Jersey pulled it off without a hitch. DNA results will confirm the body is Philip Segallo, a thirty-year-old new employee of NWT in Manhattan."

"I need to be sure. Philip was crucial in extricating Michael."

Her adopted father took her hand. "He'll have a new identity upon his arrival in Italy tomorrow. All records will prove our Philip died at dawn in a fiery crash while speeding off the George Washington Bridge and onto Route 80 West. His burned remains will be laid to rest in Saint Nicholas Cemetery."

"I believe that as Brother Thomas Quinones, a novice monk at San Marco Abbey, he will find peace and safety in Italy." Cesar added, "Like Lukas's, Philip's papers are meticulous."

"*Gracias, Senor.*" It was all she could say. She gave a thin smile and took a quick glance at Lukas, who looked nothing at all like his commanding father. Michael was broad of shoulder and tall with angular features and thick, wavy brown hair on the longish side. Lukas, who had just turned fifteen was small for his age, wiry with a mop of blond curls and a round face that had almost delicate features. But it was the boy's deep dimples and eyes of royal-blue that stood out. No. He doesn't look at all like his father, she thought, very wary about Michael's current state. Fear thundered through her chest. One blood tear had been all the response she'd gotten from Michael on the plane. It wasn't enough to convince her he'd ever come back from this.

Eight days of poison in his system and left with festering wounds. Michael's sanity will be questioned, and Lukas's lack of trust means trouble. If and when he came out of this, she wanted to know everything about his son, about this ridiculous revenge even if it took days of explaining. Because whether or not anyone wanted to admit it, Michael's actions had just changed everybody's world—and perhaps, not in a good way.

"So, dear Alana, how is your new life in Portofino?"

Cesar's question reeled in her thoughts. "My home is totally gorgeous and living upstairs from my *Zia* is a dream. I don't miss the city. Thank you, again. But that's not what's on your mind."

He gave a slow shake of his head. "Removing Michael from under Clayton's nose will have profound repercussions. I'm sure."

Her throat tightened before she blew out a slow

breath. "Clayton Mails is as good as dead when higher-up evil learns he signed the order to incinerate Michael's body."

"A fitting end and much-deserved," the ex-Guardian replied.

Her mind was jumping all over the place. "I know you helped *Zia* push through the Petition of Intervention. Monsignor Scarlatti gave the go-ahead, but—"

"The Council is aware of the Champion's history, both the good and the evil. So is every Georgian throughout the world."

She turned and snagged her adopted father's attention, "But giving sanctuary to a creature of the night has never been allowed."

"Close your eyes and rest, honey," he whispered.

As the limo sped down the two-lane highway, Lukas's blank expression bothered her. Seated next to Celia, he hadn't said one single word. "Your father accomplished something totally unbelievable. Every Guardian should be grateful. His reasons may be a mystery but the end result is extraordinary, right?" Alana hoped for a response, but got none before whispering to her father, "Will the Council see this rescue as part of the cosmic order of things or simply my stubborn need to save the vampire I once loved?"

He leaned in close. "This event obliterated an immortal Triumvirate of Evil and shut down dimensional portals they have lorded over for a millennium, honey."

"The Council has to view our rescuing him as a necessity, Dad. North America no longer has any sinister umbilical cords to Hell... at least none that we know of." Her head sank back into the soft leather seat as she sighed. Since arriving in the city two days ago, she'd gotten very little sleep. Her father's arm came up and around her shoulders drawing her to him. He had to be as exhausted as she was, and she relaxed against him with another sigh. "Daddy B, this is a nightmare. Are you sure they'll help him?" Feeling his nod, his kiss to her hair never failed to soothe.

"Michael and Lukas now have precedence over all other matters before the Council. Sanctuary is guaranteed, honey. I have it on good word that Guardians across the United States are already destroying demons trapped in our dimension as a new day dawns—because of what he did."

Cut, slashed, bruised, bled out and pierced... No. He'd never be the same after this. "He wrestled back his soul over a hundred years ago. That alone makes him worthy of sanctuary."

"Shhh…rest."

It was a gentle order, but she couldn't comply. "What about his connection to me and what went down between us?"

"That was years ago."

But it was always on her mind as if it was a scar on her skin. A constant reminder. She realized she had sailed way past fatigue. No sleep in over forty-eight hours, no peace of mind until Philip had placed Michael in her arms. A sense of uncertainty settled in her.

"Monsignor Scarlatti is a very compassionate man, Alana," her father whispered.

Evil won't touch him here. Evil won't sense him here. Her eyelids fluttered and her shoulders relaxed. But what ran through her mind felt like an Alpine avalanche—unstoppable, unpredictable.

Two nights ago, she had prodded Celia B about the days-long incredulous dream of survival. Her adopted sister had only offered disjointed smatterings but managed to confirm that Michael definitely owned the building she now called home. That particular revelation had been a surprise. He still loved her. She was certain. But after ten years of hunting demons in Manhattan, after fulfilling her mystical mission, she had craved a clean break. And when her great-aunt made the suggestion, she moved to Italy, she saw it as a heaven-sent chance to change her life. It gave her hope that 'normal' might not be out of her reach.

Alana had to distance herself and being an ocean away from Michael Malone sounded perfect. With her love for the handsome vampire buried down deep, leading a normal life was now possible. But just before pulling off the once-in-a-lifetime, gutsy rescue Celia B had insisted, "Admit it, Ally, you still love him."

What she felt was more than love. For the past eleven years, like it or not, the truth was that Michael Malone was entrenched in her soul.

Chapter 2

The limo pulled up to the back of 52 Via Amadeus in the scenic seaport of Portofino. Attached brick buildings with small specialty stores lined the front of this particular street off the piazza. As the garage door opened, Alana's body still throbbed from every nerve-wrecking minute she'd lived through during the last ten days. Pulling herself off her adopted father's chest, she whispered, "Take Lukas up with Thorn and Celia and get him settled in. I'll wait for the truck alone."

Cesar left her in the back seat and got in the front with the driver while everyone disappeared into the darkness of the garage. Hearing the whir of the elevator, she closed her eyes once more.

Michael had spared no expense in renovating and furnishing her new home. His taste, in every facet of the remodel, of turning two apartments into one grand living space, had been exquisite and bold. Modern appliances, rich subtle colors, air-conditioning... Stylish furniture filled every room of her home. Original masterpieces graced every wall. A private elevator opened onto a rose-colored marble foyer at the back of her residence from the garage behind the first-floor's trendy bookstore. Every renovation was top quality and stunning.

And everything had been done *before* she arrived last September.

Zia Rosa, her great-aunt on her mother's side,

presented her with priceless, hand-crocheted curtains. They softened and deflected the strong rays of Mediterranean sunshine in the expanded dining and living room, which was now a spacious great room with a wide wooden arch between them. During daylight, the unique curtains appeared as if illuminated by the angels themselves. At night, dark shutters attached to the outside bricks allowed different details to emerge. *Stunning works of art crafted by my grandmother decades ago. Intricate scenes created thread by thread of the hills surrounding my home. Of all the things on my mind, why am I thinking about those curtains right now?* Well, at least it brought a small smile to her lips as she opened her eyes. And for the past ten days, there hadn't been a reason to do that. At all.

Another revelation from Michael's languid dream came to mind. As soon as she heard it from Celia B, and still waiting for the Council to approve her plan, she went down to the vacant apartment across from *Zia* and easily ripped off a padlock on the door. Then she sent Monsignor Scarlatti a specific list of items to furnish it. Exactly half the size of her home, the cozy apartment would be safe and comfortable—for Michael and Lukas.

It took over a week for the Georgian Council's approval to extract him, so she dedicated entire days to shopping in Pisa to keep her mind off her rescue plan. The apartment now had everything a person needed. Besides household items and furniture, she picked out soft Italian leather loafers for Michael to wear and multiple pairs of expensive silk pajamas—all black, all for him. She shopped for casual clothes he eventually would need. Black jeans and dark shirts were his favorite style. Her small red car, another 'anonymous' gift, looked like Santa's sleigh after each spending spree.

In Michael's master bedroom, *Zia* helped her hang dark-navy, lined brocade drapes over the wall with two windows. All the shutters had been locked tight to shield every room from sunlight. The day before she left for Manhattan, a masculine sleigh bed arrived. It perfectly suited the commanding creature she loved. Trimmed in ebony wood, it stood high off the ground with cushioned panels set into a massive headboard. And for Lukas's room, twin beds and a desk were waiting. It gave her time to think while decorating the apartment—and it also gave her an outlet for the worry and concern that rumbled through her soul.

A tap on the window made her jump and jarred her out of memories. Thorn indicated that the truck had backed into the garage. *Okay, now for the hard part because no one's going to like my decision, but with any luck, they'll give me a chance to explain later— much later.*

Her stomach rolled as she approached Doctor John Baker and Thorn at the elevator. They each held an end of the body bag and rode up in silence. As the doors opened on a rose-marble foyer, Thorn gave her a very quizzical look, tilting his head but not shaking it with a curt, "No. Don't do this, dear Guardian."

Without further explanation, she simply said, "Please follow me," and led them through the hall with exquisite Florentine wallpaper and dark-walnut floorboards. Then she opened the front door, which was original to apartment. After following her downstairs, she opened the vacant apartment's door. "I'm sure he will be more comfortable in his own private space."

Instead of walking in with them, she stood at the side of the threshold as they walked into the master bedroom—and then turned to enter her *Zia* Rosa's home across the narrow hall.

Thorn shook his head, literally feeling Alana's exhaustion as well as her truly conflicted heart while directing Johnny Baker to the dark and quiet bedroom. They placed a wide rubber panel over the navy cotton sheet before lifting Michael out of the body bag and onto the bed. Not at all comfortable with this change in plans, he pulled up the covers and let out a long, slow breath. What a friggin' disaster this is, he thought.

After Baker left, Thorn tucked a thick quilt around Michael's long, lean frame. In flight, the concoction sent by Alana's great-aunt had been rubbed into every wound. Like some kind of mystical miracle, it had stopped the blood oozing out of every ugly wound. Standing at the vampire's side, he studied Michael's beaten face. For the past seven years it had been his mission to keep the vampire safe. His mind raced through a quick prayer, wondering how in God's good name Michael could come out this with his mind intact.

Michael Malone opened his eyes for the first time in days. *Throbbing pain, many deep wounds, a paralyzed body...Oh God! Why did I survive?* Anger and amusement flickered in Thorn's gentle gray eyes, and that made him blink again. Upon seeing the empath, recognition and a little bit of shock registered. His friend was leaner, definitely more muscular, and much less gentle-looking. Not a hint of a smile. Vivid recall of a particular dream jarred him further awake.

He returned a similarly intense, narrow glare, watching the huge man shake his head of curly auburn hair.

"You look like hell. Do I even have to tell you how much mayhem you've caused, you sneaky bastard? Sometimes reality resembles fantasy, but this healing isn't going to happen the way you've imagined."

Alana's scent lingered in the air, but it wasn't fresh, and these surroundings were absolutely unfamiliar. Relief and something akin to anxiety filled him at the same time. Anxiety won by a mile. Hurting from head to toe, his mouth was as dry as sand. "Where… Is…She?" That came out raspy and low, and Christ, it even hurt to speak.

Thorn sank down on the edge of the bed. "Probably upstairs with the others."

"W-what others? Where the hell am I?"

"This is your apartment, smart ass, remember? So you decided to invest in prime Italian real estate without telling me—just in case you decided to pop across the Atlantic Ocean on a midnight flight for a glimpse of her. I like what you did upstairs, turning two apartments into one was a brilliant idea. Very chic. Great taste in furniture, too."

He moaned and turned away at the sound of Thorn's somewhat over-wordy, uncharacteristic needling.

"Oh, and thanks for the heads up in your fantasy. I've always suspected you would totally provide for her. But hey—why bother to confide in me about *important* things, right? Did you conveniently forget that I was sent by Helena to make sure you behaved yourself? Nah... All you chose to see were thick glasses, timid smiles, and all those extra pounds. Stop cringing. I don't need glasses anymore. My vision's as good as yours, and I didn't particularly enjoy the stroll through your twisted mind for nearly nine days."

"Oh. Shit. You walked my dream of survival."

"It was one hell of an amazing trip. What a self-absorbed melodrama," Thorn muttered with a frown. "You were never alone, my friend. Helena fed you a tremendous amount of info—which leads me to believe she may not walk the earth anymore but she's still power-packed when it concerns you."

Silence filled the dark room. Disjointed fragments of the dream poked holes in Michael's woozy mind. "Talk to me, Thorn, you've got to tell me—"

"No."

"What was real and what wasn't? I've got to know if—"

Thorn cut him off again with a firm "No."

"Why not?"

The empath stood and walked away. "It's neither time nor place."

"Are you out of your mind? I've been out for-for—"

"Ten days."

"Ten days? Fucking unbelievable."

"Uh-huh... like Day One, Day Two, Day Three, etcetera... Can't you count?" Stopping at the door, the empath turned and glared at him. "You got that part right, by the way. It took Alana another day to break you out of NWT's cell from Hell and then another day to bring you here. There'll be *many* thank-you cards to write when those cold, vampire hands are working again. But you're safe. The kid's safe."

His eyes shot wide, which hurt like hell. "My son—"

"Is safe," Thorn said as he walked out.

A skeleton key turned in the old-fashioned lock. In a higher state of alert, he moaned. The pain was intense and he was beyond weak. *Oh God, what did I do? Is my boy finally with me, like in my dream... What did you see, Lukas? What do you remember, son? My son...* He swallowed but couldn't stop the blood tears from filling his eyes. *God, I need you Alana.*

****

Peering out into the hall, Thorn's serious expression told Alana *not* to go near Michael. Emotions warred within her, and she looked away before going back into her great-aunt's home to join her at the dining room table.

"Drink your tea," came with a caring pat to her hand. Well into her seventies, *Zia Rosa* still had shades of brown in her short gray hair. She also had a highly-developed sixth-sense. "He's right, *cara*. You can't be with Michael now."

"I understand what needs to happen, but he—"

"Wants you... Yes, he does. The poison in his system is immensely dangerous. Wait for *Monsignore* to accompany you." *Zia* shook her head. "You're still very far away and very, very sad, stuck in one particular memory."

She stopped staring into her cup and met *Zia's* gaze. "I'm... uneasy. Uncomfortable... just read my soul." She'd no longer deny what he meant to her.

"Twenty-one is very young, *cara,* and you had no way of knowing."

"Yes, I did. But I couldn't fight the desire inside me, inside my heart. I couldn't wait until the end of my mission as a Guardian. I pushed him to that point of no return."

"But the Council allowed you to fulfil ten years of a deadly, mystical mission and then you moved on. You moved here."

She shrugged, slowly shook her head. "This is reality-time, *Zia*. It can never work between us. A retired Guardian of Souls *still* secretly madly in love with a vampire? I shouldn't want him; shouldn't love him the way I still do. I thought moving three thousand miles away would help. But I couldn't let NWT keep him. Why did this have to happen now? I have a new life."

Rosa blew out a sharp breath. "What *new* life?"

"The one that includes my ever-illusive hope of 'normal.' Loving a vampire, even if he is tagged mystically enhanced, doesn't fit with 'normal'. Many ex-Guardians go on to live average lives, complete with husbands or wives, and children who play softball or take piano lessons. Why can't that happen for me? I'll be twenty-eight in September. It's not too late, is it?" Sitting forward, her elbows hit the table.

"You are a classic Italian beauty, Alana."

"Yeah all five-foot-three-inches of curves."

"You still have mystical strength, yet your touch is soft just like Stefania's was. You have your mother's beautiful hazel eyes and a lovely curl to your chestnut hair, just like she did."

Yeah , and 'kissable' lips, as Michael used to say
"Oh God. Michael..." She twisted her hair and rested it over a shoulder. "Celia swears I come off too reserved

around men." *I was never that way with Michael. Don't go there, because that night when we did what we did comes right back, front and center, every time. His touch, his kisses. The passion...*

"He speaks to your soul as well as your heart," her aunt whispered.

"As a Guardian of Souls I broke a solemn vow, and *he* paid for my transgression. When his beast-within surfaced and sank its fangs into my neck, the reality of loving someone you shouldn't hit me right between the eyes." Her hand went to two small indentations on her jugular, and she could feel Michael's call deep within. *He's here less than an hour, and I'm already being pulled as if he has a rope around my very soul.*

The sound of a wooden spoon tap-tapping against metal broke her reverie. Not even aware of when her great-aunt had left the dining room, Alana stood up and walked through the narrow arch to lean against the kitchen counter and sniffed at the pot on the stove. *Zia's* lips moved as if in silent prayer while stirring a spicy mixture that smelled odd and medicinal.

"Why, do I get stuck on that single, solitary night every time I think of him? Is it some kind of mystical signal warning me to stay away from him?"

Her great-aunt continued to stir and sniff. "There is no sacred vow to uphold anymore. Perhaps the invisible wall you've built needs to come down."

"Why? I can't have normal with Michael. He can't grow old with me. He'll be just as he's been since 1690—tall, commanding, singularly handsome, and forever twenty-seven. We can't stroll through the piazza on a sunny day. We can't walk down the aisle of San Giorgio's to have our union blessed before God."

How ridiculous it sounded... saying it out loud. "Besides, the Georgian Sovereign Council took too many days making the decision to rescue him. That says he isn't on their list of favorite creatures."

When her great-aunt looked her way, it was as if fire sizzled in her light-gray eyes. "Don't confuse self-doubt with a matter that had no protocol for us to follow. Before you left Italy to rescue him, you told me how he'd heal in *your* bed, how you wouldn't leave his side. Tell me why, Alana. What has changed?"

Sharp words so uncharacteristic but very perceptive, she thought. At first, she hesitated, and then as if she couldn't get it out fast enough, she said, "I've had plenty of time to think this over—days of listing all the pros and cons and then going over them once more to be certain. Our relationship... What I feel for him is-is over. Being this close to him is a serious mistake." *There it was. The plain and simple truth.*

Her great-aunt stopped stirring. "And what else, *cara*?"

Instantly, her eyes glistened, and she swallowed hard. "I-I never left his side after I got him out of NWT, and I held an unrecognizable body in my arms praying he would survive. Being near him tears me apart and my head screams walk away—do it now before you can't."

"But your heart, what does the heart whisper to the soul?"

She didn't answer. Her aunt put the wooden spoon on the counter and opened her arms. Her hug felt like heaven. "Sometimes it is easier for someone else to see what you cannot."

Chapter 3

The pastor of San Giorgio Church smiled as he clasped Lukas's shoulder and put a wrapped package in front of him. At the man's touch, Lukas didn't jump out of the dining room chair and curl his fists. Nor did he tense up, experiencing unexpected comfort. His gaze slid up far to study the priest's features...a full head of snow-white hair and rimless glasses over light-blue eyes. An open smile and soft lines on his face. He'd never met a priest before, at least not that he could remember.

Monsignor Sebastiano Scarlatti had introduced himself speaking perfect English. Much older than Miles Bookman, his voice was powerful but gentle, not like the researcher's soft, clipped voice. The long black cassock and purple sash made him look like a formidable authority figure. "I hear you've just had a birthday, Lukas. *Buon compleanno.*"

Of course, Lukas tore at the wrapping. When he pulled a lightweight laptop out of its box, his eyes went wide. "Thanks...like a lot! How'd you know?"

"I have my ways. *Prego.* It's Italian for "you're welcome." Miles told me you like to write," the priest added in a friendly manner before leaving him to join the other adults in the living room. Mister B, Celia, the demon and Alana were sitting quietly waiting for him.

While no one looked his way, Lukas memorized

Alana's home. It was really spacious with state-of-the-art everything, like something out of an architectural magazine. A low, glass-topped table with bowed legs stood between the beige leather couch and two matching armchairs. He knew they were really comfortable because after a not-so-hot shower, he had sunk into one of them.

Plum colored walls, oil paintings that jump out at you in a subtle way, all the wood dark and shiny. Everything said wealth and style to him, even the antique roll-top desk in the corner of the living room. The dining room had two large windows, a big wooden table with a hutch to match. It had many drawers, but classy plates and different sized vases on its open shelves.

Mister B came over, and Lukas gave a small smile. "This is way cool." He placed the laptop next to the other one on the long dining room table and relaxed back against one of the cushioned armchairs around it.

"Do you need help setting it up?"

"Nah, it looks pretty easy. Looks like you have more important things to do, right?"

"Monsignor represents the Georgian Sovereign Council, the group that is helping your father."

Totally focused on the gift, he asked, "So you work for them?"

"I'd rather say this is a way of life I've chosen. The penthouse in Manhattan is the Council's, not ours."

"Yeah, you're married, right?"

"Yes, I am. My wife, Laura, has a career, and I lecture on paranormal studies at a variety of universities. It's something many believe to be folklore."

"So, do you, like, talk about Michael in class?"

The man nodded with a friendly grin. "But most innocents don't believe in vampires or demons. They can't see what we see. The Guardians, the Georgians, you and I know the truth, don't we?"

Lukas gave a shrug unwinding the power cord before plugging it in the laptop. When Mister B walked away, he eyed the shuttered windows with lace curtains drawn closed as well. The only light in the room came from a classy chandelier over the table and recessed lights in the living room through the wide wooden arch. *I get why this place feels like a cocoon... Why Mister B says stay far away from the windows. I'm the human son of a vampire that hasn't had a heartbeat in over three centuries.* And just like his father, he had mystical strength. *That's why everyone's being so nice, not because they care. And that's why the priest is here.* The blank expression he wore served a purpose. His thoughts and worries were nobody's business.

****

Perched on the edge of an armchair, Alana heard Monsignor Scarlatti explain what would have to happen before healing could begin. Her stomach did multiple flips when he added, "With such devastation to this creature's nervous system, it is further determined that the demon existing in Michael must be removed. Otherwise, he will never regain the ability to self-heal, or for that matter, regain full sanity."

Remove the beast-within? Was that even possible? More than anxious, she glanced at Lukas through the wide, wooden arch hoping he'd be too engrossed in the laptop to eavesdrop, and like everyone else, kept her voice at a whisper. "Can this be done or not?"

"It would be an unconventional exorcism, but something we must try. And the physical area must be prepared carefully. Then, Michael must consent to exorcism—without persuasion. Once the entity is mystically cleaved from him, no dark seer will be able to locate anyone inside this newly consecrated space, no matter what brand of magic is used."

She looked to her father for reassurance, but Miles avoided her gaze, and Celia and Thorn were holding hands, doing what always reminded her of the Vulcan Mind-Meld. When her narrow glare zeroed in on them, their hands instantly unlocked.

"Once the vampire agrees," Monsignor stated, "Mystical healers will immediately purify the building. Only then will they perform the ritual tonight."

"Tonight? So soon?" Alana's stomach did another flip.

Thorn began to grin. "So who gets to break the good news to Michael— about giving up his demon parts?"

"It can be asked by any of us," the monsignor quietly replied, "Although someone extremely close to him would make it much easier for him to accept."

Monsignor's serious gaze slid to her. She looked away. *Oh boy, here goes nothing.* "I'm sorry, Father, I-I can't."

Her sister's eyes went wide. "Whoa… back up a bit, Ally, that's not what you're supposed to say! You have a way with him, a-and Thorn can't interfere in *anyone's* destiny!"

For a man in his seventies, the priest rose quickly, smoothed his cassock. His wrinkled hands folded at his waist. "*Va bene.* I shall speak with Michael."

Uneasiness, the very ache in her heart showed, but she sat there unmoved by all the odd expressions on everyone's faces. The disapproval in Celia's glistening green eyes hurt the most.

Then her adopted father stood up as well. "*Grazie mille, Monsignore*, Celia will take you to him."

****

Too stunned by the unexpected decision and wringing her hands, Celia shot up from the couch. Thorn, already at the door, looked bothered when Monsignor Scarlatti stopped in front of him and whispered, "Ah, you are the loyal soul who has experienced lifetimes of pain. The angel Helena chose wisely."

Thorn glanced at her, saying in unspoken words, "*I'm guessing that arrogant bastard's not going to be too agreeable now. By the time I'm finished with him, he'll wish I still languished in Hell instead of being here kicking his guilty ass.*" Passing him at the door, Celia gave a thin frown as he mumbled, "I only sent that one to you, honey." She led the monsignor downstairs, bursting with love for the gentle empath.

Opening the door to Michael's sanctuary, Monsignor Scarlatti followed her in. Celia unlocked the master bedroom and moved to the side of the bed to turn on the lamp on the nightstand. Michael squinted as if he were unable to adjust to even a low-wattage light.

"Oooh…sorry about that, sweetie." She sat beside him, picking up intense vulnerability and total disorientation. Unlike Ally's home, the room smaller than the master bedroom upstairs and sparsely furnished with a mahogany dresser and a dining room chair in the far corner. The stylish sleigh bed dwarfed all else. Three bland, egg-shell white walls were set off by pleated black-out drapes covering the window.

"I heard the door unlock...but only recognize one scent...yours," Michael finally whispered. The thick rasp of his voice wasn't his usual soft, controlled baritone at all. Lightly her hand brushed his bruised forehead pushing his wavy brown hair back. Blood tears stood in his espresso eyes and his angular features tightened. Never known to show emotions, she fully realized just how much the dream of survival had literally stripped and exposed him. Easy as possible, her palm traced his high cheekbone and then hooked his bruised chin. She liked Michael and tender gestures might not heal, but certainly wouldn't hurt.

"Give her time, sweetie," she whispered.

He slowly blinked and then turned his face away. "I know what you're doing, Celia. Stay out of my mind."

The ache in his soul rivaled the distress in his voice. Absorbing the excruciating, physical pain and his psychological desperation, her eyes glistened in sympathy.

"I sense how you wanted to end your existence. You thought Ally and Lukas had left your life—would be forever safe. Then, you went in for the kill." Her gentle tone belied brutal truths laid before him. "Is it possible to love anyone deeper than that? We couldn't let you have your way. You don't belong in Hell."

She sniffled back tears as she cupped his bruised cheek. His wounds were torturous and the raw emotions scorching his soul were just as unbearable. Crimson liquid sank back into the wells of his bloodshot eyes, but she caught one cool, red bead sliding down the side of his face and held it between her fingers. Celia's kiss lingered on his forehead wishing she could take away his pain. "You have an important visitor. Just hear him out, okay?"

"Why isn't she here with me?" The unsteady tremble in his voice was so very uncharacteristic.

"I'm not avoiding your question, but now's not the time."

And as Monsignor Scarlatti entered the bedroom, another tremor shook her psyche. Absolute panic had Michael glaring at the tall, impressive figure. Pulling the solitary wooden chair close, Monsignor sat at his side.

Guilt filled his soul. Fear filled his mind. Both of them sensed it as the white-haired priest dipped his head and whispered, "All is understood. *Buona sera, Signore*, I am Sebastiano Scarlatti. The Georgian Sovereign Council has placed you under our protection."

****

Michael's gaze followed Celia out of the room. He didn't want her to go—even though he heard honest compassion in the priest's voice. With a deep sigh, he closed his eyes. *I don't want to look at you. I don't want to look at anyone except the woman I love. Where is my Guardian?*

Like a snake about to strike, the pain surged to unbearable. The fucking poison gnawed at his bones and tried to devour his ability to think. Alana's absence decimated his spirit, slashing unperceived, fresh wounds that only she could heal. A warm hand came over his cold knuckles. Unable to pull away, his skin didn't sizzle from the holy man's touch.

"Come now, you must have faith in us. You had not desired nor expected to survive such a battle."

Every inch of him screamed as if he stood in that deadly Manhattan alley once again. "Let me die," he moaned in defeat, just as he had in his dream of survival.

"You must be open to what I have to say. Please listen carefully."

Fierce shards of pain slashed at him again. He cringed, gasped, and although there was no need for the air he took into his lungs, he took breath after breath.

"You give a human response, one made by the man, not by the beast-within. But you will sink into insanity if you refuse our offer. There is one condition to Sanctuary, something you must agree to and give consent of your own free will."

"What do you want of me, Father? You know what I am...all that I have done."

The priest's lips came to his right ear, and all four walls closed in like a consecrated tomb, causing the beast-within a new type of torture.

"In order for us to give Sanctuary... In order for holy women to heal your body, the demon inside you must be purged."

His bloodshot eyes narrowed. Unearthly hissing and howls choked in his throat, already suffocating from the priest's close proximity. Yet a merciful look lingered on the priest's face, in his wise, pale-blue eyes.

"Surrender the beast-within. Permit us to separate it from your soul. Only then can we be sure that you and your child will not be found by those who have done this to you."

The priest's manner was graceful, serene. And as

every tormenting pang seemed to double its intensity, Michael knew his immortal body was weakening against it.

"Is this even possible? Is this my path to redemption? A potion rubbed into my wounds on the plane gave me a brief reprieve…" The pain reached unbearable as he grit his teeth. "I'm no good at making deals. And it gets messier when something's dangled just out of my reach. I don't understand how my boy is here. I did a stupid thing to save Lukas from himself. It ate at me night and day. It doesn't take a genius to realize that as soon as I took my revenge on those bastards all bets were off. I destroyed his one chance for happiness. Lukas is as he was before," he added in disgust.

"No, your child came without a fight, just as he went to you the night of the battle."

His eyes blinked rapidly but didn't focus. Desperate to contain the pain as well as the raging beast-within, he got out, "Lukas saw me trying to end my undead existence?" The next fierce spasm silenced him as he thought, perhaps I am meant to only listen.

The monsignor shook his head. "Did you honestly believe you could destroy yourself? Helena would never accept such momentary weakness, such self-pity." The priest leaned back clicking his tongue as he folded his hands.

But the words had an effect. More twinges and jerks began that he couldn't control as if tolerance had been a mirage. Good and evil collided in his weary soul. Unexpected screams burst from his mouth as all the stitched wounds popped open and blood tears dripped down his temples. Between sobs, he whispered.

"I cannot... will not... do...this!"

The monsignor was suddenly standing over him. "There is no more time. The beast is ready to surface. Focus through the misery, Michael. *You* command this soul, this conscience. You are a child of God, not a son of Satan. I ask again. Do you surrender the demon? Do you agree, to the ritual offered by the Sovereign Council, of your own free will and without coercion?"

The sheet covering him rapidly stained. Splatter patterns of dark scarlet broadened. Blood given in-flight trickled out from every open wound. The clawed crevices on his back and the shoulder bite had fresh blood pooling beneath him. Unable to hold back, he trembled and screamed. With all control lost, he had to surrender and protect himself. His blood-rimmed brown pupils turned light amber as the beast-within howled.

"Fight back, Michael! You *are* strong enough! If the metamorphosis occurs you must be destroyed—and then your soul will be forever lost."

The frantic command was an unwelcomed assault as the priest's palm locked to his forehead. Sharp canines lengthened to form two deadly spikes in his open mouth as his lips peeled back. His head arched off the pillow. Panic surged sensing the wooden stake hidden in the folds of the priest's cassock. His amber eyes narrowed and deadly growls began. The beast-within snapped it head leering at an old woman rushing in with a thick white towel draped over her arm.

The large, steaming pot in her hands gave off a distinct odor. Spiced scents filled the room like incense swirling thick through a chapel. A familiar face on another woman, young and petite had it snapping its jaws. Just out of reach, she moved a dim lamp closer to the other nightstand's edge.

The strong-scented liquid mixture was beside him—too close. The beast-within snarled as he wrestled with its untimely emergence. Two different mind-sets brought uncontrollable fury to the surface as in a moment of lucidity he screamed, "My Guardian... My Guardian! Please... Come to me!"

Chapter 4

Alana stiffened, held her breath against her father's chest. As if Michael's pleas could come up through the floor to knife through her very soul, every terrified scream was as clear as if he were a room away in her bed. But Michael wasn't in her bed. He wasn't in her care.

Even if she tried, no sensible words would come to her. Something kept her from running downstairs. Fear or guilt—she didn't know which.

A terrified "Come to me!" made her flinch. This had to be more than he could take. *All those years when Michael fought beside me, when he placed his immortal body between me and death... Never once had he even winced in pain.* Every devastating blow from a demon had been meant for her—but he swore *his* Guardian would leave her mission unscathed. When she sterilized his ugly wounds afterward in his brownstone, she'd never heard as much as an "ouch."

He doesn't cry. He doesn't plead.

And more tortured cries hammered her heart. Not even her father's tight hug immunized against such gut-wrenching appeals. Part of her wanted to run to him. Part of her wanted to rage. She opened her eyes and saw Lukas sitting in the dining room. This was Michael's home as well. *If I didn't bring them here, Clayton would've found Lukas in Manhattan and he would've killed him.* That thought sobered her. Then he screamed again.

That last scream made Lukas wince and squirm in the dining room chair. Lost in his own misgivings and detached, he refused to let on just how his parent's anguished screams shot through his bones like bullets that could pierce skin and muscle.

Yet his fingers flew over the laptop's keyboard, blasting bright-colored geometrical shapes before they reached the bottom of the screen. Deep down, he knew this was because of him. And in the guarded space in his heart that harbored his guilt, he recalled the buzz from pursuing his unnatural parent and trying to stake him. *A year ago, that buzz kept me alive.*

Another scream brought another uncomfortable twinge of remorse. A year ago, every attack had fueled some kind of senseless hate within him. Too many times, that piece of pointy wood barely missed his unnatural father's unbeating heart by less than an inch.

Then one day, the hate didn't exist anymore. No memories of Michael or his first eight years of a happy life with Helena. *Yeah... he's fucking like this because of me.* The hellish howls kept him jittery, and he wanted to run and hide. Yet he couldn't pull himself off the chair. And like that first moment in the passageway when Lukas saw Michael battling those ferocious, never-ending Hell-beasts, some unknown force held him in place... again, against his will.

****

A saturated white towel in wrinkled hands swabbed his amber eyes. The beast-within leered at the old woman. Like hot ice, Michael heard the sizzle and felt the burn deep within his fractured mind. She pressed the soaked cloth against his fangs. Sour water drenched every crevice of his mouth making him gag as the stinging liquid trickled down his throat.

Small shaking hands braced his wide shoulders as if the younger woman with bright red hair could anchor his very soul to hers. His fingernails began to thicken into demon-like claws.

But when his icy hands were bound by the old woman that part of the transformation came to an abrupt halt. She didn't unleash them until they regained human form.

Again, the cloth swooshed in the pot. The old woman covered his bloody chest with it, held it firm to his unbeating heart. Searing heat... More deadly growls rumbled free.

Three voices morphed into one. Ancient words assaulted the beast-within, just as they had in 1890 when the angel chanted the antiphon over him.

In the recess of a less than sane mind, Michael sensed his beast-within go dormant. Celia's strong spirit flowed through her undeterred grip. The old woman was a mystical healer who sent his beast-within back to its unseen prison. And the priest's hand on his forehead stopped the demon that possessed him from stealing his last, rational thought.

He moaned and then sobbed as he closed his eyes.

****

Thorn had positioned himself at the apartment door. Minutes ago, when Celia and Rosa hurried past him, he sensed Michael's anguish on the edge of exhaustion. Breathing easier, he left the second floor but didn't go upstairs.

Curiosity over what he had experienced in

Michael's dream of survival still hounded him. Normally, he'd let his senses do the walking, but he had to see it for himself and headed down to the basement, taking the last set of rickety wooden steps slow and inhaling the musty smell of a windowless area below ground. One tug on the string of a lone light bulb, and Thorn froze.

"Now this is creepy. It's *deja-vu*, the first of many, I'm guessing."

Thorn leaned against a familiar brick wall. There were rows of old barrels and a wooden door bolted shut with steel rods at the other end. He didn't recall a door in the dream, but the layout was the same.

There is no question, right down to the dirt floor. On the exact spot where he had stood with Michael in his fantasy, the curly hairs on the back of his neck tingled. "Dear angel, give him strength," he whispered as if Helena could hear him.

The next back of the neck tingle had him running up three flights of stairs. Miles was yelling "No!" and Alana shouted, "Stop Lukas!" just as he positioned his beefy self in front of the only door on the third floor. The demanding kid looked ready to rumble.

"Fuck you. You can't tell me what to do. Why can't I—"

"No—not on your young life," he calmly stated with his arms folded tight across his chest. They locked eyes—one set angry, one set knowing. If the kid refused to back down, he was ready.

"*You* fucking saw him!"

"It's not going to happen."

"*She* doesn't want to go to him, but I do!"

"*She* has a name and enough sense to leave well

38

enough alone. It amazes me that the word 'no' isn't in your vocabulary. Sit," he ordered. One thick finger pointed over the kid's head. The sneer on such an angelic face bothered him. To see hate is such deep-blue eyes and on one so young... When the kid brought those dangerous fists up, he had to wonder just how powerful this mystical child's punch might be.

Before he could swing, the boy actually paled and his fists shot to his temples instead. Thorn's voice sank an octave. "Is this enough of a lesson for you?" Both boney legs buckled, and he caught the skinny kid before he hit the floor. *Thank you, God,* he thought as the kid's scrawny stomach settled on his shoulder. Miles and Alana followed him into the guestroom where he gently put the kid down on a bed. "Eighty pounds of confused trouble."

Miles whispered, "He's out like a light."

"But for how long?" Alana asked as they left the room. "God, he's fast."

"Fast and full of rage. Michael can't see him. One strong whiff of cranky kid and that "yes" or "no" won't be his own. Going downstairs isn't good for you either, Alana."

"Did you hear him?"

Thorn sank to the sofa and played with one trouser cuff, a nervous habit that began when all this chaos started ten days ago. Christ, he thought, her emotions were all over the place—which almost made him dizzy.

"Heart-wrenching and full of despair... I feel his fear," he mumbled. "I still see his thoughts as if they're mine. Anyone connected to him is also easier to read now...except for some unknown reason, that kid. Look, I know what's been on your mind—since before the rescue." He had to give her something, and offered in a gentle way, "During his dream of survival I came to fully understand his desire to be with you. As well as his commitment to keep the kid safe. And near the end, he created a gross, gory scene to rescue you *and* Lukas from Clayton. You're engraved in his eternal soul, Alana. Helena saturated his senses with loving you, making you the key to his sanity. Michael turned every inconsolable emotion inward. He couldn't separate fact from illusion. Plus, the poison made everything intense. But Helena sent many moments of compassion, full of detail—and you. I mean, my heart truly ached for him." He'd said enough, grateful that neither she nor Miles asked a question. "We can't sway his decision one way or the other. Every man must face his own destiny."

Further conversation was impossible. They sat quietly, waiting for a sign. It took a while.

****

The struggle between two realities continued. To Michael, these unnerving minutes felt like decades. When his howls turned into feeble groans, he teetered on the rim of consciousness. Helpless. Terrified. Alone. Lying in a pool of blood.

His sewn right thigh, where a Hell-beast's sword had shattered bone, bled profusely. But as the drenched towels swathed each wound again, fresh blood clotted, turning it a deep scarlet.

The healer whispered, "It did what it was supposed to do; what we knew it *would* do."

The priest made the two broad strokes of the Christian symbol on his forehead in a determined manner. "I vow to you, Champion, you *will not* fight this next battle alone."

Celia, teary-eyed and silent, laced her fingers through his trembling ones. The healer soothed with gentle words in hushed Italian as her hand rested on his unbeating heart. Every gesture as simple as it was, resonated full of compassion.

A labored breath came, then another—he felt no pain—simply a heavy nothingness. What if his survival brought death to his Guardian's doorstep as it had in his fantasy? What if he never healed? What if he awakened insane? He turned his face away, turned himself inward.

One sane thought jolted his conscience. Should the beast-within be separated from his soul, Alana would never again be its victim. The evil entity that defined his existence since he was sired in 1690 would be gone. He'd tell her and his son how much he truly loved them—before he destroyed himself. That made the decision easy.

As if he already knew, Monsignor Scarlatti leaned in close. Full of dread, not knowing what to expect, he rasped uneven and low, "I accept."

Will driving a stake through my own unbeating heart keep them safe and bring me eternal peace? His mind blurred. The question faded as unconsciousness took hold. Blessed nothingness washed over him. His eyelids fluttered down and a mystically-enhanced vampire surrendered—surrounded by the purest of souls.

Chapter 5

Close to midnight, Celia went back upstairs. Thorn read her relief and felt her utter exhaustion when she sank down next to Alana on the leather couch. He didn't read her thoughts. That would be an egregious intrusion.

"Michael made it through a-a critical juncture," Celia told them. Alana's expression was unreadable, and Celia glanced at him, saying to his mind, *"We're too close, honey. Please. You have to see it all and do this for me."*

He took a deep breath, let it out slow and plunged in. "So, the Ritual of Exorcism will soon be performed, and his beast-within will be history. I'm guessing that'll ease your mind." Alana looked down and folded her hands. "Now, now, avoiding the issue won't make it go away. Just say what you feel."

"I'm sure you *already* know what I'm going to say."

"Honey, I don't read minds," Miles said from the other leather armchair in the living room. "But I know something is seriously bothering you."

Clearing her throat, Alana appeared to sink deeper into the soft beige leather. "I'm glad we got him out of NWT. I'm glad you convinced his son to board the plane, Dad. We made the right decision bringing them to Portofino." She leveled an immovable glare at Thorn.

"He'll always be in my heart. He's rooted deep in my soul. But getting him through this is in your hands. I won't interfere. We can't ever be together…in the normal sense."

Thorn had to grin. "What about you is normal, dear Guardian?"

"You know what I'm talking about, and you're not making this any easier. Michael is what he is, beast-within or not. He isn't a living man like you. He can't change, but *I* can. After ten years as a Guardian of Souls, I-I want normal."

Miles studied her, eventually saying, "Perhaps the healers can take him to Siena."

Alana quickly shook her head. "No. I'm confident I can protect him and his son. Plus, this *is* his building—isn't it? I think I've always known. Ex-Guardians don't have patrons, Daddy B. No one puts out thousands of dollars to renovate an old building and insists the previous owner *and* her great-niece whom he's never met live in it. No one buys a car for an unknown tenant, and who's been padding my bank account? I'm sure it isn't the Council." She grinned slightly; her beautiful face as far from happy as one could imagine. "Plus, there's Lukas. Boy, talk about a jumpy soul. He really needs all of us, not just Michael. When I saw him so filthy and frightened in Michael's brownstone…the way he huddled against the wall? I wanted to kill Clayton myself." She looked at him again. "I'll stay clear of whatever it is you have to do, Thorn. Use my blood to heal Michael. I'll donate quarts of it. I want him healthy again, but I can't get so attached that—"

"Your heart breaks again?" Celia asked softly. "What happened is way in the past and you're *still* not over it. I know what it did—to both of you."

"And because of what happened Helena sent me to him. So I guess there's a higher purpose to my being here," Thorn added.

"I know you were the first person to see our love for one another, Celia. You didn't have to tell me."

"Thorn and I sensed the abysmal void your absence created in his world, too. I witnessed what it did to *you* on a daily basis... those last years as a Guardian in the city. Ally, I get the inner turmoil, and the misery that comes with it."

"I need to keep my distance."

Not about to share the worry in his heart, Thorn gave a warm smile. "Take all the time you need. He isn't going anywhere." Then he heard the mystical healers' unspoken message and stood. "The building is consecrated. Now it begins."

As he left, the deadbolt slid across Alana's door. Loyal to his sole purpose on this earth, he was prepared to stand guard outside Michael's apartment—in the event that six holy women needed a little muscle. Although he had never met them, like every Georgian around the globe, he'd heard stories about the Order of Catherine. The Sisters were legendary. Incorruptible. Always a congregation of fifty-four, each woman's destiny had been implanted in the depths of her soul before birth. Each accepted a mystical invitation in her own time to travel to Siena. To become part of something intrinsically linked to the battle against ungodly things that threatened innocent humans. The current Prioress, Anne Critchley, waited in Michael's living room with five others from her community and Monsignor Scarlatti.

Lacing his arms across his chest and blocking the apartment door, Thorn stilled his soul.

Chapter 6

Three days ago, Mother Anne Critchley had informed the monsignor that a unique form of exorcism had been prepared for Michael Malone. A hearty woman in her seventies with ruddy cheeks and light-gray eyes, the musicologist was well-known as a scholar of Gregorian chant. But tonight, her position as Spiritual Leader for her Order took precedence over Anne's many secular accomplishments.

"I see my idea worked extremely well for Alana, Sebastiano."

Her British heritage was barely noticeable in the superb command of Italian, and with a respectful nod, the monsignor replied, "When I told her you sensed rescuing something the evil ones thought to be already destroyed would be a beneficial distraction, it helped mold her strategy for a highly effective extraction, Annie."

She met his smile with a warm one of her own. "Getting him here was the easy part, my friend. I sense devastation—both in his body and mind. The vampire willingly brought this upon himself. Vengeance demands an enormous price, doesn't it? It's as if he purposely sacrificed an immortal existence for The Georgian Cause. Gabriella and Magdalena walked his dream of survival, as did I. Just before he gave into the poison, many in our congregation were shown to him. Helena revealed her link to his powerful bloodline, but

46

there's more that connects us to him." She handed him the document now preserved between two sheets of glass. "This is why our cloistered sisters will assist with the Ritual of Exorcism." Three veiled heads bowed in a show of respect. "It's been many years since they have walked in the secular world. Tonight is an exception. To create a spiritual balance, I believe their presence is, perhaps, even mystically preordained." As he read, she continued, "Please allow me to explain. In September of 1678, Priscilla, Rosalind, and Anne Malone arrived at Villa Catherine in Siena. It had been an arduous journey from London. To receive three from the same family into our order is unheard of to this day. Yet each possessed the distinct gift of mystical healing. A wooden writing chest stayed in Sister Anne's possession until her death at age eighty-six. Neither Priscilla nor Rosalind reached age sixty. All three led cloistered lives. Gabriella and Magdalena found the chest in the oldest part of the villa's basement. It contained a locket and this letter for their younger brother, Michael Malone."

Sister Gabriella, an extant in her mid-thirties, held the chest and said, "Maggie and I couldn't believe we actually found it… on the day Michael was incarcerated by NWT. Look at the inscription, Father." Also an ex-Guardian like Alana, Gabriella turned it around so he could see all sides of the wooden treasure. A little more than a foot wide and equally deep, the silver plaque on top was inscribed 'Malone' along with the letters A, P, R, and M at each compass point.

The monsignor whispered, "This is extraordinary." He handed the document back to Anne, who placed it in a leather case with a clasp, placing it carefully on the dining room table. "I will present the letter to the Council as indisputable proof that your order's involvement is sanctioned."

Anne sensed midnight approach. Along with the Monsignor, six pristine souls dressed in religious garb were ready to assist a vampire. Their habit hadn't changed since another mystical healer, Catherine of Siena, had walked the earth. Hours ago, casual clothes had been put aside. The healers had ritualistically kissed the blessed, black cloth before it settled on them and tied beige cinctures around their waists. Stiff white wimples framed their faces and white bibs covered each pure heart. Fashionable hairstyles went unseen, hidden beneath long black veils as each woman steadied both mind and heart for this complex task.

"Our cloistered sisters will return to Siena after the healing. Gabby and Maggie will remain here with me across the hall until the second stage of healing is complete," Anne stated.

Monsignor Scarlatti smiled at Rosa's daughter, a talented cardiovascular surgeon with a lucrative practice and considered one of the best in her field. "It's good to see you again. Taking part in this does not frighten you, Magdalena?"

"It is destined, *Monsignore,"* Magdalena, the soft-spoken nun replied.

"My sisters and I are aware that we will face untamable evil," Gabriella stated with her hands on her hips.

Anne noted Gabby's confident stance. Magdalena's reserved manner balances the other's feistiness, she thought. The ex-Guardian's expression read excitement while the surgeon remained calm and serious. "Should the demon secure itself to any of our souls, Gabriella is prepared to end that person's existence without a moment's hesitation with a silver sword through the heart." Sensing the hour, she whispered, "The empath is standing guard. We are ready to begin."

Silence hung heavy in the small living room as each healer entered prayerful meditation. Anne studied them with assurance, recalling her initial reaction to accepting her role in this midnight's mystical event. She thought about Sebastiano, about Rosa. For a brief moment, she allowed her mind to wander back to a fateful summer over fifty years ago. *Two young women on a college campus in Rome meeting a dashing, young seminary student. Both Rosa and I were drawn to his sense of peace.* Each had taken different routes to happiness in life but had remained close friends.

Anne believed in destiny. Just two nights ago, she had searched the stars in the heavens, contemplating how easy it is to spout faith, yet how difficult it is to live. *Now mine will be tested. Just as the intricate notes of a contrapuntal melody weave into a predetermined puzzle of sound, you must do this, Annie.*

Monsignor Scarlatti led them into Michael's room.

With uncommon grace, Anne said to her sisters, "It is time. May God protect us all."

Chapter 7

A thick circle of consecrated salt ringed the vampire. Anne watched as Gabriella, her mystical strength still intact, lifted Michael's body. Gloved and gowned, Magdalena used a thick towel to absorb the blood on the rubber panel beneath the vampire, carefully guiding it, along with the surgical gown and gloves, into a thick red plastic bag labeled for medical waste. The three cloistered sisters draped a starched, white altar linen over the mattress. Then Gabriella settled Michael in the center of it before unsheathing the silver sword and resting it against the headboard. Incense filled the prison of his room. Many candles of clarified beeswax, blessed and sacred, blazed in each corner. With shutters locked and heavy drapes drawn, this space sealed itself off from the world.

Anne sensed Michael barely conscious enough to hear the whispered words in a language thousands of years old. A sacred litany, slow and insistent, rose during the anointing of the wooden chest—the demon's new eternal vessel. Finally, each healer issued a mystical command for the beast-within to leave the injured creature's soul.

When the last words intoned, the beast-within stirred. Low growls sounded. Spiked canines lengthened and dark-brown pupils faded to amber, crazed and feral. His fingernails morphed into sharp claws in defense, in fear. The beast-within railed against an inexorable threat. Rage consumed it, thrusting any lucid thought within its host deeper into an abyss of hatred.

Amber eyes, full of mockery leered at the mortal innocents. Monsignor Scarlatti's lips moved in prayer anointing Michael's forehead with oil. The priest's mind merged harmonious with the mystical healers. Snarls and hisses came at him, but he anointed the undead man's eyes, lips and unbeating heart as well. Michael's brown eyes returned. Fangs retracted and his hands regained their human appearance.

The priest's glistening thumb pressed into Michael's chest and as if cords of thread had suddenly passed through skin and muscle to snare it, the entity was bound. Michael's cold flesh sizzled when the healers placed their palms, saturated with holy water, on his bloodied frame.

Beyond agony the beast-within roared. It had no ability to speak. For that, it needed a lucid vampire.

The intoned chant swelled to a crescendo and the wooden chest stood open inside the circle of salt. As if it were cut with a scalpel, the mystical thread split the demon apart from Michael's reclaimed soul. Only then did he scream—full of terror, full of rage.

The plainsong rose to an unrelenting pitch when the healers accessed the depths of their primordial souls to connect to the angelic realms of Heaven. With forceful resolve, they issued one final command.

The demon couldn't fight back. It couldn't retreat. The beast-within shot forth into its forever tomb, and Michael's shrieks stopped as abruptly as they had started.

Monsignor Scarlatti closed the chest. Mother Anne

locked it, replaced its hidden key. Another ancient chant bound the entity to a new vessel. Its sepulcher was drenched with blessed water, anointed with holy oil, and doused with salt.

Gabriella lifted Michael, and Magdalena removed the sacred linen beneath. Anne covered his body with the blood-stained sheet while Monsignor Scarlatti wrapped the chest in the altar linen, tying it with his purple sash.

She turned to the cloistered healers. "Monsignor will take you to Villa Catherine. The three of you must document the burial and the Ritual of Internment." When they nodded, she added, "I know the toll this has taken upon each of you, physically, spiritually, and mentally. Thank you, my sisters." She looked at Sebastiano. "We'll not touch him until I sense your arrival back here in Portofino."

After a gracious nod, he simply replied, "Now your vigil begins, Annie."

Thorn felt the sinister rage of a captured entity as soon as he opened the apartment door for the priest. Tired eyes met his. "I'm great with a shovel, and I have a very good reason for wanting to see this thing buried deep in hallowed ground. It'd be an honor to drive you and the healers back to Siena."

The monsignor nodded. "*Va bene*, gentle soul, *andiamo*."

Mother Anne's appreciative words penetrated his thoughts. He gave a proud grin and followed behind the silent women. It could've been Helena's voice he heard in his mind. Although as far as he was concerned, every mystical healer was like Heaven's own angel still on earth. Yet seeing Mother Anne in his mind, he thought they could be identical twins.

****

Hours passed as if the universe had decided to slow itself down. Having pulled the chair next to Michael, Anne sat alone in the bedroom. Gabriella and Magdalena had changed the bed linens and covered him with a thick comforter. He appeared peaceful, motionless. Even though he couldn't hear, she leaned in close. "For the next forty-eight hours you will sleep." She tucked the comforter around him as if tending a sick child. For a brief moment, she saw him through Helena's eyes, maternal and protective.

Still studying his bruised face, she sensed Rosa at her side with a steaming mug of coffee. "It's been over fifty years since we've taken a caffeine break together so long after midnight, hasn't it? What a far cry from a college dormitory in Rome this is."

Rosa handed her the mug. "You look exhausted."

"Dear friend, you still know me so well." It took every ounce of strength to remain focused as Anne sipped the strong brew before placing the mug on the nightstand. Even her head ached. Sensing Rosa's question, she whispered, "He won't experience pain, nor will we allow him to dream. What a most unique creature! As soon as the demon ripped away, I saw his courageous soul brimming with human desires and deep emotions. Vampires are ruled by the need to feed. They're Satan's toys. But Michael... He loves your niece and his child. *His child*... Now that is astonishing to say out loud."

"And truly troubled souls they are, Annie. The child is torn between rage and fear. Alana is torn between love and denial."

"Give her time." A slight, surprised grin appeared. "There is another like us here who is very worried about him. A very old, powerful soul! Ah…Cecelia is the researcher's daughter? Your niece has made a request through her. It is honored, of course."

Seconds later, a very determined young woman stood in the threshold. *So this is Stefania's daughter, the lovely, brave ex-Guardian who rescued him.* Both she and Rosa passed Alana in silence, leaving the bedroom door ajar.

Unnerved and unhinged, Alana was grateful they allowed her this one visit. The wait had been endless. Torn between worry and curiosity, she had begged Celia to describe each step of the exorcism. Once Celia told her Thorn was parking the car, an overwhelming urge sky-rocketed. "I need to see him, Celia," she had said, insistent, impatient. "I need to see him *now!*"

Knots curdling in her stomach didn't go away. They tightened like a vise to grip her soul. *He's unaware of his surroundings…unaware of me. That's what Celia said, and I totally trust her word—but at least he's no longer in any pain.*

Holding on to the wooden footboard, she just stood there. She had memorized everything about tonight including his screams. Like flaming arrows arching through the sky, they had pierced her aching heart. Only one other night, when a different terror changed her life, had she felt paralyzed like this. *Unearthly howls—I still hear them…. Lying beneath you in your bed at the brownstone as your beast-within surfaced.*

Just like thousands of times before, she relived the

pleasure and the pain of losing her innocence half-way through her mystical mission. What started with a kiss quickly surged to synchronized desire. That horrible night, raw need had her heart racing with anticipation. Refusing to heed the vow that defined a Guardian's mystical mission, Michael's touch had been too enticing. *So naïve, and willfully, I demanded what I knew I couldn't have.* Forbidden love led to an ecstasy never dreamed possible, before or since.

"Every detail still haunts me, my love." Drawn to him, she moved closer. Once at his side, she wanted to soothe him. She wanted to scream at him. A crooked finger brushed his cheek, not knowing which 'want' would win.

"Why did you do this? Look at you...pasty skin, eyelids sunken and black. High cheekbones so bruised and hollow...sword wounds, broken ribs, the clawed crevices and a shoulder bite so raw and...Oh, God. You *wanted* to destroy yourself. You *wanted* to leave me forever?" His thin lips, so sensual, so kissable and cool, had no color.

She backed away even though outraged at what had been done to him. *Leave him now. Don't give in to this crushing need. And how you still tug at my soul...* Her resolve crumbled like a house of cards.

For someone who had insisted that she'd walk away, she stubbornly crawled onto the bed. Tender kisses met his icy skin. Her arm snaked behind his broad shoulders to draw him close. Then her trembling fingers combed through his thick-brown waves always worn a little too long. He wouldn't hear her words or feel the rhythm of her drumming heart. It didn't matter.

"You'll always be my ultimate temptation because

you complete me. Only you can touch my soul. No one understands. They never will."

Another night came to mind, a gentler night. She blinked away the unexpected tears as a slow, small grin began. "I'd known you less than a year, but it felt as if you'd always been there to protect me. We sat next to each other on the couch at your brownstone. You said in that no-nonsense tone, "Read it out loud, my Guardian, because Romantic poems are meant to be shared." Those dark, penetrating eyes blazed through to my heart. Your arms stayed braced across your chest, but then that charming smile appeared... A really rare expression I'll never forget." And like that night so many years ago, similar and indescribable emotion drew her in. "Did you already know how much you meant to me? Your smile was like an affectionate kiss to my soul." Like a prayer, she whispered, "How do I love thee? Let me count the ways—"

At the poem's last line, a teardrop fell to his hair. It shimmered through the dimness of a solitary table lamp. She reveled in the weight of him on her breast, and sadly sighed, "Michael, my love."

Chapter 8

What occurred in Portofino had repercussions an ocean away. No one could explain it. No one knew that it happened. The demon's origin, Michael's sire, was an insidious vampire who had existed for 700 years—a shrewd, deceptive murderer. Cyril didn't drink as often as the younger ones. Centuries of turning humans into undead beings fed his need, well enough. Most of today's progeny only desired to quench their thirst, which ensnarled them in traps set by Guardians of Souls. Some lasted mere days before stake or silver blade culled them. Modern times didn't produce individuals capable of thinking long-term, and by the turn of the second millennium, Cyril Waczynska could count his undead treasures on one hand. These vampires had formed allegiances to augment their satanic strength. Such unholy deeds increased a sire's longevity. Their devotion nourished Cyril's potent beast-within like nubile blood to swell his sunken veins.

The inconspicuous hills of Vermont suited his reclusive nature. The baron, as he was often called, held his brittle hands above a roaring fire in his parlor. Almost skeletal now, a plush black velvet robe kept his aged joints warm. When he felt rage grow silent within his 'once-favorite' son, he staggered back into the chair, gripped the worn arms. Claw-like nails punctured its textured hide. He sucked air into rotted lungs, which made his call sound like the hiss of a snake.

"Edward." Convinced the servant felt it more than heard it, he smiled when the stupid man uttered, "Yes, Master Cyril." He liked being called 'master'. And Edward, rubbing sweaty hands against his pants, already appeared nauseous.

Cyril's untamed eyes locked on the human until the mortal held his wrist out. Deadly and long canines swiftly punctured a vein. Only when the quivering piece of flesh dropped to his knees did Cyril retract them. Licking his blood-stained lips as if he'd had a few too many whiskeys, he slurred, "Eat healthy tomorrow," before Edward limped out.

Once alone, Cyril glided to a window. Unearthly and crazed, he howled like an injured wolf. After all, Michael Malone had been one of his finest creations...

****

"Baron" Waczynska came to the bustling shores of New York in 1685 with his residence shipped stone by stone. Pristine forests reminded the vampire of his native Slovakia. The island of Manhattan appeared a lucrative place for trade, attracting humans like bees to the nectar of a sweet spring bloom. The Triumvirate of Evil who ruled the continent's portals quickly located Cyril, his egomaniacal essence easy to detect. A lasting bond formed. The sire fed off many but turned few, preferring a specific look—fierce masculinity, arrogance, bold ambition.

Cyril's progenies were distinct. And posing as an eccentric nobleman, his façade was an effortless draw. Handsome then, he had aristocratic features and enchanting, ice-blue eyes. Women swooned in his presence. Men envied his panache. The mysterious foreigner proved to be ever available to assist with 'certain' problems.

In December 1690, the Triumvirate of Evil sent an important fool Cyril's way. Their banker had a wife obsessed with a dashing trader. The illicit liaison caused a distraction with the sorcerers' human money-counter.

Cyril took Antoine Glenmont's gold, but the description of the woman's fixation tweaked his interest. On the night that the vampire came to drink and drain the trader, he quickly altered those plans. The demon sensed innate charm that drove women wild. The tall, handsome Englishman exuded the scent of lust—a master at saturating himself with sexual pleasures.

As soon as Cyril entered the philanderer's office, the human's dark eyes turned murderous while reaching for a pearl-handled knife tucked in its sheath. "Who are you? How did you get in?"

From the doorframe, he observed his prey. The attitude dripped of conceit. *Approach slowly; hold his gaze. Yes...very self-confident indeed.* "My name is Baron Waczynska. I have been sent by Antoine Glenmont in regards to his wife."

"Stand where you are. I do not know any Glenmont *or* his wife. Leave. I shall not hesitate to attack."

With a sly smile, he replied, "Arrogance... I like that. But unless that prized blade is pure silver and blessed by your priest, it is of no use." He allowed his blue eyes to soften. A steady hand ran across the desk's mahogany wood. "Now we come to the matter of the wife. Her husband demands your death. It is obvious how such refined features and fearless manner have caused the banker to pale considerably in her eyes."

Cyril read thought, an amazing gift for a sire, and the strapping man before him still waited for an opportune moment to attack. Cyril smiled, shook his head. "You will be dead before your next breath if you try."

Yet his victim hadn't been rattled. "You are no ordinary man. There is death in your eyes and something I do not comprehend. Stay assured. I will fight you."

Again. Such brash confidence. Only the slightest fear punched his boldness, and the vampire stepped closer. Palms pressed together as if in prayer; his fingers tapped rhythmically on his ruby lips. "Indeed, you are finely built. Healthy and strong."

"I do not fear you. I do not fear death." The grip on the knife tightened.

It is a lie... He fears both. Lust rules his desires. Quick thinking keeps him undetected by all the jealous husbands. I will give him ample time to scream, if that is how he wishes to enter my world. He wanted this one but backed away in a polite manner. This perfect specimen could be corrupted— in a roundabout way. "There is no cause for alarm. No crucifix on the wall, no such icon against your chest. This repartee crosses no boundaries with your faith in God."

The trader seemed angered, bolder. "I do not quake in your presence. No *Ave Maria* will be whispered from my lips."

This time, he tells the truth. His belief system died years ago on a summer day when three beloved women left his life. Ah, yes. His sisters. Resistant to faith in anything but himself, he eagerly seeks physical satisfaction. It was easy to glimpse those flashes of memories. Plus, he liked the rebellious nature of a man

who got through seduction whatever he wished for—
and from a multitude of women! Admit his many sins?
Cyril sensed it wasn't an option. *Confessionals remind
him of coffins, suffocating and unyielding. This one has
turned his back on God as he reasons God has turned
his back on him. How foolish to believe he will author
his own destiny.*

In a brave move, the man slapped the knife to his
desk. When both hands clamped his trim waist, his
heartbeat slowed. "Speak, demon, and leave."

An air of superiority, a challenge with useless
words… Cyril had centuries to refine this game. The
bow was a deceitful compromise. Not liking the
dismissive tone, this display of ego somewhat
captivated him. He placed the heavy pouch on the desk
with calculating eyes that never descended, purposely
locked to his next victim. "I misjudge you, young sir.
Glenmont has no knowledge of this mysterious ability
to overpower even one such as I. Pardon my intrusion. I
shall not bother you again."

As quickly as he had entered the establishment, the
vampire left. Cyril correctly assumed how the man was
too stunned to move. Michael Malone should have run
to the nearest priest with a thankful heart. He didn't.
Vanity had properly groomed this soul for tonight's
dance with a devil. The Englishman thought he was
safe. Cyril, however, had other plans.

In the days and nights that followed the encounter,
Michael steered clear of Jeanette Glenmont—not out of
fear for her sniveling husband. She looked pretty
enough, and she tasted as sweet as a ripened plum, but
the woman's refusal to use her pouty lips on his very

eager manhood had become a constant annoyance.

One week passed since the demon's late-night visit. Approaching Christmas, business was brisk enough to keep him occupied during the day. But every sunset, Cyril's words claimed his mind. Imported cognac became the preferred pacifier, and tonight, he drained another snifter, letting its smooth, smoky flavor wash over his tongue before another slow swallow.

"Why did you not kill me? Why was I spared?" His hand trembled. Cyril's lifeless, cold eyes haunted his dreams. He refilled the glass only to drain it like fresh well water, but the encounter with a demon refused to fade. "It is as if you invade my room every night to call my name. You bowed to *me*... Because I am too strong to kill! This devil has met his match. I am from a proud bloodline—a powerful one." He sneered, staring into the flames of the fireplace and finally numb. Close to midnight, a sharp knock pulled him out of these thoughts. With lantern in hand, plus a noticeable sway to his gait, he opened the door.

In the moonlight, a magnificent Friesian with a richly carved saddle stood majestic. Without hesitation, he went to the horse. A letter wedged between its saddle and sleek black coat. Pulling at the wax seal, he held it to the lamp.

"Sir, once more, I offer apology for greatly misreading you. Please accept my finest Stallion as a gift. Like the hammer that rends a man powerless, this is my Lucerne. I beg you, ride him to your destiny— CW."

A thin smile appeared as one eyebrow arched. "Indeed, I am the stronger."

Lucerne turned his long, broad head, instantly

charming Michael. A snort came when he ran his fingers over the horse's crimpy mane. "You are easily eighteen hands!" Each stroke to the horse's shiny coat heightened the desire to mount the magnificent stallion. And he did so with grace. Proudly, he sat tall in the exquisite saddle, which gripped securely where it should. The animal's sweet scent engaged, and his woozy eyes fluttered closed, whispering with passion, "I feel your power, my Lucerne."

His arms stretched wide. He breathed in chilly night air, and without warning, the horse lunged. Thrown off balance, he fisted the thick mane. Lucerne flew as unstoppable as a shooting star and solid beneath him. Long smooth strides had them at the city's edge in no time, the stallion forging a sure path through the forest. Even if he could stop such a commanding beast, nothing was familiar enough to decipher from which direction they had come. The horse maneuvered with a high step between trees, and Michael clung to Lucerne's broad body. Flapping reins whipped at his arms as if they were in God's punishing hands. An invisible force pressed him into the horse while his heart pounded a furious rhythm. Tight to the Friesian's muscular neck, blood raced through his veins, and to catch a breath became difficult.

Then, just as sudden, Lucerne slowed with a prancing gait.

Torches flickered in the distance. Many stars shone above like bright lamps in the night sky to make this more than mystifying. Fear wormed up his spine because he couldn't sit upright.

Cyril wasn't alone. Servants stood silent at his side. Glenmont, yards away and with gloved, steady hands, held a rapier that glistened in this eerie light.

Lucerne halted with an excited snort. He fell off directly in front of Cyril—as if it had been planned. He rubbed his sore arms, oddly aware of every tender welt under the soft linen of his billowed sleeves.

With a jovial flare, the sire stated, "Welcome, Michael. Glenmont wishes to win back his honor." The demon's mesmerizing gaze had him. "Ah—*now* I see the glint of terror through the enormous blush of ego."

With contempt, he eyed the banker. "You insane fool. Do you know what he is?"

"Did you need liquor to steel your nerves this midnight?" Glenmont stepped back, gingerly fanned a gloved hand under a beak of a nose. To deepen the insult, the banker removed one glove and slapped his cheek with it. "This challenge is to the death. You shall forfeit your life."

Cyril smirked. A rapier landed at Michael's feet. He didn't reach for it, and after a tempestuous look, locked his arms against his chest. "I have no desire to duel. 'Tis foolishness. You are under this demon's spell."

"A daring insult," Glenmont shouted, not believing the truth. "The baron should skewer you on the spot. Pick it up!"

He snickered. "Look in his eyes. *He* is demon!"

Poised for attack, the banker shouted, "You will say anything to hide cowardice!"

Angered, he spit out, "Cowardice? I am no coward. He *conjured* this outrage."

The fool stood straight to announce, "Witness this, my good men! The coward will not follow rules of the duel. Therefore, I, Antoine Glenmont of the New York colony, abiding by etiquette and honor, do seek justice with Michael Malone. I defend my wife's honor with my life!"

The move came swift—not untrained. As if guided, Glenmont's rapier found the deepest welt on Michael's arm, slicing through sleeve and tender skin. Blood soaked the cloth and his prey grabbed the arm.

"Soon I will taste you," Cyril whispered, allowing only Michael to hear.

"No! *This* is idiocy! I warn you, demon—"

Glenmont bellowed, "Pick up the rapier, coward!"

The fool's blade slashed his cheek. His hand shot to the wound, and he glared indignant. "I will not do this, demon."

"Then you will die, Michael. Defend yourself or he cuts your throat, and I drink *your* life-force," Cyril hissed.

Although Michael didn't reach for it, the rapier came into his hand as if he had—and Cyril grinned. The men began to thrust and parry—both sure-footed. Glenmont had technical genius, whereas Michael moved with intuitive passion, his swordsmanship instinctual. The sire watched an erotic dance of death as unsuspecting puppets played their parts. It amused him more.

Michael shouted as he fought, "Let us lay down our blades—together. I apologize, from the bottom of my heart for what I have done."

Fully outraged, Glenmont screamed, "What heart—does one beat in your chest? You bewitched my wife, you took her—" He lost his footing, and Michael's blade pierced his chest. Glenmont dropped to the ground.

Michael threw the rapier down with disgust. Out of breath, and aching, he knelt down and ripped open Glenmont's shirt to compress the wound. A gold crucifix gleamed against the man's chest caught by a singular beam of moonlight. As he reached for it, Cyril's minions lifted him away from the banker. A glassy stare of terror held Glenmont's face as the vampire ripped the icon off his neck, then bit into his throbbing vein.

"*No!!*" echoed through silent trees. Morbid sucking sounds sank him to his knees. He gagged, then vomited.

"Take him," Cyril ordered.

Steel hands cinched the Englishman's arms. Thrown across the horse, his stomach hit Lucerne's leather saddle, and with a snort, the magnificent stallion barreled sure-footed through the forest. Feathered hooves clapped against cold earth in anticipation. It knew its destination—it knew its master's home.

I am now a murderer. Never have I soldiered, nor do I particularly enjoy the hunt. Cyril grinned at Michael's panic. *Charming my way out of confrontation with ease, I live for pleasure, not death, not duels, and definitely not defending my honor.* Glenmont's blood coated his shaking hands and his voice faltered as he whispered, "Oh God, what have I done?"

"God had nothing to do with this. I did," the sire responded with a sneer. He fisted Michael's hair, which was still gathered at his neck in a strip of leather. With every stumble into Cyril's home, a merciless yank snapped back his head. It also took courage away, kept his victim queasy and hunched over. And when Cyril's boot kicked his backside, the arrogant young man sailed across the room.

Landing in front of a roaring fire quickly sobered him. He swiped his muddy sleeves across his watery eyes, and then made a discreet study of the windows.

Cyril snickered from his chair like a king on a throne, "I will beat you *severely* before the first filthy hand touches the edge of my expensive, imported draperies."

"Let me leave. I will not tell what happened."

His voice had steadied, and Cyril drummed the chair's arms with even taps. "The authorities believe you are Glenmont's killer. You will be charged and hanged. A servant delivered the body to his screaming widow while Lucerne brought you home."

With narrow eyes full of disgust, he scoffed. "This is not my home."

"I beg to differ. A bath is being drawn as we speak. Perhaps you will be less impolite afterward." Regal and tall, Cyril had strolled to a side table, returning with a delicate cup in hand. "This is chamomile tea for your sour stomach." Michael's eyes shifted to the door. Cyril leaned down watching him sweat in the sweltering room. "The key is in my pocket. Some of us see thought as if it is written on parchment with indigo ink. Some of us are very strong as you soon will be." Like a gracious host, he held out the cup.

Two trembling hands gripped the fragile china. Michael stared with suspicion at yellow liquid, aromatic and hot, but didn't drink.

"No, it is not drugged. Alchemic sedatives to keep you here are not necessary."

"What you are will remain unspoken, I swear on my soul."

"What is that useless thing worth? Look with truth, young sir. Search the vacant thing inside. Which priest hears your contrite confessions of adultery and lust?" The Slav allowed his blue eyes to sparkle, to show ageless superiority as a satisfied smirk crossed his lips. "Nothing anchors you to life. You are alone, a loss to no one."

Sitting on the floor, his victim fell silent. The herbal tea worked its magic on his stomach, but his conscience caused a different discomfort. Cyril saw it all as an arrogant sneer came at him. "What a hypocrite you are, demon, to speak of souls. Did you not offer yours to Satan when you became a thing?"

He curtly corrected, "A vampire."

After a last sip of tea, Michael bitterly repeated, "A *thing!*"

With force, he issued a punishing slap. The blow sent the china cup clear across the parlor and blood dripped from Michael's split lip. At last, Cyril saw fear. His cold finger swiped the scarlet bead, and he brought it to his lips. Its unique taste made the sire's eyes widen. The beast-within wanted it all, wanted it now. Momentarily stunned, he whispered, "Indeed, a bloodline both ancient and untainted."

"You change the subject? Tell me of your *immoral* soul!"

Cyril swallowed the growl. Instead of anger, he displayed patience. Soon enough, his new child of the night would learn correct protocol. "Such wit accompanies an interesting choice of words. Most humans cower before me, but you choose to banter. How perceptive of one so young... Or is your boldness mere foolishness? Listen well and learn," he said like a tutor. "The beast-within swallows it for eternity. You will know this and more, my child."

"I am *not* a child," Michael stated, again indignant. "I near twenty-eight."

"And *I* have walked this earth since 1305." The vampire paused, let that fact work on him. Sweat dripped from Michael's brow, and fear made it impossible for him to swallow. "I was sired late in life by a beautiful creature. I had wealth—a full, happy life. I outlived my wife and sons." He crooked his head, ordering, "Go. Your bath water steams." To further snare Michael's mind, the foyer doors opened without his touch. As if the man were a houseguest, not a hostage, he added in a cordial manner, "My minions will not harm you, but simply bring what you need."

Cyril sensed deception in Michael's submissive bow. The human followed his minions into the foyer. They were small in stature, not like Cyril, not like his victim. Long strides brought Michael midway to the stairs before he turned and ran. Instead of freedom, the Englishman came face to face with his fate. Cyril's amber eyes glittered like a tiger. His long white canines were bared. In the blink of an eye, the terrified man hit the wall, his cheek pressed to the stone. The sire's pressure on a mortal's spine was enough to paralyze.

"That was not a wise choice, my son. Lesson one: Never provoke the wrath of *this* sire."

"No! *Please*," Threads of tears dripped from Michael's dark eyes.

Fear made a man's mind easy to read. The image of his soul burning in Hell, the shock of dying was now reality. Uneven sobs filled with regret about three sisters leaving, meeting his end without an heir, a self-centered life—the absence of true love. Michael Malone's physical strength was of no use against one as powerful as he.

"Please do not do this to me," the young man cried. But the erotic rush of devouring an ancient bloodline called to Cyril. Exposed and hungry, the beast-within called. Michael choked a final sob and screamed, "*Dear God*, please save me!"

Cyril ripped into the pulsing jugular vein drawing cells of a mystical bloodline deep into his throat. Like a narcotic, he fought the desire to take it all. The thrill of his new child paling and a strong heart slowing! The fine specimen of human flesh approached death. Easily, he lifted the strapping man and flew down stone steps to a hidden room. Lined with soft black satin, a polished maple casket waited. And like an eager parent, Cyril placed Michael in it. He tore open his left wrist, forced his new child's thin lips apart with one finger. Thick, crimson liquid trickled down his child's throat.

When Michael's mouth clamped his wrist, Cyril reached near intoxication.

"Drink, my passionate child, suckle well. Immeasurable strength is in every ounce of blood we share as sire and son." Those were his exact words…

Lost in memories of that long ago night, Cyril pulled himself out of the chair and crept to the fireplace. With a flick of his wrist, the fire flared wild to reheat the room. "You are gone, my son," he hissed as his palms teased the flames.

The recall was as vivid as if it were yesterday, not 1690.

"My inhuman hands plucked you from Lucerne

and hurled you to the stones. You slouched on the stones and trembled that all-important night. I read your every thought, my son.

Then I marveled as your bright-amber eyes flashed wide before such heavy lids fluttered closed." It had thrilled Cyril as never before. "My legacy became your destiny. Someone will pay for destroying the beast-within that bound sire to son for eternity. Over a century ago, you took him from me, angel. But now, he is gone forever."

Cyril seethed, and like a man, the sire mourned.

Chapter 9

Alana watched Michael's son steadily frown at himself in the salon's huge mirror. "It's not too short, right?" Clumps of curls had already been swept off the floor.

"Holy fucking shit," Lukas grumbled. Celia shushed him before more foul language slipped out, and every old lady in Mirella's trendy hair salon stared and chattered in Italian.

"What are they saying, Ally?" Celia whispered.

"Mirella's customers want to know why anyone in their right mind would cut such beautiful blond hair and turn a sweet-looking boy into a dyed brunette."

"Ouch," Celia mumbled. "But he looks totally different."

"I told you she was the best in the area."

With a dreamy expression, Mirella clicked her tongue. "*O mamma mia*, you look-a so handsome. When *ragazzas* see to you, they will... *Como si dice...* melt a butter!?" The hug from behind came with a loud wet kiss to Lukas's cheek.

He looked miserable and ready to swear again. When Celia pulled him out the door, Alana called over her shoulder in Italian, "Just bill me, Mirella, and thanks a million!"

On the narrow street, she couldn't stop staring at Lukas. But it was his eyes, a deep-blue so vivid that one

72

was drawn to. The inheritance was definitely there, specifically in the intense way he studied everything. "Look at those high cheekbones, just like your father's," she said hoping to engage him. He didn't react. "You'll love the warm Amalfi sun. So what do you think of the seaport?"

He glanced at a group of teenagers talking and laughing on the busy piazza and didn't reply. Alana didn't read minds, but she'd give anything to know more about what he was feeling. *No friends his age. Well, that can't be helped. Nothing remotely familiar... No normal routine, school, or the city streets he knows inside and out. The way he's walking steps behind... On purpose or because he's about to make a run for it? With dark hair he'd blend in, be harder to single out as different.* She also wanted him to like her—more than just a little.

"Think you're up for a trip to Pisa? We could shop. Buy some new things that you can actually try on, Lu— uh, Evan...Evan?" His guarded gaze seemed so far away, full of trepidation. Not even a hint of a smile met her friendly one. *Too much to deal with and he isn't coping very well. The distance in him isn't awkward, adolescent hormones. He's just lost.* Doctor Chamberlain had told Miles that because of what Lukas had been through and the years of physical as well emotional stress, normal growth spurts had most likely been delayed. He simply didn't look fifteen.

Then she caught him staring at Celia. "Pisa? Yeah—I guess. Hate being cooped up."

Sweetly, her adopted sister said, "You're uncomfortable around Thorn, right?"

Hostility sailed at her as soon as Celia said the

name, but he kept following, a bit closer now. Yep, she thought, Celia B had hit a nerve.

"How about we, uh, check out the Leaning Tower," Celia quickly suggested. "A-and besides clothes, we'll check out some video games and movies. I like movies."

"It'll keep your mind off things. Mine too." Crawling into bed at dawn too troubled to sleep brought back loads of uncomfortable memories. With everyone belted in she gunned the engine. The small red car plowed down Portofino's narrow back street at a very unsafe speed.

****

Miles stood in the doorway of Michael's bedroom and gave a slight nod to Mother Anne. He glanced at the vampire lost in induced sleep. The Sisters had changed out of their habits, which he thought wise. With all the windows wide open now, if any of Rosa's neighbors across the street saw the women, they'd not raise unanswerable questions.

Mother Anne followed him into the small living room. "Michael has round-the-clock care. We've redressed every wound."

"I'll update Monsignor and any Council members who are still here. In two days, the need to feed will be a matter of survival. Research indicates that to be the point where he might struggle against your will."

"I've read your brief. We've made the twelve-hour mark without incident. This somnolent state requires our full concentration. One of us should always be close by, but I'm not taking any chances, Miles. Two will sit with him until he's brought back to consciousness."

Stopping at the apartment door, he turned back.

"I'll be at the rectory if needed."

"There is much on your mind."

"There is much to be discussed," he offered before leaving.

****

Once outside in the beautiful spring weather, Miles glanced at his watch. He had fifteen minutes, just enough time to enjoy a brisk walk uphill after the tension he'd lived through the last eleven days. Thorn's documentation—eight days worth of detailed narrative from Michael's dream of survival, made his briefcase feel like a barbell. Twelve copies in rough draft, one for each Council member that he hoped would be acceptable for today.

Only after entering the conference room did he realize that another researcher had been summoned. Deepa Chandra, his counterpart on the European Continent, accepted her copy with a supportive smile. *She has to be here. Italy's in her jurisdiction.* Very good, he thought seeing six Council members. Monsignor Scarlatti took his place at the table and motioned him to begin.

The first fact-sheet was in everyone's hands.

"From what I can piece together, this began many months ago when Michael Malone secretly created a plan to obliterate the North American Continent's three sorcerers, referred to as The Triumvirate of Evil by all Georgians. Seven years ago, as we now confirm, they had authorized the ritualistic killing of the angel Helena's corporeal presence to kidnap eight-year-old Lukas Malone—handed him over to the sorcerers in the Second Realm. Michael's plan of revenge included the destruction of NWT—New World Technologies, the sorcerers' earthly link to our dimension. Well after sunset on May 19, 2005, the vampire took action. On his orders, two ex-Guardians destroyed the sorcerers' elite vampires known as the Summoned Six."

"Who authorized the two ex-Guardians' deaths?" the monsignor asked.

"The sorcerers' human liaison, Clayton Mails."

"And the Triumvirate?"

"Michael annihilated them by fire. However, it is indicated in the dream that one of them opened the insidious dimensional hub many blocks away before burning, to call forth Hell-beasts. Said portal in a deserted passageway was located by the Champion, where he engaged these creatures in battle. It was Clayton who unleashed an enchanted creature to poison Michael. This vile act allowed his capture. Shortly after dawn, I found the boy distraught and disoriented at Michael's brownstone. Although undetected, Lukas had witnessed the end of the battle in the passageway."

Antonio DeMarra, a Council member, spoke first. "Without informing Michael that I am a Georgian, I've been employed by him to run the bookshop below Alana's home. The vampire insisted I close it a full week before this occurred in Manhattan."

"If your connection to us had been discovered?" the monsignor asked.

"Clayton may have had a reason to come after Alana," Antonio stated.

Miles nodded confirmation. "Michael made it explicitly clear that he acted solely out of revenge for Lukas, who, by the way, Alana knew very little about. I might add—her rescue strategy was ingenious. Clayton fully believes Michael was fed to the incinerator at three a.m. on Day Nine of captivity. Our last source at NWT has sent confirmation."

"Is the informant safe?" Antonio asked.

"She and her daughter have disappeared in the midlands of Scotland."

"And his son is untraceable," Cesar Gonzales added. "A fictitious dossier was created; Lukas's physical appearance slightly altered. As they say in the states, all bases covered."

Monsignor Scarlatti leaned back. "Last night, the healers exorcised the beast within Michael."

"Astonishing," Deepa whispered loud enough for all to hear. "There's no question, Miles. The vampire has *clearly* disrupted demonic activity in your jurisdiction. He's earned the title of Champion—many times over."

"The dream journal... This is a rough draft, I presume?" Monsignor asked.

Miles nodded.

****

After a short break for lunch, the discussion dragged on for several more hours. Miles peeled off his reading glasses, finally asking, "Georgian psychics also sensed the angel Helena's intervention in his dream-fantasy, am I correct?"

"Reports have come to us from around the globe. The full Council must reconvene for that matter alone. They will also study the preliminary reports from the dream of survival." Monsignor Scarlatti closed the file. "What about the child, researcher?"

Miles cleared his throat. "Everyone is concerned. God only knows *what* he suffered at the sorcerers' hands for four years. The boy does not speak about it and there is no way for me to broach the subject at this time. The dream journal gives only small insights into Lukas at age-thirteen when Michael freed him from the sorcerers in the Second Realm. Then, at age fourteen, a full year's illusion of normal life tempers Lukas's rage, but I suspect many issues still on his mind. We have no way of documenting the lost year. However, underneath his quiet demeanor, it is clear that the child is prone to rage. He needs to bond with Michael—as soon as possible."

"I am not without compassion, but I disagree," Monsignor stated. "We cannot know the vampire's condition until after he is awakened and questioned. However, I also sensed emotional instability last night—like a bomb ready to detonate."

He knew Monsignor Scarlatti to be an understanding man and gave a slow nod. "I'll talk with him. I believe Lukas trusts me." He closed his notes on the conference table, leaned forward thinking, now's the time. "There's another matter to consider, specifically, Michael's attachment to Alana."

Brother Giovanni, a monk from San Marco Abbey, had, so far, only listened to the discussion. His usual warmth and friendly demeanor weren't visible when his hands pressed flat on the table. "She broke a solemn vow during her mission—one in existence for a millennium, Researcher. Guardians lose clarity once they act upon physical desires. We're aware that Alana's strength of purpose doubled instead of dissipating after the sexual experience. The Council unanimously agreed to place full blame on the creature and an exception was issued for Alana."

The monk's righteous words captured everyone's

attention, and Miles's jaw fully tensed. "Alana's the reason why Michael Malone is a Champion, a proven weapon for *our* side, Giovanni. Carefully read the dream of survival again. You'll agree that it's not all fantasy. This information comes from a trusted Servant of Souls. It is impressive."

The shuffling of papers began. He took a moment; made eye-contact with each of them.

"None of us knows who'll be called to this mission. Yet Michael felt compelled to protect Alana—*years* before she accepted her destiny. He was near during every attack, even before he introduced himself. Alana was a year into her mission when they first spoke to one another. No one condones what she later did with him. Helena yanked Michael from this dimension because of what they *both* did the night she turned twenty-one. While he was gone, demonic activity lessened to the point of non-existence in Manhattan. Who'd have expected this, especially heading into Y2K? Never has it happened before; never has it happened since."

Silent now, they scrutinized his documentation.

Deepa looked up. "I've studied these numbers before. Miles is right—very few Guardians attacked."

Antonio added, "Is this correct? Right after Michael's return the number of vampires captured or staked shoots back up? Interesting—"

Miles pointed to more documentation. "He returns five months later, and never again approaches Alana—but continues to protect her from the shadows until the day her mission ended last September. And my daughter never had one injury during ten years—*ten years.*"

All but Brother Giovanni nodded, and two council members hadn't said a word. Deepa's expression told Miles to go for it. "The Georgian Creed is that *all* vampires must be destroyed by stake or silver blade. I ask you to consider what Michael Malone has done. I petition the Council to issue a formal document that places *this* vampire above The Law of the Kill."

After folding his hands, Monsignor Scarlatti studied Miles. "That requires a full conclave. Two hundred years of innocent death and demonic mayhem cannot be overlooked. However—I must concur. It is Day Eleven and the portals on an entire continent remain closed. New reports indicate that multitudes of portals in other countries have disappeared. I sense this to be an amazing feat... and permanent. Perhaps Michael will agree to full disclosure of his actions before reclaiming his soul in 1890."

He phrased a careful response, saying, "I understand there must be consequences for the taking of so many lives. But consider if *any* soul, who has no control over what it is forced to do, is truly responsible for his or her actions. Michael Malone wasn't a killer before being sired. We simply see a brash, self-absorbed young man. These traits don't turn a person into a vicious murderer. The beast-within did that."

Brother Giovanni eyebrows rose. "Are you suggesting *absolution*?"

"Absolution is not ours to give, Giovanni," Monsignor Scarlatti calmly interjected. "But we must allow Michael the act of atonement."

Fine. He could accept that. The discussion continued until they reached agreement.

****

Close to sunset, Miles Bookman walked back to the red brick building a great deal slower. *Another long day, and there's no black or white when Michael's the topic, with the exception of this devotion he has to Alana and his son.* The researcher in him didn't expect to defend the vampire. But many issues needed consideration. He knew Alana better than anyone. Five months after turning sixteen, Alfonso and Stefania Ciminio had tragically died. He and Laura had been their close friends since college. The Georgians made it possible for him and his wife to immediately adopt Alana, whom they had known since birth. *I know her. I know how she thinks.* She'll never stop loving Michael, he realized. According to the tastefully edited version of the dream of survival, Alana was Michael's soulmate, his beacon of hope.

Already exhausted, he still had much to do today.

****

"One more task completed," Miles said to his daughters later that evening. "The blood donation schedule is set. We start tomorrow... the three of us. Lukas has agreed to give a pint as well." Finally relaxed in an armchair, he sensed a quiet evening needed by all tonight. Ten minutes later, a loud crash and the sound of breaking glass came from the den.

Lukas strutted down the hall yelling, "You're the fucking servant, remember asshole? You clean it!" The guestroom door slammed, and he disappeared from sight.

Pure misery claimed Thorn's face as he sank into the sofa and let out a low grumble.

Dreading the reply, he had to ask. "What just happened?"

Rubbing a shoulder, the burly man groaned. "I gave him the short list of dos and don'ts. The kid came at me, fists flying and kicking like Jackie Chan! He *obviously* doesn't like to be told what to do. The lamp just missed me, Miles. I was seconds away from breaking Helena's No Interference Rule." Celia started to rise. "No, I'll clean it up," Thorn quickly offered. "This isn't going to be easy, Miles."

"Dealing with a teenager never is. I'll speak with him," he said in a calm tone.

"The kid's ready to crash and burn. That's a fact. Reading him is like putting a puzzle together without a picture and with pieces missing. He's got the left-hook of a boxer. Humph! I'd rather deal with his daddy—like any day."

"He needs time to adjust."

"He needs to be tamed."

"That too," he replied and rubbed his aching temples.

Thorn took the broom from Celia while Alana simply stood stunned. After cleaning up the mess, Miles watched the gloomy empath leave the apartment.

****

Sitting on the windowsill, staring out at the night, Lukas didn't react when Miles entered the guestroom. Experience as a parent told him to use a casual voice. Rarely, in fact, had he ever raised his voice to either Celia or Alana. "Why did you throw the lamp at Thorn?"

"Keep it away from me."

"That's not an answer. Why would you attack such a gentle person?"

"Don't know," Lukas grumbled.

Simmering anger was obvious and the lie came too fast. "Yes, you do. I won't punish you—"

"Like you think you can."

"Mind your manners, young man, and don't get fresh with me. We are guests in Alana's home. Throwing anything at anyone is not acceptable—nor are your fists." He hoped for an admission of guilt. None came. "I've noticed how you look at Thorn—"

Lukas sprang up. Both hands instantly balled into fists. "Keep it the fuck away from me, okay? This is *my* problem," he hissed, "not yours. That thing is— Ow...shit!" With a wince, he paled.

He reached out just as the boy slumped and swayed. To his surprise, Lukas didn't pull away. Fists stayed pressed to his temples and as he leaned in, he knew this behavior hid fear. Perhaps, he had gained a bit of trust. "It's all right. The pain will subside very quickly." The words came so suddenly, Miles had no idea whether or not it would happen, but Lukas didn't budge from his fatherly hug.

****

Celia's green eyes radiated love for the huge man standing outside Michael's home. "We came to see if you're okay. Haven't heard any more furniture flying, so I'm thinking Dad's gotten him to chill. So, are you, you know, over it?"

"I'm calm, but I can't say the same for the twitchy woman beside you."

A slight grin appeared, and Alana's eyes narrowed. "Back off, Adonis, because if the tables were turned, you'd be twitchy too."

One bushy eyebrow rose. "Ah, but they're not. This is highly creative of you—using the only woman

83

in the universe who turns my knees to jelly to get inside. Think you'll sneak a peek at our patient? Maybe steal a quick kiss or place a palm on his wounded chest? I might be able to get the geriatric sorority sisters to leave the room for a quick cappuccino."

As he opened the door, Alana shook her head and gave a slow smile. The timid empath she'd seen in Manhattan had been much heavier, huggable like a giant teddy bear. Well. He was still a teddy bear just not a giant one. Thorn hardly ever spoke, his gaze forever cast down to avoid reading her. Without thick glasses, his gray-green eyes shone radiant, no longer disguising the mystical ability to see into her heart. On the plane, he kept apologizing for not participating in Michael's rescue. "My mission in this world is purely reconnaissance," he had said.

Jolted from her thoughts, she stared at Mother Anne who smiled as she stood. It didn't calm her nerves—and a day in Pisa hadn't gotten Michael off her mind, either.

"He's not in pain. I didn't get a chance to introduce myself last night. I'm Anne Critchley, one of your *Zia's* oldest friends." A clear, distinctive voice, she thought, a compassionate gesture that she takes my hand. "We're halfway there."

She nodded, felt maternal goodness in the healer's touch, which felt exactly like *Zia* Rosa's. Mystical healers also read thought, but still she asked, "How long can I stay?"

"Only a minute and you cannot touch him tonight. Rosa and I must be with you."

Disappointment showed in the slump of her shoulder as she bit her lower lip. It didn't take a psychic to know this wasn't what she wanted to hear.

Ever the eternal optimist, Celia whispered, "That's better than nothing, Ally."

****

Michael's exposed right arm rested at his side. A heavy comforter tucked around his long, lean frame. As close as possible, Alana studied his bruised, handsome face. A shaded lamp next to Rosa cast a soft glow in the room, the smell of antiseptics used to clean his wounds hung heavy in the air. *Germ-free and every window locked and draped again. Oh God, I need to hear his voice, to see his dark eyes open. Why do I feel nothing and everything at the same time? Why does this have to take so long?*

"One more day… That's not too much to ask," Mother Anne whispered.

All she could do was nod once…and leave.

Chapter 10

The day of Michael's awakening didn't start out peaceful. An early riser, Miles craved the beginnings of a new morn. The dawn itself was his tried-and-true alarm clock. Today was important. With every hour categorized, his timeline for tonight's event was clear.

Pink light spilled through open windows and hoping not to wake Lukas in the bed across the room, he stood in silence. After a deep breath of refreshing sea air, he noticed the other twin bed was empty. Lukas should've been asleep, a mere six feet away. Fatherly concern soared, not to mention panic in thinking the teen had run away.

Looking around, he moved to the edge of Lukas's bed and saw the boy slumped in the corner. Blood trickled from where he'd bitten into his own arm. "I believe you. Just leave me alone. No. No..." the boy trembled and stammered as if he were in an altered state. "Please... won't run away again, I swear."

This had to be a familiar terror, something that could plunder a fragile mind. Miles crouched down, touched his cheek. "Lukas, look at me."

Glassy-eyed, the child began to wedge himself deeper into the corner. Both knees met his chest with his arms wrapped tight around them. Breaths heaved as he tucked his chin low to hide his face.

"You're bleeding, I'll help—"

With an ugly snarl Lukas shoved, and he crashed

into a dresser. Wincing, he grabbed his left shoulder and crawled back. "Please let me help you." Cowered yet glaring at him, the child's eyes dripped silent tears. Then he palmed his eyes and ran his hands down his bloodied shirt. "Lukas, do you hear me?" No answer came. "I won't hurt you. Just give me your arm."

As the minutes ticked away, he repeated his request many times. Then very tentative, Lukas held out his bitten arm. Without a fight he got him up and watched as the boy curled into himself on his bed.

"It…goes away…heals…always does."

"Well I'm not about to wait. Does your head hurt again?"

First a nod, then a moan with no understandable words. He ran to the bathroom and returned with a soapy washcloth and bath towel. Gently, he wiped streaks of blood off the boy's face and arm. Afterward, he grabbed a clean T-shirt from the dresser and helped Lukas remove the stained one, relieved the boy was cooperative, responsive.

Why he turned on the bedside lamp, Miles didn't know. Enough sun now lit the room. With a squint, he narrowed his focus and became more disturbed. Subtle discolorations covered the child's back and chest. Eclectic ribbons of scars marred his tender flesh, and a father's rage surged.

"Dear Lord," he muttered as he guided Lukas's shivering arms into the T-shirt. The early hour, coupled with the nightmare, had the child searching for rest. "No one knows about these, do they?"

"No…just you… Please, don't tell him. Don't tell him that I-I couldn't fight back."

"Shhh, sleep," he soothed, kept a hand on Lukas's

damp cheek. Tucking the blanket around, he sat with Lukas until the boy's body relaxed.

What rushed through his gut was vicious. Right now, he didn't feel like the even-tempered researcher he was. In fact, he wanted to kill.

****

Dressed in jeans and a lavender sweater, Sister Gabriella stood at the open door of Alana's home. Miles looked up from his laptop hearing, "Knock, knock, Miles... Is Alana here? Mother Anne's given me an important, ex-Guardian task," she said in a bright, cheery voice.

He pulled out the pencil wedged between his teeth, motioned her in. "I'll make myself scarce, Sister. Please, sit. My Lord, it's almost noon? I'll be in the den with Lukas. As you know, he didn't sleep well. Alana," he called as he stood.

"But he likes you, Miles. That's important." Gabriella simply smiled as she looked around.

Not at all convinced that she wanted to leave her room on what was sure to be a tense day, Alana walked into the living room...dressed in jeans and a lavender sweater. She stared at the healer who took in everything about the living room. *Short blond hair framing soft-blue eyes. A very pretty face... Great, just great. Wish she had stayed in her habit like a good nun. And just look at what she's wearing...* suddenly she was uncomfortable in her own home.

The nun gave a winning smile. "Wow... Nice place and the décor so comfy and charming."

"Thanks, but I had nothing to do with this."

"So I heard. Malone has great taste for a vamp. I'm

impressed."

Settled on the sofa with one bare foot tucked underneath, she watched the stunning nun flop into an armchair across from her—perfectly at ease.

"Oooh...very cushiony! I could fall asleep. And who'd have guessed we'd both look really good in this color? Even with such opposite skin tones and hair color. I'll shout out a fashion alert tomorrow. But I'd bet my last Euro that we have many traits in common, having been in the same line of work."

The mischievous grin made her suspicious and curious, asking, "How long ago did your mission end, Sister?"

"Four years last August 11th... And please call me Gabby." The nun flashed another billboard smile. "I kissed California good-bye and came to Siena. After what we see, you can't walk around clueless anymore. Plus, I had this healing thing going on. I used to teach Kindergarten. Show me a boo-boo and all it needed was a touch and a prayer. Hunted vamps by night, taught the ABCs by day, and promised myself how if I survived those ten years, I'd follow my heart instead of my head."

'Gabby' continued to smile. Alana didn't. Such a confident manner made her more self-conscious. Not that she wasn't confident in her mystical skills. It was every other avenue of her life that hadn't fallen into place. Yet. "So, it's the head and the heart thing again. Have you been talking with my aunt?" *Why had she been in Michael's dream? Celia said nothing about the healer being this pretty! Okay, that's catty, but why was she in his dream? There has to be a reason.*

As her head tilted slightly to the side, Gabriella's

smile faded. "We're on the same side, Alana. And no, I don't have a clue as to why I helped Michael in his dream. Don't you want to know how he's doing?"

"If something were wrong, you'd have told me already."

"Oooh...we're a little snappish, and today of all days."

"I didn't expect sarcasm." She paused to swallow what she *definitely* didn't expect to feel. "So how is he?"

"There's the faintest trace of poison left his system, but our consecrated blood will dilute it when he's transfused tonight. Mother Anne will allow you to be in the room when we wake him." Alana turned away, didn't respond. "Look, every Guardian's ten years are different. I got out of some tight spots. Knew when the water was too deep for my toes. As for celebrating my twenty-seventh birthday, I was the only Guardian in my territory to make it that far."

"I never asked Michael to protect me."

"The truth is you didn't have to. He loved you."

"There's a lot you don't know about him—or me."

"But I know love when I see it. Being a nun doesn't strap blinders on these baby blues. I've read his file. Heard the stories. He's assisted other Guardians since you left Manhattan. Okay, let's put the handsome hero looks aside. Malone is something else fighting the evil ones. That creature has conviction—*and* the ability to love."

They stared at each other...neither woman willing to back down. "So, your point is, Sister?"

Gabriella stood. "For some reason, my soul absorbs your turmoil. It's a heavy burden you carry, which I sincerely hope will be resolved." At the door, she turned back. "When we ripped the demon from him, Malone's soul emerged strong, and it called out for only *you*. That truly touched my heart. I had to make this offer. You do what you feel is best, but the invitation stands."

Before she could answer, Gabriella was gone.

****

The late-afternoon sky, sweeping over the seaport, streaked white clouds billowing against a cornflower-blue backdrop. Alana had made the reservation and Miles asked for a table with a perfect view of the Mediterranean Sea.

"I'm glad Dad suggested an early supper away from home. I think something happened this morning. He kept hinting how Lukas needed a change of scenery. I know I did." Celia nodded while she stared at Michael's son and Miles a distance away, walking the stony path at water's edge. She picked at the decadent chocolate truffle as Celia made delicate headway through a wedge of amaretto cheesecake. "You're the only person I know who can make a sliver of cake last for hours, sis."

A sweet grin came at her. "Still wrestling with yourself, Ally? I'm not sensing the usual gusto for anything chocolate."

"Isn't Vito a great chef? *Zia* and I eat here once a week. He tries out each new recipe on us. Vito's been over a couple of times, you know. Thirty-two, unattached, cute and straight—what more could a woman ask for?"

Celia dipped her spoon back into the creamy dessert. "You're dancing around the issue like an

91

expert. Do I have to use the 'A' word? The clock's ticking here, sweetie."

"I'm not 'A-voiding' the issue. See? I saved you from saying it."

"Well, besides Michael, chocolate is the love of your life, but you're torturing that thing! Vacillating vibes bounce off you like rubber balls. Listen, even a holy healing sister confirmed that he still adores only you."

"Some holy healing sister. Gabriella looks like she just stepped off the pages of *Vogue*. Not a stitch of makeup on alabaster skin and inquisitive, huge blue eyes."

"Do I detect envy here?" Celia licked the cheesecake on her spoon.

"What…me, envious of a *holy* healing sister? She's had her hands all over him." She pushed the plate away, folded her arms on the table, and stared at the sea.

"Those are *holy* healing hands, and just because Gabby's touching him, it doesn't mean she's *touching* him. You could say the same for *Zia* Ro, Mother Annie, or Sister Maggie. They've had their *holy* healing hands all over him, too."

"Do you give everyone catchy nicknames?"

"Hello, Miss I'm-still-avoiding-the-issue… Okay. I'll play. To be honest, they feel like my psychic family. We have certain gifts in common. If I hadn't met Thorn, I just might have walked that untouchable path myself."

"You've got to be kidding…really?" Celia stared directly at her, and the secretive smile snagged her attention. She half-believed that revelation until Celia giggled.

"Nah… Dad needs grandchildren."

Suddenly curious, her eyes narrowed. "Are you and Thorn planning ahead or did you EPT?"

"Like I'd need to pee on a stick to confirm it," Celia huffed.

"Wait… Thorn's an empath. Helena sent him here! He's not entirely human, is he?"

"Are you really asking this? Thorn's more than entirely human—he's mystically human! You're fixating on the 'normal' thing again, aren't you? Hello—I'm not normal, you're not normal, nothing in our *world* is normal! Yeah, we struggle through like everyone else, but *we* are different. The Georgians, the Catherines—rules of the norm don't apply to us. Look at Lukas. He couldn't have survived if he were *normal*. Anyhow, I think it's over-rated. There's a bigger picture here, and if you continue to rock n' roll between accepting who you are and wanting to be something you're not, it's major heartbreak time—not to mention the dreaded mental meltdown. Michael is in your heart. He's in your soul. Go tonight because he needs you. Forget about all the holy healing hands, and forget about normal, abnormal, or paranormal. Go with your gut this time. Oooh… Here comes the flash of I'm-so-stubborn in those hazel eyes, sis," Celia added with a prissy grin.

She leaned forward, blurting out, "You don't know what committing ten years to a mystical mission can do to you! Of course, I've made this more difficult for myself because nothing compares to the way I felt when…when he made love to me," she whispered. She inhaled deeply and blew out a long, steady breath. "All right, I confess. I take one look at Michael… Having him so close, remembering what being with him felt like, wanting him to be something he can't—it overwhelms me."

Celia gave a sympathetic shrug, took her hand. "Do what you need to do, sis. Take this whole I-love-you-I-love-you-not thing apart and put it back together seven different ways, but don't avoid this issue. It's not healthy, and it's not you. Michael didn't want to survive, but he did. That's got to tell you something! Only *you* could've rescued him and right here *with* you is where he's meant to be. Think long and hard before you decide to walk away, because if you turn your back on him, it'll kill him quicker than a wooden stake."

****

The magnificent yachts anchored in tranquil waters seemed to intrigue the uneasy teen. Radiant colors of botanical treasures, blossoming from the earth during spring, had dozens of artists lost in its beauty, sketching the harbor. Miles watched Lukas take in everything. The warm breeze felt like a summer blanket around his shoulders.

"Never seen anything like this in Manhattan… It's way cool." A gray pebble sailed through the air, landed far out in the sea.

He had to smile. "Are you nervous about tonight?"

With a quick shrug, Lukas mumbled, "I guess, a little." He handed him another pebble, which didn't go quite as far. Thinking about seeing his father clearly threw Lukas off his game. "I'll never make it past the bulldog, though."

The sullen tone caught his attention as the boy pitched another pebble.

"I can get you past Thorn."

"Yeah—Like you think he won't know or something?"

"Oh he'll know, but he won't interfere."

It took a full minute before he replied, "Yeah. I want to see Michael. Will you be around?"

"I will."

"How about the healers. Do they have to listen when I talk to him?"

"I doubt it. We'll wait outside the room while the sisters bring your father back to consciousness. Patience must kick in, Lukas." He added in a slight, stern voice, "There will be no aggressive behavior later on—just patience."

"I hear you. I can do that."

He handed him another pebble. It sailed farther out. "You'll be able to tell your father what's on your mind." The troubled expression proved that the only person this child trusted was the one handing over small, jagged stones. The way the last one flew across the water had his respect. "Your arm is amazing. For all we know, it might reach the shores of San Marco Abbey. Let's get back. I'm sure my daughters are talked out by now."

"They can talk for hours. So, like, what do you think they say to each other?"

The question made his smile broaden. "I've often wondered that myself. It beats me. They tell me it's a girl thing."

Chapter 11

Forty-eight hours had finally passed. At midnight, Thorn stood by Michael's door while Miles and Lukas settled on the black leather couch in the living room. Reading the man, he said with a laugh in his tone, "You really went out on a limb with this one, Researcher." As Miles sent him a warning look, he zeroed in on the fidgeting kid. Even though the monsignor had finally agreed that a minute with Michael might ease the pouting boy's need, Thorn wasn't convinced. With any luck, his father would come out of this with his sanity intact and all would be well.

From the threshold of the bedroom, he caught Celia's eye and she gave a nod. Alana was seated next to her in a chair by the dresser. It left little room to move around. Purposely blocking the kid's sight-line, he studied the three healers in consecrated habits and each specific task being done to bring Michael to consciousness.

Mother Anne and Rosa rubbed a gelatinous substance into his open wounds. There were many. Aromatic, rare herbs and spices engulfed the somnolent vampire like an invisible cloud. Bruises faded and cuts sealed themselves as they proceeded from abrasion to incision. Then she nodded as Magdalena guided a long needle into the sunken vein of Michael's right arm. Gabriella squeezed the blessed Georgian blood from the first bag as an ancient chant began. When the last bag drained, Magdalena leaned down to ease the needle out.

Thorn backed out of the doorway and closed the door, prepared to wrestle the kid to the ground if that bratty temper cranked up during the next crucial step.

****

Michael's eyelids fluttered. He began to move his head through the stiffness from side to side. Shallow intakes of air were exhaled as soft moans—not lascivious growls. *My dear sisters, pray for my immoral soul,* he thought as the sire's fangs sank into his neck… His fingers twitched and his fists clenched and unclenched in erratic spasms. A black shadow hovered close enough to hear it breathing, but it wasn't broad nor as tall as Cyril. On the edge of terror, he said in a hoarse hushed tone as it leaned closer, "You are not the vampire… Who are you?"

"Who are *you*, S*ignore*?" came back at him, the voice soft and feminine.

"Michael… Michael Malone. Where is the demon? I-I cannot clearly see, I do not know—" Crushing pain surged again, and he swallowed. An unfamiliar taste made his mouth feel as if grains of sand lined his throat. *I am cold beyond reason, and something else is strange…absurdly so! How am I able to hear beating hearts, each a different rapid rhythm. The scent in the air is heavy with herbs and incense…* Yet, one particular scent intoxicated his senses as never before.

Shivering, he flinched when the black shadow touched his shoulder. The warmth of her hand comforted in the purest way. Desperate to move, he absolutely couldn't. "We will not harm you, *Signore*," the woman said in heavily accented English.

"Please, I beg you, kind lady, disclose who you are. And where it is that I am… Is this the demon's house of death? He-he is at my throat as I, as I—" Each breath was a conscious labor. He blinked repeatedly yet couldn't clear the film from his eyes. "Did he blind me? Are you demon sent by him? Or was I rescued by God or man before—" He let out a tortured moan in utter agony. It couldn't be stopped as a second shadow sat at his side and took his hand. "Am I already dead? Are you sent to take me—"

"I'm Mother Anne, Michael, a Roman Catholic nun. Please allow the sisters to make you comfortable." Her accent reminded him of home. But Sisters? Had his sisters found him on the precipice of dearth? She pulled his shoulders forward as pillows piled behind his back. Then a third filmy shadow pulled him up into a comfortable, sitting position—with ungodly strength. Mother Anne's scent came closer still as her hand came to his cheek. Gratitude filled him to the point that he swallowed to hold back hope.

Could it be that he was rescued before… "I cannot see and—s-so cold," he moaned through another shiver, still disoriented as another heavy blanket was tucked around his body.

"Your vision will clear momentarily. Please do not be afraid. You've been severely injured."

Her voice held reassurance as his senses heightened. "You are British as I? Yet this is not England."

"No. It is Italy."

"Impossible… No. I am in the New York colony an ocean away." His body continued to quake, and he searched for her hand again. Instantly, she took it. Held it tight. The gesture, so maternal, soothed him. When she brushed his hair off his forehead, it reminded him of his oldest sister and with no control whatsoever his eyes began to fill. "I am saved? The demon did not end my life?"

"This is complicated. It will be carefully explained to you."

He crooked his head, suddenly very still. "How is it that I sense so many strange things at once? Someone cries. I hear her tears. She calls to my soul as—" He gasped in a mid-sentence tremble. Weak and confused, what he thought could not possibly be, something he could not accept. His hand recoiled. So terrified that he bent forward and wrapped his arms around his chest as his chin tucked low. "Merciful God, my heart—it does not beat. I did not live. Oh God—" And with crystal clarity, the likes of which he'd never experienced, his bruised, stitched arms came into focus. There were three nuns tending him, but they weren't his sisters.

The faintest utterance of "Michael, my love—" sounded less than a breath away.

At once, his head jerked in her direction, and he met her glistening eyes. The most alluring woman in the world was across the room and out of his reach. Without a doubt, he knew he loved her. Sorrow had claimed her, but then, very steady, very determined, she crawled across the bed and came to him. He welcomed the delicate arms that held him to her warm breast with tenderness. Her touch promised more than comfort, yet he choked back tears.

Does she love me as I love her? Puzzling images exploded in his brain. None made sense. Gentle kisses graced his hair as her surging heartbeat pounded against his ear. He had to look, to drink in her beauty and affection. The softest hands held his face as he moved, now able to gaze into such large, hazel eyes so full of worry. And in that instant, their souls were lost in silent reverie.

For her, he had immeasurable need.

Boldly, she kissed his lips, his brow—as if consumed with gratitude that he had awakened. An elderly woman placed a caring hand on her shoulder causing the beautiful woman to look away for a brief moment before she whispered, "Thank God you know my touch. Thank God you came back to…" The comfort of her embrace consumed him, and she seemed unwilling to let him go.

"Why does your presence ease me so? Tis as if I know your soul to be joined to mine. Yet I know not your name."

"Alana. My name's Alana."

"Ah-la-nah." Each soft vowel was a gentle sigh… Passionate desires ignited within him. "Are you a Guardian Angel, sent to rescue me from this madness?"

Her beautiful eyes filled again. "Something like that. Please, just know that you're safe."

She let go, and gently, his back met the soft pillows. A petite woman with short auburn hair approached. Dressed as strangely as his lady, she gave a sweet smile and took Alana's hand. He looked from face to face yet memorized every facet of the alluring woman he knew he loved as she left him to sit once again—in the far corner of this mysterious room.

****

The upscale London accent with outdated intonations, antiquated inflections, sentence cadences and clipped pronunciation—every word Thorn heard in his head sent chills down his spine. And outside Michael's door, he quickly snapped to attention. Full-blown panic rattled him. Looking at Miles, he quickly shouted, "Get the monsignor…now!"

Thank God the man didn't ask "the question" before running out the door. What worried him more was the stubborn resolve in the kid's glare. Still prepared to tackle him, he softened his tone. "I'm really sorry, kid. Your reunion is temporarily on hold. Please… I honestly feel for you. Believe me, if I knew more, I'd share. Don't fight me on this one, okay?"

Maybe the look in his eye triggered the unexpected response, and Lukas sat back. Relaxed his lethal hands which curved around the chair's arms instead of curling into fists.

He sweated through the minutes it took for Monsignor Scarlatti to arrive and opened the bedroom door without saying a word. Gabriella and Magdalena came out. Didn't say a word. Then Alana holding Rosa's hand followed. Celia appeared stunned, which made him all the more uneasy. And once again, as if he stood with the priest and Mother Anne in the sealed room, he heard Michael's every thought. Except he couldn't fully concentrate.

Miles studied his expression. So did the kid. *And just like that patience and self-control have come and gone. He looks too twitchy, and nobody that came out of that room is saying a word.*

"Shit," the kid suddenly mumbled. "A lame joke since the city… I fucking trusted you." Of all people, he glared directly at the researcher.

"Shhh… sit still, young man," Miles whispered as

he went over to Lukas fidgeting in the other armchair and leaned down. "Remember what we talked about?"

One punch sent the good man flying, and the kid ran out before Thorn could grab him. Miles's spine had slammed into the corner of the dining room arch, a good ten feet away and then he crumpled on the floor.

Alana and Gabriella each had an arm to guide him down into an armchair. But Thorn stood at the bedroom door rubbing his neck, trying to focus on what just happened while Michael's thoughts did a number on his brain.

"Ah… My back's on fire. The muscles just continue to twist."

Gabriella was already running her hands down the man's spine. "That boy has got more than just *a little* mystical in him. You'll feel better soon, Miles."

Wincing, Miles shouted, "Good Lord, Thorn, where did he go?"

He could barely get out, "Sorry, I just can't see him, Miles, and I can't leave."

"I can handle Lukas," Gabriella stated. "Give me a minute to change into functional clothes." The ex-Guardian sprinted out of the apartment as Celia kept wringing her hands.

"Try to zero in on him, honey," Thorn whispered as her face grew serious.

"Uh, that's not so easy. B-but we should follow the sea, Dad, and head south. He's not in danger. I-I'd feel it, right?"

Miles gave a slow nod. Another tense minute passed. Alana hadn't said a word; neither had Rosa. Even the ever-calm Sister Magdalena paced the room with both hands tucked in her habit's wide cuffs.

"Can *someone* please tell me what has happened? The healing worked, didn't it? Michael is awake, isn't he," Miles asked.

"If I hadn't seen it, I wouldn't believe it," Celia answered.

Stumbling over specific English words, Sister Magdalena said, "No beast, *Signore* Bookman, only the dying man is returned."

"The dying man... I don't understand what—"

"That explanation can wait, Miles," Gabriella said entering the apartment in a sweatshirt, jeans, and sneakers. "Lukas couldn't have gone too far. I'll run up and grab Alana's car keys. Meet me around the corner."

"We must find that child...and quickly," Miles stated, still looking confused.

"Oh Dad, the little sweetie is so upset, and Michael's head is such a mess," Celia answered.

Watching them walk out, Thorn muttered, "Mess is too kind a word."

****

Everything fascinated him. Lights never flickered and didn't come from oil lamps. A soft mattress, smooth bedding, evenly sewn, masculine quilt... These details and many others had Michael in awe. Warmth, but no fireplace and walls uncommonly smooth, covered with a color he'd only seen on an artist's palette.

Every sense tingled. The motherly nun answered numerous questions about every nuance he observed. And he still held her hand, as if letting go of might bring Cyril walking through the door to drag him back to... *Vivid, terrifying screams in a hallway of death.... Held flush against the stone wall and bitten. How have*

I gotten from there to here? And where exactly is here?

Everything confused him, and although embarrassed to admit it, Mother Anne's presence brought immense relief. With every sense keener than humanly possible and vision better than 20/20, his full attention turned to the tall priest who entered and studied him.

"This is Monsignor Scarlatti, Michael," Mother Anne said.

In respect, he inclined his head as his father had taught him to at the age of four in 1669.

Incense lingers on his cassock. His racing heart belies outward composure, yet I seem a thing of curiosity, not a demon to be feared liked Cyril.

"It is good to see you awake, *Signore*. I know there are many questions." His manner had a calming effect, his English schooled and clear. "Perhaps straight forward responses will best address this dilemma. I will not shield the truth." He paused before saying, "More than three centuries have passed since you walked the earth as a living man."

Pushing through fear, his eyes widened. "What is the year?"

"2005. The world has changed in many ways, but creatures like you remain the same."

"No. It cannot be… Creatures like me? I am *demon*?"

The priest nodded as he pulled a chair close. "A vampire."

The very word shook him. "If that be true, then how is it that the good sister soothes me and you, Father, may be so near a creature of the night? Has the world changed so much that one such as I may be in your presence?"

"You had become a *unique* creature of the night in 1890, Michael. This is documented fact. You are different."

"Is this why you are here, Father, because I am different?"

A kind smile appeared. "The question is difficult to answer in a few sentences."

"You appear at peace around a vampire."

"Do you not recall our last conversation? The questions I asked you?"

Slowly, he shook his head. "No. I do not recall a conversation."

"What is your last memory?"

"It is clear in my mind—rather sobering at the same time. Last midnight, I-I was forced into a duel. I... I did not mean to kill him... when he fell to the ground I—"

"December 14, 1690... The night you met undeath. Antoine Glenmont was his name."

His brows drew tighter. "You *know* of the deed? I swear before God, I did not murder him! I was tricked by a maniac, a *demon*—Baron Cyril Waczynska." The name on his lips brought another uncontrolled shudder. "I was taken, could not escape, powerless against him. He held me to the wall and I-I—"

Mother Anne patted his hand. Although appreciative, he fully cowered when the priest leaned closer to say, "He bit into your vein."

"He bloody *tore* into my *neck*!" Although angry, his tone trembled. "Such searing pain, hot— unnatural... I wanted to live! I cried to God!" Thrusting his head back, he turned his face away and blinked his eyes against the gathering moisture that blurred his crisp vision. His jaw remained tense, his lips sealed tight. *I am damned for eternity!*

Touching his shoulder, Mother Anne whispered, "No, you aren't, Michael. Nor are you to blame. I can read your soul."

"Cyril read my thoughts that night as well. I felt bottomless terror. Yet that you can do so brings peace. You know I do not lie." When a tear slid down his cheek, Mother Anne caught it on her thumb. He found the courage to look at her and became overly curious as she glanced at the monsignor. "Why do you study a simple tear?"

"Because it is not a blood tear."

Although her answer made no sense, he didn't question it. Slowly, he shook his head and looked up at the ceiling. "Oh God, I have killed!"

"The demon that corrupted your soul was the killer, not you," the priest calmly stated. "Search your mind, Michael. Don't you see the rest of your actions as a vampire?"

More confusion, a prickly uneasiness... "I recall my life. I have no other memories."

"Do not have or will not see? Which is it?" Mother Anne asked. "This is a significant question. Your response is crucial."

Captivated by her light-grey eyes, he replied, "You expect honesty, good sister. I… I search my soul, my mind. Many sins haunt me, but they are not the actions of a-a demon."

"You have a steady stream of conflict within. What you are experiencing is all quite complex, unexpected as well. Understand that it is *because* you are different that we offer sanctuary. Now, it appears, you are even more unique." He nodded, hung on her every word. "A vampire has no access to life-memory. But you recall only a man's existence, not the vampire's. This significant fact sets you far apart from other undead creatures. As Monsignor stated, for over a century, moral thought has determined your actions, and your very soul remains in—"

"*My soul*!? Satan does *not* own my soul? How is it possible? Is this why I have so many wounds? Did I fight the almighty Devil to keep it mine?"

"Yes, in a manner of speaking. It's why you're here. Why we choose to harbor you."

"Swear you speak truth," he demanded. Yet they had no reason to lie. Full of ungodly aches, he sank deeper into the soft pillows, and as if he were still among the living, he took deep, even breaths. Clarity eluded him. Nothing, not even this conversation made sense.

"Will you trust us, Michael?"

Without hesitation, he replied, "Yes, Mother." His face turned to the door; his thoughts turned to...

"I'll tell Alana you're resting comfortably. Monsignor will stay." Crossing the bedroom, Mother Anne whispered, "This has indeed been a difficult, long day—for all of us."

Amazed how he could hear every utterance, every strange sound coming from different rooms in this house, he felt something still within him. For the first time, his twenty-seven years of life had clarity. His eyes closed, seeing himself as overconfident and willful. Each transgression against his Christian upbringing had to be confessed aloud—for his soul to be saved from the fires of Hell. From eternal damnation. Mortal sins plagued his conscience and he found himself fearful of facing the priest alone.

Full of regret, he whispered low, "I chose to lead an immoral life. I did not pray for nor seek forgiveness for my sins. A vacant thing is what Cyril called my soul. He spoke the truth." Swallowing hard, his eyes filled once again. *I lost my faith in God years before my death.*

"Will you…hear my sins, Father?"

"I am here for you, my son." He heard the priest's cassock crinkle as a steady hand raised in a blessing.

****

Walking into the living room, Anne sank into an armchair and took the hot cup of coffee from Rosa's hand. Her mind closed. No one would read a thought, not even the empath standing guard at Michael's door. "Where are the others?"

In anxious Italian, Magdalena explained what had transpired before stating, "The child ran, Mother. He believes his father is gone. We are all worried."

Wearily, she sipped the refreshing liquid. Tension was well off the charts in the quiet living room. Although the child shouldn't have been able to leave the consecrated building, apparently, he did, she thought. Nevertheless, it was what happened in the bedroom that disturbed her more. "Everyone in the bedroom saw what I saw. Neither the boy's father nor the documented Champion appears to exist. A terrified young Englishman brutally murdered in 1690 has somehow returned. What an unforeseen outcome—almost unforgivable."

"You said it yourself, Annie, this has *never* been

done before," Rosa quickly whispered, "You couldn't know what to expect."

"But I feel responsible, and those kind words are appreciated."

Alana shook her head and finally looked at her. "Why is he like this?"

"I wish I had a definitive answer. I'm very aware of your concerns. We won't leave until he's prepared to face all that is on his soul. Certain results are clear, though. Most important is the successful extraction of the beast-within. But *this* immortal knows nothing of his undead existence. Yet his reaction to you is completely genuine, Alana. He simply cannot place you in his mortal life." She glanced at Thorn. "The child—has Celia found him?"

"No, not yet."

His voice had caught, and she gave an understanding nod. "You are seeing into his soul again."

"I'm right there with every unfamiliar feeling, Mother. Michael's awfully confused, wave upon wave of honest-to-goodness fear."

"He'll need you, Empath."

Leaning back, Alana's hand gripped the couch's arm. "How, Mother Anne? You knew immediately."

She gave a slight grin. "His speech pattern isn't modern—and being from London helps." After a sigh, she added, "Lukas will be found soon. Sebastiano will further ease Michael's fears. There's nothing more I can do for him tonight." Her mystical energy directed toward Lukas Malone as she thought, this is a very long day, indeed.

Chapter 12

No stars, no moon visible in the cloudy sky as Lukas found a clearing far down the coast and sat in coarse sand. Huddled against the rocks, he shivered, enveloped by the sea's chilly mist. He had no idea where he was, and he didn't care.

Anxious memories had tears burning his eyes. He knew he shouldn't have run. But hiding in Michael's brownstone for eight days, believing Miles Bookman that he would be safe, then coming to Italy—nothing got the one result he wanted. He swiped his runny nose and palmed his eyes. Even though he liked Miles and Celia, mistrust was his comfort zone.

"No connection to this fucking world for me and there never will be. I needed you to wake up, to call out *my* name. Maybe I'd see in your eyes what I saw in the passageway. So now you're gone…just like that." His fingers dug into moist sand. "When the Hell-beasts disappeared, I should've grabbed you from those fucking men before they took you away—fucking bastards."

He started to cry, very ashamed of why he had run back into the old factory so frightened. The thought of being recaptured and tortured made him cower deeper into the dank space. It had even brought the nightmares back. Sobbing at the hollowness in his heart that overpowered reason, he banged his head against the cold rock until his brain shut down…and then, blessed peace.

****

Like a drag-racer, that's how Gabby handles Alana's car in the darkness around every deep turn, Miles thought as he gripped the bucket seat in front of him. She sped down the road that shadowed the Mediterranean Sea and his anxiety level rose. "I can't see anything with this mist. Damnit! He couldn't have gone this far in such a short time," he whispered looking out the window.

Only when she pulled onto the narrow shoulder did his grip loosen. His daughter was just as quiet. But when he lowered a window with a press of a button, both women simultaneously sucked in a breath.

Gabriella got out, started for the embankment. "We go the rest of the way on foot."

Celia waited as he fished through the glove compartment for a flashlight. "He's way too upset, Dad. Lukas has got to relax, like ten minutes ago. I've got him on the old psychic radar. He's close." Her hand stayed in his. "Keep it aimed at your feet, okay? Gabby's worried about you. So am I. You can't rely on a sixth sense like we do… to keep from slipping and falling."

They made it to the water's edge. Nothing but the rhythm of lapping waves… A quick scan of the wet rocks, and he caught a glimpse of a white sneaker reflecting the narrow beam. Gabriella was standing by the shivering boy. Running over, he squatted down to aim the light at Lukas's head. "Good Lord, you're bleeding—"

"Get away! Don't touch me!"

With firm hands under his arms, he pulled Lukas up brushing off the coarse sand. "No, I will not get away! You're like ice, damnit!"

"He wants to run, but he can't. Good work, Celia," Gabriella whispered. Instantly, the ex-Guardian hooked Lukas's waist, getting him up the embankment and into the backseat. "Maggie examines the gash as soon as we get back, Miles. Even if he self-heals, it's best to be on the safe side."

Scrunched in the narrow seat he held Lukas tight. He had no jacket or blanket to cover the sniffling child. His daughter handed him a wad of tissues, which he used to gently wipe the tears on his face and swipe his runny nose. Miles mumbled, "He's still shaking."

Gabriella put the car into gear, then turned with a frown. "Well, that's what you get for taking off like a bat out of Hell on a chilly night. Too bad I was so preoccupied with his dad. I would've tackled him *before* he jumped the stairs."

Celia quickly shook her head. "Don't blame yourself, Gabby. We were all a little freaked-out before."

"I have to know," Miles asked during the tight U-turn on the deserted road. "How strange was it in the room—on a scale of one to ten?"

"If ten's the highest, go with a hundred."

"It was that out of the ordinary?"

"You have no idea, Dad."

He studied his daughter's silhouette against the darkness of the road before them.

****

Monsignor Scarlatti raised his hand in a final blessing. *I've read everything ever written about this vampire. The Champion has never been known as a talkative creature. But tonight, many insights poured out of Michael soul.* Unknown facts about that December night included events that led to a duel as well as the young man's attempt to flee from Cyril. *Humbled by hopeless fear for his soul, he is raw, full of human emotions.*

With heart and mind open, he had listened to every regretful stammer. This had always been his way. He sensed a contrite man, not a three-hundred-year-old vampire. Mired in theological and philosophical queries and as Spiritual Leader of the Georgians, there were no documents to study. No experts to ask. The lost soul, sitting in the bed so broken and battered, still looked to him for guidance. He couldn't offer anything but absolution for human sins.

The researcher's request to grant Michael leniency now weighed heavily on his mind.

****

Thorn experienced Michael's gratefulness when Monsignor Scarlatti gave the final blessing of confession. Leaving the silent women, he went upstairs with an interesting thought: Alana's scent may bring the memories back. He carried down the Queen Anne chair from her bedroom, and Alana actually managed a smile when he entered Michael's apartment.

As soon as Monsignor Scarlatti left the bedroom, Thorn gave a grateful nod and took in the chair. It barely fit in the snug space between the draped wall and the wide sleigh bed. When he repositioned the small nightstand, he also grabbed a few more frightened thoughts.

This was one befuddled soul Helena had sent him

113

to serve. Crossing the room, he closed the door before sitting beside Michael on the high mattress. Most of what had just been explained about his undead existence hadn't stayed in Michael's mixed-up mind, but one fact had become clear. "You feel better knowing that you still have your soul."

"Do I know you?" Michael asked with a glib expression.

The formal British accent made him grin. "Thorn's what everyone calls me, and I'm a, your, uh, servant. How about we get some clothes on you?" No answer. More curious stares. He grabbed a pair of black pajamas from off the dresser. "There's no need to be concerned, Champ. I'm here for you."

"Why do you call me this...Champ?"

"Well, you call me Empath... It's a term of endearment." Michael's eyebrow arched, which had him quickly adding, "But *not* in the way you're thinking."

The sudden, wide-eyed stare held genuine inquisitiveness. "You see thought as Cyril did? And you are just as inhumanly strong. Why come in here now? Are you—?"

"One at a time. We can build up to Twenty Questions later. Ah, you *demand* immediate answers? Let's just say I have a talent, especially when it comes to you, Michael."

As if in control of the situation, he scoffed. "I do *not* grant permission to be addressed by my christened name, servant. 'Tis Master Malone and no forwardness will be tolerated." A quick, sucked breath followed. "You dare smile? Lower your eyes and bow deep! Remember your station in life, manservant."

Yep, this is gonna be fun. He cleared his throat, tolerated the smug expression. "Sorry for the offense, *sir*. Now, may I dress your buck-naked body? Kindly give me your arm, and all will be well—only God knows when." He pushed the heavy blankets away and was careful with Michael's many injuries, especially his right thigh, which was shattered by a Hell-beast's sword. "Uh-huh, soft, silk pajamas and not nightshirts are the current fashion-trend in men's sleepwear." The blank stare confirmed how Michael didn't have a clue as to who or what he really was.

"This chair you bring... *Her* scent is on it. Where is my beautiful lady?"

"My beautiful lady, huh? I'm catching every x-rated picture, too," he mumbled while piling extra blankets on the shivering being.

"I hear your whisper. I warn again, do not read my thoughts. 'Tis the filthy trait of a *demon*... *Not* heavenly like the saintly Sister!"

Lacing his arms against his chest, Thorn sat on the bed again. "Listen, snippy superior attitudes are *way* out of line with me. So is your yen to 'bed the beauty'. That's a total no-no at the moment." After clicking his tongue, he tempered his tone. "Trust me when I say I know *exactly* what's in your head—whether you forbid it or not. Call her Alana and not 'my lady' or 'my' anything."

Buttoning the pajama collar, unspoken questions kept coming along with a familiar arrogance. "And there's no way you're doing *that* with *her.*" He read every question like a pro. "No. A looking glass won't do you any good. The short version is—you won't see anything anyway. Yes. You look dashing and no, your wavy hair isn't long enough to bind in a leather ribbon. You have two black eyes and tons of purple bruises on your face, which further enhance your already rugged-handsome good looks."

Michael's bristle didn't hide his panic—because Thorn knew those were his exact thoughts. And he frowned as he rolled his eyes. "No, I'm not a deadly creature of the night. I'm something close to the complete opposite. All right, enough! I swear I'm really *not* Satan himself." But then, he allowed a bit of gentleness to seep through. "You're in God's good graces, Champ. I'll send her in. Just remember to behave yourself."

****

The beautiful woman settled against the exquisite floral pattern of the chair near his bed. With a tilt of her head, that luscious long brown hair was swept over one shoulder. Her head rested against the high back to frame her lovely face. *She is mine, a vision of loveliness...full red lips, expressive eyes the color of a precious gem!*

Each individual feature stirred passion in his hazy brain bringing his body to the edge of excitement. Renewed desire for her touch raced through every fiber of his being. Alana's scent enticed, beckoned. And he wanted her. He'd hold this beauty and bring pleasure to her—enough to make her sigh. He knew every inch of her curvaceous, supple body. To straighten his slumped position, both fists bore into the soft mattress. Sharp pain shot through his chest, and he gasped.

She gripped the chair's cushioned arms and leaned toward him. "Are you all right? Should I get Thorn? Can I help you? Where does it hurt? I mean I-I'm sorry.

I know that sounded—a little silly," she murmured before exhaling a slow breath.

The rise and fall of her breasts had his full attention. "Needless concern on such an enchanting face… You are distressed. But alas, I am fine, my lady. I have four broken ribs that heal as we speak! Truthfully, I see them in my mind," he declared full of wonder. Then his tone softened. "You care for me. Your heart quickens."

"Yes, I do, and yes, it does."

"I have loved you. I have made love to you." Her body warmed, and his confidence soared. Now if he could only touch her…

Even though the schooled British accent threw her off, that last statement made Alana blush. "Yes, you have and yes, you did." *Thank God I didn't add "my love." That's a discussion neither of us could handle right now. Two minutes, and I'm already losing control!* His eyes held a sensual glimmer, and she hadn't seen such a charming grin since—*Oh no, no, no… I'm in trouble here.*

"Though it is rather impossible to move with ease, I will not deny it. This body remembers you. It yearns for your delicate hand. Will you come to me? Will you sit by me, darlin'?"

A curious expression swept his handsome face. And her heart lurched. *What did he just say!* It had been seven years since she heard "that word" and his voice had taken on the same liquid lilt. *How did this Michael know to say it? It's the one word he only used on me… Oh God! He knows I'm special to him. I want to leap into his arms and…* The room felt a bit too warm.

"Darlin'?" she asked. The look of innocent curiosity on his face was one she'd *never* seen before. Had to force herself to sit back. "I'm sorry, is that what you just called me?"

He sank deeper into the pillows. "I-I apologize, my lady, I do not know from where this comes. Yet, when I see you, I sense this word. Please. Sit by my side?" He patted the mattress. She studied another never-before-seen look—awkward shyness.

Don't do it! But how can I turn him down? Look at the glimmer of hope in his eyes. He's so handsome. He'd turn heads in any century. But getting closer might reveal much more than I care to have him know. And there she was, suddenly sitting next to his hand. *Okay... You can handle it, right? Just breathe!*

The way his cool fingers brushed down her jeans, and then the way his hand cupped her knee. "Why would a tailor sew this type of clothing for such an alluring woman? I quite admire the even stitches, the material so strong. Yet this might be worn by a man who works the earth, not a fine lady." His dark penetrating stare strayed below her waist. His grip tightened on her knee. "I see no buttons or laces of any kind to remove them. How this fascinates me!"

Go for a simple explanation and find an excuse to... Quickly standing, she stammered, "Clothing's changed a lot since 1690. Everyone wears jeans today. A-and this is a zipper. It goes up and down. See?" If anyone walked in right now, they'd definitely get the wrong impression. Very self-conscious, she sat again...next to his hand.

His gaze dripped desire as he stared at her breasts. "And this odd bodice, my lady? 'Tis finely spun wool, the shade of French lilacs in bloom. Such color, such quality of craftsmanship demands closer study. Do you knit?"

The black silk pajama top she'd purchased in Pisa hung from his broad shoulders as if tailor-made, just for Michael Malone. And that hushed, sensual tone had her wanting to melt against his chest and kiss his thin lips until... *Yep, I'm in trouble!*

"My lady?"

"Huh? Oh. No. I shop. It... it's made by a machine, just like my jeans."

One hand reached out, then instantly recoiled with a courteous, "May I?" It took a second to realize he didn't mean what she *thought* he meant.

"Oh! The sweater... Sure, go ahead."

The conversation had passed uncomfortable; headed straight to comical. When his fingers now ran down her arm, she tingled. When he whispered a soft, "Ah..." low in her body, a flutter began. Then he smiled as the back of his hand swept over her wrist and strayed to her lap.

Her flush deepened. Her body roared to react. The room grew hotter still. Now she *fully* understood why she'd kept away from Michael the last seven years, even when they had lived in the same city. Goose bumps dotted her skin and the unconscious yearning within throbbed like a torturous ache.

On the plane, the sight of him so injured and unconscious had squelched these desires. And two nights ago, all she could do was hope and pray while cradling him close. This was different. To hear his voice. To feel his touch. *We're now very far into the danger zone!* Whether or not *this* Michael remembered their history, closeness was more than she could handle.

With a quick turn away, she closed her eyes and barely whispered, "Michael, my love."

He brought her wrist to his neck, and with determination, tugged her to his chest. "My need for you burns like an incessant flame, never to extinguish." Breathing deep, he nuzzled her adding in a sexy low voice, "The scent of a woman I know I love."

Kisses found her lips. Urgent enough to tease the longing that entered both of their souls. Her kisses were just as deep. He groaned, pressing her to him, and it shocked her how he was able to pull her over and to his left side.

Their lips stayed locked together. Their tongues twirled together in a passionate frenzy. She didn't want to break away from this sensual moment. The temptation of every caress caused a restless need to blossom. She could feel his arousal; he could sense hers.

A sure and steady hand parted her thighs as he whispered, "Indeed, you are only mine." He fondled her pulsing core and a whimper escaped, suddenly lost in his intimate touch. More searing jolts began when his hand pressed harder against her through the thick fabric. Such a possessive hold. A long-denied primal response sprang awake. The uncontrollable reaction felt like a warm pool. It flooded her senses and a rush of heat swallowed her as the craving instantly swelled.

His kisses turned more self-absorbed, and she arched her back, the need to feel him inside of her all-consuming. A hand crept under her sweater. One breast fit the width of his grasp. She wanted more... And then her eyes filled. Short breaths came fast.

Oh God, what am I doing? Why can't I stop him? There's no way to explain what I feel to this man. I can't even explain this to myself! Stop. This isn't right. He doesn't know me! Doesn't remember— Every conflicting emotion rushed back. A full breath hitched.

He pulled his hand, his excited body away. After a tender kiss to her cheek, he whispered with devotion, "My Guardian...my love." Once again, confusion bathed his dark espresso eyes, and timidly, he added, "I am once more puzzled by what I do not understand."

Inch by inch, she crept off the other side of the bed until out of his reach.

"I offend you, but I know not why."

Clear your head. Don't confuse him anymore than he already is. Somehow, she managed to walk back to the upholstered chair and sank down. Once again, she gripped its arms. Self-control would've been ancient history if she had spent another second next to him.

"No. Offend isn't the right word. And I-I shouldn't have allowed this to happen."

Unable to explain further, she leaned her head back and shut her eyes with a sigh.

He knew he had caused her discomfort. Unfamiliar phrases full of unfamiliar words, their meanings far out of grasp raced through his mind. Yet he didn't want to understand them. Deep distress at knowing he had caused her to become upset as well as the agonizing throb of full arousal had him completely bewildered.

Pulling himself up, he leaned heavily against the cushioned headboard and folded his hands over what he did not want her to see. *Yet, I know that I love you, have lain with you. I know your body as if it were a part of mine.* Half a minute later, every wound on his body rose from dull ache to excruciating pain as if to demand his attention. *Did my passion for you trigger this...this—* Unable to think, unable to move, a fierce gasp erupted. Terror gripped him. Some unfamiliar need ached so badly it dulled his vision. Craving surged. Something he didn't understand—again bringing him to the rim of consciousness.

"I-I...cannot, I cannot—" Words ceased as he shivered.

He heard her calling his name as though he were in a long stone tunnel...

"It's all right. I've got him," the servant assured. He had a glass carafe and a full crystal mug in hand. "Your hunger is surfacing. This is new to you—in a way."

The scent of human blood made his senses swirl. Low grunts erupted as Thorn cupped the back of his head and held a crystal mug to his lips. As if compelled, each greedy swallow eased an inevitable need until the carafe stood empty. Only then did the appalling reality become clear. His fingers shook as they rubbed against his lips, and full of disgust he refused to look at the servant.

"I drink *blood*? *This* sustains my existence? *I* must rip into a human's vein? No, I will not! 'Tis an unholy act!"

The large paw of a hand braced his sore shoulder, eased him back against the headboard. "Let's not get overly dramatic now. Bring a little levity to this newly discovered fact, all right? Once you're back in action, you can switch to animal blood. You've developed a taste for it."

These words of reason only made him more obstinate. His arms threaded tight to his chest. His jaw set as he glared at the idiot. "I will not kill to sate my need!"

"Oh no. No you don't," the servant dared to scold, "No signature pout, no unbendable brood because you aren't getting your way. Did I say you'd have to grab a bow and arrow and run across the street to take down the neighbor's dog? Weren't there butcher shops back in 'the day'?"

Insulted, he cringed at Alana's grin. Silent, he simmered and refused to respond.

****

Lukas sat on his own bed in clean sweatpants that Mister B insisted he change into. As soon as the gray sweatshirt came over his head, Sister Magdalena walked in to examine the washed wound. He eyed the quiet nun listening to her habit rustle when she moved. The smell of spices and herbs wafted off her, too. The stethoscope was cold against his chest and back. He hated it when she made him open his mouth to look inside. Her two fingers on his wrist were smooth and warm. But avoiding the disapproval on Mister B's face and her sympathetic looks, he gave one-word answers as she questioned him.

After disinfecting his scalp, she said, "*Molto bene…* Skin is closed already."

"Don't you think I know that?" He yanked away as Miles shook his head gravely.

The other nun blocked the doorway. Both fists stayed locked to her waist. "Hey kiddo. I carried you in here like a sack of potatoes and I can drop-kick you like a soccer ball into the living room. You gave us all a jolt tonight. Let Sister Maggie do her thing and do not give her bratty. Or I'll have to show you just how strong I really am."

The scowl remained, but he gave a half-hearted, "Sorry."

"Did you give yourself another headache?" Sister Maggie asked flicking a light in his eyes.

"No," came out drawn and reedy.

"No, Sister," Mister B said in a stern voice.

"No, Sister," he whispered.

She smiled, hooked his chin. This time, he didn't yank away. "There is no concussion. *Ma per favore,* no more midnight runs, *capisce*? Good boys stay home with their papas, yes?"

Even though her touch soothed, he muttered, "Yeah, right."

He heard a "Thank you, Sister," come from Mister B, but as soon as they left, the man moved in with a piercing parental stare. "Look at me, young man. Let's discuss your reaction."

Fidgeting, he shrugged. "Let's not and say we did."

The next glare accompanied one raised eyebrow. "I don't care for your fresh mouth, young man. You owe me an apology. You have assaulted me twice in a twenty-four-hour period. You do not send humans flying across the room."

He looked away. "Sorry."

"Come again?"

"I'm sorry, Mister B."

After making a sound in his throat, the man said, "Apology accepted. Next, you were too quick jumping to such a foolish conclusion about your father. A *wrong* one, I might add. He didn't disintegrate into dust and bone. He is awake—but without recent memories."

His eyes narrowed. "Like, you mean he doesn't know who I am?"

"I don't believe he knows you even exist, but we won't be certain—until he sees you. Your father only recalls his human life in the seventeenth century, which is, in itself, quite remarkable."

Lukas gripped the edge of the mattress as he stared at the heavily draped window. "If he doesn't know me then I did lose him."

"You've just jumped to a conclusion again. When you see him, Lukas, the last thing your father needs is an angry outburst—from his son!" Words like father, son, and angry outburst made him edgy. The desire to run away again really looked good. And this time, they wouldn't find him. "Do you hear me, young man?"

"Yeah, I get it—*when* I see him. So when is when?"

Mister B didn't answer right away, but then met his gaze. "We can go downstairs right now—if you're ready."

His palms began to itch. "I can talk to him? You really mean it?"

"I have never lied to you, and I'm certainly not about to start with something as important as this." For once, the parental demeanor made him feel a little closer to safe.

Chapter 13

The bedroom door was ajar when they entered the apartment. Miles nodded to Mother Anne who immediately stood. "I wanted to wait for you, Miles. Alana is walking Monsignor Scarlatti to the rectory. She'll be back soon."

His attention turned to Lukas, who had taken one look at the healer sister and instantly froze. The boy's eyes watered, and Miles knew that his guard had gone up again. "It's all right. Lukas, this is Mother Anne." After swiping his eyes with the sleeve of his gray sweatshirt, the boy stared down at his sneakers.

She held up a hand, motioned him to say no more. "I'll be across the hall, should you need me."

Thorn came out of the bedroom just as the healer was leaving. "I, uh, oh Lord, I'm so sorry, kid. The resemblance to Helena threw me for a loop, too. I could kick myself for not mentioning it. I'm guessing that you'd be happy to do it, right Miles?"

Totally miffed, Miles replied sharply, "To say the least." As Thorn stepped aside, he could hardly swallow his outrage. *Can this day get any worse for this troubled child? Helena was the only mother the boy had ever known and if there was a resemblance, I should have been informed.* The boy came off sad, obviously emotionally raw, which said Lukas was more sensitive than he let on. When Miles touched his shoulder, there was no pull-away or stiffening. Without looking up, Lukas mumbled, "Can I go in there now?"

"Of course," he replied, leading the way.

****

A voice. A familiar scent. Inexplicable anxiety hammered Michael's subconscious mind. When the boy entered, many strange feelings surfaced. He couldn't easily move, but his ungodly strong hands and arms immediately flexed tight. Why was there something familiar about this child? Ill at ease, they studied each other with equal intensity. "Who are you, and why keep such a firm hand to this boy as you approach?"

"My name is Miles Bookman," the stranger said with diplomacy. "This is Lukas."

Jealousy and blessed relief battled inside his mind. Yet he didn't know why. "Come closer, please. How old are you, little boy?" But the child didn't move, stayed out of reach, shifting foot to foot.

"I'm fifteen."

"Truthfully?"

"He turned fifteen on May 19th," the older man offered as if it were an important fact, an important date.

"You appear younger, perhaps by two years..." Then his eyes narrowed. The way the child studied him. *The scent of sand and fresh blood... A wild heartbeat...*

"You know what I am?"

"Yeah."

"It does not frighten you?"

"No."

He sniffed the air. "There is something unnatural about your hair."

"It's really blond and curly, not dark-brown and wavy—like yours."

He glimpsed the servant and Alana near the door while saying to Miles, "Why does the child look to you for approval before he speaks? You are not his blood. I sense you protect and worry, but he is *not* your son."

The man gave a dry grin. "No, he is not."

He glared until the hand left Lukas's back, and then grew irate when the man didn't move away. Lukas looked directly at him as if he had something to say. And as their eyes met, he whispered, "No. This cannot be nor is it possible."

Miles brought Lukas to the edge of the bed. "Let me get to the point quickly. You must state precisely what you assume to be not possible."

He reached out and his thumb connected with the warm smooth skin of Lukas's hand. Then the child gripped his hand as if to hold it. "You do not pull away from what I am. Such unnatural strength, yet it is a most natural bond." Staring into the darkest blue eyes imaginable, he stated with absolute certainty, "Truly... you are mine." It made no sense, yet he was positive, sensing it deep in his soul.

A small, dimpled smile began on the boy's angelic face, and Miles stepped back, stating, "You've chosen most appropriate words."

Of course, he found immense satisfaction in the bright smile that now graced Alana's lovely face. The manservant, however, did not grin.

"A unique bloodline... Cyril had said those words. Dear God, none of this makes sense," he whispered. Their hands stayed threaded together. *His* child sat on the bed and showed no fear. Pride filled his soul now, too overwhelmed to question this impossibility any further. He pulled Lukas closer. Intense emotions spiked within him when willingly, Lukas leaned over and rested his head upon his chest. As he basked in the scent of his son, he ran a hand down the boy's slender back. There was an immediate jerk against his hand and then the boy's body stiffened.

Disjointed scenes flashed before his eyes. *The terror in his eyes… filthy clothes shredded on his back. The scent of blood…* He had to know if what he saw was true, and he held his son an arm's length away. "You must remove this," he ordered.

"You are upsetting him," Miles quickly said.

Instantly, the boy twisted to break free. He would not allow it, and roughly pulled until the material tore, exposing the left side of his slender chest. Still compelled, he took advantage of the next twist and held Lukas down, lifted the cloth up to his neck to study the boy's back.

Each discolored scar infuriated him. "Who did this to you?" Grabbing both boney shoulders, he looked his boy in the eye. Murder loomed in Michael's soul as those deep-blue orbs glistened with tears.

"Let go of me," Lukas screamed flailing in his grip.

Shaking his son, he barked, "Who did this!? You will tell me!"

Both slender arms shot across that angelic face. "You're not him! Let me go!"

Full of fury, he shook his son again and shouted, "Answer me!"

The manservant wrenched his wrists off his son and wrestled him back to the headboard, pinning one thick arm against Michael's bruised sternum. "That wasn't a smart move, Champ."

Lukas scurried off the bed, and Alana pulled him

close to her before the boy wormed out of her hands and ran out of the room. He fumed and cursed, struggled and yelled, "No! No! He is mine! Lukas, come back to me!" Unable to budge, a bitter glare stayed on Miles Bookman. "You know! You know! *Tell me!*"

"Calm down and I will explain," the man answered, rather heatedly.

"No! You will tell me *immediately!*" Still trying to unpin himself and seething, he hissed, "Release me, you ignominious jackal!"

"Not a chance… Like the man said—Calm down." His fist slammed into Thorn's broad chin, and just as quick, a brisk slap across *his* bruised cheek stunned him in return. "What is it with you and the kid? Do I look like a punching bag? You'd think the pressure of my elbow against your sore ribs is punishment enough. I guess not. The slap shocked you quiet, though."

An exaggerated groan of pain escaped, but his servant's thick elbow didn't budge. Then, he met Alana's icy glare. "Do it, Michael. Calm down *now!* Thorn, where is he?"

"Celia's got him."

"Celia? Who is Celia?"

"Not now," Thorn bellowed.

But the name brought a sense of relief, told him that his son was safe—and he didn't know why. Alana settled into the upholstered chair. Scowling, he slumped to the pillows and rubbed his cheek. Thorn's elbow eased off, but the man's glower intimidated him into compliance. Now he was effectively boxed in with sharp looks on both sides of him.

At the foot of the bed, Miles had the audacity to

glare like a bull ready to charge. "Now that you've managed to upset an innocent child, let me be candid. What a positive shame this is! I don't believe your pig-headedness. If you'd exhibited even the slightest bit of self-control this would have been fully explained!"

The brusque indictment had him tense. Annoyed. Purposely, he turned away only to come face to face with Alana. "I don't care what century your brain is in. How could you do that to your son? You know what he's been put through—Oh, God! *You* don't know," she added in a breathless whisper.

"Then tell me!" He braced his arms to his chest, waiting for more cutting words, having no idea why he'd been so rough with a distraught child… his child.

Miles's hands clamped behind his back as he paced by the footboard. After another glare, the man yelled, "This egotistical propensity of placing your own *selfish* need above everyone else's, *regardless* of how it may affect them, truly appalls me! I could slap you myself!"

"I regret upsetting *my* child, but I demand to know why he has been beaten and bloody scarred! Will *someone* oblige me? These injuries I have—they are connected to my son, are they not!? What in God's name did I battle? Who brought this wrath down upon me?"

Thorn shook his head. "Here we go with Twenty Questions again. But the answer to the last one's really easy."

"You did," came in rapid succession—from *each* of them!

His gut clenched. The simple response did more than turn him silent. Cascading guilt merged with the most alarming terror he had ever known. It filled his soul.

****

Hours later, Thorn sank down at the foot of the bed. "There's nothing at all current in his mind, Miles."

The long, tedious discussion had both calm and heated moments. One unearthly fact led to another. Innocent questions required complex explanations, which obviously make no sense to someone who couldn't accept the fact that he had existed as a vampire for over three centuries. And even though Michael seemed to cringe at the thought of being a merciless killer for two hundred years before taking back his soul, they had witnessed dismissive scoffs and dozens of sideways glances. Thorn realized that *this* immortal couldn't recall *that* existence.

"He's not giving up those archaic beliefs of Heaven and Hell—of angels and demons, Miles," he again repeated. "And he's gloating because none of us can explain how a vampire fathered a human child. Uh, no... You didn't stump us, Champ, so lose the satisfied smirk."

Miles said, "Helena allowed you to reclaim your soul in 1890 and Helena sent Thorn to you seven years ago." Michael simply stared at him.

Alana yawned. "We've been at this for hours, Dad."

Thorn read his latest thought. "Yes, she is his adopted daughter, and yes—I'm sure as hell not just an ordinary man."

Edging his feet away, Michael gave a nasty sneer. "Thus. Like Cyril. You *are* demon."

"I'm as human as they come—just mystically-enhanced. A very old soul lives in this body with the added talent of seeing things—especially in you. To use an old cliché, you're my reason for living."

"Then why did you not save me from myself, servant? You are a failure. And you are dismissed!"

After a chuckle and a snort, Thorn stood. "And I thought only the vampire thing made you such a conceited pain in the ass. You were seriously in need of an ego intervention—even before Cyril took a nibble at your jugular."

"Do you *dare* to jest with me? You are not *my* equal." Michael pointed to the door. "Leave!"

Miles shook his head while Alana met Michael's gaze, wide-eyed and waiting. The last comment did it, and Thorn leaned down poking one thick finger at Michael's tender chest. "The correct term, my wayward friend, is Servant of Souls. I watch out for the fluffy thing inside that you can't see." He jabbed again; caught scenes from a life cut short by undeath. "You've been damn near perfect since 1890 because Martin Malone taught you right from wrong. Let's see. Ah! …About Lukas's age when your sisters left. They'd be *mortified* at the piece of work you turned into!"

Michael swatted his hand away. "Stay out of my memories, demon, and do not speak of my family!"

"How could you have been so outraged? Your sisters followed their hearts. They had a unique mission in this world. Things didn't go your way, so you tortured your saintly mother like some devious wild-child? Pushed your father's buttons the way you're pushing mine tonight? Every moral he instilled, *you* foolishly ignored. Then, instead of learning your lesson, you chose to become a self-indulged man who could charm any women to the point of ecstasy! Lust isn't love. There's a huge difference."

"Of which I *am* aware. No doubt, you are sent by Satan to trick me, *demon!*"

"Weren't you listening before when I told you what I am? Look at me, Michael." Caring swelled from the depths of his heart. "I know this terrifies you. But look into your soul. See *all* you've become."

Michael's gaze drifted down. "You say you have been at my side for seven years. Tell me truthfully, servant, why do I need *you* to care for my soul?"

Alana let out a sigh, looked directly at his bruised face. "I get the feeling it's my turn to play jog the memory. I'll take it from here, Thorn, by myself. You need sleep, Dad." Whispering words of support, Miles kissed her forehead before he left. Concern and regret were on the ex-Guardian's face, Thorn thought, as if it were etched in her very soul.

With a small grin, he stated, "I'll take my leave, *master.* But I'm right outside the door." When he turned away, the grin faded. Without a doubt, his own grave concern began to grow.

Chapter 14

Lukas checked the alarm clock on the dresser. *After nine a.m. and Mister B is still snoring? Because of last night and what happened...* Emotion exhausted him, and he had fallen asleep with his father on his mind. No recognition, no memories that included him. But for once, he had no nightmares about the four years he had been held captive in the Second Realm.

With clean clothes in hand, he tip-toed out of the guest room, held back a sneeze until he got into the hall. Another sneeze shook him as he entered the bathroom. The warm shower felt good, but like ghosts grabbing at him in a wet mist, the lack of recognition in his father's eyes haunted him. Then the fierce expression on his face when seeing what marred his skin..

During an entire year of being somebody else, he had never even noticed the scars on his chest and his back. Soapy water ran clean down his chest, but the scars wouldn't be erased. He remembered being beaten by the guards in the Second Realm. A lot of times—before being pulled from the sorcerers' dimension, crazed and full of rage. Michael had rescued him, and then what did he do? He turned on his own father, tried to stake him—for an entire year.

Then came a year with no memories, and he had been happy for the first time in a long time. Until that illusion of a normal life ended on the night of the battle in the Manhattan passageway.

He needed to talk to Michael. He needed to tell him so many ugly things. He needed to apologize. His eyes burned—and not from soap.

And what Lukas kept deep inside made him want to puke.

****

The house was still quiet when he came out of the bathroom. Lukas glanced at Alana's door and gave Celia a shy smile.

She motioned him to the kitchen's round, mosaic table and placed a plate of scrambled eggs and toast down. "Ally stayed down by your dad, sweetie. My dad came up just before dawn. I made you breakfast *a la* Celia B! Eat up. There's plenty more on the stove."

Her green eyes sparkled when she smiled and began to nibble a piece of toast. He dove into the tasty dish and swallowed before asking, "Did your ESP tell you I was up?"

"Nope—I heard the sneeze."

"This is really good. You can cook." He scooped up another mouthful.

"I'm a regular wiz at eggs and my organic rice-pudding is scrumptious." She paused as a blush pinched his cheeks. "Wow, you should smile like that more often. I love those dimples. You're going to have your dad's drop-dead gorgeous looks—I'm *totally* certain!"

That something about him looked like Michael stuck in his head. He smiled with more warmth this time. "Is that your ESP talking?"

"Nah, just feminine intuition… Seriously though, your dad knew you were his?"

The strong hug, the love in Michael's eyes, the deadly glare and how he ripped the sweatshirt... It all spilled out of his mind, along with a spectrum of emotions.

Celia rubbed the corner of her eye and cleared her throat. "Uh, yeah... Dads have their own kind of ESP, sweetie. They know if you're hurting—if you need them."

But he doesn't remember me. The fork raked through what was left on the plate. He pushed it away. "I'm full."

She leaned across and touched his shoulder. "No, you're not. And Michael loves you more than you'll ever know. There's real goodness in him. I know how far he'd go to make you safe. Trust me, sweetie, he'd give up his existence for you. Now eat."

Celia handed him the fork as he studied her. *Kind...as caring as her father.* Honesty was written on her pretty face.

****

The aroma of coffee, fresh and from an old-fashioned perk pot came at Thorn. His eyes stung like hell as they opened. Mother Anne placed the mug on the coffee table and sat across from him. As he pulled himself up to sit, Rosa came from the kitchen. She gave a caring smile before she left.

Mother Anne folded her hands. "Rosa has prepared something for him. Her recipe will supplement consecrated Georgian blood. I take it you were up all night. How's Miles?"

He rubbed an unshaven chin, still trying to focus. "Thoroughly exhausted... Alana stayed with Michael."

"So many days without sleep isn't good, Empath."

His arms stretched wide before he gulped down the coffee. "Did you catch the conversation from Hell?"

"You know I read you." She gave a grin. "I read him as well, and you were right last night. Nothing current is in his mind. No one thought his human life could resurface. Something's not right."

"You saw what happened with the kid." He winced, shook his head. "And I do apologize from the bottom of my heart. I'm surprised Lukas didn't bolt again when he saw you."

"Perhaps the resemblance to Helena is purposeful, meant to force repressed memories out of him. The child found comfort in his father's arms and experienced devastation when he found the scars."

"Talk about running the gamut of your emotional range—Michael went berserk. But not even that shock catapulted him forward a couple of centuries. I'm seriously worried."

"So are we all. Monsignor wants Doctor Chamberlain to examine him. I agree."

Sitting back, he groaned. "Hopefully, he won't be as abrasive with the specialist as he was in his dream. And just in case it's another *deja-vu* moment, I'll make sure the kid stays away from the good doctor, too."

"Lukas concerns me," she quickly said. "Can you read him?"

"No, and it's frustrating. Helena warned I was never to look inside the kid's mind, even when he stalked his father. Why the angel forbids this is a mystery. His need for Michael is furious, but I can't see into this kid's heart."

"Celia can. She's tremendously gifted, with a soul as old as yours. You are blessed, Empath."

Grinning, he answered, "In more ways than one, Mother, in more ways than one. I've had many lifetimes to get it right. And I wouldn't be lying if I said ours is a match made in Heaven." He paused. "Ah, I'm needed in a few."

He waited until the healer left before going into the kitchen with another loud yawn.

****

Michael studied the beautiful woman still asleep in the chair.

My guardian angel—peaceful in rest yet ready to spring into action if needed. Loving Alana is my only certainty. Whenever I think of you, my soul quickens. My need for you is…is—

His mind went blank and without warning, every muscle tensed. Pain wrenched his chest and limbs. His eyesight clouded like a heavy fog as the room spun wild. His teeth clenched against the new assault and as his body shook, he turned his face into the pillow to absorb a scream of agony.

A massive hand braced his head. His face pulled off the pillow as cold, thick liquid was held to his lips. Openly panicked, he grabbed the mug and greedily swallowed. The haze cleared, and unable to speak, he felt thankful that she still slept. Weak and needy, his body slumped down. Then he was lifted out of the bed, resting limp against a broad, barrel chest.

****

Settled in a soft armchair, a bright-colored, knitted blanket was tucked around Michael. Shivers thundered through his body, making it hard to relax against the thick, soft leather. Thorn handed him another mug, which he took and drained quickly. When his mind cleared and the shivering stopped, he studied a small parlor. One wall had a broad wooden arch, and through it, a dining table with four wooden chairs and two covered windows. He sensed the cooking area off to the side, filled with hums and unknown scents. Fresh air streamed through grates on stark white walls. Strange sounds, round lamps that were cut into the ceiling. Smells of lemons and spices mixing in a pleasant way.

Once again, everything intrigued him.

Thorn towered over him, and unable to hide embarrassment, he whispered, "It is appreciated…your kindness, your knowing."

"I'm a bit worried here, Champ. Yeah, she's still asleep. I put her in your bed. That'll probably be a real eye-opener when she wakes up. Yes, of course I closed the bedroom door."

Although he appreciated the assistance, he warned in a low whisper, "Stay out of my thoughts. I am not comfortable with unspoken word."

"The other you doesn't like it, either. Let's get something else into you, okay? Alana's great-aunt made it special, just for you. Give me your hand, and I'll help you to the table."

His head shook and adamant, he looked away. "No. No. I will not—"

"Yes, yes, you will!" Thorn insisted, mimicking his inflection.

"You cannot order *me*, servant. Nor will you mock. My right leg is all but shattered. I will stay in comfort while you explain all I do not understand."

"I don't think so." Thorn hoisted him over one burly shoulder. The pain in his belly made him groan.

Set down with care and now seated in a chair at the table, he gripped its arms and cursed. "Watch your mouth, and don't give me a hard time today."

"You lift me as if I weigh nothing—and I will say what I please."

"It's another God-given talent, and you'll watch your language. See? Shivers are already gone. You'll learn to sense the thirst thing."

A narrow-eyed glare followed Thorn into the cooking area and back. A steaming bowl was placed on the table. The thick brown puree smelled savory. Full of curiosity, he sniffed at it. "I eat food as well? Ah, 'tis animal blood! Will this appease my craving?"

"If it did, many species would be extinct, don't you think? You *do* know that there are other vampires in the world?"

Wide-eyed, he asked, "Do other vampires keep their souls as do I?"

"No. You're one of a kind. Obviously, you don't recall the taste buds of a creature of the night, either." Thorn handed him a spoon. "Look, animal blood doesn't pack the same punch as the human variety, which has been very much off your menu for over a century—but it'll do the trick."

Trustful for once, he took a brimming spoonful. Immediately, his mouth burned and with a sour scrunch of his face, he spit it back into the bowl. "'Tis bitter… 'Tis putrid!"

He pushed it away. Thorn pushed it back.

"'Tis nutritious—'tis good for you. Don't gripe." Refusing the offered spoon, Michael leaned back and laced his arms across his chest. "You know, I haven't had a decent night's sleep in thirteen days because of you. What did I say about giving me a hard time?" Of course, he gave no reply aloud. "Oh I will read your mind and I've never heard you utter such nasty words. Listen up, immortal being. This has healing herbs, yummy vegetables, and gobs of animal blood. All the things a creature in your condition needs to get back on his feet. No, you're not in charge here and yes, you *will* eat this."

A huffy groan dismissed the authoritative tone. No servant spoke like this, like a parent with an errant child. But that thought forced recall of his father's stern demeanor.

"Ah, yes… Shall we see how fast I make you wail, little boy?" His father's exact words stunned Michael. His eyes went wide as the servant sat beside him at the table. "I'm normally even-tempered, good-natured. Have another not-so-nice thought and injured or not, I'll do what Martin did. And it's Thorn, not servant!" Michael snatched the spoon from his hand. "God help me," Thorn mumbled, "It's another *deja-vu* moment."

****

It took an hour, but Michael finished the pasty soup. He'd admit to no one that each sour mouthful brought more range of motion. Cramped muscles loosened. Internal healing quickened.

But when Thorn took the bowl to the cooking area, Mother Anne entered and sat at the table.

Something close to panic and a sense of helplessness entered his mind. Obscure images sputtered before one face formed distinct through the haze.

"Yes, Michael, I believe Helena and I look alike."

"Helena…" he whispered, not able to recall who

she was to him.

She nodded and placed a large leather case on the table before him. "We'll speak of the Old One another time. I believe this has been waiting over three centuries—for you."

With uncertainty, he stared at it—made no attempt to open it. At his side, Thorn unhooked its metal clasp and set the contents before him. Both of his palms pressed flat on the table. He could *not* move. He watched Thorn unfasten four brass clips to remove the glass. Trembling and shocked, his fingertips inched toward it and then ran over the pristine parchment. A familiar gold locket lay beside it undisturbed.

"When you are completely well, I'll provide a detailed explanation of how this came to be in my possession," the kind Sister stated. "But for now, let me offer this. Many days ago, at our Motherhouse, the two sisters who helped awaken you found a wooden chest with these items inside."

In an eerie low tone, he whispered, "My sister's writing chest... How can this be? This is indeed Anne's script."

One finger slid over her signature as he read silently:

Beloved brother,

I have unbearable anguish in my soul. Priscilla and Rosalind come to me in tears of terror. You are taken from us this night. No words describe the decimation to our hearts. Torn away, thrust into an undead world where you are the hunter and we the hunted. Yet we will always love you.

Loving brother, tender child we held to our breasts with such joy. This twist of fate, this tragedy should not be. Retribution will bring redemption and your soul will triumph. As life appears before you from dust and bone, seek a path to salvation, not damnation. Grandfather's chest, made with mystical hands, will free you of a burden none can endure. The locket is a symbol of our love. Present it to another with devotion. A child will lead you on a journey. The journey will lead you home. You shall be delivered from evil.

Your devoted sister, Anne

Witnessed 14 December 1690 by Priscilla & Rosalind Malone

Her words blurred. The corners of his mouth turned down as he clutched the locket to a heart that could no longer beat. Pulled back to 1678, he saw it all as he cleared his throat to speak. "A foggy summer morn… My chest aches from sobs, and I lay my head on Anne's lap. She strokes my hair as Priscilla and Rosalind kneel beside to soothe, to hush my cries. But fury has my heart. No one will explain why they dare to leave my life. I press the locket into Anne's hand begging, 'Do not go. I will never see you again.' I sense this and cannot accept it. Priscilla takes the locket and whispers she will hide it in the chest. Rosalind, often silent, kisses my cheek. But it is my beloved Anne who I study. There is serene resolve on her face—And my heart shatters. Father's harsh pull from the coach angers me. Mother is too heartbroken to speak. But I have never known life without their love."

Unraveled, raw distress poured out as Michael palmed his eyes and tried to find a sense of composure. It would not come. Honest misery at who he'd lost. Memories the healer had said should never be recalled. So many aches within his soul. Her hand came over his as she whispered his name. But he closed his eyes tight and shook his head. That day in 1678 had defined his life. Even his loss of faith.

Thorn gripped his shoulders. "You have to let it go."

He could not. "As I took my final breath as a living man, I saw their faces and hated myself for never finding them."

"And now you have." Mother Anne refastened the thin glass over his sister's letter. "You must move on, Champion."

His throat closed. His eyes filled again. This had pierced his soul. Folding his arms on the table, he buried his face clutching the locket as if it could bring back an unfinished, mortal life. Shattered, he muffled his sorrow as his shoulders shook. Mother Anne brushed his hair back. He could not look at her. Comfort shimmered though him and embraced his soul in understanding.

Yet he was terrified; slow to respond. It took every ounce of control to finally straighten his back. He forced his shaking hands to his lap, and although his eyes misted again, he met her sympathetic gaze. "I hear your unspoken request, but I swear to you—I *cannot* see it."

More resolute, she leaned forward. "The beast-within dominated your thoughts, but it didn't abscond with them. You *must* search again."

Unable to stem the flow of life-memory, he came to the untenable decision, just as any moral man would. "It is *my* soul that will forever burn in Hell for a demon's deeds. There is no salvation. *I myself* will destroy this body."

"Not on my watch, Champ," Thorn firmly stated. "A good woman loves you and a troubled kid needs his father." Thorn looked at Mother Anne. "I'll find a way to fast-forward his brain. I don't know how, but it'll come to me, sooner or later."

"I have every confidence, Empath." She stood slowly after the reply, and her warm hand came to his cheek. "You *must* do this, Michael. You must accept your destiny."

****

Several minutes passed in silence. Fractured feelings were all he had, none of which made sense. Alone with Thorn, he composed himself enough to whisper, "Please take these away."

When Thorn came back into the dining area, his broad hand stretched out. "Take it, Champ. Your right leg is slow to heal, which makes it unsteady. It won't support you."

He had to get away from this room, from this cumbersome sadness. As if strength of mind could force these feelings back down, he grabbed Thorn's hand, then his arm, and stood. "Good, now we're making progress. First, we walk to the bathroom. Come on... Push through the pain."

Stubbornly, memories of a life he'd never finish would not leave. He hobbled with a pronounced limp, and Thorn had most of his weight. To protest or complain didn't enter his muddled mind. "I am not malodorous," he said with a sigh.

"Have you gotten a whiff of your breath lately? Onions, garlic, blood—you need to brush with gobs of toothpaste."

Grateful for the humorous tone, he asked from a

fog, "There is paste for teeth?"

Inquisitiveness lessened his somber mood, and the short walk took some time. He stared at the thick Persian carpet under his bare feet as each soft-wool fiber felt like a massage. In the small, shiny room his fascination piqued. Longing to stand without assistance, both hands locked to the black pedestal sink. His eyes scanned the looking glass, and he preened, turned his head from side to side.

"Why such an odd face, servant? Ah, you notice. My hair does not even graze my shoulders. 'Tis too short for my liking, yet still full of familiar brown waves. Rather pleasant to look at. Tell me, is this both modern and fashionable?"

Thorn's expression changed as he muttered, "Oh boy."

"And the looking glass is crisp, clear for my reflection," Michael added in full amusement.

Chapter 15

Moving the living room furniture against the walls, Thorn had another *deja-vu* moment. The Persian carpet had enough space for Michael to freely stretch his six-foot, three-inch frame well enough, and exercise would relieve his stiff joints—maybe jog a memory or two.

Well, one could hope, he prayed.

Stopping often to let him rest, Thorn guided Michael's very shaky moves. This version of Michael didn't bring up either letter or locket, nor did the thought of either item take hold in his old-world mind. Fully focused on independence and strengthening his injured body, at least he now somewhat resembled the self-sufficient vampire he had known for seven years.

But by mid-afternoon, it was evident. Michael couldn't take much more. Repeated gasps replenished oxygen to his atrophied muscle. Sprawled on the floor, the black silk pajamas clung to his lean frame. And once Thorn got him upright, he couldn't help but stare at the sweat dripping off Michael's temples.

Okay, another thing I've never seen on him…ever! Do vampire's sweat?

"Now this body is malodorous," Michael groaned.

"After a shower, you'll have another helping of Rosa's soup." The sour expression returned, and he clicked his tongue. "Now, now, let's not lose the gold star for today."

"Perhaps you should taste it. Truly, your manner of speech puzzles me, and I rather doubt that even a creature like *you* could fly to the heavens and present me with a golden star. For this shower, how have you gathered rain water?" Michael started to fall, and as they moved down the short hall, Thorn's grip tightened.

"We don't gather rain. Just turn a knob to set the temperature and lather up with a bar of soap. I'll leave fresh clothes outside the door. This limp is still a bad one."

"The bone in my thigh does not mend. It is indeed tender." He stopped hobbling and asked in a confident tone, "Will my trousers have a zipper?"

"A what?"

"Are you dull in the mind, servant? It is called a zipper. It has shiny silver teeth that go up and down as if by magic. My lady showed me this."

The dry frown was classic Michael. Swallowing a laugh, he replied, "Uh, let me just show you how the shower works."

****

When Thorn closed the dresser drawer, Alana bolted up into a sitting position and rubbed her eyes. "Okay, how did I get in his bed and what did you do with him?" Over one arm, Thorn had a white sleeveless undershirt and black sweats. "Hey... I bought those for Michael in Pisa."

"And they'll fit perfectly. I put you there, and he's in the shower."

As she smiled, both of his bushy red eyebrows rose. "Oooh... You're enjoying this, aren't you? I'll bet he's just full of questions."

"You don't know the half of it. Oh, and he wants to

know if his trousers have a zipper."

Her blush deepened. "He, uh, got a little inquisitive. You know, Celia said that Michael's business included selling silks and satins, buttons, thread to sew dresses, jackets, and…and etcetera!"

"I'm sorry, I couldn't resist."

"Seriously. How is he today?"

"Pathetically weak and emotionally raw."

Hugging her knees, she yawned, didn't react to the statement. "What time is it?"

"Three p.m. Listen… Please tell Miles that I need him down here—like right away."

"Why don't you do the telepathic-telephone thing with Celia B? I know how much the two of you enjoy it."

"She's keeping the kid's mind off his father. And you should go before—"

"You don't have to tell me twice." She forced herself to leave Michael's bed. *Being emerged in his scent comforts me, even if he doesn't remember…* "I'll give Dad the message," she added.

In the empty hall, she looked at the stairs and sank against the wall. No one *ever* used words like pathetically weak or emotionally raw to describe Michael Malone.

****

The hot trickle of water felt good running down Alana's back. Sleeping for hours in the upholstered chair and not being able to relax around Michael had taken its toll. Afterward, she grabbed at her knotted hair with a favorite pink towel to squeeze out the excess water before twisting it up with a plastic clip. Shorts and a cropped top would be perfect for a run through the steep hills.

That might put him out-of-mind for a while. Hopefully, it'd lessen the anxiety building inside like a volcano ready to explode, maybe even halt the gnawing desire to see him again. This being—and only God knows exactly what he is now because I sure don't—his soul's the same. As soon as Michael opened those dreamy brown eyes, she had felt it. *He knows I'm special to him, and he feels the connection as deep and intense as I do. Nothing is lessening this relentless worry...* With sneakers in hand, she entered the living room. Lukas flopped on the couch. "Let me guess. It's either *Raiders of the Lost Ark* or a 70s *Star Wars*. My sister has a major crush on Harrison Ford."

"Old movies are pretty cool. I kind of like the third *Indiana Jones* one. Where are you going?"

She tied a sneaker thinking, *now that's a loaded question!* He wore a cooped up, ready-to-explode scowl. She met his broody gaze that reminded her of... "You know, it doesn't take a psychic to sense antsy. Feel like a run up the mountain? It's an awesome workout."

"I wish," he grumbled. "Like they'd let me."

"Who are 'they'? Give me the short list."

His deep-blue eyes rolled. "Mister B might, but not, you know, *him*."

"You mean Thorn? What's he got to say about it, anyway? There isn't any demony thing in Portofino. The villas aren't full of the devil's minions waiting for you to jog by and wave hello. Get your new sneaks on. I'll tell Celia."

"Really?"

The hint of a dimpled grin thrilled her. "I'm not

gonna offer twice, babe." She went to do just that, and when she came back into the living room, Lukas was ready. He started for the foyer at the back of her home.

"Nope—we go out the other way."

Hesitant and fidgety, he asked, "But, like, why not the elevator?"

She motioned him to follow and started down the steps. On the second landing, Michael's son stopped and stared at the apartment door. It was closed.

****

Weaving a path to the dining table by way of the wall and strategic pieces of furniture to hold, Michael slowly limped along. Although his ribs had healed, the bandaged right leg hurt like hell. The shoulder bite and clawed crevices down his back throbbed merciless with every move.

As soon as he sat at the table, the shivers began. As stubborn as an old mule he avoided the man's serious expression. Miles Bookman reminded him of his last tutor: stern, smart, and unrelenting. Last night's discussion was hazy, but he clearly recalled those curt comments and irritated glares. The way *his* child had looked to Miles for reassurance hadn't left him, either.

Thorn placed a bowl with the putrid puree in front of him. Not willing to show displeasure to this particular visitor, he refused to cringe and swallowed each spoonful without a pinched face. The craving... the thirst surfaced. He had to face the disgusting need. Fresh human blood filled a crystal mug. He brought it to his lips, eventually draining the tall carafe.

"This is progress, Champ," Thorn said. "Pretty soon, you'll sense it and get to the fridge all by yourself."

"These trousers are made of the same cloth that my child wore last night."

Miles stared at him. "They're called sweatpants and that's a cotton undershirt, oddly referred to a tank top."

"Get the kid off your mind," Thorn warned.

He chose to ignore both of them. "The waist gathers and stretches as did *my* child's."

Folding his hands on the table, Miles leaned in. "It's called elastic, one of the many conveniences we now have along with electricity, mini-vans, and cell phones. I'd explain DVDs, radio talk-shows, and space shuttles, but hopefully you'll enter the Twenty-First Century sooner rather than later. Is anything back?"

The incessant probing was too persistent for Michael's taste this afternoon and his smug turn away was purposeful—to deepen Miles's frustration. After a decent wait, the man stood, walked to an open window. With his hands tightly clasped behind his back, which also reminded him of his tutor, the man shook his head, stared out at the daylight. "I cannot imagine what could be so important that you needed me immediately, Thorn." Curious himself about the street below, Michael pushed off the table and took the few steps to his side. Immediately, Miles huffed out, "Oh, Good Lord—"

Thorn chuckled as he joined them at the window. "You can say *that* again. He's got one hell of a first-class reflection, plus he sweats up a storm. Standing in sunlight? That's three hits right out of the ballpark."

He noticed his skin shades paler than both men. Basking in delicious rays of warm sunlight, he then looked down in awe. "How fascinating this modern world is. How wondrous! The road below is smooth. What are those objects on four black wheels? So many colors and shapes." He leaned out farther, unconsciously resting all weight on his right leg. Instantly, he teetered and lost balance.

The servant's massive arm hooked his chest. "Steady now. We wouldn't want to test the flying thing, now would we?"

Quickly, he asked, "Do I fly?"

"Not exactly, but a long leap isn't out of the question. And hitting the pavement won't kill you because... Let's leave it at not exactly." Thorn had eased him into the closest dining room chair with arms. "Celia wants me, Miles. Could you babysit for a few?"

The man gave a nod aiming a curious thin grin Michael's way. It seemed pleasant enough, and he said in a conceited tone, "You are amused by me?"

"That I am." Sitting next to him, Miles opened a black, rectangular object, which instantly whirred. Intrigued by the new sound, he leaned over and in. "This is a computer," Miles explained in a dry fashion. "It functions like parchment and pen with memory and—" He paused to put his glasses back on grumbling, "Sweating skin, tolerates daylight, a reflection...total mysteries to me. Truly remarkable."

Suspicious print flashed across the device. Then, a silver dragon in a gold circle appeared. Michael sprang back, too proud to ask the meaning of this insignia. He eyed a different chair, which was at the head of the table and maneuvered through aches and pains into it.

After a sideways glance, Miles mumbled, "I shouldn't be surprised. How interesting. Some arrogant habits never seem to change." Glass spectacles rimmed with thin wire now perched on the man's straight nose. His eyes widened as Miles rapidly pressed square buttons. "These are called keys... each represents a letter of the alphabet. When I press the letter, it appears on the page. May I ask a few questions? As a researcher for the Georgians, insights to your human life would be invaluable."

"My human life," he whispered, once again pulled back in time. Yes... He saw his life—and he saw his death. When their eyes met, only encouragement showed on the man's face. He could feign exhaustion, but that would be a lie. "It is... It *was*...an extraordinary existence. I am birthed in London, the fourth and only male child of Martin and Rebecca Malone. The year is 1663 and it is the beginning of May."

Slowly, his voice grew more confident.

****

Thorn leaned back and handed Celia the empty plate. "What would I do without you? That was just what I needed. It's been a brutal thirteen days, but you already know that." She kissed his cheek and set down a fresh cup of coffee. He held up both hands. "No, honey, I need to stay away from all things caffeine. God only knows what I'd do to him if I get too jittery."

Sitting across the kitchen table, another work of art, another example of Michael's exquisite taste, she touched his arm. "I've never seen you so frustrated. It's really that freaky?"

"Last night was freaky. Today is surreal. I keep thinking any minute he's going to snap out of it, but I don't see an iota of who he is in his head."

"What are you getting off this Michael?"

155

"Well, there's stubborn arrogance, just like our Champion. Financially secure and clever in business, he certainly didn't go looking for the fast-track to Hell in 1690." After grinning, he shook his head and let out a sigh. "Alana's on his mind. His soul screams for her…and he's sneaky enough to try and get your father to talk about Lukas, which means he wants to see the kid again." Thorn stood, adding, "When Mother Anne produced his sisters' letter, he just broke down, couldn't hide *any* emotion. I mean, you know him, Celia. He's as controlled as they come. You never get a-a bright smile *or* a blood tear—ever. This Michael is completely unraveled."

"You're just as close to unraveling, and without a clue as to what to do. I'll come with you."

"This shouldn't be happening. Maybe I've missed something. I mean, he's changing right before our eyes, and it doesn't make sense…just shouldn't be able to happen."

She leaned in, and his arms folded around the petite woman. "Don't feel this way."

"What way?"

"Useless, sweetie, because you never were, and you aren't now."

"I keep replaying the last twenty-four hours and I just don't see it."

"Michael scared himself with this whole 'I can take on the sorcerers and I'm gonna make them pay' macho attitude. Without you? He's fair game. This Michael isn't able to recognize danger." Thorn kissed the tip of her nose, basking in the love radiating from her beautiful green eyes.

****

When they entered the apartment together, Thorn sensed Michael's reaction to Celia. Immediately, he saw warmth and gentle respect in the soft expression on Michael's face. And both of them caught every thought when he flashed a bold, utterly charming smile—something far from ordinary.

Sitting close at the dining room table, Celia took his cool hand. Michael brought her hand to his lips and kissed it but didn't let go. "Hey, sweetie, how are you?"

"That voice, so loving and kind—you are Celia!"

She smiled. "I most certainly am."

"You are close with my beautiful lady. It was you who soothed my child last night. I know this to be truth."

They both sensed scattered, incomplete notions of what had occurred last night. Together, they sifted through an abundance of useless information no longer needed in this century or the modern world. Other than that? Silently, Celia, sent the message, *"You're right, Thorn. Oh my God. Nothing's there. Nothing!"*

When she asked him how he was feeling, Michael seemed very eager to converse with her, and his aptitude for flirting revealed itself. The tilt of his head, holding her delicate hand, the mystique of his dark-espresso eyes... Thorn studied what he'd never before seen. Miles was having a field day documenting all of Michael's reactions, near hilarious comments, and unexpected openness. Yet Thorn's frustration grew... by the minute.

****

As the sun set on the first day of his new existence, and drawn to Celia's sweetness, Michael felt pleasantly relaxed. But when the downstairs door opened and closed, his eyes narrowed and his nostrils flared. His eyes shifted as Thorn grabbed Miles's arm saying in a low voice, "You can't, Miles. The calm before the storm is now officially history."

Hobbling to the door, he felt the stares of everyone at the table. Boldly limping into an unfamiliar stairwell, his scowled deepened. He grabbed Lukas's arm, pulling him into the living room, ignoring Alana's demand to let go.

Lukas broke free of his weak grip with his fists flexing at his sides as he backed away farther into the living room. "I don't get it. Why the fuck are you so mad at me?"

Furious at the brazen tone and the curse word, Michael demanded, "Who gave you permission to leave this dwelling?"

Lukas glared as Alana confidently stated, "I did."

He leered at her, saying, "Positively scandalous. Cover yourself, woman! You show *skin*!"

"Skin is good," she replied, which absolutely astonished him. Grabbing the afghan from the chair, Michael threw it at her. She threw it back, landing it at his feet.

With a lurch, he stepped over it and his tone sank low. "Shameless and in such a state of indecent undress you dare defy me? You have been reckless! The boy is *not* safe in the streets of an unknown country! He might have been taken."

"Taken by whom?" Miles quickly asked.

His temper accelerated. Something within snapped. "Damn it! Didn't I tell you to *stay put*? Answer me, little boy! Do it now!"

As the manservant placed himself between father

and son, Lukas punched the man's broad back, yelling, "No you didn't! Fuck it, demon. Get out of my way!"

Coldly, Michael hissed, "Step aside, Thorn."

Keeping Lukas behind his looming frame, Thorn's legs stayed wide, his feet firm on the carpet. "Before you go making an ass out of yourself *again*, answer the researcher's question. Those two little words "stay" and "put" sparked a memory. I'm warning you, back off, Daddy. The kid's okay."

Alana gripped Michael's arm, pulled him back. "And I know this scene. I read that dream journal twice. Calm down and get over it."

Her sharp tone had him speechless. Fire danced in his eyes when his son's fist *again* jabbed Thorn's back, hissing, "I'm as strong as he is, asshole, get the fuck out of my way!"

Thorn didn't budge, holding onto his son. "Simmer down, kid. This is why I'm here."

"Go to Hell. Like I *care* why you're here. I didn't fucking do anything wrong!"

Sternly, Michael stated, "Enough, little boy! Your temper will not be tolerated. State an apology this instant and… and… go to your room. Go." In his mind, the small living room morphed into a much larger one and his voice took on an unfamiliar tone. "I told you to stay put! Clayton knows we're *here*, damn it! When I tell you something, you listen. And lose the attitude or I will absolutely get parental. Now go!"

Miles shook his head. "This is from the dream, Michael, and it will not play out."

Lukas screamed, "Yeah. Right like you think you can!"

Quickly, Miles said, "Lukas, stop. Your father's

confused." A glare shot to Miles before he turned his attention back to his son. "*Listen* to yourself, Michael. Whose words are these? Who is Clayton? How does he know you are here? *Think*!"

"I said go—right now, little boy!" Grabbing Thorn's shoulders, Michael hoped to toss him to the floor. It didn't work. One huge hand splayed across his chest, and in a quick move, Lukas sprang around.

Thorn grabbed an arm and shoved Lukas behind again, warning, "That's not going to happen either, kid."

"Don't do this, Michael, just stop." Alana cinched his waist, and with one pull, he landed hard on the floor, two feet from the front door. Fierce pain ran up his spine and down his right leg.

Wincing, he muttered, "You are *immensely* strong for a woman."

"You got that right, buddy," she answered. The last word she said irked him, but the pains shooting through him had him unable to move. He was forced to simply sit there and watch.

Lukas cursed continually at Thorn, who finally bellowed, "I told you to simmer down! This isn't the family reunion you're hoping for, either. In the dream, Daddy had you over his knee and crying, so think of this as me *literally* saving your skinny behind."

Celia slipped a hand over Lukas's curled fist, which instantly unrolled. "Come with me, Lukas, it's all going to work out, right Thorn?"

Thorn nodded as they moved away, and then he crossed the room. Sinking down with a serious expression, the huge man crouched in front of him. "That's strike two with the kid. You spooked him again. What you did last night still bothers you. Want to get it off your chest?"

The soft tone defused his anger, and confused, he whispered, "I'm so sorry, Lukas. I-I didn't know—"

"*What* didn't you know?" Coming over, Miles stood over him. "Think, Michael! You've lashed out at your son not once, but twice. *Why?* Search your soul, damn it!"

Lukas let go of Celia's hand, palmed his eyes, and ran out. Miles called his name and followed up the stairs. Thoroughly lost, Michael wished they *all* would leave.

"Take my hand," Alana said. He didn't look at her as she knelt behind and rubbed his tense shoulders. "It'll all come back. It has to. I love you too much to lose you again."

Her touch ignited need in his soul. He swallowed, afraid to speak. He didn't want to understand where this outburst had come from and why his manner of speech had changed in an unfamiliar way, only craving the comfort she offered. Slowly, he eased back to rest against her breasts. The soothing scent, the nearness of her meant safety.

"I want to be alone with him, Thorn."

"I don't think it's a good idea—"

"I do." Sweet Celia said as she took Thorn's hand. "Call if you need us, Ally."

"I seriously don't think you're going to—"

"Make the situation any better, Thorn?" Her embrace tightened. "Yeah, I know. This is your mission and all. But unless you have a better idea...do you?"

Once alone, she didn't try to talk to him. She just held him.

Chapter 16

Miles had followed Lukas into the den and watched the boy aim the remote and turn on the television. No displays of anger, no heated words exchanged, just a bothered look. He came back into Alana's living room and made the call. As he hung up the phone on the antique secretary, Thorn and Celia entered. They sat on the couch as he walked over. "Chamberlain will be here tomorrow morning."

Thorn shook his head. "Is he a licensed demon shrink? Because Michael's problems aren't physical anymore."

"Arthur's the best in his field. Maybe he can explain this memory lapse. Michael recalls direct quotes from a dream but will not address reality. Perhaps his fantasy showed us one crucial truth. Perhaps certain blood will have a similar effect in the real world."

"Giving him a taste of Alana or Lukas would be risky just now," Thorn replied. "He's nowhere near his former level of strength *or* self-control and his responses are all over the place. In his dream, all memories were intact, right? There's no telling what he'll do like this. I got a little nervous when he slipped into the scene with the kid. Confusing him could get dangerous."

Celia asked, "Do you think Ally can open his mind?"

"No. And it won't help matters."

"So, what do we do now?"

"I was about to ask the same question," Miles said with a sigh.

"You're feeling the intensity of everyone's mood, Celia. The kid's ready to rumble, Alana doesn't know which way is up, and your dad's about to haul off and punch Michael's lights outs. Am I right, researcher?"

Thorn had accurately nailed his feelings. Miles sank into an armchair. "This is, without a doubt, a most exasperating situation. We have to do something and soon. In his dream, we mixed their blood."

"Give Ally a little time with him, Dad."

"Alana's his security blanket right now, Miles. I'm not sure their blood will have the desired effect."

"It's been twenty-four hours of this," Miles stated.

"So it's time to try anything? I don't know, maybe you're right."

Celia quickly said, "He won't voluntarily drink their blood, Dad."

"He will if he's thirsty. I'll get him moving around a bit before we spring the midnight snack. How do you think the kid's handling this latest run-in?"

Miles rubbed his temples. "I'm not clairvoyant, but I understand children. I am genuinely concerned, Thorn. Celia's calm suggestions will only work on him for only so long. Lukas needs stability. He needs his father."

"I'll go sit with him, Dad. We're pretty tight." She kissed Thorn's cheek.

After she left, Thorn said in a serious tone, "Okay, researcher. Let's you and I go over this one more time."

****

Alana kept him in her arms a long time. He hadn't moved, and when he finally grabbed the edge of the couch to haul himself up, he sank down slowly to the cushion, leaned forward with his elbows on his knees and his hands covering his bruised face. The slump of his broad shoulders looked as if he'd given up trying to find a misplaced but valuable object. She didn't know what to do. "Can I get you something, a-a glass of water, maybe?"

Having to get away, she went to the kitchen before he could say "no". *Even if he doesn't drink it, he'll recognize an act of kindness. Oh God, I'm...* "Very worried," she murmured. She came back in, set the glass down on the coffee table between them and avoided his gaze.

"Sadness consumes me. I am not the one you love."

"That's not entirely true."

"I apologize for needing you the way I do."

"There's no reason to apologize."

"I am not the one you love," he repeated with defeat etched in his tone.

"You're a part of him, but not all of him."

"He is truly fortunate to have known your love."

"And I'm a lucky woman to have had him in my life."

"You want him back." So tenderly said, his response touched her heart. Regret couldn't be hidden as old wounds opened.

"I told you last night that we haven't talked to one another for almost seven years. We were extremely close for a long time, but then... Let's just say we purposely avoided each other."

"Because of the demon that is no longer in me?" He held her gaze, and the meaning of 'emotionally raw' and 'pathetically weak' came at her full-force. "Delicate shoulders and a womanly figure belie such tremendous strength. You are unique, a mystical gift to the world...to him."

If I were foolish enough to sit next to you, I'd already be in your arms. "The demon... That's one major factor, but there are others."

"What are they, my lady?"

She leaned forward. Simply his voice sent waves of desire crashing through her. *I know you better than you know yourself, and nearness only makes this more disconcerting.* "I'm not comfortable sharing them with you."

"Would you share it with him, darlin'?"

His tone... the way it slid into sensual. *Please, please, please just ignore the last word...* "Michael, you *are* him. You just don't know it yet." She reached for the glass. His hand gripped hers; his fingers wrapped around hers. She did not move. *I can handle being alone with him—as long as he doesn't have that pleading gleam in those gorgeous espresso eyes—as long as I don't feel that persistent yearning tug at me.* Her heart pounded. The room felt too warm.

He whispered, "My Guardian...my love."

Don't breathe. Don't feel. She stared at the glass...at his hand, which tightened. Every unwise want nudged as she met his commanding gaze. "Do not do this. It isn't right. We'd be taking advantage of each other."

"I must admit the urge to take you in my arms

persists." His hand pulled away. "Hear this earnest plea from the depths of my soul. I want you; I need you, and I love you."

Sit back, force yourself to remain calm. You read this in the dream journal, too. "Love won't work between us. We both know it. This relationship can't ever be right."

He looked about to cry as he sat back and laced his arms against his chest. "I will honor your words, my lady, though I do not accept them. Indeed, he is a lucky man. I shall never know such loyalty of a woman, such gracious love. Even on my best and brightest day of walking this earth as a living man, I would never be worthy of someone like you."

His response chipped away her resolve. *To be in your arms, to kiss away loneliness...I want you with every fiber of my being—body and soul.* About to give in to his need—her need, Thorn walked in. Quickly, she stood. Without looking at him, she softly said, "Good night, Michael." This time together had unnerved both of them. *We exist in two different worlds, two different points in time, and neither of us can act upon our feelings without destroying the other.*

****

A little edgy, not at all convinced it'd work, Thorn rubbed his palms together. An annoyed expression appeared on Michael's face, but he kept a positive attitude. "Let's put that lover's angst to use. Get up. It's training time."

"Your untimely arrival forced my lady to depart. I will not forget this. And thus, with neither broadsword nor rapier in this room, I refuse your challenge, servant."

"I'm not giving you a weapon, Zorro. Up." Glancing over, he caught Michael's uneven limp to the arch—and the egotistical smirk. He moved the furniture again—one heavy piece at a time. Michael's deliberate steps in the opposite direction. Catching the annoyed pose… Thorn sensed the next quip coming.

"You have demon strength."

"I have mystical powers."

"But you are demon."

"You still don't trust me, do you? So now, let me guess. You and your new, unnatural knowledge of all things creepy declare it to be so because of the way I move furniture? Stop goading me. I'm *not* demon. Please share that info with the modern 'you'. Unlike the creature you are, I'm a living, breathing, mystically-enhanced man with a *fully* functional body. Don't bite necks, don't fly, and I enjoy loving my Celia!"

More than bothered, Thorn slid the small coffee table out of the way fast.

"Even in the dream, you landed way off the mark. For seven years, you actually believed I was a *demon*? This proves what an oblivious character you are! When you're all here, we'll have a serious chat because I'm highly insulted. So what if I like to sleep under the stars? I don't burrow into your garden like a-a pod-person!" The explanation was useless, and he didn't care for Michael's mischievous smirk.

"Perhaps this rant is another sign of demon within you."

"You know, Helena never clued me in on this particular part of my mission. But then again, no one figured you'd go postal on three evil sorcerers, either." Gazing upward he added, "I think one day of this is my limit."

"I find your manner of speech interesting. It is rather humorous for a—"

"Don't say it!" The satisfied grin was more than irksome. He cleared his throat, took in a deep breath and then blew it out slow. "We'll start with push-ups—*silent* push-ups."

Michael only appeared to struggle for a minute. *The body has a memory of its own,* he thought while sweeping that jumbled mind once more. *Nothing is back, and Celia is right.* If *this* Michael couldn't recognize a threat, he wouldn't survive a fight with other-worldly demons. The evil ones would surely find him, and Michael Malone's existence would be over.

****

An hour later, and pushed to his limit, Michael stretched out on the floor, again coated with sweat. "I-I need sustenance, please." His words came shaky but respectful, and when helped to his feet, both legs buckled.

Catching him, Thorn said, "You did really fine tonight."

As they neared the table, he was still breathing hard when Miles entered and handed something to Thorn. Opening a leatherbound book, Miles sat across from him with pen in hand, saying as he wrote, "It's almost midnight."

Arrogantly, he answered, "Day or night means nothing to me. Yet once again, you are documenting me."

"Dripping strands of sweat, a pale-pink flush on your face and the look of exhaustion—all human traits indicating significant change."

Thorn took the empty seat next to him and set a large carafe before him. It contained a blend of blood types, but two unique scents stood out. Instantly, Michael's senses spiraled and barely able to think, what stirred within terrified him. "I-I hunger for this blood, more so than ever before."

"It's much more potent, and you already know why. Drink it please," Miles stated.

It took a two-handed grip to hold the crystal mug. Not about to bring it to his parched lips, his jaw tightened, his eyes narrowed. He set it down in full refusal and hissed, "I will not drink."

Miles leaned across the table. "You must. It's an established fact that Guardian blood has an extreme effect on a vampire. Alana is very special to you. Lukas is your very bloodline. Both individuals are intrinsic to your survival. Thorn knows it from the dream. I know it from my research. This will speed up the self-healing process, quite possibly restore all memories."

An insistent glare began. "Tis an abomination—an act of horror!"

"It is the truth, Michael. This is no time for squeamishness. It's an absolute necessity."

Leaning back, he shook his head, wiped his sweaty brow with an emphatic, "*No*."

"Then we'll simply transfuse you. But we *will* get this into you, one way or the other—tonight."

Thorn kept the crystal mug even with his mouth. "You won't like that, Champ. I'd have to hold you down, and let Miles shove a long, painful needle deep into your vein. You have to drink, to remember." Softly, he added, "Please. Just drink."

Still hoping to resist the draw, he lowered his head.

"No! I ...*will not* drink." But it was intoxicating. It made his body scream, struggle for sanity. Feelings of an unknown terror, so very foreign to his soul, were impossible to interpret. Barely able to speak, to think, he whispered, "My life as a living man—it is simple, justifiable. But to reclaim the legacy of undeath, to recall centuries of a predator's existence—they would, then, be made real." Yet the primal need soared and screamed within him. "I will not accept the vampire's sins as my own, do you hear me? They belong to the demon! *It* is responsible ...*not* I. This blood of those I love... I beg you...Do not force it upon me." More frightened of seeing each ungodly act than of dying with a silver blade to his neck, both hands flew to his face. He rubbed his teary eyes raw. "*None* of it is *my* fault. Truly, I fought Cyril to the very end of life!"

"We know. And you didn't look for death." Thorn brought the crystal mug closer now.

"You were simply a young, self-absorbed man, but you didn't have the heart of a murderer." Miles said in a softer tone, "You must drink."

Craving obliterated his defenses. He nodded once, looked to Thorn—for courage? For a reprieve, perhaps? But a reprieve from what? With no ability to fight them or his need, both hands locked around the mug. He brought it to his lips—and Thorn refilled the crystal mug many times before it slid from his grasp.

The diluted genetic blend worked its magic. Immediate changes occurred. The chalky complexion of his hands vanished as if this potion absorbing through his starved veins held living vibrancy. On his arms, cuts and bruises faded. The ugly shoulder wound sealed right before the two men's astonished eyes. But the physical changes weren't as dramatic as the internal ones.

Staring into a void, Michael's shaky palms pressed into the table while scenes whipped through his brain.

"I use charm to lure and drain faceless victims. Bend them to my will. For two hundred years, lust is my narcotic, but then I approach the portal." A distance filled his words, and a long sigh escaped when he saw the angel in his mind. "But what is the purpose to this new existence, Helena? Why have you changed me? That I may seek atonement? Redemption? A century passes, yet night after night I stand in the passageway and ask the same questions."

His hands clenched into tight fists as his eyes narrowed. "The dark seer insists what lives inside her womb is punishment for taming my beast-within. How can this be? As life leaves her, I cut into her to save *my* child. I draw in air to breathe life into the still baby boy. His feeble cries fill me with awe. When Helena takes him from my arms, deep sadness swallows my soul. Every night I return to the passageway. Meaningless time passes until the young girl walks by with her father. Years later, I rage when her destiny is revealed. She will be *my* Guardian to protect, and the need for her survival fills my empty soul."

The next bizarre vision forced a dark scowl. "The snake of a liaison tells me my son is with the sorcerers in the Second Realm. *When*? *How*? *Why*? In defiance to all that is evil, I jump through a portal and steal him back!" Full of anguish, his fists slammed the table. "Why is there such hate in your heart for me, Lukas?" His shoulders lurched back. "Oh dear God, please, no more!"

Pulled out of tumultuous bits of reality, Michael's eyes flew open. Trembling, his fingers raked his damp hair. He stood and limped to the window. The murky night sky held his fractured attention, and after a tense minute, he made a deliberate turn to face Thorn and Miles.

"*How* the *hell* did this happen to me?" His voice held an unfettered sharpness and it filled the small dining room. Long strides, a steadier gait brought him into a strange living room. Slamming the apartment door shut, he nervously gripped the top of a black leather couch wondering why he was this anxious. "I'm waiting. Can *somebody* give me a believable answer? How did I get to Italy! This is Italy, right? What the *hell's* going on? And you, Empath, when did you take up weightlifting? Did you lose your glasses again? Damn it!"

"No trace of the young Englishman's old-world accent *or* naiveté anymore, Miles. And these aren't the composed, controlled mannerisms of the Champion either," Thorn barely whispered.

"I hear you, Empath."

"Uh, exactly what do you remember, Boss?"

Just shy of total annoyance, he approached them. And his right leg hurt like hell. "Not fucking enough, that's for sure. I feel funny... Like I've got a bitchin' headache. Care to tell me why?"

Not even looking at him, Miles kept writing. "Give us facts, Michael."

"Nice to see you too, Researcher. When did you start wearing reading glasses? Why are we on the Amalfi Coast? Wait... Did we slip through a portal?"

Thorn's glib stare continued as he said, "Alana got

you and Lukas out of the city."

Furious, his words spewed out as his head throbbed. "She did what!? And Lukas is *here* trying to kill me? Did he go after Alana, too? Is she safe? Shit. I never explained my son to her. He'll use her to get to me. And why does my leg hurt so bad? Christ! Did I lose my mind or something?"

"*Something* would be the right choice of words." Thorn quickly added, "Why am I here with you? Do you remember?"

"When did we get here?"

"Ten days after you drugged me and took out three immortal sorcerers. You know— those big, evil idiots at NWT? You cooked up the devious, now-I'm-getting-even scheme with Robert and Danny."

"That's crazy! I don't talk to ex-Guardians who—"

"And then you made sure I stayed clueless. That was some feat, by the way. How'd you pull it off, I wonder? You didn't, by *any* chance, use a little of that dark, nasty magic, did you? It always has a vicious kick to it, especially if you have a *good* soul."

Michael cringed but ignored the meaningless words. "The difference in you is… I mean that paunch is gone, not to mention chatty *and* complete sentences. You barely mumble "hello" and I steer clear of that demon company," he said in typical arrogance. "And I know better than to use dark magic on a *mystical* being. What's going on here?"

Miles closed the notebook. "How old is Alana, Michael?"

"She's twenty, and you know how old your adopted daughter is!"

"Alana will be twenty-eight in four months."

"No. She'll be twenty-*one*."

"How old is Lukas?"

Each ridiculous question irritated him more. "What is this, a fucking quiz? Thirteen, and that's one dangerous little boy who'll get himself killed coming after me like this. Three filthy sorcerers brainwashed him. And Clayton's a bastard! He *knew,* damn it! They slaughtered an angel and kidnapped my boy! I took him back! They're all gonna pay. Mark my words!" The fierceness that sizzled inside had him close to insane.

Miles leaned forward in his chair. "Listen carefully. Your timeline doesn't mesh with what is real. Lukas is fifteen, and you did something about his rage. You must remember."

"Remember what!? Oh God, please tell me I didn't hurt my boy."

"No, you didn't. But everything's far from all right with Lukas."

Both men looked uneasy, as if they fought to remain calm. "He's *here*...you said he's here. Alana's here too? I want to see Lukas, and then, I swear I'll tell Alana about my son before she thinks I'm the one who made him crazy."

"No!!" they both shouted. Starting for the door, he gave a dismissive frown. "Yeah, right... Back off and let me handle this."

Thorn grabbed his arm, blocked his path. "You're too furious and far too sure of yourself. Sit down." He pointed to the dining room chair.

"*No way*, and where'd you learn to move fast like that?"

"You're searching for answers that aren't there yet."

Full of frustration, he limped to the head of the table and sat. Nervously, he thumped the chair's arms. "What the hell's going on?"

"Do you remember certain things we told you last night?" He didn't answer. Because he couldn't. Thorn looked at Miles. "This isn't an act. There are enormous gaps in what he knows. What time is Chamberlain coming?"

Pulling off the reading glasses perched low on his nose, Miles rubbed both eyes. "Nine a.m. Good Lord, *this* is bloody maddening."

"Who's Chamberlain? Did I see Alana last night? I was at the brownstone, wasn't I?" He palmed sweat of his forehead and stared at the moisture on his hand. "What the hell... Am I sick or something?" Then both elbows slammed on the table. Rubbing his aching temples, he felt desperate, whispering, "Oh God. Talk to me, Thorn."

****

A small village existed down the coast, neither modern nor attractive. Not popular with wealthy visitors to the Amalfi Coast, time had forgotten these run-down shacks inhabited by people who never could seem to get out of poverty. If someone had the opportunity to leave, that individual did so, vowing to never return.

Serafina Ravento's unbearable life dragged on day after monotonous day. But tonight, naked and defiant, she stood in the center of a five-pointed star drawn on her bedroom floor with a piece of charcoal. Her mind opened to the voices calling to her. They'd take her away from the disaster her *Nona* deemed a 'good life'.

Everyone called the seventeen-year-old a half-breed bitch. They spit at her, taunted her, swore she possessed "the evil eye". Serafina would swish her long, raven-black hair and spit right back. *Nona* said pray for them to see the error of their ways.

Prayer wouldn't do it. Prayer never worked.

Two days ago, the mysterious star popped into her mind while hanging the old woman's shabby black dresses. And trudging into the decrepit shack called home, it had beckoned as bright as the Star of Bethlehem.

But this image came from a different god—one with dark, potent magic. When she drew it on a wrinkled paper bag in the kitchen, *Nona* blessed herself repeatedly. Then the fearful old thing grabbed a broom and beat her until she cried. Serafina didn't forget this insult from a fanatical holy-roller. *Nona* ordered her to run and confess this sin to the white-haired monsignor in Portofino.

That didn't happen.

Midnight approached. She knelt in the precise middle of her pictogram with a starving mind. Wanting this with heart and soul, she chanted, "I am Serafina. I call to you, dark god."

Then she heard it. A chorus of fallen angels singing in dissonant chords, "We need you, Serafina!"

Chapter 17

After an hour of listening to gibberish from two worn out men, Thorn stifled a yawn, saying to Michael as if he were a ten-year-old who had asked a difficult question, "So that's where you've been for the last twenty-four hours. Give or take a couple of centuries. At least you're somewhere closer to today now."

His head didn't ache as much anymore, but a two-finger tap continued on the edge of the table as he leaned back. "I actually screen devious clients and collect a *seven-figure* salary from NTW?"

Miles dryly stated, "N. W. T."

"Yeah, *whatever.*" He stood and limped around the small parlor. "And this building belongs to me? I take care of Alana and that's a good thing. But *this* place—"

Thorn groaned out, "What's wrong now?"

"It's kind of cramped for my taste, you know? There isn't one masterpiece on the wall. No floor-to-ceiling bookshelf, either." He gave a loose shrug, started for the door.

Thorn sprang up and beat him to it. "Whoa, where are you going?"

"You're the empath. You tell me."

"It's not happening on my watch. You're not all here, and Alana doesn't need to see this. Then there's the fact that you've already messed with the kid's head twice. Strike three and you're out—for good."

"Since when do *you* give me orders?"

"Since *you* began jumping time periods. Take a cold shower. Get Alana off—"

"Yeah… *After* I see her and my—"

Thorn grabbed his arm and pulled. Michael reached for the couch before he landed on it. "I out maneuver you by a long shot right now, so just *stay put*!"

He rose with a steady glare as pain shot through his head. "*What* did you just say?"

"These twisted *déja-vus* from the dream have got to stop. Plant your ass back down fast and *stay put*!" He blinked several times, totally confused as something flickered in his brain. "Go with the vague image. The kid got fresh. You got parental. Does this ring any bells? Are you picking up what you did in the dream or what just happened a few hours ago—either will do."

The throbbing in his head intensified, and he sank into the couch. "*Damn it!*"

With notebook in hand, Miles stood at the door, saying before he left, "It will come back to you. It has to. She loves you too much to lose you again."

His head thrust back against the soft leather. "Alana said that to me, didn't she? I swear… I heard her say it."

Settled in an armchair, Thorn straightened a trouser cuff. "I want you to relax. I'm very serious. Stand under the showerhead for a few. Call it a night and tomorrow we start fresh. But don't try to walk out of here, Michael. I won't be too far away—not for a minute."

He nodded, limped unsteadily through the living room. In the tiled bathroom, he closed the door and gripped the pedestal sink for support. Rarely if ever, did he take an absentminded glance. But this time, he reached out to touch the mirror.

Terrified, perfectly still, he whispered, "Oh, my God...my reflection?"

****

Looking up from his new laptop on the dining room table, Lukas studied Miles's slow nod to Alana. Seconds later, Celia whispered, "I'll go down, Dad. He's really frustrated," and she left immediately.

From many feet away, Lukas listened to the hushed conversation. Mystical hearing gave him the advantage. Miles had his arm around Alana, softly saying that *this* Michael will be even harder for her to deal with.

He didn't want to feel anything right now. *Another fucked up version of my father to screw up my head. Celia said they were trying something different downstairs. Guess it didn't work.* But what he had seen on his father's face earlier tonight still bothered him. Instead of playing a game on his computer, Lukas continued to read from a disc that Alana had given him. She had journaled her years as a Guardian.

And it wasn't hard to close his mind to the conversation in the living room, either.

The first year of Alana's mystical mission as a new Guardian of Souls read like science fiction. He finally understood what she was *really* capable of, what the calling entailed. This journal started on 9/20/94, a day after she turned sixteen. He checked the menu for the last entry date: 8/28/95, a full month before she met Michael, just as Alana had said.

She has wicked writing skills, similar to Mister B's, he thought. Detailed accounts of tracking and fighting evil creatures was something he could identify with. Self-healing, enhanced senses, super strength… They had those gifts in common. *Only one deviation: Alana went after any demon. I only hunted my father.*

He thought about the crazy scene earlier tonight and began to fidget. Something different caught his attention—the thick, black binder labeled *Michael Malone: Dream of Survival,* sandwiched between two discolored folders.

He took a quick glance at Miles with Alana, and with a swift, perfect grab, he had it in hand. Nine days of information organized like a narrative. The laptop's wide screen was ample cover, so he flipped to *Day One* and read:

Helena guides Michael's mind into believing Lukas is standing over him. Lukas smells animal blood flowing from each wound, nauseated immediately. "What did they do to you? I've got to get you out of here. I've got to get you out of—"

"The light of dawn," Miles Bookman replies.

****

Holding his drenched undershirt, Michael strode into the living room thinking he could disguise the throbbing limp. The pain shooting up his right ankle settling in his thigh just wouldn't quit. A burgundy towel hung around his neck and the comfortable black sweats hung low on his waist as he made it to the living room. He eyed Celia close to Thorn—holding hands? His thin grin deepened. More charming than ever, he flashed a wide smile at the petite psychic. Her delicate bone structure and short red hair reminded him of a pixie, but Miles's daughter had always been a powerhouse of personality and goodness.

Immediately, he felt indebted to her. Didn't know why... "Sweet Celia B. Did I miss something? Do the two of you have a love thing happening?"

"Hi. How's it going?" Celia craned her neck up as he approached the couch. Thorn's thick arm draped her shoulders, like he could crush her with one squeeze.

"Ah, that voice sounds like a song. Not too well, according to your, should I say, boyfriend—and thanks, by the way." Innate charisma sailed over the top, hoping to snare her.

"For what?"

"I'm not sure about that part, but I know I owe you my life. Care to—"

"You won't get it out of her."

Yeah. That pissed him off. "Why not and stay out of my head, Empath."

"Generic info is all we offer. You get to fill in the details by yourself. So say good night to this lovely woman and go to bed."

"I've walked this earth for centuries. You don't get to tell me—"

"But my soul is *very*, very old, and yours isn't," Thorn said as if he'd won. "Therefore, in the grand design of all things mystical, I'd do as I'm told. It hasn't dawned on you yet, but I only call you Boss because you like me to. Remember, I serve a greater purpose in this world. Empath, Servant of Souls, bigger-better-being—and you're my mission."

Ignoring the 'mission' part, he replied with confidence, "Yeah, so refresh my memory. Why exactly are we friends? Care to share, pal?" His gaze stayed dreamy and glued to Miles's daughter. "What— no sarcastic quips in front of the lovely little slip of a psychic? He's been mean to me, Celia B."

"Needling him doesn't work," she said with a signature giggle in her voice.

Thorn kissed her, got up, and stood toe-to-toe with him. The empath's look pierced his soul, caused an uncomfortable flinch. Their voices harmonized in his head, *"You're worn out. The day's had too many challenges. It's time to dream a peaceful dream."*

"Good night," he whispered and limped into his room. On the dresser, the locket caught his eye. One finger brushed over the gracefully engraved 'A'. Although he recalled nothing of his awakening or how he'd been injured, his beloved sister's words had been burned into his conscious mind. "You'll be close?" he said to Thorn, very hushed, very unsure.

"Always, my friend… Good dreams tonight—only happy thoughts."

The light went out. The door closed. He trembled in the darkness, very uneasy, very lost.

Thorn sank down on the couch, next to the woman he loved. "There's unfathomable emotions imbedded in his soul."

"You're exhausted," Celia whispered as she rubbed his chest.

"God, what he's put himself through. We owe him, you know?" He kissed her cheek with pure devotion. "In spite of his soaring arrogance, that's one good soul. I can't figure out why it didn't all come back to him."

She snuggled closer. "What do you think, maybe a little reprieve for both of them tonight?"

Thorn kissed her lips, and then watched her stand. "I guess I'll see you in the morning."

****

Celia clicked her tongue. Lukas startled and closed the binder. "Oooh…what a nosey little boy you are, kiddo," she whispered. "You didn't get to Day Three yet? And I thought you were a super-speedy reader! That's a lot to take in at one sitting. You should know better than to go around snooping—especially where that cute nose isn't allowed!"

The gentle scold made him blush, and he leaned back with a charming, I'm-sorry expression. Celia kept a stern face, which she wasn't very good at.

"Gonna tell on me?"

"Nope. Now put this back *exactly* where you found it. I'll give you the entire scoop—tomorrow when we're alone in the den. I promise. It's been another whacky day and night, so hit the pillow."

His yawn came out of nowhere, and that shocked him. "You really *are* mega-cool with the ESP!"

"Yep, I'm the real deal." She hugged him from behind, kissed the top of his short brown hair. "Oops, you let a thought slip, huh? I'm too old for you. Plus, I'm spoken for." She hugged him tighter. After replacing the binder, he got up and actually mumbled, "'Night" to everyone before closing the guestroom door. Dog tired, Celia stared out a living room window.

"Any progress," Alana asked.

"Nope. That's one vacant vamp living his distorted version of 'happily-ever-after'. You should've seen the look on his face when Thorn kissed me. It was priceless." She turned with a smile. "You look kind of beat, Ally. Gonna call it a night?"

"That sounds like a plan. Are you sure Michael's okay?"

She sent a thought. Alana gave a small grin. "Yes, Celia B, I'll *try* to have a happy dream. And you know I'm really not comfy with mental conversations."

"*Neither* of you are—go figure," she replied with an innocent shrug.

****

Alana tossed and turned for exactly five minutes before soft satin sheets against her skin made her feel as if she was floating on a billowy cloud. Tension slipped away. Her mind relaxed, thinking about Michael, thinking about loving him, thinking about dim light from the street spilling in, the curtains wide to let warm spring air fill her bedroom. Sweet smells of the sea and budding flowers.

Naked in each other's embrace, as lovers we are free of inhibitions…free of doubt…

Her body is as inviting to him as his is to her. "I've missed you, my Guardian. You're all I think about," he whispers.

His serious expression tight, his thin lips make his handsome face more attractive. An affectionate nuzzle allows him to take in her scent. Her heart races against his smooth, broad chest. Cool hands trace to her waist and his lean frame presses to hers. Against his chest, she finds the comfortable niche, craves more of his touch. Yearning fills her.

"I've waited too long to be in your arms again." She speaks straight from an aching heart. "I can't lose you again, my love. When we're apart, my soul longs for you."

No answer is necessary. He feels the same way. Light kisses taste her lips. How he searches her eyes for approval, for permission. The next kiss reaches into her, expresses his need to love only her. A flurry of nibbles graces his chest, his neck, his very inviting mouth before her arms lock around his neck. Every nerve throbs with anticipation.

No more delays. Neither could bare it.

Lightly her fingers thread through his wavy brown hair, so thick in hand like spun silk. A sensual groan emerges from deep within him. The broadness of his shoulders keeps her in his shadow—to obliterate moonlight as if obliterating thought.

This man holds my heart—owns my soul. We have the same need. Desire takes root. He straightens his back, sweeps her up his aroused body and into a possessive embrace. A low, rolling groan demands that her many senses awaken. The firm tip of him waits against quivering warmth and calls her innocent body to blossom.

It has been a long-concealed wish and at last, he comes into her. Sighs of delight assault a silent night. Deeper he drives to possess the very core of her. *Become one. Consummate years of loving him and make this a reality.*

She feels him move inside—a long-awaited pleasure, ripples of indescribable delight. Devotion has never wavered. It is confirmed when they reach the ultimate state of bliss at the same moment in time.

When he slips from her, instant emptiness pleads his return. He insists she wait. Cupping her bottom, stroking her back, his embrace is so tight, so secure. As he moves to the bed, the new sensation of taut muscles against her dampness brings an impatient whimper. Her coated body sinks to the firm mattress. He hovers over her as fresh hunger begins.

I can't speak, can't think, so in love with this man. Just the sight of him has me lost in the desire to join with him again. On her breasts, the coolness of his tongue makes her writhe. On her open thighs, the grip of his firm hands brings something far beyond rapture. Every temptation teases and need surges as love bursts through both souls. He probes, thrusts, races to claim her in passion's climax. It is their destiny to see each other's thoughts—know each other's fears. After such sweet surrenders, they lay wrapped together. They are at peace.

Emotion claims his revelation, "I've always loved you, my Guardian. I'll always need you. I want nothing more than to face eternity at your side."

Only she will see this private side of the courageous Champion. Gentleness, tenderness—it's always been here, waiting for her to release it. He is her soulmate, her completion. Tender showings of affection exist only for her. Her voice, no longer absent, has become strong, determined. "I love you, Michael. I am yours—forever and always."

She is the powerful woman who belongs to him, as he, a powerful man, belongs to her.

Joined with him, she sees who she is. There is no more doubt.

Joined with her, he is finally home. He'd walk through the fires of Hell for her.

Chapter 18

Plastered to the pillow, Alana's thick lashes fluttered. Her eyes were slow to open against the assault of strong morning sun. Rolling over, a conscious panic forced her to sit up. Eleven a.m.! She blew out a long, weary breath. She'd overslept and completely missed Doctor Chamberlain's visit. Pulling on a robe, she raced into the living room, stopping short with an uncontrollable yawn in front of her adopted father.

"Before you say anything, you picked the perfect day to sleep in," he said in a calm tone. "Arthur wanted to read Mother Anne's preliminary report first. You have some time, honey."

Relieved, she kissed his cheek. But still uneasy, she thought, okay, so what happened last night because it felt so totally real... A large mug of coffee came into her hand. "Thanks, Daddy B. I, uh, need to shower." She padded back into her bedroom, closed the door. Leaning against it, she closed her eyes.

****

Dressed for the day and raring to go, Alana found Celia in the den with Lukas. She crooked one finger and arched one eyebrow, motioning the sneaky psychic over. They ended up in the sunroom, which her sister always claimed whenever she visited.

"How'd you sleep?"

Not buying the innocent expression, not letting the

big, green eyed innocent look deter, she leaned against the door with a nervous huff. "As if you don't already know? Did you have anything to do with—with *that*? Come clean, sis. Is *that* what you do with Thorn while you're in England and he's in Manhattan? Because I'd swear Michael was in my room last night. We were talking, we were... It was so, so real. No, it felt *more* than real." A melting sigh escaped. "And then we, uh, I don't think I've *ever* had such a peaceful sleep. I *never* sleep 'til eleven. I don't function well when I sleep 'til eleven. And I wasn't that tired last night. I got this weird tingling in my head when you said happy dreams. I felt his touch, his, his... This is—I'd swear he was there, and we both know that he couldn't be, because—"

Celia's splayed hands waved her quiet. "Okay, take a breather because you're on a roll that'll turn into a ten minute I-can't-believe-we-did-that monologue!" Alana took a breath, but the drumming of her heart continued like it would never stop. "So first, yep—it *really* fills those lonely nights when you're thousands of miles away and you need to, well, let's just say snuggle with your honey. Second, I'm glad you slept. Michael did too. These have been two weeks of Hell!" Celia reached for the doorknob.

Alana held her arm. "Not so fast, sis, I asked if it was real."

Celia's eyes sparkled again. "He's your soulmate whether or not you admit it. Can you blame me for wanting to ease things just a teeny, tiny bit? I know you're confused. But all the pent-up passion vibes are straining my psyche, and so I just...gave us *all* a breather."

"Will he remember it? I have to know."

"Did *you* remember it?"

"Down to the very last, sensual detail," she said with misery in her heart.

Her sister's hug didn't calm her down, either. "How about a not-so-cryptic easy answer? The same desire was in both of you at the exact same second. That's all I'm gonna say." She opened the door and marched down the hall hearing Celia mutter, "Okay… That wasn't too bad. No need for long, detailed explanations. In this instance, simpler is better."

Nope, Alana thought, it really isn't!

****

The dream didn't leave Alana as she followed her father and Doctor Chamberlain down the stairs. Relieved that Michael wasn't in the living room, she sat across from Miles in one of the armchairs. Thorn disappeared into the master bedroom with the specialist and closed the door.

Miles opened his laptop on the low table between them. "I assure you, Michael's in good hands. I've known Arthur for years, honey. We met soon after he left the army. He'd been a medic then, fresh out of an internship—certainly witnessed all types of atrocities humans inflict on each other."

Okay. This could keep her mind off Michael. "Was he already a Georgian?"

"No, but he sensed a greater evil in this world. A few years later, he took a post with the coroner's office. That's where he autopsied his first vampire victim. I had begun to lecture on paranormal studies in the city. He sought my advice, and then came on board. Arthur's been the lead scientist for the Georgians for years."

Well that didn't work. She settled in for the wait, pushing scenes from last night out of her mind. *Muffled voices from the bedroom, low hissed words...* She winced. Even through thick plaster walls, Michael sounded too irate.

"I reread a particular dream scene yesterday. You don't think he'd dare assault the doctor, would he, Dad?"

"Thorn's in there."

"Oh. Right," she drew out with a sigh. Nevertheless, she stayed on edge until the door swung open. Michael limped out behind Thorn and sank into the other armchair—staring at her. At least an end table stood between them. To avoid his eyes, she focused on her father. *Daddy B's taking everything in. A thorough man, a researcher of the highest distinction... If he doesn't have pencil and paper in hand, his trusted laptop becomes an extension of himself. Thank God he can't read minds.* She glanced at Thorn who could— and quickly looked away to see Michael smiling at her. *Dark gorgeous eyes dripping with devotion the way they did when— Okay, focus, Alana, focus on the doctor!*

Oblivious to the discussion, Michael couldn't stop reliving last night's dream. Like a nomad who'd found an oasis in a desert, he wanted to fill himself with Alana, to feel her in every cell of his being.

"—And our lab can't break down the toxin compounds. That poison destroyed his system for nine days. Chalk this one up as a win for us, thanks to Divine Intervention," Chamberlain said to Miles.

"Clayton left him exsanguinated with his wounds

festering, Arthur."

"You wouldn't know it to look at him now. Except for his leg, he's in good physical shape, but psychologically, well... That's a different matter."

"Is the memory lapse a residual effect of the exorcism or the poison?"

"In my opinion, it's both and neither. He's happy in his delusion."

The specialist's flippant tone burst through Michael's absorption with Alana's womanly body, and on the defense, he barked, "I'm *not* playing amnesia victim."

"I'm sure you believe that," Chamberlain said in a clinical way. "But you're fresh out of a demonic combat zone. Think of a tortured soldier standing alone after a devastating siege. He appears fine physically, but what's happening in his head? Repressed memory of the battle, time distortions, and sequential deviations—some of the symptoms you're experiencing."

He slipped back into more thoughts of this gorgeous woman and didn't respond. He'd carry her to his bed, rip off her clothes and slowly, sensually—

"I know you're hearing me, Michael. You woke up with the mind of a terrified young man who died savagely and then only recall your humanity? You're the only undead creature who's now aware of *why* he was killed by *whom* he was killed. Let's move on to examine the emotional attachments to Alana and Lukas."

With a dismissive groan, he leaned back. Even Chamberlain's facial expression was annoying.. "I don't need a fucking therapy session, you quack."

Thorn's glare had him sinking lower in the armchair. "Well—*I don't!*"

"Let's add uncharacteristic nastiness to your long list of symptoms," the specialist stated as his tone heated up. "This is a multi-faceted psychosomatic trauma. To shield thought from a Servant of Souls? How you managed that is a mystery. To reach a point where you're willing to sacrifice yourself out of vengeance? That was one *hell* of a ballsy shot. Then you pull off a classic David and Goliath, but two brave men died."

He shot the doctor a disgusted look. "I don't know what you're talking about."

"We both know you do. You're so far in denial that what you did in Manhattan isn't real to you. And why be scared senseless? Because you survived. Face reality. Face *all* of your feelings."

He sneered but stayed silent as Miles shook his head. "But his imprecise delineations of time and events—"

"Actually, they're in sync. His mind is in a safe zone remembering Alana and Lukas up until it becomes complicated. There's logic in his selective memories, Miles."

About to call Chamberlain a few more choice names, he caught Thorn's serious scowl, and he closed his mouth as Thorn said, "So put the memory thing to the side for a minute, Doc. In the formal Council report, how will you classify him?"

"I don't understand the question."

Irked more, edginess stoked his temper. "I do! Care to tell me what I am now? Let's do the list…clear tears, stands in sun, and a reflection—that's a start. Body temperature high enough to make me fucking sweat, and I *don't* have a beast-within that begs to drink and drain. Blessed blood? Not a problem! Goes down really easy. And I'm actually able to digest this-this *grotesque* puree. Want to take a stab, Doc? Am I demon or not, vampire, manpire or freak?"

Chamberlain didn't wince once. "Where's this attitude coming from? Your file suggests a rational being, a true gentleman—never *overtly* edgy or confrontational." In a professional manner, he stated, "As long as you drink blood the classification remains "vampire." We already accept the mystically enhanced tag. Add the fact that the demon within, which *should* be keeping you alive and undead, has been extracted— but you're still here. It's uncharted territory. So I'll state the simple conclusion with measured certainty. You're beyond undead."

With a sardonic grin, he repeated, "*Beyond undead*? You're making this up as you go along. I've never heard such a bizarre term."

When Chamberlain stood, the doctor glared down at him. "And I've never heard of a not-so-chilly vampire with a soul who sees his reflection in the mirror and stands in the sun. You're asking a scientist to give definition to that which does not, *should* not, exist." He placed the thick chart in his briefcase. "This is an altered state. Let the memories return—all in real-time order. Then come talk to me."

Michael shut his eyes and leaned his head back. He didn't want to hear anymore.

****

While Thorn went across the hall to speak with Mother Anne, Miles walked Chamberlain upstairs. In

Alana's foyer, he stared at the rose-marble floor, waiting for the elevator doors to open.

"Will you update the Council at tomorrow's meeting?"

"I'll be ready."

"Arthur, I'm concerned about him. Be candid. Did we miss a step?"

"No, Miles. You gave assistance to an ensouled creature. Michael has earned the title of Champion, his actions for our side are heavily documented. Guilt has this immortal petrified. When the event is fully studied, facts will confirm how he single-handedly accomplished an unimaginable feat. But I wouldn't want to walk in his shoes. It's got to be a very lonely place."

****

Everyone had left, and when Michael leaned across the end table that separated them, Alana realized that it wasn't a good idea to be alone with "this" Michael.

"More beautiful than I remember, you've become an alluring woman. And you survived the mission without a scratch. I'd like to think I had something to do with that."

"You sure did," she answered, hearing pride in his voice and hoping he didn't remember last night's dream, which still made her tingle.

"My Guardian, I can feel your heart race. Is something wrong?"

His tone, his concern dripped tenderness. Casually, she shrugged. "No. I'm just relieved your brain sprinted forward three centuries. The clipped, oh-so-proper accent threw me for a loop. I'd forgotten that originally you came from England." The reply came off awkward, but she couldn't think of anything appropriate to say. And when he stood and approached the sunny dining room with slow, uneven steps, she held her breath.

"You're avoiding me, darlin'," was all he said.

"No, I'm not," she answered, innocent enough. *Even his voice is sensual. Those broad shoulders I clung to last evening are… almost in full afternoon sunlight? Oh God! Stay calm…stay in the chair.*

He came back into the shadow on a deliberate path. "Yes, you are."

"*No,* I'm not." Damn desire tugged, and she tingled again.

A hand stretched out and in a sexy, playful tone, he said, "Prove it."

Touching is definitely out of the question! Folding her arms, she answered, "I don't have to."

Bending down, his fingers wrapped her wrist. As her temperature rose, she protested with a curt call of his name. But his full-strength grip said power. No amount of resolve could withstand his touch. In less than a second, she was up and against him. His dreamy espresso eyes drew her in as obsession sizzled in his expression. A slight dip of his chin, and their lips would … "I've wanted to do this for a long time." The first kiss was gentle. Then his lips crushed against hers. Soft, sensual, he sighed. "You intoxicate and comfort me at the same time. I dreamt about you last night." Her body stiffened as she drew her face back. "What's wrong? You know I'd never hurt you."

But his tone was rough. Full of annoyance. That's it, she thought, letting out a sharp breath—more than convinced how certain facts weren't there.

"You pull away? What's the matter, my Guardian?

Miles said your mission ended months ago! We won't breach any sacred trust. I said I'd never hurt you."

"This can't happen. I-I won't do this."

"Do *what*?"

The sharpness in his tone worried her. She shook her head. "You don't remember everything." When she pushed completely out of his arms, he looked furious as well as wounded.

"I love you! Isn't it obvious? I've waited *ten years* to—"

"No! You didn't wait! *I* didn't wait! Search your soul! It's got to be there!" Out of reach, she continued to back away. "You remember *this*, you don't remember *that?* Chamberlain's right. You're terrified and more aggressive than ever! This is crazy. I explained it all just two nights ago! You've chosen to *conveniently* forget the last seven years between *us*! No. I won't do this!" Darting around him, she rushed upstairs with him on her heels, sharply shouting her name. As they burst into her living room, she turned to him insistent. "Go back downstairs!"

"No!"

"You *shouldn't* be up here!"

His rage knifed through her heart as he shouted, "*Why, damn it?*"

"Because of me," she heard Lukas say.

Michael reeled back, couldn't stand steady. His leg twitched in agony from running up a steep flight of stairs. Speechless, he stared at his son's short brown hair. Clean clothes, eyes that matched the color of twilight. A healthy complexion. He wasn't a devious child, always dirty, disheveled, and full of rage. His son stood there staring, without a trace of wild hatred. But his eyes read guarded. Very guarded. Lukas still looked thirteen, not like a fifteen-year-old close to manhood. Without a word, Michael turned. Stormed out of the unfamiliar apartment. He wanted to fly down the stairs, but each attempt at a quicker step had him hissing and kept his gait uneven.

He limped inside the second-floor apartment as every hidden emotion erupted like hot lava. Brutal punches cracked the thick plaster wall as his knuckles bled. Guilt smothered his soul, crushing like it weighed a ton. The courage to look inside himself, to understand "why" wouldn't come. Slowly, the rage inside faded as his sweaty forehead hit the brittle cracks.

He scented Miles and Thorn as the deadbolt twisted. Thorn's wide hand clamped his shoulder, which calmed his urge to scream. Despair filled him and bitterly, he said in a low voice, "I can stand in the sun, see my reflection, and shed unforgiving human tears, but I can't face my boy or the woman I love without wanting to shove a sharp piece of wood though my own miserable heart."

****

Alana shook her head and blew out a slow breath as Celia ran into the living room. One look at her sister and they both realized that simply the sight of Michael had wreaked havoc with his son's more than fragile emotions.

Celia went straight to Lukas, cupped his pale cheek. "Are you okay, sweetie?" He turned his face away. "How about you, Ally?" she asked with similar concern. Impossible to describe what she felt, she kept her focus on Lukas, who looked as lost as his father.

Softly, Alana said, "Your dad's not himself yet. He needs time—"

"I wouldn't have let him hurt you."

"He wouldn't have done anything to either of us, Lukas."

"Mister B said to give him time."

"And I agree," she answered. Helpless, she looked at Celia. *This confrontation did it to me, Celia B. Being in his arms threatened and baffled me at the same time. Here's a new mental list, a long one. Seeing his terror and guilt even when he can't face it in himself. Being convinced something was happening three thousand miles away, and I couldn't stop him. Rescuing him from the bowels of Hell on earth. Not to mention the unnerving wait until I held him on the plane. So many seriously dreadful days and now this!*

Memories yanked her toward completely undone, and the huge living room began to shrink, no longer big enough for each twisted vignette racing through her.

"Oooh Ally," Celia said with excitement, "Are you thinking what I'm thinking, you know, change of scenery? I've *got* to get out and into the sunshine for a while." Her sister tapped her forehead as if receiving a signal from "The Great Beyond". "It's a perfect day for cheating with chocolate. You on the same wavelength?"

She couldn't clear her head as she studied Lukas, tried to hide a sense of loss. "A chocolate binge sounds perfect, Celia B."

Celia gave a look and a nod. "Hey, kiddo, want to join us?"

He shrugged and mumbled, "Yeah, I-I guess."

"But I want *special* chocolate! Oooh—chocolate ice cream! Got any suggestions, Ally?"

The sweet idea was perfect, and to see Lukas smile again, she would play her part like a pro. "How about a drive *way* up the coast? There's this great gelati place with a spectacular view. Have you ever tasted *real* Italian ice cream?"

"Uh, I thought ice cream was, you know, ice cream," Lukas mumbled.

Somehow she mustered a convincing smile. "Oh boy, you're in for a treat. This is a chocolate lover's dream."

This time, they'd *definitely* take the elevator down.

Chapter 19

Moonlight would soon illuminate the sky. Serafina darted across the highway and hurried barefoot through prickly bushes. Down a steep embankment, she saw the sea. On the stony beach, she begged for guidance.

It took a long time to locate the rock. Her tongue lapped the dark, dried stain. A raging boy's sorrowful tears emblazed her mind, and she smiled. "A magical sign comes from you, Master. I will be rewarded!"

Tasteless blood swirled through her saliva. When the stone was clean, her wrist rubbed her lips. Like an evil angel, one toe raked the coarse sand to create her altar, a five-pointed star. "Serafina has it inside her," she sang slow, reaching a disturbed frenzy.

Clawing at the shapeless cotton shift, it shredded, fell away to set her free. With her naked limbs spread wide; she positioned her head toward Portofino.

Voices chanted, "Serafina."

She squirmed as if a handsome lover now devoured her. His murky image sharpened in her mind—a beautiful god, tall and blond. Her hips rocked when he reached inside to sample the boy's blood. The god's ice-blue eyes bore through her last, sane thought.

Full of macabre pride, the voices reached a crescendo to proclaim, "Serafina is ours!"

Like thunder, her heartbeat rolled. Repeated gasps didn't help. Instead of air, her lungs filled with blood. Life slipped away. Serafina's soul went straight to Hell.

****

Zoltan Vashkar fed from a sixteen-year-old Guardian who had been eager to prove his new mystical abilities. The pimple-faced teen grossly miscalculated vampire strength. Virginal blood gave him additional focus. Considered royalty among demons, Zoltan had just returned from Manhattan where he had dealt with Clayton Mails.

Walking the grounds of his estate under the canopy of shadows from dense trees, the Hungarian plotted a new course. NWT was beyond salvage. Vashkar Enterprise would absorb all remaining, measly assets. *The European Triumvirate has offered every earthly resource to locate the child. It took less time than expected—fourteen days since capturing the father, six since the vampire's untimely trip to the incineration chamber.*

Malevolent minds, tortured souls ripe for the taking, were the raw nerves, the quivering ends on the tentacles of evil. One dead girl was insignificant. Zoltan's ice-blue eyes sparkled when he saw the nest. *Retrieving the boy will be my crowning achievement.* His muscular arm reached up to strangle a baby bird in first-flight. After placing it on the ground, he pulled a silk handkerchief from his breast pocket to wipe off the stain on his hand. *Together, sire and son will obliterate an ancient bloodline. Unless...*

He snickered. "Another possibility will insure Cyril's participation."

****

Michael eyed the researcher's notes lined up and organized on the dining room table. He studied Miles cataloguing each hand-written description. "Again, I believe Alana can take care of your son," Miles stated.

Still tense, he turned back to the window and repeated, "It's already dark. They should be back by now."

"I'd know if Celia faced trouble," Thorn said from the table.

The empath's calm reply irritated him, too. "Well, I don't like it, damn it! Alana couldn't get a driver's license in New York *or* New Jersey. What the hell is she doing driving around Italy? You should've stopped her, Miles. Then they'd be here in the protection of my building." He walked through the arch and sat on the couch's arm with his hands locked to his knees. "Portofino's prime property. This is worth a fortune. How many apartments again?"

"Three and a bookshop downstairs—for the third time," Thorn muttered.

"And her aunt, Rosa Bellini, lives across the hall? Is that her mother's sister?"

Studying a particular page, Miles dryly stated, "No, she's Alana's grandmother's youngest sister. That makes her a great-aunt. Alana calls her *Zia,* which for the third time, means aunt in Italian." Miles paused. "We seem to be jumping around quite a bit tonight."

"Oddly talkative," Thorn mumbled.

"Alana's place looked bigger, plus it's sunnier."

Thorn narrowed his eyes, turned to face him. "Are you actually comparing sandboxes? That's because it *is*. In my opinion, you went a little overboard with the original artwork, but hey, I don't enjoy a stroll through the Metropolitan Museum the way you do. You could've gotten her a bigger car, purely for safety reasons."

"I bought the car? Why didn't you stop me?" A grin accompanied his quick mood switch. "So, Empath, how would you know if Celia faced trouble? Does Miles approve of the lovey-dovey looks you give his daughter…or did I just out your secret?"

They both glared, Thorn appearing more annoyed. "I don't feel like explaining anything to half a vampire again, so let's save this for a later date when *all* of you is paying attention."

"Who's the touchy *demon* now? Come on, big guy. Tell me why Helena gave you to me."

"The angel didn't *give* me to you. And for the tenth time, since you seem to suffer both long *and* short-term memory loss, I'm a mystical being just like you. Remember? We're imbued from above to keep the forces below from getting snuggly with humanity. You're a good creature, and I'm an amazing Servant of Souls. I think you're enjoying this too much. The slap-happiness is wearing thin. Maybe a swig of the blessed blend will sober you."

He came over, leaned his good leg against the table. "Speaking of blessed things, why haven't I met the holy healers? Rosa's the sweet old lady who came for the empty pot, right?"

While Thorn and Miles stared at each other, he limped to the kitchen and opened the refrigerator. Intrigued by the automatic action of doing something he'd never done he took a glass container and broke the wax seal. After draining the bottle, he limped back to the men with a smirk on his face. "Would they be hiding across the hall…afraid of me?"

"They're not hiding. They're doing exactly what I'm doing." Miles said.

"Why? Don't the Georgians trust a researcher's version?"

"Each 'version' will validate the other. It's called qualifying the evidence and it's done with every Georgian study of paranormal events." Miles pulled off his reading glasses. "Lose the tone, Michael. I've met the real you. That man came off rather impetuous, but quite charming, perhaps sweeter, for lack of a better word."

His leer sailed at Miles—full force. "I was *never* sweet."

Thorn gave a nod. "Yes, you were, and too young to die. Although you talked a good game. Come on, Champ, do what he asks. Put it in neutral. You're not yourself right now because you actually prefer clueless. But you'll feel better if you stop fighting it."

Not wanting to hear any more, Michael went to the window, stared into the night. Thorn walked out of the room. When the faucet turned on in the kitchen, he made his way through the wooden arch. Bothered and edgy, he sank into one of the comfortable armchairs.

****

The night dragged on, and close to eleven, Michael heard movement upstairs. Restlessness left him, as if the wired energy of so many hours had taken its toll. The sound of a piano, an old baby grand came from across the hall. Languid intricacies of a Chopin nocturne soothed his soul. Someone's hands delicately mastered the keys. Romantic trills, arpeggios, and elaborate cascades of anticipated harmonies, softly pedaled and executed with care, wrapped his cloudy mind in a blanket of peace. In a minor key, the haunting piece sang sorrowful. Each passionate motif reawakened his need for Alana. Impelled by feeling and not by reason, he ventured into the hall thinking it odd that no one stopped him.

Rosa's door wedged open. He pushed it, hesitating in the threshold. Strong sensations of acceptance came into his mind and drawn to what curiously felt like a familiar place, he entered. And after a few steps, he froze. Two nuns sat on the sofa with their backs to him and facing the piano by the window.

The sister took her hands off the keys and turned with a shy smile. Softly, she said, *"Ciao bene, Signore."*

She hands my dying boy to me from the back seat of a white van. We speed down a highway to Siena. Her heart fills with concern for Lukas. "Don't let him die, Sister Magdalena," he whispered.

Another nun stood up and faced him. Her hands locked a trim waist. "Good evening, Malone."

"The villa was crawling with guards, Sister Gabriella, and you fought at my side. How do I know this?"

Then the third stood, and her approach was steady. The serenity on her face captured him. She held his gaze and said with compassion, "How are you tonight, Michael?"

A familiar voice whispered, *"It is not your time, Champion."*

"Helena, please let…me…die." On the precipice of fear, he shook his head. Fractured segments full of screams and distorted faces. His legs trembled, and as he sank down, a massive arm shot across his chest.

In a sad manner, Mother Anne inclined her head. "Now it is in your hands, trusted Empath."

****

Thorn practically carried him across the hall, eased him down onto the couch. "I know you don't need to breathe but take a couple of deep ones anyway. You're that shade of undead-pale again, and I don't know how to revive a passed-out vampire."

Perched on the edge of the cushion, Michael scrubbed his face. "My God, they exist? I saw two of them in a dream, my dream. It was a dream, right?"

Miles came beside him. "Yes, it forced you to survive eight days of captivity. Focus. Let it come."

"No! Don't want to see *any* of this! It… it doesn't matter…just a delusional fantasy!"

"It sustained you," Miles firmly stated.

Michael had the nerve to point to the door. "Go. Both of you! Just leave me alone!"

Although he was unhinging before their eyes, Thorn wasn't about to stop. "Yeah, like that's going to happen anytime soon."

"I didn't *want* to survive! You had no right to interfere, Empath!"

The way Michael cowered when he grabbed his shoulders and hauled him to his feet made Thorn furious. "Too bad. You did survive. Deal with it! And shame on you for taking the easy way out. Just had to do things *your* way! Do you know how torn up Alana is? How mixed up that poor kid is because of you? Want to hear what you did to me in Manhattan, so you could destroy yourself without an empath siphoning the *ingenious* plan from your head?"

Trying to twist out of his grip, Michael hissed low,

"Get your hands off me."

"Stop squirming because I'm immovable. I was always strong, you egotistical ass! This debacle is *your* creation. *You* slinked behind my back, and two ex-Guardians, two good men paid with their lives. It never crossed your willful brain to ask for my help with the kid, did it? You had a mystical being at your service, but instead, you trusted the truly evil Triumvirate to fix his life!"

In a flat tone, Miles said, "Let him go. He simply doesn't remember. Perhaps tomorrow we can try—"

"Not a chance, Researcher!" He glowered at Michael, beyond livid. "Look at you! It's like there *isn't* a huge problem here? Letting this go on so long says I've failed you." He shook his head, a deliberate pause with no options left. "Get in the bedroom." When Michael refused to move, one good shove drove him into the doorframe. "Forget it. No way will you overpower me."

He watched Michael sprawl on the bed staring at the ceiling and rubbing his shoulder. "You son of a bitch. You couldn't have helped me. I had to do it myself, didn't I?"

"It's a little late to be asking yourself that question, don't you think?" He turned to see Miles's startled expression.

"There's been decent progress today, Thorn. He is simply not ready."

"Well I am." Angry at himself for losing his temper, Thorn stomped into the kitchen and came back with two specifically labeled glass containers. This had to end right now—with a healthy dose of reality. "I stayed in his dream for a reason. Evil isn't sitting around the campfire singing songs about how they finally got rid of one very cocky vampire. Every action has a consequence—we both know it, but he's the one who needs an epiphany. Game over. Now we get down to business." He stopped talking long enough to soften his next statement. "You know I'm right, Researcher. I love Celia with all my soul. If anything comes down upon this house with *her* in it, I'll spend the next millennium back in Hell because I didn't have enough courage to accomplish what I've been sent here to do. Michael's too comfy in his self-stylized purgatory. Until he's aware of *everything* he's done, he can't leave this building. And if *that* doesn't happen, Lukas and Alana *will* die."

Miles stared at the containers. "But that blood—"

"Will either bring him back or push him over the edge. There's only one way to find out which it's gonna be."

"I'd like to stay and help."

"I'm sorry, Miles, but no. It's better if you're upstairs with them. He's safe—as long as he's with me. I'm convinced with each passing second. There's no easy fix for this. So let it be done the hard way." Thorn watched Miles leave. Then without hesitation he entered the bedroom.

****

Out of the corner of his eye, Michael saw Thorn take a deep breath, lock the door, and drop a skeleton key into his shirt pocket. His fingers laced tighter behind his head as Thorn placed two jars on the nightstand. Each stood eight inches tall. Each contained blood.

"You reek of I'm-not-willing-to-face-myself… so

don't do casual-aloof. Let's have another glimpse of your dream. Don't say a word, just drink."

The stare was as cold as his voice, and adamant, Michael didn't move. But just like a man, his gut knotted. "I'm not thirsty. And if you come at me again, I'll wrestle you to the fucking ground."

"That's faulty logic."

Thorn pulled him off the bed. His right leg gave out and he hit the floor. Instantly, inching away, he murmured in an unsteady voice, "You beat me till I wailed."

Crouched low, Thorn met him eye-to-eye. "Keep that dream scene inside your scrambled brain. Look very, very carefully. These are punishing arms, another gift from Helena. If you don't drain the container, count on what happens next."

Shaking his head, he got out, "I need time. Not strong enough yet. Why right now?"

"Because another night like the past two is *not* in your future." Thorn's thumbs hooked the belt's silver buckle. "You have until the count of three. Then I take it off and swing. One, two—"

He cringed when Thorn stood, quickly scurried to the upholstered chair, and pulled himself into it. Thorn grabbed a glass container, ripped off the seal, and his eyes shot wide. The scent of his own bloodline made him twitch. Yet a queasiness churned in his gut as the empath shoved it into his hand. "Oh God, please no… He's my boy."

"And he needs you. Drink."

It came to his lips, and each mouthful of Lukas's blood quenched a ravenous hunger. Missing memories anchored to his mind. Rescuing his son from the sorcerers in the Second Realm. The deal made with Clayton for his son's very sanity. The night he held his raging boy, whispering a dark incantation, and then sadly kissed his forehead, unwilling to admit his solution was morally wrong. Ripe with regret, he faced an uncomfortable truth. "Memories aren't meant to be erased. I sold his soul for my peace of mind." Slouched in the chair, a ripe nausea overpowered him, but not from Lukas's blood. Rather, from his own actions. Full of uncertainty, he said, "I need my son here. Please, Thorn."

"Over my dead body."

"I just wanted him to forget. I am so sorry."

"Good. But trembling won't make me stop." The snide remark cut deep as Thorn broke off the second container's seal. "That's one guilt-written window open. Let's continue."

Michael flinched, shut his eyes. As if he could vomit, he gagged and coughed. Folding inward, his arms stayed tight to his aching stomach as Alana's scent, sweet and seductive, flooded his enhanced senses. "No. It's too powerful. I'd never drink from her."

"Stop the lying. Tear down every mental roadblock because this charade will not continue. Trust me, it'll taste familiar."

His eyes locked to the empath's while shouting, "You're wrong! I'd *never* drink from her!" The container came closer to call and repulse him in alternating seconds. Thorn's unwavering authority thrashed his shredded psyche. Doubts lashed his soul.

"Here comes the prickly I-know-I-did-something-I-shouldn't-have. This sends your senses into overdrive, doesn't it? The craving won't stop, so just give in. You're like a druggie twitching on the stoop outside your brownstone. The guilt's conspicuous, and I have no sympathy left, so take it. Face another truth. Alana will *never* come to you again—until you reclaim all that you've done." Ready to crack, the thought produced full-blown panic, and he shifted in the upholstered chair. "Helena went easy on you in the dream, so you'd stay sane. Your full existence as a vampire—those crucial facts were kept to a minimum. Alana's affection for you fueled the fantasy. But what *this* holds is brutal and raw."

"Please, Thorn, don't." His body shook as his jaw clenched.

"I haven't been sent here to coddle you. Helena allowed me the privilege of a human life to match your needs. You've become a powerful creature. A Champion, brave and strong. I've always been a *more* powerful creature—devoted and faithful. Who's gonna win this one?"

Remorse swallowed his soul as he accepted the second dose of veracity. His Guardian's blood held rich memories. *Love, mystical strength, sensuality...* These and more realities entered his conscious mind. With need beyond control, he longed to feel her smooth skin, her hot breath on his neck when he took her with a passion no fantasy could diminish.

The drained container slipped from his hand as full recall of one forbidden night carved forever on his immortal soul. He slid off the chair. His shoulders curled down and both arms locked over his head. *I stole her innocence. I bit into her tender flesh to taste life from the woman I love.* "Oh God, no—"

This truth alone paralyzed… And there were many, many more. His undead existence pounded its wicked signature upon his soul with the force of a thousand hammers. Hundreds of faces danced an insane ballet in his brain. Cruelty. The abject desire to destroy each victim… Twisted lust, misguided passion—all etched within for eternity. Uneven gasps punctuated the stillness. "God help me," he whispered, "I cannot make amends."

Wrestling his own despair, Thorn knelt down and placed a steady hand on Michael's shoulder. The jolt to his mystical mind was a physical shock, but something still wasn't right. Compassion escalated to alarm as he swept Michael's thoughts. This was all Michael could stomach, but it wasn't complete. Thorn's eyes glazed over, and pulling him up off the floor, he sensed sadness far beyond sorrow "Come on, Champ, dig deeper."

"This is over. I can't face them. I didn't want any of this back!"

What now, the empath thought. *I've done all I can.* In anxious frustration, Thorn let go—and Michael ran. One outstretched hand strained for the doorknob before Thorn dragged him back to reach the nightstand. Choking down sobs, fully desperate, Michael clawed at the arm pinned across his chest.

"I want death! I welcome it!"

"No, I won't let you die. Helena won't let you die." He grabbed a drained container. The tall jar shattered when it hit the corner of the nightstand. This would be the hardest truth to face. Cuffed in an unyielding lock, Michael trembled, and stared at the jagged piece as

Thorn slashed his own arm. Scarlet ribbons of blood oozed through his shredded skin—dripped to the carpet.

"Drink," he ordered, sensing many emotions unravel in Michael as he struggled. He didn't stop, jamming his bloody arm to Michael's lips, refusing to pull away. In unwavering loyalty to all that was good, he whispered, "Now you'll remember it all, my friend."

He was a Servant of Souls, powerful and courageous. He was Michael's last chance.

Part Two - Housekeeping

Chapter 20

As Thorn's slowing heartbeat softly thudded, Michael ripped his mouth away, and like a boulder, Thorn began to sink. Thorn's legs had stayed locked until the last memories from his mystical mind were fully absorbed by a still somewhat-distraught immortal.

Full strength of a Champion. Total recall of all he'd done. Michael guided the brave Servant of Souls down into the upholstered chair with care. Resting Thorn's broad head against its high back, Michael finally heard a moan, and after a slow lick of the jagged wound, the ugly incision began to close as shredded skin knit together. Reaching into Thorn's shirt pocket, he took the skeleton key and unlocked the bedroom door, walking through the threshold with a steady, signature gait.

When he came back, Thorn took the bottle of water he offered. Drained it in three swallows. He sat on the mattress across from the upholstered chair to study the empath. Then his head hung low, rubbing the back of his neck and calmly saying, "I recall every aspect of my existence—alive and undead, past and present."

"Extraordinary measures for an extraordinary being."

"I'm sincerely concerned. Are you okay?"

Softly, his friend sighed. "I live and breathe. But I see a couple of steaks in my future."

The humorous pun turned his worried expression into a typical, thin smile. Leaning back, both elbows supported him, and he scrutinized Thorn's watery eyes. "A little TLC from that green-eyed healer who loves you with all of her heart wouldn't hurt, either."

"You caught that, huh?"

"You shared the *entire* dream with Celia B? That whole angst thing stays between the three of us, Empath. So now, I know exactly how you feel about the woman who fell in love with you the first time she saw you. Why didn't I ever catch it?"

"We were discreet."

"Very, I'd say. I respect you immensely. You're one hell of a man, and I owe you and Celia in a big way."

"Seriously... Can you handle everything? I still sense sadness in your soul, but you're back, Champ, whole and well."

The calm, controlled manner in which he spoke, the sure way he carried himself was evidence enough. "I killed the bastards who brainwashed my son. I destroyed NWT, shut down the portals. Clayton's as good as dead. Those are the plusses." He walked to the locked windows. Pulling back the drapery, he opened them both and pushed their wooden shutters to the outside bricks. After a full breath of sea air, he searched the multitude of bright stars in a dark night's sky. "I let two brave men get in over their heads. Rob and Dan died without mercy because of my vengeance."

"They saw too many innocents die. You didn't have to ask them twice to get involved."

"It's on my soul. Mine alone. I have Lukas back, which I didn't expect. Do you think he'll ever understand why I did this?"

As he turned, Thorn crossed a leg and straightened a trouser cuff. "Sure, but the kid's a firecracker. You'll have to dig down deep and quick to grasp the meaning of fatherhood. Celia kept the kid's mind occupied for his own good. I seem to bring out the worst in him—immediately."

"I'll get through to Lukas. Too much is buried in his head, in his heart."

"He's got some immediate issues. Talk about obstinate. Lukas has you beat by a hard mile, plus he's a pro at temper tantrums." Thorn paused. "What about Alana?"

"Ah, my Guardian… my love. I've put her through a special kind of Hell. Do you think she'll forgive me? Will she even *talk* to me?" Thorn didn't answer, and devastated, Michael whispered, "Oh, God. I've lost her. Go ahead. Say it. I should've told Alana about all of this, at least that I'd always love only her. What a selfish, *stupid* fool I've been."

Thorn rose slowly. "I can't disagree with you there. So what are you going to do about it? Please don't take the self-pity pout and brood route. I've had enough poignant peaks and valleys tonight."

"I admit I've made a mess of things, in every sense of the word."

"Oh no. Here we go. Get a soapbox and a hankie. Crank up a Mahler symphony to augment the *mea culpas*."

"No. Lesson learned. I know your intervention just saved me. My sense of purpose has been missing for weeks. At least I can think clearly now. I'll take this one step at a time. First, Lukas has my full attention."

His voice softened. "My Guardian knows how important she is to me, in many different ways. I believe Celia showed her one last night."

His right eyebrow arched when Thorn chuckled. "I'll come to her defense about that one till the day I die. Like you, she's a romantic at heart. Plus, she happened to be right."

"That little slip of a psychic and I will have a conversation about overactive imaginations—and very soon. There's one more thing I need you to do, though."

Thorn followed his signature strides into the living room. Grabbing pen and paper, he spoke as he wrote. "This is Christenson's number…my accountant in Manhattan. Tell him to get all my finances out of the city, just as I did in the dream. Have him contact Mary Kendrick to forge Lukas's birth records and clean out the brownstone. I need an international driver's license and a passport in my hand by noon. Christenson has to bring his family here as soon as possible. This has to look subtle—above suspicion, Thorn."

"No problem. But then Celia and I need some one-on-one time. You, uh, well, now you know exactly what I mean." Thorn stopped at the door, gave a gentle grin. "Uh, she'll tell him. I'm sure he'll jump the staircase."

Avoiding the mirror in his bedroom, he pulled a black v-neck sweater out of the top dresser drawer and changed into a pair of black jeans he found in another drawer. He slipped into leather loafers he saw in the corner of the room. Although not his preferred footwear, they fit perfectly. After opening the dining room windows, his palms rested steady against the farthest wooden frame. Taking a deep, determined breath of fresh air, whether or not he was ready, he knew he had to connect with his son.

A soft thud in the hall made him turn.

Lukas appeared nervous and approached in a tentative way with silent footsteps, then stopped safely out of reach. He didn't act on the overwhelming need to wrap this troubled child in a long-overdue embrace. He kept his arms braced across his chest and his tone gentle. "I've hurt your feelings. Both times, I was seriously out of line. I deeply apologize."

Avoiding his gaze, Lukas's face was aimed down at his sneakers as he shrugged while shoving both hands into the pockets of his gray sweats. He observed everything, memorized every move his son made. When the boy finally looked up, the expression was one of uneasiness—perhaps not knowing what to say or what to feel.

Michael's soul melted with love, at the same time filled with pride as he gave a careful smile. "I hear Portofino's pretty lively at night. What do you say we walk to the piazza?"

"Maybe, you know, we should stay here."

A rapid heartbeat, sweaty palms. Stay beyond calm, he told himself. Crossing to the door, thankful his son hadn't run upstairs, he turned. "I could use the exercise. I want you to come with me. Ready?"

After another shrug, Lukas finally met his gaze. "Should we, like, leave a note?"

"Celia will know exactly where you are."

He took the stairs faster than a human. His concern grew until he heard his son do the same. He twisted the lock without hesitation and stepped onto the familiar street from his dream. For his son, he narrowed the width of his strides as Lukas fell into step at his side. "Genetics are a cool thing."

"Yeah, way cool," his son mumbled.

"Dad" will come, Michael hoped with a sigh of relief as they headed toward the sea.

****

Alana watched from her living room window. "Seeing them together is good, but maybe I should follow?"

"No, honey," Miles said to her.

"What if something happens?"

Thorn was already sitting next to Celia on the beige leather couch. "Nothing's gonna happen, dearest Guardian. Take a long, well-deserved sigh of relief with us. Michael can handle a fifteen-year-old." As Celia rubbed Thorn's right forearm, Alana saw his hand stay over hers.

Miles took an armchair. "How did it go downstairs?"

"The event's over. Just like in his dream, Lukas's blood triggered certain memories. That took the wind out of his sails very fast."

Alana raised an eyebrow. "Michael drank voluntarily?"

"Let's just say he remembered a certain scene."

"Not the one in his brownstone…with the belt? Please tell me—"

"Well, I didn't use it on him. I just gave a sharp glower and watched his guilty mind do the rest. I never thought *anything* could make him shake like that. He's carrying around loads of baggage in his brain. Martin Malone made a lasting impression on his son."

"Fathers tend to do that," Miles said. "What

happened next? The Council will want specifics."

"I gave him the other container." When Alana turned away, Thorn added, "It's as uncomfortable for you to hear as it is for me to tell."

"The whole truth, Thorn, give it to Dad," she stated.

Thorn cleared his throat. "What Michael did to you ripped his soul apart, that's for certain. And every hideous act of the beast-within came back with a vengeance—two centuries worth. It broke his spirit. Love for you is directly intertwined with guilt for everything he's ever done." She turned and they all stared at him. "I can't lie, Miles, so don't ask the question. This will satisfy your preliminary documentation." As if overly eager to dissuade her father's dogged interest, Thorn's demeanor changed.

Miles stated, "So he drank from you."

"He left me no choice, Researcher. Michael saw the dream of survival, the battle and everything else." Again, Alana looked away. "And dearest Guardian, it's all there again, the way it should be. Now he can move forward without me looking over his shoulder."

Celia softly sighed. "Oh God. What happens now—to you...to *us*?"

Full of tenderness, Thorn put his arm around her sister. "I'm not going to vanish into thin air or have a massive heart attack and keel over if that's what you're afraid of. As long as Michael walks God's good earth, so will I. But I'm yours, Celia. I'll be with you throughout eternity."

She kissed his cheek. "There isn't a doubt in my mind."

Alana felt only happiness for two special people

who belonged together. Their love was visible. But her heart remained heavy, her future cloaked in mystery and inconclusive. I've created as many obstacles in my heart as any woman could imagine, and what I want from him can never be, she thought.

"You don't know that." Thorn suddenly said, "He's an original. Strong soul, moral conscience, and not hard on the eyes either, uh, strictly speaking from a woman's point of view. He's the total package. Destiny's a funny thing, you know. You can't deny it. No matter how hard you try."

Celia came out of his arms and walked over to her father. "We've booked a room on the piazza. Someone special needs my undivided attention, without the weight of the world on his shoulders."

"I believe he does, honey. I'm exhausted just looking at him." Miles stood and his arms came around both her and Celia. "The Council meeting is tomorrow morning."

"And you'll have the room to yourself. Michael will take care of Lukas, so don't worry, Dad." Celia walked with Miles into the guestroom as Alana went back to the window.

Thorn met her there, sweetly kissing her knotted brow. His thick arms came around in a caring embrace. "Hugging you is like hugging a soft, gigantic teddy bear," she said close to tears.

"I have some words of wisdom for you. I don't think you've ever wrestled any demons as fierce as the ones harbored in your heart. You've always won, you know. So boot them out and say amen to that for once and for all. It's time."

After Thorn and Celia left, after all the hectic

happenings of the past weeks, all the emotional ups and downs, she felt uncomfortable this alone. Thorn's words repeated in her mind, and she said out loud to no one, "Fierce demons *are* harbored in my heart. And this time I'm terrified I won't win. They've been in there too long."

****

Like father like son, their footsteps made no sound approaching the building. After the piazza stilled, they spent an hour in hushed conversation at the edge of the sea. Each had carefully phrased his words to feel the other out. Nothing was said about what had led up to the battle with Hell-beasts almost two weeks ago. The son had avoided all sensitive issues, as did the inexperienced father.

Different information came out of Lukas, and Michael proved he could be an attentive listener. The guarded teen talked about his one year of life as an uncomplicated someone else. He didn't come off nervous describing normal day-to-day activities, which Michael sensed he desperately wanted again.

The only freshman to win a spot on the fencing team, Lukas had been an honor student with loads of friends. His son admitted he loved writing, to which he confessed intense dislike for the laborious task, no matter how his enhanced mind afforded the smallest detail's perfect recall.

Taking the stairs two at a time, Lukas seemed eager to continue talking. He'd give him a permanent home, a much-needed sense of order in this safe haven. Certain his son would now thrive, he proudly pushed open the door to the other bedroom and hit the light switch.

"It's late. Let's call it a night. Tomorrow we can—" Observing Alana's lack of symmetry and style, although good intentioned, for the first time in centuries he could've fallen into an uncontrollable fit of laughter. They both stared at twin beds against opposite walls—with frilly pink, floral patterned bedspreads. A dusty-rose patterned lampshade on a nightstand between the two beds was positively hideous, and the red Persian runner between the beds clashed with the overly feminine décor.

Lukas eyed a pair of pajamas on the left bed that had colorful race cars all over them. Picking the pajama top up, he whispered a breathy, "Wow."

With a quick clear of his throat and no trace of a smile, he said, "You can sleep in your sweats tonight. Go online tomorrow morning. I'll give you a credit card number. Feel free to order what you and Thorn will be okay with."

His son's eyes darted to the other bed. "Wait... No *fucking way* it's in a room with me."

"What do you mean by it? The man's name is Thorn."

Lukas's palms were already squeezing his temples. "Forget it. I'm staying upstairs. Mister B snores, but he's no friggin freak."

The tone brimmed of disgust and the abrupt mood swing shocked him. He sat on a bed full of alarm and braced himself thinking, here comes the part I know absolutely nothing about—how to be a good father. He kept his voice calm. "That's not the way it works. Home is here. That's your bed. Unless he's made other arrangements, this one's for Thorn."

"I'm not sleeping anywhere near that fucking

thing."

"Thorn's not a *thing*. He's a good friend."

Pulling off the bedspread, Lukas flung it to the floor. His son propped one pillow against the headboard and the other sailed across the room hitting Michael square in the face. Coming down with force on the pink sheets, his son bounced around before locking his hands behind his head and crossing his feet. "I stay upstairs with Alana," he muttered with a scowl.

"No… You'll stay here with me—and Thorn." He stood. Handed back the pillow.

Lukas swatted it away. "I stay where I want and it ain't here! Or I'll live somewhere else. You never found me in the city. You won't find me in Italy, either. I fucking *hate* him, Michael!"

"I'm Dad now, and you don't make the rules anymore. I do."

"No fucking way," Lukas muttered, and like some switch had been flipped, rage was rushing to the surface.

He studied every wince, every fidget. Flushed face, tight fists, he thought, plus a rapid heartbeat. How Miles had gotten his son to Italy without incident absolutely mystified him. Why has this temper flared so suddenly, he wondered, yet fully prepared to get to the bottom of the reaction, especially when he heard, "No fucking way" again.

"Stop using that word," he said a bit stern, flying blind and going on instinct. "We're not on some abandoned street in the city anymore. You think I didn't watch you the year you hunted me? Always filthy, huddled in condemned buildings, stealing clothes and food. I've seen it first-hand. Something's triggering your temper. I want to know what it is."

His son's eyes narrowed as he scowled. "No *fucking* way I'm staying—!"

"Like it or not—yes, you will. Try to run and every Guardian in Europe will be alerted. And when one brings you back—"

"Yeah, what? You yell? Send me to my *fucking* pink prison?"

"Absolutely, little boy—right after I put you over my knee and make you cry like a baby. Thorn stays. So do you."

His son lunged at him, wildly punching and kicking. He stood and grabbed him around the chest to keep his feet off the floor. Lukas's head pounded against his chest. Pinning him tighter, he kept repeating, "Shhh… It's all right. I've got you," until the rage turned into dragging breaths and sobs. He sat on the bed and held Lukas on his lap, his son positively clinging to his neck. "Talk to me, little boy," he tenderly whispered, "I'm not letting go. Just talk to me."

"I see it when I look at him." His face stayed hidden, his voice shook. More sad sounds, full of distress, came from his son. But he held on tight.

"What do you see? It's all right. You can tell me."

"No. It isn't all right. I did something really bad," Lukas cried. "I looked into the portal after Helena sent you back. And he saw me."

Clayton Mails, that bastard, Michael thought. The sorcerers' liaison's devious face blazed in his mind. All along, his instincts had been right. But Helena only revealed a partial truth in his dream of survival. Cradling his boy, rocking him, and rubbing his back was all he could do, But the way his son shook and sobbed terrified him.

"I did it. I killed an angel."

"No, son, *Clayton* killed an angel and then you were manipulated by three evil sorcerers because of who I am. Oh God," he sighed. They had slowly, methodically turned an innocent child into an unnatural weapon full of rage. "You did *nothing* wrong, nothing to deserve—"

Lukas pulled away swiping his eyes and sniffling. "He said crazy words. Cut her deep. I swear that's what happened. But I had Helena's blood all over me. And then I was standing in a different place, strange and dark. I couldn't fight them. They said I killed Helena, the only person I loved, because like my father, I am a demon."

Envisioning the scars, he had to know. "Who hurt you, son?"

Between hitched breaths, Lukas answered, "The guards. Every time they found me after I ran away. They beat me with their belts."

And Michael wanted to kill. Cunning Clayton had orchestrated all this misery. Rocking his crying child, he kept his tone soft and calm. "No one will ever touch you again and live. And you didn't kill Helena, little boy. This wasn't your fault."

"I found where you were hidden. Your amber eyes… Howls like a wolf every time you tried to grab me. I had to look at you."

"Because you knew you were mine." It all came back to one forbidden night with a chaste Guardian. He had stolen Alana's innocence and then hunted her for weeks. Celia opened the portal and Helena yanked him through it. For the second time in his undead existence, the angel forced him to harness his beast-within. That Lukas had seen what lived within him was one of the revelations in his fantasy, his dream of survival. And now, every jagged sob from Lukas, every drip of a tear was branded on Michael's soul.

After another hitched breath, his son whispered, "The sorcerers said you purposely led the man to Helena because *you* wanted her dead. And I hated you. I hated me." The way Lukas cried meant he was in a total meltdown, and Michael rocked him steady, held him tighter.

"*They* lied, never anything more than evil, deceitful things. Nothing in any dimension, any universe could make me do that. I'm so very sorry, Lukas."

Michael's eyes glazed over as his jaw tensed. Clayton had waited four years before leading him to Lukas. The thought sickened him, filled him with bitterness. By then, every happy memory had been ripped away only to be replaced with rage.

"You could have been killed the way you hunted me. I found a way to make you forget those horrid years. To forget I was your father. I wanted you safe. But I should have gone to Miles. I should have crawled on my knees and groveled before the Georgian Council. Instead, I chose to do the wrong thing."

Lukas peeled off his chest, his drippy eyes red and swollen. "I had to find the passageway. I had to find *you*. I didn't hate you anymore. You needed to know."

His thumbs brushed the tears away as his palms held his boy's damp cheeks. "I swear, I never wanted any of this to touch you. I can't make these memories go away, son, the same way I can't deny what I am. The easy way out never works. Thank God you're here.

Thank God you're safe," he whispered. When Lukas rested against him again, he prayed the protection of a father's tight embrace would heal such a troubled mind. As his son's racing heart slowed, he realized what an impossible gift his son was. With more concern than he let on, he asked, "Feel better now?"

"Yeah, Dad." One little word brought with it an undeniable, new emotion.

"And you're okay sharing the room with Thorn?"

His head bobbed. "What color does he like?"

"Anything but pink," Michael replied with tremendous love in his guilty soul as he rocked his son in his arms and kissed the top of his head. He never wanted to let him go. Not ever.

Chapter 21

Thorn held his soul mate close. His massive chest dwarfed Celia by its sheer width. Like the branches of a sturdy tree, his arms enfolded her as she slept. Her breaths came even, full of peace.

His heavy eyelids belied the alertness of mind. Helena built many fail-safes into Michael's dream to insure survival. Misplaced guilt had all but crippled the kid. *No doubt, Helena was there when my blood dripped to the carpet.* He sensed his mission would change but didn't quite know how yet. *Michael's heroic, albeit complicated deed ushers in a new era in the eternal war between Heaven and Hell. The Georgians will have to pick apart this event. Guardians will cleanse the continents, cut off the heads of the perpetrators.*

Eventually, they'd appreciate the actions of an arrogant vampire. Fantastic accounts of how Michael forced evil's hand one hot, humid night in May would abound.

Celia shifted in his arms. "Hey, sweetie." Her voice was thick with sleep. "Where's your busy mind?"

"You made my name the catalyst to end the kid's suffering, didn't you?"

She played with the tufts of red hair on his chest. "A little backup is a good thing. I saw where I could help, and I went for it. That was *my* mission. I gave Lukas a few insights from Michael's dream." She kissed his chin, snuggled closer.

Tenderly, he whispered, "It's taken me lifetimes to find you, my dearest angel."

"Ditto," Celia replied, falling back to sleep in the comfort of his arms.

****

Alana twisted and turned, fighting the wine-colored satin sheets as if they were purposely trying to strangle her. On the alarm clock next to her bed, the hours ticked by slowly. She eyed the open window wanting to float away on the soft, serendipitous sound of the sea. *That would relieve the conflict in my soul. No decisions to make...just a normal life with a normal guy who loves me.* Oh, who am I kidding, she thought. *It's not an elusive dream. It's an excuse.* Her destiny would never include "normal." Finally, her heavy eyelids closed; her brain shut down. She couldn't think a clear thought even if she had to.

Then at two a.m., she awoke again. The air had chilled. With a shiver, she stood, grabbed a terry-cloth robe. *This never happens in Portofino. Nothing's ever cold here.* The room looked bare without the Queen Anne chair in its usual spot. Lost in thought, her arms hugged her body as she sighed, "Michael, my love." *You just had to say his name out loud, and once again I'm wide awake.* Walking to the window, she leaned against its polished frame. The night turned cloudy with minimal starlight as if the heavens had become secretive. As if the sky was purposely cloaking its clarity tonight.

You didn't come to me. I was positive that after you got Lukas settled, you'd be knocking on my door—or breaking it down, depending on your mood. Oh God, poor Lukas... She closed her eyes. With the windows open, the sound of his son's cries had travelled. It had upset her even more. "Oh God, I could just imagine," she whispered, "Michael holding his son, easing his troubled, young heart as only a father could." She had seen those ugly scars on his chest and his back. It had outraged her as well. *No. Michael's absence makes perfect sense.* His son was a long overdue priority.

She left the window and walked back to her bed, snuggled under the covers and spooned a soft pillow wishing with all her heart that it was Michael in her arms.

****

Michael didn't leave his son's side, even after Lukas had finally closed his eyes. Curled on the bed and hugging a pillow, the sight of his boy brought a weary grin, endless love, and bottomless compassion. Like any father, he wanted this unnatural burden erased. Gone. Never to return.

Even in darkness, he could see a peaceful expression, perhaps full of safe dreams for the first time in many years. Reaching down as he had in his dream, one light hand rested on Lukas's chest. Steady thumps of a brave heart were the rhythm of life to fill his soul.

This isn't a dream, of that I'm sure. Never again will you be a target. "I'll kill man or demon that makes you suffer for being born to me. I'll forfeit immortality to insure that you regenerate Helena's bloodline—our bloodline." Just as he'd done a year ago, his lips brushed his son's forehead. *A similar kiss made him forget his troubled life, forget me. This one has no deals attached, no vows of vengeance.* "I'll do whatever it takes to keep you safe. This is a solemn promise, my son."

He tucked the bed covers around his son's slender frame. Left the room and closed the door. In his bedroom, he walked to the upholstered chair. Alana's scent filled his senses. He tried to clear his mind, but *his* Guardian stole the next thought. Because he had to see her.

I want her, need her…love her. She's my compass—my way home. An old habit surfaced. He paced the small living room before going up the stairs. Fully aware it would be an invasion of privacy; it wasn't possible to stop. He had made up his mind. He had to see her.

****

The antique knob yielded to his touch. Twisting it, Michael smiled. Had she left the apartment door unlocked on purpose? Did she know he'd come to her? Vision didn't need to direct him. He entered her bedroom, feeling cool breezes from the chilled air, hearing gentle waves lap at dark-gray stone. He closed the window.

Soundless strides brought him to the four-poster bed. Even in sleep, her heart beat strong and powerful like a song of life he wanted to share. Her soft supple curves, the outline of one breast peeking through a thick robe that had opened in tossing and turning… It excited him. Her nearness intoxicated him as never before. To slip under the covers, pull her naked body next to his and pleasure her with sensual kisses, passionate caresses.

I'd ride the rhythms of your heart and let them guide me to fulfill your most-secret desire. It will be my surrender that takes you, claims you as mine for eternity. Sensual scenes spun through his mind, but he didn't act upon his need. Another realization, full of devotion, replaced passion. *Now is the right time. Nothing stands in our way. Love is strong. It's resilient. With you, it's forever. Sleep my Guardian, my love. When you awaken, I'll be waiting.*

****

The private jet taxied down an airstrip tucked away in the hills of Vermont. Zoltan folded his long frame into a waiting black limousine. As it wound through narrow roads, he further refined his plan.

The limo turned down an unmarked lane. Full of bumps and potholes, the ride to the main house infuriated the vampire. Cyril never cared about the finer things, like paving roads or laying fresh stone over mud—or electricity.

Seven hundred years of riding a horse is more the sire's style. Modern modes of transportation are as foreign to him as needing breath to live. He imagined the difficulty of convincing Cyril to board the jet. With a tight grin Zoltan decided that either by his own volition or nailed in a coffin, his sire would eventually understand. The ultimate prize was within his grasp.

Chapter 22

Michael leaned in a casual way against the hall wall, his arms and ankles crossed in a comfortable way. Miles had come down the stairs with a bulging briefcase in one hand, a travel mug in the other. "Nice suit—did you get that in New York?"

"Pisa, a few days ago," the man proudly stated.

"Let me freshen that for you, Researcher." He took the mug before any dry protests as Miles followed him into the tiny kitchen.

"I see you're up and about."

"And thanks to Alana I found a tasteful but typical dark shirt and a new pair of black jeans in my dresser."

"That smells heavenly. Did you make it yourself?"

"I have brewed coffee for centuries, Miles." Fresh, steamy liquid filled the mug before he snapped the lid in place. "A caffeine rush is an eternal pleasure."

"Yes, I imagine it would be. All memories are back?"

Leaning against the counter, he admitted, "Every last one. I have a hell of a lot to thank you for, especially with my boy. I never considered you a trusted friend."

"Until it involved Lukas's well-being... You understand that because of what lived inside you, even if you had access to your conscience, I couldn't encourage my daughter's attachment."

He met Miles's gaze. "And now?"

"I know the dream, Michael. Thorn's report is very

thorough. Documents were prepared granting me custody of Lukas should your existence end. That shows a full understanding of the man I am. Your fantasy had it correct. I harbor no ill will against you. And now, I know the original Michael Malone." Miles took the mug from him. "Never a creature to engage in personal conversation, your actions consistently reveal exactly who you are. Devotion to Alana and Lukas is indisputable. Suffice it to say, you are very welcome. But be *better* than good to my daughter, or I swear before God that I'll have Thorn hold you down while I use my own belt on you."

His eyes immediately narrowed. "Does everyone know about that dream scene?"

"It tends to stand out in spite of Celia's tasteful edits. I wouldn't cross Mother Anne, either. I'd imagine she packs a good wallop." He flinched just as a timer dinged. "Is that cinnamon toast in the oven? What a very home-country aroma. Ah yes, we do share the same heritage. Did your mental romp through the 1600's reveal additional memories?"

"Of my family, the loss of my life… But now, I've a growing boy to feed and a woman I hope to serve breakfast in bed to for eternity if she'll have me." An unreadable expression appeared on Miles's face, and Michael quickly changed the subject. "I'm going to dig out the old apron and brush up on my culinary skills. I'd appreciate it if you keep that out of your report, by the way."

The typical dry grin appeared. "Oh I plan on giving the Council *everything*, down to the last mundane detail. However, I'm duly impressed. Coffee, cinnamon toast… Perhaps grocery shopping's next."

Unable to hide his pride, an unusual, broad smile appeared. "Got to the market as it opened," he stated.

Miles shook his head, and Michael heard him mumble as he walked out the door, "I wonder how long it'll take before he acquires a healthy tan."

"Now wouldn't that be a sight to see," he said as he set the table.

****

A delicate pale-pink rose, the first thing Alana saw when her eyes opened, rested beside her pillow. The note written in his familiar, old-world script read: "Breakfast awaits. You know the way." Gently she caressed the vibrant bud, its scent subtle and sensual.

He remembered her favorite flower. Her favorite color.

Fighting the urge to run to Michael, she showered and dressed for the day. She chose comfortable jeans and a thin sweater that matched the flower's hue. In front of the mirror for a final look, her nerves did a jangling dance. Thousands of dreams about talking to him again. Now? All she had to do was walk down a flight of stairs. In a moment of uneasy weakness, she went to the window to view the cloudless morning. She took in a sharp breath of fresh sea air thinking, am I ready to face you?

****

When Alana entered through the open door, Michael stood by the dining room table. She noticed the leather loafers she had purchased, something he'd normally never wear. Slow and determined, he approached already probing her expression for a sign. With a lean down, he kissed her cheek. The brush of his thin lips didn't feel cold, which intrigued her.

Another rosebud graced her plate. "I remember buying these table settings for you in Pisa. Now, it seems a lifetime ago."

"And the clothes you chose are exactly my taste. Thank you, my Guardian."

With the manners of a true gentleman, he seated her. A cup of coffee had been prepared the way she liked it, on the dark side without sugar. A bowl of fresh berries stood next to the plate. He put two slices of aromatic cinnamon toast on her dish and spread a small amount of sweet butter across them.

He knew her preference.

Neither spoke. Neither could. Michael sat across from her...five feet and a world of regret away. With his arms folded on the table, he took in her every move—in silence.

He sipped his coffee. She did the same.

"Please, eat something."

Her stomach did another dance. He'd always been a very good cook, and not wanting to insult him, she took small bites.

Lukas came into the room, gave a care-free "Hello." She'd never seen such an easy smile.

"Are you joining us?"

"No. He already fed me. That toast is way cool. Can I go upstairs for a while? I need to do some stuff online."

"Sure," she said, smiling back. "But you know you don't have to ask."

"Yes, he does," Michael said.

When Lukas left, she gave a grin. "Was that "parent-speak" I just heard?"

He pointed to the plate with a grin. Another ten

minutes full of awkward silence passed as she tried to eat. Then suddenly, he stood. "More coffee?"

"Thanks."

When he came closer to fill her cup, her heart skipped a few beats. Bathed in morning light, he looked more than handsome. The sight of him thrilled her. So did his charming smile. When he sat in full sun at her side, she tried not to stare—aware that he wasn't planning on returning to the other end of the table.

"Pretty amazing, isn't it?" As he placed the pot on a folded towel, his smile disappeared. "I'm so very sorry for what I've put you through."

He looked as nervous as she felt. Sitting back, she willed her hands to stay flat on the table. "I hear the sincerity in your voice and the last thing I want to do is argue. I know you, Michael. I understand your need for revenge. But you should have told me about Lukas. You should have told me why you went to NWT. You didn't and—" Defeat swept across his face.

In direct sun, every intense, chiseled feature seemed more pronounced. Small lines on his strong brow, the warmth of his eyes framed with thick dark lashes, the angles of his face... It was difficult to breathe.

"Alana?"

"I'm sorry. This-this doesn't seem real. We're not having a conversation *after* sunset."

His not-so-chilly hand gently came over hers. "Can we, darlin'?" Another flutter of her heart happened upon hearing that word. "Can we have a long, truthful conversation? I've missed you more than you'll ever know, my Guardian."

Slowly, her head shook. This was exactly what she

wanted, but only on her terms. "You have years of explaining to do. Unless you're willing to answer every question, to fill in every detail, I'm not interested in vagaries that have no meaning. I want to hear it all."

"That would take a very long time."

"I've got the rest of my life."

Leaning back, he nodded. "Warm sun on my shoulders is something I never expected to experience again. But being with the woman I love is more than a dream come true." The look he gave kissed her soul. "I'll regret what I did to you after that September night for eternity. But this story begins long before I talked to you."

Just as his soulmate requested, he didn't leave out the smallest detail.

****

The pervasive urgency bothered Miles in the rectory's conference room. A full assemblage of the Georgian Sovereign Council. Twelve of the purest souls who walk the earth was a rare occurrence. Each member, specifically chosen, possessed acute intuition. Decisions and decrees were guided by a power greater than all of them. Miles hadn't been summoned before a full conclave in close to seven years. He acknowledged his good friend. Deepa Chandra, who had also been summoned this perfect morning, indicated the chair next to hers at the far end of the table. He set his briefcase down, and Monsignor Scarlatti called for order.

Neither mysterious, sacred protocol nor mystical prayer opened the conclave. A simple minute of silence began the collective focus of astounding minds. Monsignor handed everyone a copy of the special decree. Miles noted ripe tension on each face when the wise priest stated, "Our first purpose is to discuss the newly created Document of Atonement, something as unique as the creature for which it is meant…Michael Malone, the mystically enhanced vampire."

****

Miles had read every word on the many pages. "This is extremely thorough."

Brother Giovanni reminded him, "This is not absolution."

Closing the document, he looked at the monk. "But it is, nonetheless, a compelling gesture of acceptance."

Monsignor Scarlatti gave an austere nod. "He will have two days to acclimate himself to this changed existence, Miles. Then you are instructed to present this and explain its meaning. Before further discussion, I'd like to address the vampire's healing."

Before he could even digest what had just been said, Mother Anne gave a day-by-day account. The discussion that followed included precise details of the unexpected results. Council members studied affidavits from all six healers, which gave them fresh perspectives on the incredible journey of Michael Malone.

The next question came from an America scholar, Joseph Atherton. "Mother Anne, many of us are thinking the same thing. I've read up on this creature. Do you now suggest he's no longer a vampire?" Atherton looked down at his notes. "Doctor Chamberlain, is it even *mystically* possible?"

"I believe he's beyond the known description of a vampire. Significant differences exist. A reflection, sun tolerance, and his tears are clear. The blood tear of a vampire is legendary. But Michael's are as human as yours. Plus, he perspires like a man, which suggests his body has altered. We're dealing with a singular being here. His system tolerates consecrated blood, along with a nutritional puree…and he's thriving."

"The removal of the beast-within has changed him. I truly believe this," Mother Anne added. "I respectfully suggest Michael cannot be classified "vampire". Too many anomalies now exist."

Chamberlain nodded agreement as did many Council members.

Antonio DeMarra, the bookstore's proprietor, motioned to speak. "There's more to consider about this creature. What happened on the North American Continent is unprecedented. There are three less sorcerers in this world and no NWT. Michael is like a-a lethal weapon who has proven full allegiance to The Georgian Cause."

"Other factors should also be considered." Cesar Gonzalez added, "My daughter, a second-year Guardian, has been assisted by Michael. He has protected the newly called as well as the seasoned warriors who end up in compromising positions."

Hiro Kuma of Tokyo, the newest Council member, quickly raised a finger as he glared at Cesar. "What does this have to do with what we are discussing?"

Courteously, Cesar responded. "Doesn't it prove loyalty to our cause with or without Alana Ciminio being a demon's target? Let's not forget. Michael did *all* of this with Clayton Mails breathing down his neck."

Through the many hours, Miles carefully noted the pros and cons about presenting the Document of Atonement to an immortal creature.

In the end, the secret ballots were tallied. Monsignor Scarlatti stood to announce, "The vote is unanimous. Michael Malone will be the only undead being in the history of the Georgian Council to be offered irrevocable Sanctuary. May it bring peace to his uneasy soul."

****

They had spent hours talking. Michael did most of it, open and brutally honest with Alana. A point came where both had to stop for a while. She cleared the table; he went upstairs for Lukas. Happy in conversation with his father, they then walked into the smaller bedroom.

Michael called out to her, "That suit your father had on this morning… He said he bought it in Pisa. Do you know which store?"

"It's down the block from the tower. Why?" With dishtowel in hand, she walked into Lukas's room and her eyes grew wide. The blush on her cheeks matched the sheets. "What the *hell* was I thinking? Ugh! This is totally embarrassing!"

Lukas smoothed the bedspread—obviously out of practice. Then he bent down, grabbed the pajamas and shoved them under the pillow. "That's okay, I, uh, like pink. Pink's pretty."

"Feel free to laugh. I completely understand if you want to replace all this—like today. Especially those pajamas." She followed Michael into the living room, fully embarrassed.

Flopped in the armchair, Lukas stared at them as Michael asked, "Did you buy me a suit?"

"No, only casual clothes, you know, the functional kind."

"Do you mind if I put a few items on your credit card? I'll pay you back."

"I think it's more like the other way around. I should have suspected this was all you—apartment, car, the cash in my checking account—long before it crossed my mind to question who the anonymous donor could possibly be."

"You don't owe me a thing. I, however, owe you for saving me, for safely bringing my son here."

Standing so close, Alana felt the perfect fit, as if they were a normal family having a typical discussion. She caught Lukas still staring at them together.

"Dad," he softly said, "Like, if you go to Pisa…you know—the road trip? Can I come?"

Before Michael could answer, her hand came to his arm. "Dad and I wouldn't have it any other way." Dad smiled, too.

****

A clock on the conference room wall confirmed the mid-afternoon hour. Miles had spoken privately with many Council members during lunch, but as soon as Philip Segallo walked in, he suspected something was up. When the ex-Guardian now known as Brother Thomas approached, Miles's jaw tightened. "It's nice to see you here and safe, Philip. Your assistance in Michael's rescue was invaluable."

"Ally's strategy in Manhattan was something else, Miles."

"How's life at the abbey?"

Philip's serene expression said it all. "Good, my new life is good. My parents are visiting next month. Thank Ally for sending Celia to tell them the truth before you guys left for Italy."

"Alana asked the Kendricks to assist them with your funeral arrangements."

"No Georgian tracks, right? I appreciate it. Mom and Dad are old, you know? I owe Ally for this one."

"I'm rather curious. Were you specifically asked here today or is this a coincidence?"

An easy smile appeared. "My presence was requested. Do you happen to know what would require a novice monk to attend a Sovereign Council conclave?"

Miles shook his head, more concerned with one particular Council member. The woman of stature in the Slovakian government continually stared his way. Petite, with short, gray hair, Margaret Smirkovska's vivid-blue eyes sparkled like pieces of cracked crystal that could cut through to one's soul, determining truth and seeing motive in every thought. She was also one of the most gifted psychics of her generation.

Monsignor Scarlatti reconvened the meeting and stated, "Brother Thomas will please join us." A chair had been placed for him between Miles and Deepa Chandra. "When the Champion accepts this document, the ex-Guardian will become his only link to the outside world." Monsignor's gaze then locked on Miles. "There has been a change of plans. Michael Malone will sign this on the altar of *San Giorgio's* in my presence alone. By his own volition, he will proceed with Brother Thomas by launch to San Marco Abbey and reside there in solitude until what we ask is received. As his running journals are sent, Council members will review them. At the appropriate time, Michael will be summoned. If we are in unanimous agreement, then, and only then, will our signatures be attached. Once Michael signs the last page, he'll be free to live out his immortal existence in any way he so chooses."

Margaret's grave expression made Miles's chest tighten. "I don't understand, Monsignor. Seclusion was never discussed. Michael's not—"

"There is more, trusted researcher," the priest interrupted. "Deepa will assume the post of Researcher for North America, effective immediately. Cesar's daughter Kayla, a young Guardian, will relocate to Portofino. Alana will be her new mentor. You are reassigned as Researcher for the European Continent and will be posted at the Hampton Hill estate in England. All personal items from the Manhattan penthouse are already en route, and Laura is awaiting your arrival."

"My wife?" His voice sounded shakier than he'd have liked. "I don't understand. Was this Council not pleased with my work?"

"We hold you in the highest regard, Miles, and are extremely pleased indeed. You handled this event with flawless decorum. This Council commends you. What we now ask is much more difficult. Let it be known that Miles Bookman is to be entrusted with young Lukas Malone."

Quickly, he stood. "I am to be *what*!? There's no reason to separate father from son! I'm compelled to state for the record, esteemed Council members, this is not only unnecessary, it is unconscionable!" Margaret's gaze snared him again.

"You will leave for England within the week," the monsignor informed. "Your daughter, the Servant of Souls, and the child *will* accompany you. He'll be known as Evan Bookman, your nephew." Seeing his look of protest, the priest held up a hand.

Margaret Smirkovska nodded agreement. Why, he had to wonder.

Monsignor continued in a serious voice. "During the Champion's self-imposed exile, the child will abstain from all contact with his father. So it will be for Alana as well. You will inform Michael Malone the day after tomorrow. Not sooner, not later. These determinations are final and shall not change. However, I do not believe Michael will challenge our demands. In fact, he will insist it be so."

"Monsignor, with all due respect, I cannot comprehend—" he didn't finish his sentence, stopped by Margaret's cool gaze. He saw disguised fear in her as well.

"And you would be right, Miles. Lukas left the protection of a consecrated building in anger three nights ago."

"Yes, yes… But he had been outdoors before."

"Lukas didn't spill his blood in any of those locations, did he?"

"There was nothing I could've done, Margaret. I apologize for not—"

"I'm not blaming you, Miles," she said in a sad tone. "Nor is it my wish to make you feel as responsible as you clearly do. This was unforeseen by all of us. Let me clarify. Something as insignificant as an angry outburst will appear as a glitch to dark seers. If it turns into rage and comes from the missing child of a mystically enhanced vampire whose blood is found on a stone…" With a tense look of disgust, she leaned back. "Now you understand. Remember that I assisted Celia in keeping Lukas safe during Michael's ungodly battle in Manhattan. Lukas's terrified face was as clear to me as my own grandson's. We believe a command had been sent to every half-crazed mind—to do Zoltan's bidding. Yes. You recall his history. Please refresh this Council's memory."

All color drained, *never* expecting to hear the name in conjunction with this event. "When Cyril learned that an Old One had tampered with his favorite child of the night, the sire returned to Slovakia and started a killing spree as reprisal. He murdered scores of Guardians after 1890 and sired dozens, trying to create a similar protégé. Count Franz Vashkar was pure Magyar. Zoltan, his youngest son, seemed as arrogant as Michael. One fact set the two apart. Michael never aspired to warlord status. Zoltan did."

Both hands locked behind his back as he started to pace, an automatic action when his mind worked at tremendous speed.

"Many exotic rumors buzzed about his association with Cyril…all false. In 1891, Count Vashkar vowed that when he saw Zoltan again, he'd kill his son for treacherous disloyalty. Instead, the new vampire drank his entire family and assumed the Vashkar fortune. Zoltan is considered an extremely dangerous creature." Sitting down, he hoped to regain composure. "May I ask why—"

"Zoltan is killing Guardians in Hungary," Margaret stated, "He knows the child is in Portofino. So now, have you assumptions, Miles?"

His blood pressure rose and glancing at the beautiful spring sky, his brain sped into overdrive. Then, he faced the stunned Council members. "Lukas is again in grave danger and Zoltan is intrigued that he's here. In all probability, Zoltan has already killed Clayton Mails, which sends a clear message to anyone standing between him and what he wants. If he knows Lukas flew into such a rage, then it follows logically— only one creature could produce such a response. He has confirmation. Michael was *not* incinerated two weeks ago."

Margaret nodded. "Your mind is amazing, Miles."

"Michael needs to know this."

"The day after tomorrow," the monsignor reminded.

Margaret looked just as shaken as he. "I can only offer what I see in my mind's eye, Sebastiano. Spur-of-the-moment vengeance is not Zoltan's way. The Hungarian is a meticulous murderer who likes an audience. Michael must be ready."

"He'll be more than ready," Miles said with confidence as he organized the files in his briefcase. This meeting was over.

****

In silence, Miles walked with Mother Anne and Rosa back to the red-brick building. His mind didn't slow down. Although he had not been given the significance of waiting forty-eight hours, he'd never question a Council directive.

Standing alone in Alana's living room, he remained lost in thought. *Explain the document to Michael. Disclose Zoltan's possible involvement…much easier said than done. I hope with all my heart that Lukas can accept another separation from his parent. With any luck, Laura's waiting by the phone for this more than necessary call.*

Relieved by the solitude, he sank into an armchair, rubbed his forehead and whispered, "Good Lord, when will this end?"

Chapter 23

Michael looked at Thorn next to Celia on the couch as he and Lukas walked in. Loaded down with shopping bags, Lukas gave a shy smile and hurried into the master bedroom.

Thorn handed up a note. "I found it under the door."

Michael sank into an armchair, and after reading it, tapped the folded paper against the wide arm.

Celia slid a large envelope across the coffee table. "Won't it be fun at *Zia's* for dinner? The Sisters are leaving for Siena tomorrow—and we found this on the doormat."

Grinning at her, he dumped everything out. The driver's license and credit card went into a new leather wallet he had just purchased, and then he studied his digital photo in the passport. That slid into the back pocket of his jeans as well. "Tomorrow morning, Thorn, get a safety deposit box at the local bank and put my son's papers in it."

"Will do, Boss. What about tonight?"

"We make sure the healers know how appreciative I am. Find the most expensive champagne and order four bouquets of white roses from the local florist. Take care of the cards for me if you don't mind. One should be a thank-you from the man they awakened. Just this once, a stroll through my thoughts is allowed."

"I hear the words as you speak."

Again, he smiled at Celia. "Have Lukas sign his own card. Will you do that for me?"

"Not a problem." Her green eyes narrowed. "So why the gorgeous black suit, exquisitely tailored in the garment bag that's hanging in your room?"

He gave Celia a charming grin. "I'm going to ask Alana for a date. I want it to be very upscale. What hotel did—"

"Oooh, I know another one! Ally's always talking about it. Yep, I'll make a reservation. Whoa!" She stared at the stack of euros he pulled from the envelope and placed in her hand. "That's more than I've ever held at one time."

"This is going to be a special date. Now get out of my mind, Celia B."

Thorn cleared his throat. "I'm curious. Is that a watch on your wrist? You know exactly what time it is down to the minute. One day in the sun and suddenly you're craving all things human?"

The perceptive question turned his charming grin mischievous. "Absolutely, Empath, I'm craving *everything* human!"

****

In spite of the typical teenage whine, Lukas changed his clothes. Shortly after sunset, father and son stood at Rosa's door. Michael dressed the part for this important occasion. In expensive black trousers and a matching silk shirt, he thought he looked even more put together than usual. The buttoned collar made each striking facial feature stand out. He eyed his son, who rubbed a finger under his stiff blue collar. "The button-down and new khakis look sharp on you."

"And if I get bored later, I can leave, right?"

"Absolutely not and don't do the pouting thing, either."

Rosa's door opened, and they both smiled.

Alana's hair was up. Graceful tendrils framing her face exaggerated her large, hazel eyes. A soft, sensual scent of jasmine and cherry blossoms clung to her tanned skin. He recognized it instantly, taking in everything about her. The muted-rose blouse hinted enough cleavage, and the tight black skirt showed the curve of womanly hips. His gaze lingered on the turquoise cross threaded through a velvet ribbon that banded his Guardian's long neck. Silver earrings shimmered as they danced through wisps of chestnut hair. Every piece of jewelry she wore had been a gift from him. In his eyes, she rated beyond beautiful. He started to speak, but his son won the glory of her pretty smile.

Still blushing from Alana's kiss, Celia suddenly pulled Lukas into Rosa's home saying, "Oooh...let's help *Zia* together."

Michael watched him leave, and then studied Alana once again. The dark-wood threshold could've been a frame on a perfect portrait. "You are lovely tonight," he said in a voice both mellow and rich. Her heart raced when he leaned down to tenderly kiss her cheek. Her hand took his, and she led him into *Zia* Rosa's home.

Michael had never seen the healing Sisters in casual clothes. Their lively conversation with Miles and Thorn stopped when he entered the dining room—the same size as his across the hall.

"You, uh, have a-a certain commanding presence," Alana whispered. "That particular aspect hasn't changed. And the almost-human, healthy skin tone adds to your singular, um, good looks." He simply stared at her, wanting more than just a squeeze of the hand.

As he'd been taught centuries ago, Michael greeted each sister with a respectful bow and a reverent kiss to their hands.

Rosa's smile was as radiant as Alana's. "You have prepared a beautiful table, *Zia*," he said to her as she indicated the head of the table, a place of honor in an Italian home.

Expensive champagne Thorn had purchased waited at every setting, and Mother Anne raised her glass in a toast. "To your continued well-being, Champion."

Everyone expected he'd do the same, but instead, Michael looked at each person in the room. "Thank you isn't enough. What I feel is far beyond any word that exists. *Zia*, you were the strength in my dream. In reality, I don't think I'd have gotten back on my feet so soon without you. *Signora, grazie, mille grazie*."

Rosa whispered a soft "*Prego.*"

"Sister Magdalena and Sister Gabriella, in my dream and in reality, the two of you have healed me. You possess an angel's touch. Thank you for taking such excellent care of me and my son." The women, one shy and one spirited, accepted his gratitude. Overcome with respect, his gaze found Mother Anne. Humility filled his soul. "I'm not even worthy to be in the same room with one so wise. Your tender words eased the soul of a terrified man who awakened in a strange world. I will always believe you are an earthbound Old One. It is all appreciated, Mother. Now I have answers to questions that have plagued my soul for centuries. The Order of Catherine will want for nothing as long as I exist." He searched her light-gray eyes. "Please, will you honor the request?"

Mother Anne inclined her head. "You will be shown the way."

Lukas had the glass to his lips. With a stern look, Michael stopped him. His son shrugged staring at the empty plate. Hearty laughter erupted, breaking the austere mood. Michael laughed as well. "There hasn't been enough of this sound lately." His manner turned serious as he studied Miles, Celia, Thorn, and finally, Alana at his side. "I've put each of you through Hell—each in a different way. You have my gratitude and respect." He leaned into the woman he loved and added, "For eternity." Only then did his glass rise. "Here's to everyone's continued well-being." During dinner, he caught Miles's tension. Michael expected all of his worry lines to be gone. But this evening? They appeared to have deepened.

****

The ancient demon bristled as Zoltan led him through a grand foyer and into the library of his estate near Budapest. A fire blazed hot. Cyril sat. Long, skeletal fingers gripped the arms of a black velvet chair that resembled a throne. Zoltan covered him with a fur blanket.

Noisily, the sire sucked in air to rasp, "Why did you destroy my horses?"

"Everything was a liability, Father. You have all you need here. Sleep above ground in a luxurious room, my Sire, and drink from nubile Guardians."

Cyril bared rotted teeth. "You dare to bring me across an ocean nailed in a pine box?"

Cowered like an expert, Zoltan kissed Cyril's icy

fingers. When a jagged fingernail tore open his left cheek, blood trickled from the expected wound. The baron growled, licked the tantalizing liquid. His mood only brightened when an unsteady woman appeared in a minion's rough grip. She moaned, and Cyril grinned in anticipation. Zoltan exposed her neck, and the sire tore into the young Guardian.

****

The enjoyable evening wound down slowly. Laughter, great conversation, and music had been continuous. Magdalena played an intricate Chopin ballade, passionately executed.

Alana kept glancing at him from the kitchen while Celia wrapped leftovers. Michael seemed centuries away, captivated by its minor melody. She also eyed Gabriella, still sitting right next to him. Tonight, the healer's animated manner along with quick, witty comments got charming smiles and interesting grins from Michael.

"Even in a turtleneck and jeans she's stunning! Look at her, sis! She really could be a model, don't you think?" Alana mumbled.

"Admit it, Ally, that green-eyed monster is ready to roar."

From the sink, she craned her neck back to catch Michael staring her way. A devilish smirk spread across his lips, and he stood, still talking to the stunning nun.

Celia giggled, clicked her tongue. "Now you're in trouble." She made a fast exit.

Alana felt the blush, nervously turned on the hot water to scrub the sink with a soapy sponge…again.

Michael came in, leaned against the counter, crossing his arms and ankles in a causal manner as he watched her. "It looks pretty spotless to me."

Rinsing out a multitude of bubbles, she dried the porcelain with a soaked towel. "I just want *Zia* to sleep tonight without anything on her mind. It's an old Italian tradition—clean kitchen, clear conscience. You liked the music."

"I love every Chopin composition. Stefania played them just as beautifully."

Alana looked at him. "You heard my mom play?"

"I listened from the street...to her Bach and Beethoven as well. You, however, sounded less than enthusiastic with your execution of the classics," he added as if he were an expert.

A glare preceded her smile. "I had other things on my mind."

"Perhaps you were too enthralled with one particular piano student—the tall, skinny kid who lived upstairs. I believe I'd classify that as a major crush. What was his name?"

She opened her mouth to answer but let out a long breath instead. "You sneak. My parents could've had you arrested for stalking or something." A sensual smirk appeared on his handsome face, which she thought totally inappropriate for the kitchen in *Zia* Rosa's home.

"Two years of sitting on the piano bench close together and without an inch between. I'll bet that by the tender age of fifteen, you secretly thought him your boyfriend. Admit it. When he moved away you cried for days. But a few years later you met me...and what's-his-name was ancient history." He leaned closer. Kissed the tip of her nose.

Neither pulled away, and her gaze was as intense

as his. No words came out until he rested back against the counter. She could still feel his gorgeous eyes on her. Continually, she folded and refolded the dishtowel. "And why exactly did you come in here?"

"To ask you out on a date," he softly stated. "Are you, by any chance, free tomorrow for an excursion to Siena? We'll make a day of it. Then have a quiet dinner at that quaint hotel on the piazza?" He hesitated, grew serious. "Please. Will you come with me to visit my sisters?"

She saw Michael's insecurity—another first. "You've had an incredible few weeks. Maybe you should wait another day. Do you think you're ready?"

"Are we talking about the date or visiting my sisters?"

His slow grin began. Playfully, she tapped his hand, but Michael caught her wrist, pulled her close until she leaned against him. Ready to melt, she replied, "You know which one I meant. I'm not quick with a witty comeback like that holy healing sister in there."

He kissed her. His lips so inviting. She didn't want to pull apart, and they stayed that way for a long, enchanting moment. "I prefer a particular Italian brunette with fire in her eyes. She's the only woman I will ever want. Is it a date?" Another dip of his chin, another kiss to her burning cheek.

The sensuousness of his rich baritone voice suddenly made *Zia's* kitchen stifling. "Yes," she whispered.

"I'll call for you at nine."

He smiled. Another skipped beat of her heart! When he left, she turned back to the sink, hearing his mellow "Good night" to all. Immediately, the melting woman opened her aunt's refrigerator. She moved the wrapped leftovers around. A slow, half-dozen forced breaths of cold, cold air was necessary before joining Celia on the sofa, calm and collected again.

Miles glanced at his cheerful daughter before staring out Rosa's dining room window. The street was quiet, the fresh air inviting. Tremendous sadness filled his heart. For Alana. For Lukas. For Michael.

Mother Anne came to his side. "How are you going to keep this a secret, Miles? Michael looked your way during dinner. I sense he already suspects something's not right."

Softly, he replied, "One more day of happiness, after all of this, is most unfair."

****

Thorn heard Lukas flop on his bed saying, "The pink goes tomorrow."

He yawned and stretched. "It's soft, it's here... I'm tired. I couldn't care less if it had purple polka-dots." Studying the quiet teen, he asked, "So, kid, we're good?"

"Yeah, we're good. I'm really sorry."

"Apology accepted. No more headaches?"

"Nope, not even a twinge tonight when I talked to Mother Anne. It was never really you, you know."

"You don't have to explain," he replied in a gentle way. "Mystical empath, remember? With you, it just took a little extra help. You sure did capture my Celia's heart."

"She's awesome, Thorn."

"Well, she's head over heels in love with you. If you were ten years older, I'd have to fight you for her.

Now that's a nice smile. Dimples and all. It looks good on you, kid."

Lukas flew up with excitement in his eyes. "Maybe Dad could buy the building next door. I mean, it's like already attached. You and Celia, and Mister B and his wife can live here, too. We can always be together." A mischievous chuckle escaped. "Yeah… And we all live happily ever after."

"Get some sleep. And I snore, by the way, really loud." He watched Lukas grab a pair of clean pajamas and leave. His smile quickly faded. Happily ever after was nowhere in sight.

Thorn didn't see it. Didn't feel it.

****

Michael heard Lukas come out of the bathroom. He sensed his son approach as he stood by the window staring at the dark hill's steep incline behind the red-brick building.

Turning, he met his son's gaze. "How'd the apology go?"

"We're cool. Alana looked way hot tonight. Jeez Dad, I just say her name and you grin. So fill me in. Did you ask her?"

"Yep… And we'll be spending all of tomorrow together. Speaking of grins, I see the dreamy looks from Celia. She's pretty sweet on you." Lukas sighed when he clasped one boney shoulder. "Will you be okay without me for a day?"

"Yep," he replied with the same inflection.

"No bad-boy behavior of any kind, right? Because if you forget, I'll prove just how parental I can get."

"Hell, I won't step out of line."

A no-nonsense expression stayed on his face.

"Good, because I'm strictly old-school... Punching, kicking, or biting is banned from this home. I see it, and just like any normal fifteen-year-old, you won't sit too easily."

"I get the picture, Dad. I'll be cool. Swear on my soul," he stated with conviction.

Wrapping his son in a tight hug, he bristled. "Whew! The stench of hair dye is atrocious! How long before it fades?"

"How long will they keep looking for me?"

The reality of the innocent question sobered him. Dangerously still, he concealed a murderous desire with a thin, typical smile. "Go to bed. It's late." Relaxed, his son padded of to the bedroom. The door closed.

He shut his eyes, saying in a low voice, "Lukas Malone, the child born to a commanding vampire, a mystically enhanced creature. My little boy is not out of danger. Dear God, he never will be."

****

As soon as he sensed Lukas asleep, Michael slipped out. Determined strides brought him to the edge of the piazza. San Giorgio's Church came into view, and he walked around the building to the back door of the rectory. The sound inside came from a late-news television broadcaster giving an account of world events at the end of a typical day.

The door opened, and Monsignor Scarlatti ushered him into a stark parlor. The priest settled into what appeared to be his favorite chair. "You are troubled. What can I do for you, *Signore*?"

"I am, Father. I-I want to thank you...for hearing my confession." He sat on the edge of the couch cushion, searched the priest's intuitive eyes for something, not knowing exactly what.

"It was important to the man you were before undeath took life away." Monsignor paused. "Why are you here, Michael?"

"I'm spending the day with Alana tomorrow." He stopped talking, again seeking something in the priest's kind eyes and compelled to be totally honest. "I've made a reservation for dinner...at one of the hotels." Awkwardness gripped as he looked down.

"What is it that you need to hear from me?"

"Alana's years as a Guardian are behind her, and I—I love her, Father. I have to be sure her soul won't burn in Hell for loving me in return. I know this is on her mind. I heard the sadness in her voice during a conversation—"

"The first night here and through thick walls, you heard her speak about you with Rosa." The monsignor folded his hands. "You wrestled with unimaginable pain yet heard every word. In the hour before my arrival your soul begged for Alana. Ah... You do remember everything, don't you? Down to the slightest glance, the softest hush of a whisper."

He nodded, not at all bothered as the saintly man read him. "But *this* wasn't in that dying man's soul, Father."

"What wasn't?"

"The sins of the beast-within... And what I did to her."

"You stole a young woman's innocence and then tried for two weeks to kill her."

"Yes, Father."

"Who does this specific transgression belong to? You or the beast exorcised from you?"

"Me. Only me." More guilt consumed him, and yet he was forced to look the wise priest in the eye, the truth there to see. "Your goodness humbles me, Father. At my most vulnerable point, you offered Sanctuary without recoiling or revulsion at what I am, at what I've done."

"You are changing, *Signore*. Therefore, I choose my words carefully. With a clear understanding of both right *and* wrong, think on them. When you were young, many fine principles were instilled by your father. They've always been inside you, whether or not you chose to follow them during your mortal life. Yet, to encourage a Guardian's love—to place temptation before her and steal her innocence—these were your actions. To allow the beast- within to surface after more than a century of dormancy—that was your reaction. At the very peak of human pleasure, this realization hammered at your moral conscience. But Alana's solemn vow had indeed been broken, and thus, you punished yourself. Just as you had the ability to control the demon imbedded in your soul, you also had the ability to call it forward at will." The explanation hit home, and he nodded, looked away. "So now, who is it that asks forgiveness?"

"I do. I'm the one who hurt her."

"My next question may be unexpected, but your honest answer will reveal who you truly are. Do you forgive yourself?" Searching his soul, he couldn't answer. "It is the wise man who learns from his mistakes and the fool who repeats them, Michael. Find the courage within to ask forgiveness and be willing to accept her honest response. Are you prepared to walk away if it is Alana's desire?"

It took a moment before he responded. "In truth, I'll honor any decision Alana makes. But I will always love her."

The monsignor stood and walked him out a different way. "You shall use the front door when visiting me again, Champion. Have a wonderful time with the lovely *signorina* tomorrow." He stood on the top step, Michael at ground-level. The kind priest began a blessing.

Full of uncertainty, his hand moved with the priests to make the significant symbol, which once would have burned something like him. The door closed. The light went out.

A glance at the darkened church showed him what he had to do. It made perfect sense.

Chapter 24

Alana awoke earlier than usual. Sleeping at all, she considered a huge accomplishment. The dress she chose, purchased in Pisa days ago, was the deep-yellow color of a sunflower. Its bodice gathered under her breasts and flowed delicately to mid-calf. Soft-spun, summer-cotton felt perfect for such a beautiful day. She clipped her hair at the base of her neck, slipped into worn, favorite sandals to pose in the mirror many times before leaving the bedroom.

Through the arch, her father appeared serious while studying something. But when Miles saw her, the leather folder closed, and he gave a warm smile. She refilled his coffee mug and poured herself a cup before joining him at the table.

"That color is positively radiant on you, honey," he said with adoration.

"It's stylish and I feel good in it."

"Are you excited about today?"

"You already know my answer, Daddy B. I *still* don't believe this is happening." She took a slow sip, craving conversation. "I never dared to dream… He's been very open with me. This is the real deal, isn't it?"

"Only you can know that. But I sense loving you comes naturally to him. What has you so worried?"

Not knowing where to start, she stared at the coffee swirling in the cup. "We're going to Siena this morning."

He handed her a small envelope. "This is for Michael—from Mother Anne. What else do you have planned?"

She slipped it into her handbag. "He didn't give any details, except dinner." Indecision hounded her. When Miles took her hand, she gripped it tight; hoping the doubt she felt would dissolve.

"I'm compelled to give some fatherly advice, honey, so please accept an old man's ramblings. Laura and I were close to your parents long before they married. Alfonso and Stefania loved each other deeply. After they died, well, we already considered you family *before* the legal system made it official. Love is a precious gift. When I met Laura, I sensed completion to my existence. Your father and I talked about it often. He felt the same way when he met Stefania. That's what I sense in Michael when he talks about you, when he simply *thinks* about you. But you have to sense it as well. If you wish to walk away, do so immediately. Don't lead him on. Don't look back. Search your soul carefully and prepare to close your heart forever if that's your choice. What Michael's been through, well, he's now a *much* different individual than when you first met him eleven years ago."

"I've thought about only him and nothing else." The next question she whispered, not knowing if it was to her father or herself. "Is this what love feels like?"

"Love comes from the heart and the soul, not the head, honey."

Zia had said it first, then Celia, Gabriella and Thorn... "I've heard that before—way too many times."

"Maybe you *need* to hear it...way too many times,"

he replied.

****

Michael stared in the dresser mirror. As if last night's visit with the monsignor allowed him to see more of his soul, his reflection was clearer. Besides a healthy complexion, another difference was visible. One palm ran across his chin. He hadn't willed facial hair to grow the way he could as a vampire. Full beard, turn-of-the-century mustache—these were simple accomplishments. The day-old growth was stylish, ruggedly modern. He studied the cut of the black suit trousers and crème-colored shirt. A vampire's pallor didn't go well with light colors.

"Not today," he said to himself, and slipped barefoot into his leather loafers thinking that in footwear, Alana had very good taste. He studied the action of fastening the expensive watch to his wrist. With reverence, he slipped his sister's locket into his shirt pocket. One hand lingered over his unbeating heart. "If only," he said in a hushed voice.

A soft knock on the door brought him out of the master bedroom. When Michael opened the door, Rosa stepped into his home and handed him the mystical recipe. "Giacomo will keep a fresh supply of all the ingredients. You have enough to last through tomorrow, *si*?" He nodded. "I will be honored to bless it. But *Signore,* I don't mind preparing it for you."

"And I hoped you would say that." He gave an easy smile. "*Mille grazie, Zia…* You're certain?"

"It is my pleasure. Ah, how romantic your plans are."

"I love her, *Zia*. She is my destiny." He sensed Rosa searching more than his face.

"Love is a commanding healer. What is given in love should never be taken lightly."

"You said that to me in the dream. I hear the warning, *Zia,* and I appreciate your acceptance." Uneasiness surfaced. "I know there are certain things she wants, which I cannot give."

"Your mind is clear now. You'll know what to do." Taking his hands, she added, "Ah, they are no longer cold! It's a good sign. Go. I'll be here when Lukas wakes up."

****

Miles saw him standing in the threshold and unable to hide a curious grin, motioned him inside. "You actually look nervous. Nice suit," he said with a touch of sarcasm. "Did you have it sent from New York?"

"Pisa," Michael dryly replied. "Where is she?"

"In her room. Do you and I need to have a talk?"

He noted Michael's uneasy shift. "Is something wrong? I saw it in you last night."

Artfully, he avoided the question by asking, "Will Alana be home tonight?"

"You caught me off guard with that one."

"I *am* her father."

"Should I have...asked... your permission?"

"Answer the question please." He clasped his hands behind his back.

"I'm not going to lie. I'm hoping no, but we'll be back before nine...a.m. that is." Michael took a step forward. "Well do I have your permission?" Embarrassment as well as awkwardness claimed his face. "I can't believe I just asked you that."

"I can't believe it, either. Just remember what I told you yesterday morning. I meant every word."

Alana entered, and Michael's expression changed as he met her near the couch. "You look beyond lovely."

"Thanks." Alana pulled the car keys from her handbag.

Michael immediately handed them off to Miles saying, "You won't need them."

"Why?" she asked as Michael led his lovely daughter out the door.

He heard Michael casually reply, "Because I want to get to Siena in one piece, darlin'."

Of course, Miles fully agreed.

****

One glance at the directions to Villa Catherine—and Michael had it memorized. The slate-gray Mercedes sedan sped down the highway, sunroof open, with him at the wheel and a beautiful woman in the other plush bucket seat. No heavy conversations—just soft music and gentle words. He would make this day perfect for Alana in every way.

When they arrived at Villa Catherine, Mother Anne greeted them, her demeanor cheerful and warm. After leading them down a path and over a hill, they left the elderly healer sitting on a stone bench near the cemetery gate. His dream of survival had shown the location—a high wall behind and fragrant lilacs to shade his sisters' resting place. Three names chiseled on a white marble cross. Once more, he lingered in thoughts that shouldn't be in his head. Holding tight to Alana's hand, his brow creased, his eyes glazed.

"I loved them with all my heart. I was Lukas's age when they left England...when they left me. Why didn't I know what they were?"

"Maybe no one did. They truly loved you," Alana whispered.

The sight of their names brought many emotions. He refused to bury them, allowing this woman to see them all. "Father hid his loss. Mother became distant. If they only knew." He brushed the pristine stone as if he could touch them again. "They wouldn't have been proud of the man I became. Anne, Rosalind, and Priscilla Malone... My sisters who reached through time to save a guilty soul will now rest in peace." His voice broke, resembling a tender sigh. He felt for the inscribed locket, another precious memory. "Anne knew someday I'd find you."

Leaning into his embrace, Alana's touch was pure tenderness. "How do you know this?"

"Soon, my love," he whispered. "Very soon you'll understand."

Hand in hand, they strolled back to Mother Anne. "Thank you from the depths of my soul."

Tenderly, she placed her wrinkled hands on his cheeks. "Your bloodline is strong, resilient. Go with God."

****

Instead of returning to Portofino, he drove to Siena as Alana marveled at the beauty of the region. "I've never been here."

"I have."

"You have?"

"Well over a century ago. Much has changed."

After a slow stroll through medieval streets, they stopped at a cafe on the *Piazza del Campo*. The waiter, an older gentleman, poured another glass of red wine for him while she picked at a small salad.

"You don't usually play with food if that's what you call a plate of greens. Why didn't you order a real lunch?"

"I'm not hungry," Alana replied, very self-conscious and leaving out the fact that her stomach had tied in knots.

"You're always hungry," he said with an engaging laugh.

"I'll finish every last leaf. Will it make you feel better?"

"Yes, but I'm only partially satisfied. Tonight, you will eat."

"Now you can stop with the 'I'm-in-control-and-you're-not' look." It had been years since she'd seen it on his handsome face—aimed at *her*. He buttered a piece of bread and flashed a stern look while handing it to her. She remembered that look, too. She glared back, but took it, bit into it.

Suddenly, he wore a charming grin. "Ah, darlin', some things just never change."

Her heart quickened when he said *that* word again! *His smooth, sensual voice gives it a liquidly Irish lilt— no dramatic drawl or Texas twang. It just rolls off his tongue with ease.*

It made her special. It made her his. She looked away as the tingle in her very core came back with a vengeance.

****

So far, the day's been perfect, Alana thought as she put her cell phone on the console between them. "Celia says he's fine. Thorn rented a boat and they're fishing up a storm."

The Mercedes swerved onto the unpaved shoulder

of the highway and skidded to a sudden stop. Michael's palms smacked the steering wheel. "My son is in a *boat*? What if he can't swim or the boat capsizes pulling him under? *Damn* it! I said keep him busy—not risk his life! I'll kill Thorn with my bare hands."

"Whoa... Back up, buddy."

"Alana—"

"Lukas couldn't be in better hands, *mystical* hands at that!"

"Call Thorn and tell them to get to shore! Do it!"

"I can't believe this. Are you giving me orders?"

His groan deepened. "All right, *please* call and *ask* Thorn to get to shore."

"No!" She wrestled the phone from him. "You're in a parental panic. I remember the rare times when Dad had those attacks. Count to ten. It'll pass." Michael actually glowered, saying her name in a familiar way. "How dare you use that tone on me! What?!"

He slouched forward, but she remained ready to challenge. Traffic whizzed by. The Mercedes didn't move, and finally, she shook a finger at him. "You're still furious, but I'm just as stubborn as you, and I'm not on a feeding schedule. I can pout longer too, so stop being irrational." No look came. No answer, either. "Great," she mumbled, quickly changing tactics. "Why are you so worried? Lukas is having a *normal* experience. I'm sure he can handle being in a boat on the Mediterranean Sea. Please don't be one of those "*O Dio Mio*" dads, like Philip's father. Daddy B always let me breathe."

"I'm not Miles, and Lukas is far from normal," he stated, just a tad calmer.

"But Lukas is super-special, and everyone loves

him, including me."

His dark-espresso eyes captured hers. "You do?"

"I really do."

"Do you love me, too?"

Here it is, she thought, my first moment of truth.

"Do I even have to dignify that with an answer?" He didn't reply. He looked uncertain. *Oh God...I do!* In one breath, "I love you so much that *I* would walk through the fires of Hell for you so can we get on with this date now because I've been waiting *years* for today," spilled out.

"That's all I needed to hear. But you stole my line." His kiss was sweet affection, his deep voice sensual.

"Okay. I confess. I've read that dream journal so many times, I think I've memorized it."

With a very sexy smirk, he winced. "You know that's the edited version, right?"

"Don't worry. I filled in every missing line with my *own* fantasies," she admitted, certain of the fact that the rest of her life waited only two exits away.

****

Michael parked the luxurious sedan in front of the garage. Starting for the piazza, he slowed his long strides to match Alana's leisurely step, just as he'd always done on the streets of Manhattan, always after sunset. With a hand on her elbow, he tried to move her on, but she turned back to study the Mercedes.

"That color is unbelievable! I've never seen such a shade of gray. Or is it blue? Wait!" She stopped. So did he. "Won't the rental agency take the cooler? What about your sustenance? What if they find the empty blood bottles? Want to go back, maybe store them in the garage and call Thorn? What if you wait too long? What are you doing about feeding later?"

"I can't tell you how much I've missed the multiple-question quizzes, my love. The car isn't going anywhere. It's mine. I like it and I'm keeping it. As for feeding, and I truly wish you'd find a-a less catchy word, it's taken care of." They resumed their stroll. "And the room has a refrigerator. By the way, what I charged yesterday is in your checking account."

Stopping again, Alana studied him. "You're really running at top speed. You don't owe me anything. When do we switch?"

"Switch what? I'm not following."

"Apartments…you know—homes."

"No, darlin', I don't take back gifts."

"But you and Lukas would have more space and—"

"No, absolutely not. The second floor is fine. It's closer to work."

"You're going where? *What* work?"

"I own the best bookshop in Portofino. Remember?"

"No, that's Antonio's… And I can't believe I'm just getting this—"

"While in bright sunlight, strolling to the piazza?" Mischief made his eyes shimmer and he hurried her along. "Did you really think I'd let you move three thousand miles away from me and *not* hire someone to keep an eye on you? Antonio DeMarra is making a mid-life career move. He'll care for my European investments. My accountant will be in Portofino shortly."

Never speechless, she could only stare up at him.

"You really do move like a bolt of lightning! You've only been *you* again for forty-eight hours."

"Forty-one and six minutes," he corrected in an arrogant fashion. "One of the perks of this new existence is the need for very little rest, my love." He held the door and ushered her into the hotel's quaint lobby. In its old-world charm, he looked very much at home.

****

A few minutes later, the beautiful woman he loved stood in a most exquisite room with walls the shade of springtime sky. Etched glass doors led to a balcony that overlooked the sea. He would always treasure her against this backdrop. A vision of splendor in the vivid-yellow dress—the one she wore in his dream. Like a Mediterranean princess, his Guardian was both alluring and sensual. He secretly enjoyed the way Alana glanced at the bed. A crocheted coverlet matched two ecru-white boxes on it, each individually tied with muted-burgundy bows and ribbons. Inquisitiveness brought her closer to study them.

He still couldn't look away. "We have an appointment at sunset. I bought you something special to wear."

"I recognize the boutique... That's a very up-scale name embossed on those boxes. Were they in the car yesterday?"

"I had them delivered here earlier." She reached for them, and his hand traced down her shoulder, whispering, "Not so fast, my love." He led her to the balcony. Standing in late-afternoon sun, he captured her gaze. "I knew I loved you the first night we spoke. I vowed that *my* Guardian would live a long, happy life.

But what I let happen could have destroyed your soul. I'm asking your forgiveness."

A kiss brushed his lips, a soft palm held his cheek. "That night, I could have stopped you, but I didn't. I had to feel you inside of me. I knew in my heart it was wrong. Michael, there's nothing to forgive."

The very old-fashioned move was chivalrous, romantic. He knelt on one knee before her, looking for the smallest doubt on this woman's face. "I love you, Alana. I may not be able to give you everything you want, but I'll die trying. This decision is yours. If you ask it of me, I will leave your life. I will leave your heart."

She stood over him, speechless—almost unable to breathe. Then he heard the murmur, "No demons in my heart." Her hand came to his shoulder. "Imagining my world without you in it is an unbearable thought. I know it in my head and in my heart." Softer, she added, "And if I ask you to stay?"

As eager as he was for a response, he was fully prepared to accept rejection. He took a leap of faith. "I will be the very best man, being, creature—whatever you want to call me, forever and always—for you."

Her smile lit the room. "You stole my line."

His most sensual smirk appeared. "I'm waiting for an answer, darlin'."

"Did you really think it could be anything but yes? My heart only belongs to you." Alana paused. "I-I think you can get up now."

Quickly he stood and kissed her deeply, passionately. Then he left her and walked to the closet saying, "Now you may have the first box." While slipping out of the loafers, Michael changed his shirt, aware that Alana hadn't moved. In a playful way and without turning around, he said, "You're watching me." An audible breath made his soul quicken as his sister's locket slipped into the starched white shirt pocket. Sitting in the chair, he pulled on black socks and classic black shoes. "Only the one closest to me is for now. Go on. Open it."

She tugged at the wide ribbon. The lid came off, and she held up an exquisite dress. "It's the color of the roses! What a stunning neckline and the beadwork...so subtle, delicate." When she held it to her body, she moaned as the fine material brushed her skin. He watched her move to the dresser mirror, and when he came behind her, she jumped with an odd, "Oh my!"

The reaction made him smile, and Michael kissed her neck. "So, darlin', now you can cross stand in the sun, stroll the piazza *and* see his reflection off that list." He didn't let on how their image, together as never before, thrilled him as well.

Her eyes grew wider. "You *heard* that conversation with *Zia*?"

"Guilty as charged."

In the mirror, she searched his face. "Michael, this is, this dress is—"

"One of a kind, just like you." He wrapped his arms around her waist. And when she turned, her heart drummed wildly against his chest, making his deepest regret surface quickly.

"I'm sorry. I can't do anything about certain things."

Steady palms rubbed across his chest as if she had read his thought. "You have a metaphoric heart that beats as bold and strong as mine. I love you so very much."

He kissed her again, and then pulled away with a distinct glimmer in his eye. "Put on the dress, darlin'. We've got someplace to be." Not wasting a second, he unzipped the soft yellow fabric, which fell around her tanned legs like a circle of sunlight. The pale-pink chiffon fluttered over her unclipped hair to hug her curvy frame. After reaching into the suit jacket, he fastened a bracelet of sapphires and diamonds around her wrist. Matching earrings dangled in his other hand. More kisses grazed her soft shoulders as she fastened them to her ears. With a last amazing look at them together in the mirror, he grabbed her hand and started for the door.

"Wait a minute," she squealed. "My sandals aren't—"

"I don't care if you're barefoot, darlin', we've got to go… right now!"

****

As they entered San Giorgio's, she dipped her fingers in holy water and made the sign of the cross asking with the cautious whisper, "What are we doing here?"

"We're crossing things off your list, remember?"

Fading daylight filtered through age-old, stained-glass windows. Firmly, he held her elbow to walk her down the aisle. Hand in hand in front of the altar, just as the sun set, he faced her.

"What I feel for you, my Guardian, reaches the depths of my very being. You have my love throughout eternity. My soul belongs to you alone. I'd walk through the fires of Hell for you. This is my solemn vow."

He fastened his sister's locket around her neck before a respectful kiss to her full lips.

She touched the delicate gold. Her eyes glistened when she met his gaze. "My hopes, my very dreams exist in you, my love. In my own voice, I seal this promise. You alone have this heart. You alone complete me. I choose to love only you throughout eternity. My soul is joined with yours, forever and always. This is my solemn vow."

They clung to each other for a long, peaceful minute. Michael glanced at the sacristy. The compassionate priest had blessed them. Theirs was a sacred union.

****

Hand in hand, the couple strolled through the bustling piazza. Heads turned. People stared. Everyone noticed the attractive man and the serene woman so in love.

They didn't notice. They only saw each other.

Pleasantly at ease, dinner conversation stayed soft, languid. Each moment convinced Alana how this would be as close to 'normal' as she'd ever get. *Celia's right,* she realized, *being honest with myself feels so much better than fighting with destiny.*

The quiet atmosphere changed slightly when they heard the smooth piano and unhurried double bass. Michael led her to the small dance floor. Slowly they swayed to the brushed beat of the music. "This song has always reminded me of you, darlin'." Softly, he whispered the lyrics, "You're everything I hoped for, everything I need. You are so beautiful to me."

When the song ended, she kissed his lips. She knew his desire, and almost breathless with anticipation, she could hardly contain her own.

****

With balcony doors wide open, their room held the evening's comfortable warmth. Resplendent stars in a clear sky were their only light. Standing behind his soul mate, Michael slipped an arm around Alana's waist. His chin dropped to her right shoulder.

"How am I doing in the list department?"

Her hand covered the locket as she studied the moon. "From this day forward, I have no more lists."

In a sensuous way, he asked, "Ready to open my other present?"

As if this were a dream, she sighed, "Yes", and approached the bed. The box had remained untouched during these last, incredible hours. Thick ribbons yielded, and she lifted the lid. A negligee, the same pale pink of the dress came into her hands. Pearl buttons hooked the bodice, making it all the more unique.

Michael waited until she entered the bathroom before he drank the sustenance, which had been placed in their room while at the church. Cool and pure, it satisfied his need. No matter what the circumstances, he vowed to never again drink in front of those he loved. Sitting in the chair beside the dresser, he loosened his tie, undid the stiff collar, and waited for her. When Alana came to him, he pulled her onto his lap with a kiss.

She unknotted his tie. "I've never slept in anything so elegant. Did you bring those sexy, silk pajamas?"

"No," he replied with the slightest smile.

She unbuttoned his shirt and pulled it out of his trousers. Her hands rubbed his shoulders. One by one, she undid the cuffs, slowly sliding the sleeves down his arms. She stood to place it on the bed, and he reveled in the outline of her supple body through clinging satin. But as enticing as this woman was, he didn't hurry his desire.

She knelt, took off his shoes and socks.

Softly laughing, he let his head fall back. Playful kisses fluttered across his chest, and his belt pulled through the loops. When her hand reached for the button at his waist, he guided Alana's arms up and around his neck.

He stood, slid her up and off her feet. Their bodies molded together. Each kiss built upon the last, slow and passionate. Tiny pearl buttons loosened down her breasts. Then, his hand drifted lower to gather the gown. With a sigh, her toes returned to the carpet. He pressed his palm to her warmth. The heat against his hand, the shiver of her body brought a gasp from her that fully aroused him. But gentle dissuasion met her stubbornness when she tugged at his zipper. Placing her arms back around his neck, he whispered, "No, not yet."

Excitement engulfed Alana. Remembering him, preparing for him, bold confidence shot to the stars. She tried again and this time, proudly accomplished the task. Michael's trousers dropped to the floor. She'd drive him to the edge of self-control. He groaned, saying her name in a cautious way. Breathless, she replied, "This isn't all about me, my love."

He pulled her closer still. "I disagree, darlin'. This has always been about you—wanting you, needing you, loving you."

Pushing off his broad chest, she gave a feisty look.

"Are we going to argue? Because you know I always get my way."

He had her waist. He gave a stern "No" as his silk boxers joined the trousers. Indignant shock appeared on his handsome face as he lifted her, firmly stating, "Not this time."

The sizzle in Michael's eyes heightened when her legs wrapped his waist. Gripping his wide shoulders, her brow kissed his. The feel of him through thin satin brought unexpected pleasure so overwhelming that she gasped. Raw need clawed at her. Every part of her body screamed and throbbed, instantly on fire. Tight hands supported her bottom. They held each other's gaze. And when he began a slow stroll to the bed, the friction teased enough to fully coat her without mercy.

Settled on the center of the bed's crocheted coverlet, each row of twisted thread prickled her skin. She wanted to cry out. He nuzzled her neck, took his time unhooking the rest of the pearl buttons on the gown. Frenzy built within as it came off her shoulders to free her hungry body.

Urgent kisses bathed her waist, her hips. With a groan, his lips moved lower and when they came to her core, her eyes shot wide. The rub of his unshaven skin swathed her in unbearable pleasure. This intimacy, this possessive act of physical love, left her breathless. She fisted the palette of pale pink satin draped around her. Then her trembling fingers ran through his wavy hair, the texture tickling like feathers against her burning thighs.

Every hidden spot his tongue tempted brought delirious desire for the ultimate completion. Yearning soared when a throaty moan escaped him. In fragrant sweet surrender, she sighed his name. His hand was wide, splayed across her heart to keep her still as he suckled the hidden bud. She would remember this sensual awakening with love.

Pleasure beckoned and no doubts existed within the woman he loved.

He felt the rolling sensation within Alana and sensed his Guardian would be just as powerful a lover as he. Physical. Mystical. With slow control, he kissed his way up her body. He captured each excited breast as she whimpered. The tip of his erection brushed against her dampness. Untamed, innocent passion within the one woman he loved seemed to demand release. Full of roughness, his mouth devoured hers.

And with care he eased into her. Her back arched, accommodating his path to probe deeper. Silky heat within her tightened around his erection in a way he never expected, and he soared beyond desire. No physical passion had ever felt like this—love, total completion of body and soul. The thumping of her heart so close to his chest brought a new sensual satisfaction.

Her fingers gripped his shoulders, her legs settled on his hips. With energy equal to his, she drew him in to the deepest part of her. The rhythm of two passions became one, and the burst of orgasm lingered timeless as if this act of love could seal two destinies already intertwined.

Her core tightened, begged him not to leave after release. And when he withdrew, she cleaved to him with a sadness he would never understand. Easing to her side, she searched his burning eyes. Nestled against him, he kissed her lips, held her tight.

Passion ignited many times during their first night together. Gentle conversations and playful moments made it a perfect keepsake. In the silent hour before dawn, her eyes fluttered against his chest. She greeted sleep softly saying, "Michael, my love."

His eyes drifted closed as well when he answered, "My Guardian...my love." But his simple response brimmed with more emotion than he thought it ever possible to feel.

Chapter 25

Miles looked up from his notes. As promised, they walked in at nine on the dot. After an affectionate kiss, he heard Michael say, "Rest. I've got some things to do." His daughter's expression read pure love as she closed her bedroom door.

Michael came over, sat across the wide dining room table. Looking like the most satisfied man in the world, Miles wondered if he'd be able to focus on anything but Alana. Such healthy vibrancy was an astonishing thing to see on a creature with over three centuries of history, and it appeared literally impossible to tell him apart from a living man. Taking off his reading glasses, he stared at the only object on the table, a black leather folder. What concerned him more was not being able to predict Michael's reaction to what he now had to say.

"I assume my daughter is comfortable with her decision?" He cleared his throat noting Michael's slight blush—another anomaly.

"You would be correct."

"Would I also be correct in saying you visited San Giorgio's? I had a *very* specific feeling last sunset."

In typical arrogance, Michael leaned back crossing both arms and legs. "I thought that skinny slip of a psychic is supposed to be good at keeping secrets? I sensed a private ceremony was best, the honorable thing to do. Your usual dry smile is barely visible this morning."

"You both have my blessing, you know."

Michael's dark eyes had locked on him. "You cannot disguise such seriousness. Why the worry lines? And don't deny that something's wrong."

He slid the folder across the table. "We have much to discuss. I'm truly sorry for having to do this right at this moment, but the Council has made a request. I've prepared a list of explanations, should you need them."

Michael read The Document of Atonement; examined each phrase, each paragraph, often referring to the researcher's miniscule script in the margins. No questions came as it closed. Miles watched him stand and walk to the window. Michael's hands gripped each side as he shook his head slowly.

"Monsignor wants you to know—whether or not you agree to this, the Council is forever in your debt."

When he turned around, nothing showed. "This is all they're asking? Describe each kill and say I'm sorry."

"Yes."

"I don't believe you. And Alana—does this accept our union?"

"This only addresses your actions as a vampire. It doesn't affect your decision to be with her. When what is asked is completed, you may live out your existence in any way you so choose. Those are Monsignor's exact words. The document will be permanently sealed."

"Your heart rate just soared, Researcher. What aren't you telling me?"

Miles leaned back, gave a weary sigh. "There's another matter—a most urgent one."

"I already know I'm not going to like the reason

for your hesitation." Michael came back to the table, resumed his previous pose, no doubt seeing the tension on his face. "Let's hear it...all of it. I've just been through Hell on earth, so nothing can make me shake in my boots at this point in the game—which isn't over, I'm guessing."

Searching for words was never an issue, smooth speech his signature. Miles knew what had to be said but recalling the love on his daughter's face made this more than difficult. "It's been brought to the Council's attention—" Michael's elbows hit the table. Locked hands supported his chin. "The... the night you were brought to consciousness... Lukas was distraught."

"Alana said my son ran away. But you found him."

"His blood was left. On... on the stone, dark seers became...aware."

Michael's brow tightened. "They *know* my son is in Portofino?"

Never suspecting Michael could pale this quickly, he stated, "The European Triumvirate has enlisted an undead thing to avenge the loss of their North American assets."

"Who? Who's coming?" Through gritted teeth, Michael hissed with anger, "The Hungarian. We met during the Depression. Zoltan's a sadistic bastard. Picking victims was an art form for me. Every kill brimmed with lust. But the Hungarian makes humans insane before he drains them. Is this because of what I did to NWT or because I rid this dimension of three deadly things? Damn it!"

"Zoltan has a diversified need for power. He gambles with The Triumvirate and always wins. He brings them many macabre offerings to show fealty.

Hours ago, my source in Manhattan confirmed Zoltan has disbanded NWT. And for allowing your untimely incineration, he burned Clayton alive."

"But destroying me gets me out of their evil way for good."

"Apparently, your sire had hoped to re-educate you in the killing way."

"Cyril?" Beads of sweat dotted Michael's brow as he stood and leaned across the table. "What's really going on, Miles?"

"Lukas flew into a rage. Only you could make him do that."

With wide eyes, he leaned closer. "They *know* I'm still on this earth?"

"They must assume so... Yes."

"And Lukas—how does my son figure into this?"

His throat rapidly dried. "Zoltan may see your son as a-a suitable candidate... There's no doubt. Lukas has uncommon abilities."

Michael's expression hardened. "Only when it comes to *me!* Lukas has never attacked anyone, any *thing* else!"

"But those skills are there. Lukas summons rage in the blink of an eye. The entire year he hunted you, Guardians couldn't capture him. He tracks. He senses. There are innate traits. Think of the monster they could create. An angel-faced demon—sired by an ancient turner."

Michael's scowl turned murderous. "*Sired?*"

"That's only my educated guess, a logical progression from point A to point B."

"Your educated guesses are too often written in stone. They are *fact*! Siring a child before sexual

287

maturity has never been successful. Madness is instantaneous! Death in a matter of hours!

"But Lukas is different. If he survives, those two would be worshiped as gods. And the mortal world would be introduced to the most dangerous killer *any* innocent might face."

He recognized a father's panic as Michael sank into the chair. "My God… And when were you going to tell me? When that tall, blond son of a bitch came knocking at my door?"

"Monsignor refused to present erroneous information. Now we have facts. Cyril's in Hungary. His Vermont estate burned to the ground. You should also know that six Guardians near Budapest are missing." He paused. "I must with all honesty tell you—there's more."

Michael's trembling hands gripped the sides of the wide table. "Why am I not surprised?"

Beads of sweat dotted his forehead and he drained of all color. Uncontrollable shakes and unfocused eyes…

Something was wrong, but Miles had to continue. "The Council has a plan."

"It better… include… get my son out of Italy… fast…"

Michael swayed as he stood, and Miles reached for him as Thorn and Celia rushed in. Immediately, Thorn had him back in the chair. The empath fought to hold a glass container to Michael's mouth, supporting his head and forcing him to drink. In a hushed tone, Thorn said, "I can read every desperate thought, Champ. Loud music's blaring from his room and the kid hasn't heard a word of this."

Celia brushed away dripping stands of wavy hair from his forehead. "Hey sweetie, we're here. It's okay." She glanced over. "I'm sorry, Dad, but the anxiety levels are way off the charts in both of you."

Michael pushed Thorn's hand off his shoulder, roughly demanding, "Get it out quick, Researcher."

"Lukas will be thoroughly protected at the Georgian Estate. So will all of us. Alana will stay here to mentor Kayla."

"Cesar's daughter…" He appeared more guilty than shocked. "Manhattan's *that* dangerous for everyone involved in this chaos I created? What about Philip and the other informants at NWT?"

"All are safely out of the country. Phillip's in Italy with a new identity. You will reside at San Marco Abby, and he'll be our contact while you write The Document of Atonement."

"Oh God… When does my son leave me?"

"You have a few days. As a father, I cannot accurately express how deeply I feel for you. We'll protect Lukas with our lives. You know this."

"And it's my fault—again! My son will never have an uncomplicated life. *Damn it!*" Terror as well as rage came at Miles when Michael threw the glass container, which shattered against the wall.

Thorn grabbed for him, but Michael stood. "It's a good plan, a smart plan."

"It's the *only* plan," he yelled. Like a caged animal, he paced the room. "Son of a bitch! All I do is screw up his life. There's no safe place for him in this world!"

Celia approached, saying softly, "You got Lukas out of Manhattan."

"No," he shouted, "*You* got Lukas out of

Manhattan! *I* painted a big, red bullseye on him—on everyone! Rosa…the healing Sisters! What about every Georgian who laid their life on the line for me? What about Alana?"

Coming to Celia's side, Alana said, "What *about* Alana? Michael? What's wrong?"

Michael's narrow eyes darted, and he stiffened as she reached for him. Instantly he moved away with his hands up and fingers splayed, and then a furious gaze locked on the black leather folder. "Tell Monsignor Scarlatti I'll sign it as soon as my child is on a plane to England. Whatever your council asks, I'll do. As long as I know *everyone* is safe."

Michael's face never softened as he stormed out. Thorn followed on his heels.

Alana started after him, but Celia held her arm. "Let's sit and talk, Ally. I'll fill you in, okay? Go Dad. He needs you."

Miles was already on his feet.

****

Before Michael could open the door to his home, Thorn grabbed his arm. "Think clearly before you go in there. Just take a moment."

"I'm just as strong as you now so get your hand off of me."

"If you want to throw a couple of punches, that's fine, but you're not seeing it."

"What's 'it', smart ass?"

Pinning him to Rosa's door in less than a second, Thorn's low tone rumbled, "If the kid sees even an *iota* of panic in you, he'll high-tail it out of here. Tell him *you* want him to go to school in England. Discuss your decision from any point of view *other* than panic."

"He's quick. He'll know."

"Only then do you insist! If he runs, you'll never forgive yourself."

Still furious, he looked away. "Leave my son. Leave Alana. Oh God," he bit out ready to scream, running his hands though his hair.

Miles came running down the stairs. "You know how I feel about your son. Laura will welcome him with open arms. And the Institute will tailor a program to fit his abilities. Then, we'll tell him the entire truth. All of us will help him to understand."

Thorn eased a hand off his chest. "I know you're struggling with this 'only' option, but you have to accept it."

Michael glared at both men. "I just got him back, and I don't want to leave him. How do I do this? What do I say?"

"Every good parent must simply leave out certain information to shield his child. Right now, it's imperative."

"A good parent... I don't even know how to *be* a parent."

"You know your son and you're not afraid to be the father he needs."

"I can't do this, Miles."

The researcher nodded. "I'll help in any way I can."

"What if he doesn't buy it?"

Thorn's hand was on the doorknob. "Believe me; he won't get out this way."

Misery clenched Michael's soul, but his son's safety was more important than his discomfort. He walked through the door, counting on the only experienced parent among them to help him explain why he had to send Lukas away.

****

Alana tried to smile when Rosa walked in. "You know, don't you? Did you sense all this, like Celia did?"

"I heard them in my mind...and in the hall. I'm very concerned for you, *cara*. Such devastation after a day of joyful peace comes to your heart."

Even after *Zia's* gentle words, the sadness in Alana's expression didn't change. "What is it with us? Two weeks of Hell, twenty-four hours of happiness, and then its right back to danger and mayhem?"

"Put this aside and focus only on happiness for a moment. What you will do to help him will become clear. Tell us about yesterday."

Drawn to comfort, she said, "I never realized just how many good souls we have on our side. Not my side or his side, but our side." Her fingers clutched Anne Malone's locket. It was a piece of Michael she'd always treasure. "Who'd have known that we share the same first initial? Michael said it's a sign."

"And I agree."

Celia squeezed her hand. "Those vows were perfection—and oooh, the dress!"

The thrill of last night's sunset still filled her soul. "And you both heard our vows, kept us in mindsight, didn't you?"

Zia sat at her other side. "It was witnessed by all of us who care about the two of you. Maybe it wasn't the grand wedding you longed for, but it was blessed all the same."

Curled on the couch, Alana slowly shared many

details of the day…not the night. Afterwards, with clarity her mind began to switch gears.

Rosa whispered, "You were called the fearless Guardian, no?"

"Oh *Zia*," Celia said with confidence, "You should have seen Ally in Manhattan."

"Mystical strength is still with you."

Yes, it most definitely is, Alana realized. "I've read accounts of the Hungarian when he plagued Manhattan in the 1920s. Thank God he preferred Europe over my territory. But Old Cyril's another story altogether—no activity noted during my ten-year mission."

Her great-aunt's face became grave. "He's one of the oldest known sires. Very few have survived, but I must caution you, Alana, he has mastered the Dark Arts as well as his sixth sense."

"Michael can shove a stake through Cyril's heart."

Celia leaned in. "Whoa, Ally… A vampire can't take out its sire, can it, *Zia*?"

"It's highly improbable. Only a creature stronger than Cyril could do that. But Michael can destroy Zoltan."

Celia added, "And being from the same sire, can they sense each other?"

"No, sis," Alana stated. "The beasts-within sense each other."

"Well now, Michael's is gone." Celia smiled. "He's off the vampire radar and that's good."

"But Michael won't be able to locate any of them either," Rosa replied.

"And that's bad," Celia whispered. "Is there something we can do to help?"

Rosa shook her head. "Not that I'm aware of. But

Michael's a true Champion. He's unique in so many ways—especially now."

Determination created a familiar type of energy within her. It morphed into the seedling of a strategic plan. "Then we'll support Michael with Georgian strength. He has our blood in him. That's an unbreakable bond. You said Kayla's coming?"

"This afternoon," Celia confirmed. "Why?"

"She's two years into her mission, very smart and super strong. Suppose Michael had *mystical* back up. How many Guardians in this region, Zia?"

"Perhaps a handful."

"How many ex-Guardians?"

"I have no idea."

"Sister Gabriella helped Michael in his dream."

Celia grinned. "I see where you're going with this, Ally. It's ingenious!"

"Will Monsignor allow Guardians to meet in the room underneath San Giorgio?"

"I don't see why not," her *zia* answered.

"Ask him for a list of local mentors and call them, *Zia*. See if they'll agree to meet with me tomorrow morning."

Resolve strengthened her commitment to the mystical mission that had defined ten years of her life. *If the scum of the earth could scan the minds of every lost soul on this planet to locate a troubled boy, then the good souls of the earth could do them one better.* As if her *zia* heard her thoughts, Rosa nodded. Now totally awake and focused, Alana stood, assuming her adopted sister had just read her as well.

Full of enthusiasm, Celia's thumbs shot up. "I like it, Ally. I like it a lot! Let's gather the wagons and take another shot at evil."

"Want to take a quick ride to Villa Catherine, sis? Gabby should be in this one." Celia's nickname for the stunning nun rolled off her tongue with ease as she thought, *I'm ready to face my destiny, just as strong in spirit as the commanding love of my life.*

****

A handsome man stood in a luxurious hotel suite in Rome, holding the latest cell phone and waiting to hear his manager's sexy voice. The flashy lifestyle that came with being a famous concert pianist also had professional demands. Photos had just arrived by private courier, and one in particular held his full attention.

His manager's sexy voice snapped him back to pressing business. "Hey, beautiful," he said in perfect Italian. "Yes, I'm looking at the restaurant right now. Is this where the piano is? Right on the piazza?"

"The stamp inside it reads 1847. He's sure that Liszt performed on it. That fact alone makes it a priceless antique. You'll be a dear and check it out for him?"

"I hear Portofino is very romantic, yes?" He zeroed in on the picture again—two somewhat familiar women at a table underneath the restaurant's name.

"I booked a balcony room at a five-star hotel, of course. Call when you arrive. He owns both of us, *capisce?*"

"Definitely, beautiful, and you'll join me there?"

"Ugh! I've mounds of work for your tour. Do this for me, Gregor. It is important. I'll transfer you now."

"Yes, yes," he quickly said, bringing the photo closer. "*Ciao, bellisima.*" Her kiss was his reply and five seconds later, a heavily accented voice droned, "Vashkar Enterprises." With full-throttle charm he stated, "This is Gregor Manieri. Please inform Mister Vashkar that I leave for Portofino in an hour."

He pressed the red icon, laid the phone on the Steinway. Like Greg, the piano had a certain, self-centered flare. The photo now stood in front of a new composition he'd been asked to study. Such a mundane task would wait till he had more time. He couldn't stop staring. "This is crazy," he said aloud.

Gregor Manieri's amazing hands mastered the keys, brilliantly fingering the opening measures of Debussy's *Claire de lune.* It had always made Ally Ciminio swoon. Her mother, his first piano teacher, had set him on this glorious path. A smile started, remembering how his first girlfriend would insist he follow the Debussy piece with Stefania's favorite oldie.

His hands switched position and *Blue Moon* filled the air.

Staring at the photo he whispered, "Life was simpler then. Sometimes I think this company owns more than my fingers."

Chapter 26

Called into the living room, Michael glanced at his son. Dressed, in a new blue T-shirt and black sweatpants, the boy looked comfortable in the leather armchair with his legs dangling over one of the arms. He studied every nuance of Miles's seasoned parenting skills. Lukas had all the right questions. Miles answered each with cheerful finesse, and a detailed discussion of the Georgian Institute followed before his son asked to be excused. Very reserved, Lukas had given an easy, dimpled smile before slipping tiny headphones into his ears and walking back into his room.

Unlike his son, he considered total silence a necessity to sort through what Miles had disclosed this morning. Danger could be anywhere. In anyone, whether it was noon or midnight. This building was now their only sanctuary—just like in his dream of survival.

Simply the sound of Cyril's name had terrified him. The beast-within had raged frantic whenever his sire was near. That high-speed signal didn't exist anymore. Then he thought about last night. Only what he now shared with Alana brought peace to his soul. And fully aware of his brusque behavior earlier, he called the local florist as well as the Mercedes dealership.

****

At the noon hour, bright sun spilled through the

arch. Michael walked into the kitchen, reached into the fully-stocked fridge and broke the seal of a fresh container to drink the necessary liquid. The blessed Georgian blood soothed his nerves. A sense of accomplishment grew while fixing his son a healthy sandwich.

Putting a carafe of cold water along with a glass on the table, he called Lukas to the table and then had to call a second time. Placing the plate down, he eyed his son's stroll to the table. His sweats were low, just barely hugging his hips, while his boxers were flush with his waist. The T-shirt they purchased yesterday now had cuts all over it. The short sleeves were gone, and it looked as if inches had been cut off its hem as well because it barely covered his stomach. Bewildered by his son's idea of fashionable dress, he said, "Pull your sweats up to your waist where they belong."

"Later," his son muttered, dragging the dining chair out far enough to flop into it. Lukas picked at the crusty bread then pushed the plate away.

"You cannot be full."

"*Zia* always makes me fresh pasta for lunch."

Aware of the spiteful tone and dig, he replied, "Well, today it's roast beef."

A disinterested shrug came at him and sitting across from his son he waited. And waited. "Aren't you going to at least take one bite?"

"No," with a roll of his eyes came at Michael. He took the plate back to the kitchen. Lukas followed, and he turned to see an icy, narrow glare. Keeping a casual tone and stance, Michael leaned against the counter. "Want to take a ride with me? I have an appointment in Florence."

"Why would I want to go anywhere with *you*?" Lukas's arms locked across his slender chest. "You're a liar."

"Excuse me?"

"I said you fucking lie."

"The other night you said how much you missed going to school. I'll only be a phone call away."

"And y*ou* said you'd never fucking give me away again."

"You'll make friends, and I'll join you as soon—"

"Bullshit! You just don't want a kid around."

Was this anger? Insecurity? Either way, he'd handle it. "That's far from true. Later we'll talk. But right now, stop."

"Stop *what*? Shoving the truth in your face? Some caring father you are. You're good at giving me up and getting all sorry about it after."

"That's not true. And you're not going to make me suffer a decision that has to be made. Later, when you're willing to listen, we'll discuss your classes."

The sneer tightened. "No. You really don't want me around. You're sending me to lame-ass England while you fuck—"

"Watch your mouth."

"You want me and then you don't give a shit. Make up your *fucking* mind."

He quickly switched to a parental tone. "I am *not* giving you up, Lukas. Stop with the language and drop the attitude."

"Stop with the language and drop the attitude," his son mimicked.

"Yeah, and tone down the rudeness."

"This place sucks, you know." Both middle fingers

shot up.

"I don't like to repeat myself."

Instead of another rude remark, Lukas turned and strutted through the arch. The apartment door slammed, and Michael ran after him. Down the stairs, his son had the outside door open, his feet ready to walk. If honesty would stop this behavior, then he'd give the real reason why Lukas had to leave Portofino. Slamming the door shut, he snagged Lukas's arm, and a high-speed right-hook clipped his throat.

And there was the rage. Full-blown and untethered. Undeterred, with an arm around his son's chest, he put up with the flailing until they were back in the security of the apartment. He pointed to the sofa.

His son scoffed, saying, "You don't fucking scare me!"

"No? Well, I should. This temper of yours—"

"Fuck you!"

"Now you're punished. Sit down and stay put." When he turned to close the apartment door, a swift kick to the back of a knee threatened to send him crashing into it. He turned just in time to block a rapid succession of punches. Sharper this time, he warned, "Stop this rage—right now."

"*You* stop! I'm just as strong as you, asshole!"

"Think again, little boy," he stated in a low tone. Of course, the punching didn't stop. Plus, his son landed a few. Then, as if realizing this assault wasn't getting him anywhere, Lukas stepped back with his fists still flexing. They glared at each other for a full five seconds before he said, "Am I getting through to you now?"

"Like I give a shit! I hate you!"

With the next mumbled, "Fuck off," he grabbed his son's boney arm so fast that when let go, Lukas lost balance. "This is me you're dealing with now. If you want to learn this lesson the hard way, then fine. Keep pushing my buttons. You know where you'd end up and —"

With a lunge, his son came at him again. Not really prepared to follow up on his threat, Michael grabbed him and held on tight as his son's head banged against his chest. "Stop it. Calm down," he kept saying. It didn't appear to register. "I'm warning you one last time, little boy."

Nope. That didn't work either. So he hooked his raging son under an arm, pulled out a dining room chair and sat him down firmly. Lukas shot up, and fully astonished by the brazen move, Michael wrestled him into the chair again—only to watch Lukas spring back up and scream another sharp "Fuck off." This time, he snagged him, put a foot on the chair and hauled his son over his knee, hoping it would do the trick. When the raging and cursing continued, he yanked those sweats *all* the way up to his skinny waist and smacked his backside until it thankfully came to a halt. Still gulping air, Lukas's face was a deep shade of red when he stood him up. Removing his foot, he sat his son down again, abruptly lifted the chair to bring it closer to the table as a long rolling "Owww" began.

Keeping his hands next to his son, he hovered over him, more than a little nervous. "Don't move. Don't bolt. Or I'll smack your ass again. Now say it."

Tears dripped down as both elbows hit the table. With his face buried in his arms, Lukas choked out a rapid, "I'm sorry."

He sweated the minutes it took for the sniffling to cease. "There are certain lines a man doesn't cross unless he's ready to face the consequences of his actions. Is this clear now?" Still hiding his face, his son's head jerked a single nod. "Good. Now I'll tell you why you're going to England without me." He picked up a cloth napkin that should have been used after a pleasant lunch and dangled it in front of his son. "Sit up straight, blow your nose and dry your eyes."

Taking the napkin, his son's shoulders drifted back, and he did as he was told. And it took tremendous self-control not to wrap Lukas in a hug. Pulling a chair next to him, Michael began very softly, "I truly don't want to let you go, and I promise this is *not* giving you up." With careful words, he explained the move, but didn't disclose anything about Zoltan. In forty-eight hours, Lukas would be safe. Calm and composed, he answered a bunch of questions about the ugly task that awaited him at San Marco Abbey. Then he waited for it to sink in. "Do you understand what I just told you?"

"It could take years, Dad."

He gave a low groan. "Try thinking in terms of weeks, okay? In order to do this, I have to access what I really don't care to remember. You already know how I feel about writing." The lost expression Lukas wore tugged at his soul, but at least he was making eye-contact. A fair amount of hurt still showed. Michael reached over to gently rub his narrow back.

"Is Alana gonna help you?"

"No, son."

"So then it's like you're leaving her, too?"

"It is. But she can handle it. So can you."

"And after you do this, you'll come for me,"

slipped out very fast.

"Absolutely. Everyone really cares about you. And by the way, Thorn has my permission to keep you in line. Are you getting this picture?"

"Yeah," he mumbled with a shrug.

"I hope I never have to punish you like that again. But if you crank up into a rage —"

"It just comes out. I mean, I can't control it."

"After what just happened, you'd better learn how to control it because *your* father has no problem with a hands-on approach."

Lukas shifted with a wince. "I know. I'm really sorry."

"Good. So can we move on now?" He stood, leaned against the table and cleared his throat. "I have an appointment in Florence. How about you and me— cruising down the highway in the Mercedes."

"Wait... You have a Mercedes?"

Those wide, deep-blue eyes made him grin. "With retractable sunroof and a sound system to die for. Go change into something more presentable. And then we'll go." As his son left the table, Michael closed his eyes and let out a sigh. What he just saw in his son had terrified him. Lots of love, a firm hand, and endless patience, he thought. This parenting thing was a new kind of Hell.

****

Celia drove to Siena, and Alana wondered why she'd been assigned direction-giver. She didn't question Gabby's request to drive back to Portofino, the nun's skill behind the wheel fully revealed in Michael's dream. Gabby didn't take the kind of chances she took, but no one suspected the small red car could maneuver like it did… Or go this fast. As they flew down the empty highway, she filled her in on Zoltan.

Once home, Celia went to meet Miles at *Zia Rosa's*. Gabby stayed with her on the third floor. Both ex-Guardians smiled as they came into the dining room. A stunning bouquet of pale-pink roses stood alone on an empty table. She sighed and opened the card, which had a single word: *"Tonight."*

Instantly, Gabby's face buried in the robust flowers. "Oh these are so fragrant. Some roses don't have that smell today. Congrats, Ally. Love has certainly put everything into perspective."

"Does it show?"

"The vibes are humming a rare form of harmony today. Your souls were joined before you took that leap of faith yesterday."

This new mission takes precedence over the green-eyed monster, she thought. And in a way, she doubted it still existed. "Thanks for everything you did for him—for me."

"It was destined." Both warriors kicked off their sandals. Facing each other, their legs dangled over the leather armchairs. "Okay, so evil's coming. What's the plan?" Alana laid it out and then Gabby added a few more facts about the Summoned Six of Europe, Zoltan's playmates. Focused and all-business, the nun said afterward, "You've got some sound reasons behind each scenario. I like the way you think, Guardian."

"We have to do this, Gabby. Michael *was* there for me every time I needed him."

"And this time we'll all be there…for him. An army of innocents backing up a beyond dead being—it'll be another first. Definitely count me in."

****

Buttoning his shirt, Michael followed Doctor Chamberlain out of the private examination room attached to his office. The specialist sat behind a cleared desk. "Your color is amazing, not a scar left. Are you keeping the five o'clock shadow? Because it makes you look older…by years, not centuries."

The comment made him smirk. "Not sure… Listen, Miles and I had the conversation."

Chamberlain instantly frowned. "Good old Zoltan. That's one sadistic son of a bitch. I've autopsied many kills; seen some horrific things. But what he does before he drains a victim turns my stomach. It's a brutal signature kill."

"He needs to be taught a permanent lesson."

"Are you seriously considering another impossible mission? Leave this to Guardians."

His expression turned to ice. "Not while my son's the target. No. This vamp goes down. I'll dust both with one stake."

Leaning forward, Chamberlain repeated, "*Both*? Cyril's on a much higher level of evil than Zoltan. Certain sires can't be killed. Guardians have tried and died."

"Everyone said the same thing about the three clowns whose miserable, corporeal existence I ended. Those portals in North America are still closed, right?"

"Cyril is different."

"My sire wants my son. *It's* not going to get him. *It* has to go through me, and that's not going to happen. After all the Georgian blood I've ingested, who knows what I'm truly capable of?" He started to scowl. "I'm guessing Zoltan will have help."

"You know this for a fact?"

"I'll bet my reflection on it. He'll utilize the European Summoned Six. But my son and my Guardian are two humans Zoltan will *not* be sinking his teeth into—not while I exist. I'll let you know how it goes."

They both stood. Chamberlain walked him down the sterile hall where Lukas leaned against the wall. As they approached, his son pulled out his earphones and put down a recent scientific journal. Chamberlain shook his son's hand, and Michael saw the scientist wince while saying, "That's the grip of a seasoned Guardian." Sheer adoration and a significant dose of fatherly pride settled on Michael's face. "We didn't get a chance to talk the other day."

"Thanks for helping my dad."

The respectful tone impressed him, and polite openness replaced the guarded looks Miles had described.

"You're very welcome. He's a Champion, and you're a very special young man. Take care of each other." The specialist then shook his hand as well. "And you, Michael, are definitely in a league of your own."

As they left the research facility, he narrowed his wide strides for Lukas. Glancing up at the third-floor office window, Michael caught Chamberlain studying them. He gave a nod and continued to the car with his son at his side.

****

In spite of the disastrous way the afternoon began, father and son had candidly talked about many things during the drive home. As they approached Portofino, new questions began. "What you did in the church,

306

does that mean the two of you are, like, married now? Should I call her Mom?"

This one absolutely made him smile. "You'll have to discuss that with her."

"So, are you twenty-seven…or three hundred and forty-three? I mean, you're like either too young to be my father or way ancient."

Briefly, he glanced at his son. "I've walked this earth for a long, long time, and even though my body doesn't age, my mind has centuries of knowledge stored, except when it comes to certain things." Like being a parent, he thought. "I may look young, but I have years on the oldest living individual that calls himself Dad. Can we lose the inquisition now?" To his relief, Lukas actually stopped. Again fiddling with the radio, his son settled on what he didn't consider music. And while parking the car, he discovered the *real* reason for headphones and an iPod.

****

In the hall, Michael read Alana's note wedged by the doorknob. "We've been invited to *Zia's* for dinner tonight."

With a narrow stare, Lukas crooked his head. "Why is Sister Gabby back without Sister Maggie? And there's a female, not much older than me. Who's the girl, Dad?"

He dropped the car key on the coffee table. "I've had enough questions to last a lifetime. When we go over there later, you can ask her yourself."

His son shrugged, went into his room. Within seconds, the same music blared. Tuning it out, Michael scanned the quiet backstreet at the window. Every heightened sense would kick into high gear at nightfall.

As he came back into the small living room, Thorn entered. "Relax. I've a good poker face. Lukas won't detect the slightest nerve-wracking twitch."

"Decline the invite," Thorn whispered. With a bothered expression, the empath sank into an armchair.

"Why? Then I'll get more questions. I answered at least a hundred in the car."

"He'll pick something up. The kid's smart."

"Well then what the hell am I going to do? I can't say I'm not worried."

"How about a boy's night out in Pisa or La Spezia? We take a slow ride in that fancy car; find some real Italian pizza, maybe a movie with sub-titles. Anything but dinner across the hall and the possibility he catches wind of what's coming."

Full of frustration, Michael sank onto the couch's wide arm. "I can't get him out of Italy fast enough. Look, Lukas can't read minds." He caught Thorn's eye. "But Celia reads *his*. She'd let me know if he suspects anything."

"You mean like scratch her nose for 'no' or tug an earring for 'yes'?" Thorn straightened a trouser cuff.

"You only do that when you're nervous."

"This is dicey, Champ. Let me be the first to admit how we gave you the wrong advice. Tell Lukas the whole truth. All of it."

"No. I'm sure you caught what happened here before. I swear to God, what I saw in my son bothered me as much as what I had to do to stop his rage. He already knows more than he should. I'll take my chances. We'll leave *Zia's* early. Celia can make him— I don't know, maybe feel queasy. Then he'll crawl in bed, fall asleep, and *not* hear the discussion."

"And I'll stay with him." One bushy eyebrow rose. "It could work. I'm getting used to this babysitting thing—first you, now him. It seems I do it very well."

"I owe you for that, by the way. We haven't had a chance to talk."

"Yeah, yeah, it'll come—sooner or later. Let him have a good dinner, though. That'll be enough time for his curiosity to be satisfied, and he won't be starving anymore."

"What do you mean—starving?"

Thorn stood with a serious grin. "He barely touched the sandwich. But you got his undivided attention. I told you he could be a spitfire."

He shook his head, gave a sigh. "I *really* didn't want to do that. Of course, I tempered my hand."

"Celia says he's still sore. Maybe self-healing doesn't happen when you need to teach him a life-lesson. Like in your dream of survival."

"Sore, huh? Now that *is* interesting. Celia's sure?"

Thorn's eyes stayed wide as he nodded. "But get some food into him."

"I didn't even realize—I should have. About the other matter—"

"We'll work on it," Thorn said as he left.

****

At dinner, Alana insisted Lukas sit between her and Michael. Not a care or worry showed on anyone's face. Genuine affection had developed between the two people he loved.

Kayla's sweet nature charmed his son, Gabby made him blush, and *Zia* smothered him with a grandmother's affection—before he left with Thorn. The gentle empath loudly praised Celia's video choices as he walked Lukas across the hall.

Michael's winning smiled sailed across to Celia. "Just add that to my tab, Celia B. But did it have to be *Lethal Weapon*? Whatever happened to light, romantic comedies?"

"Trust me on this one," Celia replied with a sneaky grin. "That boy will relate! He'll be so hooked on the action that he won't hear a word."

Before the discussion started, Alana offered to clear the table. Michael, who appeared too edgy to sit, brought the plates to *Zia's* kitchen. "I've missed you, my love," he whispered as she loaded the dishwasher. "Your place or mine?"

He handed her a rinsed dish. A familiar flutter tugged at her soul, made her smile. "Your bedroom's under the den. I think it's safer, unless of course Lukas—" Their hands touched. She gazed into his dreamy brown eyes.

Lightly kissing her lips, he gave a devilish smirk, "Celia's taking care of it."

"Neat trick," she whispered. "I'm assuming he won't hear the discussion, either? And after the movies, he'll fall right asleep? Oooh, the many talents of our Celia B… We owe her big-time." Michael's smirk turned very sexy.

****

When they came back to the dining room, every face lost its happy expression. Voices became hushed. Michael and Miles sat at opposite ends of the table. Alana stayed next to her soulmate, simply content to be near him after a full day apart.

Her father's face looked full of disgust. "Eight

drained Guardians' bodies were found on the outskirts of Budapest today. One in Paris, three in Rome, and five unaccounted for in Florence."

"Florence? Why so many?" Alana asked.

Michael mumbled, "That's another story for another day."

"Zoltan has moved quickly."

"Zoltan has declared war." Michael countered with equal disgust.

"I've heard from four Guardians and one ex-Guardian. We're meeting tomorrow morning. After the info swap, I'll have a tight strategy in place. We'll be ready."

"No demony vibes around the seaport yet," Celia confirmed. "But as soon as they're detected by any of us in the good-soul psychic community, I'll let you know."

"The flight from La Spezia to Gatwick is cleared for the day after tomorrow," Cesar said. "There's a forensics conference in London, which is Medico's cover."

Michael shook his head. "That's a day too long. What about leaving earlier?"

"Impossible. Air traffic is tightly controlled because of terrorist threats. British authorities are touchy when it comes to abrupt changes in flight-plans. We can't involve government agencies in our work, and land travel is far too risky."

"I owe you... For all you've done, Cesar. I'll watch out for your daughter. No harm will come her way in this," Michael added with respect.

Leaning close to Cesar, Kayla whispered, "I can take care of myself, Papa. And I can be very quick with stake or silver sword, Michael." The young Guardian grabbed her long hair and twisted it over one shoulder. Draping down to her waist, it resembled a black mantilla. The bubbly smile she gave contradicted a humble personality.

To Alana's surprise, a very parental expression appeared on Michael's face as he said, "I know what you can do. But you'll have to think twice as fast and not be the initiator. The vampires Zoltan will use aren't your normal, run-of-the-mill variety. You've never gone up against anything like them in Manhattan. These are the turners, the vicious ones. The Summoned Six are fully juiced by dark magic. They don't run when you show them a stake. You'll strike fast and have only one chance." He turned to Cesar. "Are you sure you want her in this one, *Senor*? I've seen your daughter in action, but this is your call."

Cesar placed a hand over Kayla's. "She's gifted, Michael, and she accepts the risks that come with her mission."

"You don't have to do this, Kayla. You know that," Michael added in a gentle tone.

Liquid-black eyes, full of determination, captured Alana's attention. He knows that look, she thought. I had the same one at eighteen.

Kayla stated, "It's an honor to fight along-side the Champion and his Guardian."

"So now we wait?" Gabby asked Alana from across the table.

"And plan from every angle." Seeing Michael's expression change, Alana asked, "What's wrong?"

"I *can* do this myself. To place so many Guardians in danger—"

"Nope." She knew preparation and execution. She had lived it for ten years. "Zoltan and his satanic six are taking out Guardians. That's my department. When these killing machines go down, we'll be right there with you, buddy, doing the staking."

Michael fell silent, either from her stubbornness or his dislike of the word "buddy".

Gabby sat back. "It's true, Malone. They started it. We finish it. The word is out, Ally. More Guardians will show."

"*Seasoned* Guardians, Sister," he said. "No yearlings. They'll be drained before we can cover their necks. I don't want to be the reason for you losing one sixteen-year-old who overestimates his or her power. Can we agree upon that point?"

Miles nodded once. "Michael's right. This isn't a training exercise. Shall I handle the mentors, honey?"

"Thanks, Dad. And Gabby takes charge of training. This plan will be perfectly solid. Count on it." After certain critical issues had been resolved, Rosa brought a fresh pot of perked coffee to the table. Then she outlined one specific strategy. Her Guardian skills peaked, more confident than she'd ever felt before.

****

In his bedroom, Alana tried to appear relaxed in the comfy Queen Anne chair, but her fingernails tapped against the arms in a fast, furious rhythm. "There's no way in hell I'm changing my mind," she stated in an even tone as Michael slipped off the leather loafers.

"I want you to consider this carefully, darlin'."

"Do not *darlin'* me right now. That won't do it. I suggest we table this discussion."

As he unbuttoned his shirt, those intense, espresso

313

eyes leveled at her. He sat across from her on the sleigh bed. "If that's what you want, I'll comply. But we will continue this tomorrow morning over breakfast—here in my bed." He gave a sensual smirk. Her head drifted back and a slow, satisfied grin began. The dark silk shirt fluttered to the floor, and he leaned back on his elbows. "The first time I saw you in that chair, I was a seventeenth century man. I couldn't take my eyes off you."

An adoring sigh escaped. "Oooh… He was such a sweetie."

"I was never sweet. Why does everyone use that word?" His insulted glare snagged her. "I specifically remember my lady lying right here on this very spot ready to pounce, to have her way—while giving me passionate kisses."

"I deny that accusation! That's not how *I* remember it. *You* begged me to sit on the bed. *You* pulled me over your beaten body and held me down! Those *sweet,* innocent hands immediately roamed." His tease made her want him more than ever. She wouldn't admit to uncontrolled desire then. And right now? She had just as hard a time—when he smiled.

One eyebrow arched and his expression dripped sensuality. "You're a deeper shade of pink than the roses I sent today, my love."

"See? What a *sweet, sweet* thing to do!"

"I recall how a certain zipper went down and up. The naiveté of your demonstration turned me on." A hand reached out. Gracefully, she took it, this time settling next to him—*fully* prepared to have her way with him. "There, that's better," he said in a low, sure tone.

His arm stretched back to turn off the lamp on the nightstand. In the moonlight, his kisses made her breathless. The slow way he removed every piece of clothing from her flushed body, the way his fingers teased. As she tugged off his jeans, the feel of his warm skin made her blood sizzle. Suddenly brazen, she had him on his back and straddled. Lacing their fingers together, slow nibbles traced down his chest to his waist.

"I'm a quick study." She loved the shock on his face, and each deep groan gave her chills. "I follow my instincts."

"I never…doubted it…for a second." Her tongue traced his erection in a bold, new exploration. It had a definitive affect. "I want you right now, darlin'."

The gruff command made her quiver. In a slow, seductive way, her lips left him to whisper, "You are such a *sweet, sweet* man."

Suddenly, she was pulled up and under him. The calculated move had been swift. "Shall I prove how very wrong you are?" His roughness revved her need even higher.

She drowned in his passion, craving every deep thrust. Bursting with love, her heart as well as her soul yearned to stay joined with him forever. The sadness which claimed a woman's body when her lover left that hidden place would always be there.

We both feel this love, she realized, so powerful together—in more ways than one.

Chapter 27

"Where's Ally?" Lukas asked as he came to the breakfast table.

The forlorn expression had an odd sensation of guilt jab at Michael's soul like a thousand needles. "She has a meeting. The morning is all yours, little boy."

Thorn walked through the open door and sat across from Lukas. "Ah, breakfast. I smelled it in the hall." Before Michael could offer, he helped himself to fresh melon and French toast. "So what's on today's agenda, Boss?"

Michael eyed his son. "I'm so glad you could join us, Empath."

Thorn grinned. "Only if I get to play the demony attacker."

Full of curiosity, Lukas studied Michael's easy smirk. "I'll clear the table, and then you do your thing with the furniture."

The dream of survival had given him the idea. He would be able to see exactly what his son could do. After breakfast, and as he had done just days ago, Thorn turned the living room into an open workout space. Lukas, already dressed in sweats that came up to his waist, the way they were meant to be worn, happily played victim-with-a-twist.

****

It was already noon. Hours of sparring, and he hadn't broken a sweat. Michael watched his son outmaneuver the empath every time. "You're accurate and sure-footed. If Thorn were a vampire, he'd be dust and bits of bone right now. You ducked out of that hold pretty quick."

Beaming proud and breathing hard, Lukas had sprawled on the floor, huffing out, "I told you... I could... take care of myself."

"Miles will allow you to train with Guardians at the estate. I'll see to it," he assured.

His son strutted across the room. A few minutes later the shower started. They reset the room, and Thorn sat heavily in a chair as he walked to the window with a worried look.

"I'm catching huge, jittery thoughts."

"If Zoltan gets to him, I'll lose my boy. Twenty-four hours—that's all I ask."

"I'm not seeing that last part. Neither is Celia."

He approached with a cold stare. "Look harder. God knows, you're not a fighter. He'd better be able to defend himself...if I'm not around to protect him."

Thorn's massive shoulders slowly shrugged. "You know my gifts. Battle-smart isn't one of them. I'll lay down my life for the kid, but combat isn't part of the package. My heart's not in it. I'm a gentle soul."

Sinking onto the couch, he stretched out his legs, resting them on the coffee table. "You could've fooled me a couple of days ago."

"That's what I was put here to do." Wiping his brow, Thorn's expression softened. "Maybe Helena's giving me a second chance at happiness."

The statement had him curious. Knowing Lukas couldn't hear them, he relaxed enough to ask, "Because you've met Celia?"

"Because I've *known* Celia…her soul, at least. Suppose I say she was my connection to you…long before we met." A shy smile started. "Threw you a bit, didn't it?"

"Well that's an understatement. I'm listening."

"The winter of 1890 was a mild one."

"I remember it well."

"So do I."

Michael's eyes narrowed. "You have memories of all your go-rounds on this earth?"

Thorn nodded, settled deep in the armchair. "I couldn't serve your soul if I didn't know mine, and I mean all of it—good, not so good, and disastrous mistakes. Different body…same soul, and many go-rounds, as you so easily put it. I only saw you once. It was enough."

"And I'm suddenly feeling more guilt. December 1890—go on."

"In my last life, I was a professor of anatomy in Manhattan. The Dean forced a graduate assistant on me. Her name was Lydia. At thirty-five, I was a confirmed bachelor—withdrawn and comfortable with the laboratory cadavers. I balked, but I took Lydia on… And fell madly in love. I had found my soulmate."

"Celia's soul?"

"One and the same. We were careful at school, leaving cryptic notes to meet where no gentleman or fine lady would be seen. Very daring and asking for trouble." Thorn gave a distant sigh. "Examination papers were piled high on my desk. I chose to ignore Lydia's note and stay to grade papers. Snow was falling when I finally made it to our secret rendezvous. The lamplight was out by the passageway."

With dread, he asked, "Would I know this particular passageway?"

"Uh-huh… Christ, my heart pumped so hard I thought, so here's the heart attack. You leaned against the factory wall less than ten feet away. The amber glow in your eyes faded and you turned up your coat collar, totally oblivious to the cowardly man glued to that lamppost. I stared at the alley for God knows how long, *too* long. You didn't drain her, you see. Immediate medical care, which I was fully capable of giving, would've saved her life. It was me who let Lydia's precious life slip away." Thorn shook his head and paused. "I carried her body through the deserted streets to the medical building. Stoked the coal furnace in the basement and watched her burn. At dawn, I hung myself. My soul went straight to the eternal fires."

All he could do was whisper, "Oh God, Thorn."

"Remember your dream of survival? You were right. Helena *did* yank my soul out of Hell after a century. This shell of a human lay alone in the same passageway taking a last breath. Its soul had already escaped. Helena gave mine another chance, God gifted me with mystical abilities and a new Servant of Souls was born. When I met Celia, my soul knew hers. You're my mission, but she's my salvation. This time, I'll get it right."

"Seven years ago, did she recognize you…your soul?"

"My Celia has enormous skills." Thorn's smile stayed sad as he massaged his temples. "Don't ask if you and Alana will be together forever. I don't read destinies. Your souls are much younger than ours. As for Rosa and Mother Anne, well, now you're talking

Old Ones on earth."

The revelation stunned and stung at the same time. "So many lives I took. Hundreds of deaths. Countless families I've destroyed. Lukas is right. It'll take years to complete The Document of Atonement. Will Alana—"

"Of *course* she'll wait. You are soulmates. You got that part right in your fantasy, so don't screw it up," Thorn warned.

****

In her mind's eye, Celia saw her sister's victory. The turnout far surpassed what Ally had imagined. Chairs cluttered the room beneath the church. Mentors. Guardians. Ex-Guardians. Gabby was screening them all, turning newbies away without hesitation before Ally interviewed each one. Sitting in the back corner, Dad sifted through piles of Georgian documents about Europe's Summoned Six, keeping Ally in view with full fatherly pride.

Celia sat at the antique secretary in the living room viewing available real estate records on her sister's computer. Three empty villas intrigued her. One, midway up the mountain, surrounded by overgrowth. *Is it me or does something here look familiar? Where are you, sweetie? I need you.* It took longer than expected for Thorn to come upstairs. His gentle eyes appeared dull. "Need an aspirin?" she whispered.

"I don't think an entire bottle will get rid of this headache. What did you find?"

She pointed to the screen. "Why do I keep coming back to this one?"

He didn't answer, and she sensed him shielding his every thought. It rarely happened. *So do migraines,* she realized.

Then a slow groan began. "Oh, dear God. Click on the floor plan. Marble foyer, kitchen with a servant's room on the left, and a back door... this is from Michael's dream." A lower groan followed. "Check out the basement's wine cellar. Look... the stone room. I wish this one was already swallowed by Hell," he added in a bitter way.

****

Early afternoon, the best time to stroll the piazza, Alana thought as she hurried to meet Michael at Vito's restaurant. Happy to be in sunshine after such a tense morning, she scanned the crowds but didn't see him. And it took a few minutes to notice the man smiling at her from her favorite outdoor table. The fact that he looked somewhat familiar interested her. Well-dressed, suave and handsome, he leaned back in his chair while scrutinizing her, and springing up he called out with a wave, "Alana? Ally Ciminio? Is it really you?"

Her eyes grew wide, her smile wider. Memories of loving parents and a happy childhood shimmered to life. *His voice is deeper...sexier, but seeing him takes me back to another place and time.* She ran straight to him. "Greg? Greg! What are you doing here!?"

Leaning down, he kissed her on the lips, sat her close beside him. Suddenly, Greg Manners was holding her hand! "I could ask you the same thing." His easy laugh made her giggle. "It had to be you... Those pretty hazel eyes still as bright as the night we played our final, gut-wrenching rendition of *Heart and Soul*." He placed one hand dramatically over his heart. "Remember the night before my family moved to Jersey? The two of us slaughtered every duet on Miss

Stefania's old baby grand."

Everything about Greg is as perfect as I remember! And those long fingers...Mom called them piano hands... "My parents went upstairs to help your parents with the move."

"We played on and on until they came back down. You had tears in your eyes. Admit it."

He put an arm around her and a blush flooded her cheeks. "I had such a thing for you, but so did every girl on the block."

Greg's smile turned into a sensual smirk which resembled Michael's, which made her voice unexpectedly hard to find. He held her hand like he didn't want to *ever* let go! "W-what are you doing in Portofino?"

"I'm checking out something before the tour starts."

"The tour?" Perfectly manicured fingernails...with a buffed coat of clear polish? Well that was different, but his laugh, as always, sounded infectious, inviting.

"I'm a concert pianist. Why? Did you think I fell in with some racy, avant-garde bohemians after moving across the Hudson River?"

"What? No! I mean, I...well you know what I mean." *His* hazel eyes mesmerized her.

I feel fifteen again, an innocent time before I said yes to my mission...before I met—

Greg's thumb stroked the back of her hand. "You know, I told everyone at my school how you were my girl. What is it about you that still makes me smile?"

The passion in his eyes matched the shock in hers. He charmed so easily that she couldn't look away. "Yeah, right... Tell the truth! I was just one of a dozen gawking groupies with a gigantic crush on the most popular boy on the block."

"You haven't told me what you're doing in Portofino."

"Oh… I live here," she said with the immediate hope that he wouldn't question further.

"A perfect backdrop for a radiant woman… You look amazing!"

Is he giving me the sexy once-over look? She tried to take her hand back, but her arm wasn't working. His touch felt sensual…*very* sensual.

"So tell me, how's my favorite piano teacher? Your mom started my amazing career." With an arrogant lean back in his chair, he looked like he was memorizing every detail of her. "I owe Miss Stefania everything."

She sobered in an instant and managed to pull her hand away. Her bright smile faded.

"Oh… you-you don't know, I mean, you couldn't, right? Both my parents died—almost ten years ago." More visions of her mother seemed real enough to touch. The happy expression on his chiseled face turned sympathetic. Greg's soulful straight-from-the-heart look melted her.

"I'm so sorry, Ally." He took her hand—again. "I feel like a fool. I can't even imagine what that must have been like for you."

"It was a long time ago, and I had lots of help from Celia B's family."

Greg looked about to ask a question, and then stopped. First Alana smiled, but awkward silence descended for long, painful seconds. She blinked, sure that her mother stood right behind him, smiling at them.

"How about dinner tonight? We can catch up."

The glimmer in Greg's eyes and everything about him said comfort. Stronger now, Stefania's melodic laugh rang around Alana. "I-I've interrupted your dessert. Isn't the truffle heavenly?"

"Chocolate *anything* has always been my favorite…yours, too. Remember the home-made chocolate place between our parents' stores?" They both laughed at the same time. "Seriously, Ally, let's have dinner here at seven. I insist."

She opened her mouth, but no words came out. Torturous seconds passed. "Sure… But I-I'm with someone. As a matter of fact, he's supposed to meet me—"

"Better late than never," Michael said in a strange tone.

They stood face to face. Two gorgeous men…same height, same broad shoulders, equal intensity in two sets of determined eyes. *Both passionate, and neither is saying a word.* Her heart skipped a beat.

****

Annoyed with Michael's tone, Alana frowned as he followed her down the church's stone steps. "It's only dinner."

"I don't like him." He didn't sound arrogant. He sounded murderous. At the bottom of the stairs, another glare came at her. "Night time's not the right time to be out on the street. You *know* that, my Guardian. Tell him to swing back next year. There's too much going on. Do we agree?"

Even though he was right about the timing, she ignored him. Too many anxious faces stared at them, and she put Greg out of mind.

With a slow scan of the room, he mumbled,

"They're young."

"They're powerful," she countered. "Gabby confirmed ten veterans and twenty-four active Guardians and mentors." With a tight smile, she added, "You have the floor, my love."

He'd remember every face. Young or old. Male or female. To say the group gaped with curiosity would be an understatement. Everyone sized him up. The Champion, a *vampire,* had closed portals. Destroyed three ageless sorcerers! They looked eager to go up against the unknown.

"My name is Michael Malone," he began in a not-so-friendly way. "I'm here to tell you that everyone in this room is fair game once this begins."

Except for his serious voice, you didn't hear a sound in the room.

****

A few minutes after seven and oddly annoyed, yet determined to keep the dinner date, Alana quipped, "I'm already late," to Michael's disturbed reflection in the mirror.

Then blocking the door to her bedroom, he demanded, "Call the restaurant. Cancel."

The drab blouse buttoned up to her neck. A shapeless skirt met her ankles. The unflattering outfit had been his ridiculous request, but she complied without a fight—refusing to admit how now she felt more than awkward about meeting Greg. Going to him, she played with the collar of his plum-colored shirt. Although defiant, she rested her head against his broad chest for a different approach.

"Guardians are playing tourists in the piazza, and I'm sure that you'll be watching Greg's every move.

You know I'm right. You're that kind of individual." She kissed his tense chin. It had been years since the no-nonsense expression was meant for her. "Which dark corner will you lurk in? Right or left?"

"Celia and Thorn agree. This is too unnerving to be a coincidence. Should I mention how he has distracted your focus? I listened with an open mind about concert tour crap, but this is no random occurrence."

"You have no proof."

"Someone suddenly appears thousands of miles away from where you last saw him—after so many years? Someone you know nothing about?" His kiss was rough. The unflattering skirt hitched up and a planned brush of his hand met her inner-thigh. "It's always a telling sign to be fashionably late."

Alana's eyebrow arched at his gruffness, but the cool tone had a sensual edge, enough to make her tingle. Barely able to speak, she repeated, "A telling sign?"

"It's telling him you are mine." His palm found the very core of her warmth. Instantly, her body responded.

He maneuvered her to the wall; shut the bedroom door in the process. The matronly blouse came unbuttoned and this time, she glared. "You are not. Going. To win. This round."

"Don't. Go." His command sounded more like a mellow plea as his fingers feathered beneath her lace panties.

It set her on fire, and she turned away denying a need as great as his. "I have to. I don't know why, but I have to." *Mom standing behind Greg at the piano in our house… She's calling me over.* She stopped herself from reaching out and blinked. When she refocused, fury showed in his eyes. The set of his jaw tense. His hand dropped. The skirt snagged her ankles. She tucked the blouse into its elastic waist while he angrily buttoned every single button on her blouse.

Then, without a word, he walked out of the room.

The knot in her gut tightened. Ignoring it, she left her home.

****

Very annoyed, Michael strode into his dining room. At the table, Celia read the screen of her father's laptop. "Did you find anything yet?"

"Yada, yada, yada, Paris Conservatory… A slew of scholastic achievements, Summa Cum Laude graduate, Doctorate in Piano Performance. Blah, blah, blah, studio work, public appearances, concerts in Europe… Pages of reviews, awards, praises about Greg Manners a.k.a. Gregor Manieri's interpretations of Romantic Era piano pieces. He's exactly who he says he is."

Lying on the couch, Thorn rubbed his face. "Seems pretty odd how old Greg never played Carnegie Hall, doesn't it? I mean, he grew up in Manhattan."

"There aren't *any* appearances in the states—ever," she confirmed.

Pacing the small space, he felt absolutely trapped. "What about family?"

"There's not much. Parents still live in Franklin Lakes. His brothers didn't stay close. One's saving icebergs in Alaska; the other's a yoga instructor in Michigan. No marriages, kids, sex scandals with smut or kinky affiliations whatsoever." She looked at him. "Ally left ten minutes ago, and no offense, sweetie, but you're making me crazy."

"Keep googling! Record label, management firm,

parking tickets, I mean the guy has to have these, right?"

"The record label is reputable. The management team is—" Celia sat up with a breathy, "Whoa." Over her shoulder, he scanned last month's article in *International Times Online.*

"Bingo. Does the name ring alarm bells with you, too?"

Thorn sat up, calling though the arch, "Share the info, dearest."

"Gregor Manieri, concert pianist of Parisian fame, was sighted at the opening of *Madame Butterfly* at the Paris Opera House with a stunning Roman beauty on his arm. When asked about their reported romance, he offered, "My manager is more than a lover. Aren't you, beautiful?" Michael, look at her!"

He'd kill this man with his bare hands if Alana was harmed in any way. Yet another connection to his dream of survival, thanks to Helena. "Anyone up for dinner on the piazza," he hissed, already striding out of his home with Celia and Thorn close on his heels.

****

From across the hall, Lukas heard his father's footsteps. Politely, he asked *Zia* Rosa and Miles if he could go get his iPod from his room. The hum of the laptop lured him to the table. Hitting the spacebar brought its dark screen back to a news article.

After a quick scan, he gave a disinterested shrug. The pianist could've been world famous, but he still wouldn't know him. He had a different definition of "good" music. But he stared at a name under the photograph.

"That's weird. Loretta, Conchetta, gotta-get-a—"

he rapped with syncopated beats and very bothered. In the next panicked second, he sprinted upstairs and opened the dream journal to a specific scene Celia had mentioned. "Clayton's European counterpart, Valetta Russo, drove a spiked heel into the man's throat." He muttered with a cold glare, "Gregor Manieri. So who the hell are you?"

Furious, he jumped the staircase and rushed back to read the whole article.

"What are you doing?"

Hearing Miles's voice, he shot up. "Yeah... uh, Celia left it on, and I was just—" Innocent, but insistent, he asked, "Mister B, you ever heard of Gregor Manieri?"

"His real name is Greg Manners, an old friend of Alana's who's in Portofino. Why? Lukas, tell me—"

"Where's Dad?"

"There's a rather odd urgency to your question."

"Where did Dad go?"

"Suppose you tell me why you need to know... The truth, please."

"This guy's manager—her name's Valetta Russo."

Lukas saw total shock as Miles whispered, "Good Lord! If Michael knows, then Alana's safe."

"Why?"

"She's having dinner with him." Miles grabbed his arm. "Don't even *think* about going after your father, young man. You must protect Rosa."

With arrogance similar to his father's, Lukas hissed, "I can do that."

Every heightened sense zoomed as he walked across the hall.

Chapter 28

Greg had ordered an expensive merlot, which the waiter poured into Alana's glass as the beaming odd-couple ran over. Her back stiffened at Celia's high-pitched, signature squeal, sure to get anyone's attention in a six-foot radius. "I can't believe it's really you! When Ally said she was meeting you, I just couldn't resist."

Greg stood with a shocked smile, kissing and hugging her sister. "You didn't tell me the green-eyed gossip was here! Wow, Celia B, I'm thrilled to death just seeing you again!" He shook Thorn's hand with great interest. "Hi, I'm Greg."

"Theo Thornwell," her accomplice replied. Sitting at the narrow table beside Alana, the empath wore a friendly smile, obviously not picking up anything devious in *this* mind.

Celia sidled into the other chair next to Greg. "Oooh, Ally says you're, like, really big in Europe. How super-special is that?"

The animated adoration threw Alana off guard. With an amused smirk and a tilt of her head, she listened to Celia chat away about everything and nothing at the same time. Alana studied Thorn, who studied Greg, who occasionally interrupted Celia. She scanned the shadows. Even through darkness, her ex-Guardian vision was better than 20/20. Greg's wasn't. Sweeping the piazza, she found Michael sitting in a relaxed, yet egotistical pose on the other side of the harbor. A menacing scowl leveled directly at her.

"And I read an article about you, and oooh... What's her name again? You know who I'm talking about—that sexy lady-manager of yours?"

Celia's kick to Alana's shin startled her. Although close to fuming, a plastered smile was friendly enough to disguise a desire to scream.

Suddenly, Greg gave a devilish smirk. "You mean my wonderful Valetta Russo? She's a classic, Roman beauty."

In less than a second, Alana knew Michael's warning rang true. That name meant this chance-meeting wasn't a coincidence. Reality felt like a brisk slap, and she gulped downed the merlot. The waiter brought two more glasses to the table, and Greg filled each. "More wine?"

Alana's hand shot out to cover her glass. "That's a definite negative," she whispered, only seeing Michael's smug expression.

Thorn sensed full innocence in Greg's reply. Nothing screamed "evil threat", but something didn't jive. In that non-verbal way, Celia told him, *"I'm very good at this, sweetie."* Her sparkling gaze stayed on Greg. "So just how romantically involved are the two of you?" she asked. "Even in a picture she's drop-dead gorgeous! Did you find her, or did she find you?"

"Valetta was part of the package when I switched labels," Greg answered off-handedly.

"What label did you switch to?" Thorn asked. "I'm extremely interested in a business way. My partner likes to sniff out artsy companies to spotlight in the global market. He's a rich kid, a collector of art with a fondness for Chopin. He's the one to know in certain circles."

"Hungarian Rhapsody Recordings... It's the best move I ever made."

Celia kept a ditzy, empty-headed look, still smiling beyond adoration. "I remember now! You loved Liszt! You used to play it for me and Ally to show off those long, boney fingers!"

An arrogant grin started. "It's owned by the wealthiest Hungarian on the planet...hence, the name. My career took off like lightning as soon as I signed last year."

I'll bet, Thorn thought. "I don't know any Hungarian billionaires. Do you, Celia?"

"Oh sweetie, just because you traipse all over the world doesn't mean you know everybody who's anybody!" She leaned into Greg as if to tell a secret. "Wealthy business types—they always try to impress. Name dropping's an art form." He was ready, and Celia forced him to say the one-word Thorn sensed.

Charmed by her, Greg said, "Well, Zoltan's a recluse."

Alana had heard enough! A cutting glare sailed to Celia. Her cell phone chimed, and glancing across crowds of tourists, she brought it to her ear knowing Michael had heard every word.

Coldly he growled, "Leave. Right now!"

Greg's last statement may have just cost him his life. She jumped up. "I'm sorry, it's my sickly aunt. Sorry, Greg. I'm not comfortable leaving her alone. I-I—"

Greg instantly stood. "No, no. I completely understand. I'll stop back before Paris."

"That sounds great," she replied with the most excitement she could muster. Celia smiled up at her as Thorn gulped down the full glass of wine. "I-I've got to hurry. Please excuse me. It's great to see you again." She kissed his cheek. He kissed hers. Alana couldn't begin to describe what she felt and said softly, "I'll see you back at the house, sis. On second thought, maybe you should—"

As Celia got to her feet, Greg offered to walk them home. "*No!*" both women shouted.

Leading him to the red-brick building is asking for more trouble! Alana quickly said, "What I mean is—"

"That's what I'm here for." Thorn rose. "You can't be too careful these days. It was good meeting you."

Grabbing a paper menu, Alana pulled a pen from her handbag. "Look, here's my cell number. Keep it handy while you're here...just in case. I mean, maybe if you know when you're coming back—or something." *I hope 'or something' isn't a terrified call in the next few hours.* She ripped off the corner, shoved it into his hand.

Greg took it, but a subtle expression swept across his handsome face. "Seriously, Ally, I would've looked you up—had I stayed in Manhattan. It's terrific seeing you again...maybe more than you'll ever know." His tentative smile lingered as they walked away.

As soon as they were out of earshot, Thorn whispered, "He knows the fine print in his contract: no relationships, no lovers, only romances orchestrated by Vashkar Enterprises."

Michael fell into step beside her, held her elbow to

pull ahead of Celia and Thorn. More hurt than angry, she choked back tears. "*Don't* say I told you so. He's as good as dead. I'm right, aren't I?" His hand slipped into hers, and although Michael didn't answer, she knew it would've been "Yes."

****

The two women hurried past Lukas, who stood outside Rosa's door. Michael saw anger in his glare. "Dad, I read the article. Valetta Russo—she was evil and in your dream. I thought you made her up! If she's real, then this piano player means trouble."

Pointing to the door, he ordered, "Inside. It's truth time. Sit down and don't interrupt." This time, he'd leave nothing out. Thorn sat across from Lukas as he explained the threat.

"So the *real* reason I'm leaving you is because some vampire wants me dead?"

"And that's not going to happen."

"Your dad's right, kid," Thorn interrupted, "We need to get you the hell out of Dodge."

"So what… I disappear? No way! That's not who I am, Dad!"

"Bravado is not what I want to hear."

Lukas ran up to him. "No. No way! I don't want to—"

"Go… Yeah, I guessed that one. Too bad—get over it and uncurl those fists, little boy. Think long and hard before taking your best shot. There's no time for this."

"No! No way! I won't leave while you—"

He had controlled his voice, his own fear long enough. "Do you *not* remember what I did to your backside yesterday?" Lukas's fists crammed into his back pockets; but Michael felt close to wild. "You will board that plane tomorrow. You will stay alert and get away safe! This isn't running, Lukas. It's turning your back on every *miserable* thing those bastards did to you. I took out three evil things. I can take out one more."

"Like killing one vampire will end this," Lukas mumbled.

"*This* will *never* end! Learn well in England. Get past every rotten memory and grow up pure of heart and spirit—*then* go after the evil in this dimension and you'll win," he yelled. "Think clear and do things the right way. Not like what I did in Manhattan."

Lukas looked down and shook his head. The truth didn't lessen his son's unhappiness, but it had stopped the rage. Michael touched his shoulder, and his son curled into his embrace. *A new, forced separation with no contact whatsoever. Unwanted tears would soon follow.* Hearing a hitched breath, he tenderly said, "Please do this for me. I need to know you're safe."

"What time?" Lukas whispered.

"Noon tomorrow," Thorn said.

"What about *Zia*? Will Gabby and Kayla watch out for her when we go to the airport?"

His hug tightened. "Absolutely. That's why they're here. *Zia's* a most special person to all of us." Softly, he added, "I love you, little boy." Before he let go, he forced the unwanted moisture from his eyes. But Lukas didn't look at him, going straight into his room and closing the door. Michael palmed his face and then ran his fingers through his hair, hearing each muffled sob. Fury still had his soul. "He's all yours, Empath."

"I'll guard him with my life. You'd better go to

her. I'll stay in case he needs to talk." Thorn paused. "Listen, Michael, Helena wouldn't have forced you to survive Manhattan if your destiny is to end up a pile of dust and bone at Zoltan's feet."

In the doorway, he turned to face his loyal friend. "I trusted you with my life. Now, I trust you with his. What I did in the city had to be done. That battle was about a child... *my* child." Slowly, he climbed the stairs.

****

Like a crazed cat, Alana didn't stop pacing her bedroom when Michael entered. Visions of Greg became her mother at the baby grand talking to her! Her vibrant smile haunted as if she could reach out and touch Alana one more time.

"I can't believe this is happening! I've got to warn him."

He gave a fierce glare. "Absolutely not. You will have no further contact with him."

The stern order had no effect. "Then you do it! Greg's not a part of this and he'll die if I don't help. Go to his hotel and get him out of Portofino, Michael, please." She didn't care if it sounded irrational. Michael looked ready to scream, and rooted by the window, he simply stared in her direction. "Forget it. I'll assign Guardians."

"I don't want to bicker, but your request... He's not an innocent, Alana. You know it, I know it, and he knows it. The man is fooling himself. When you make a deal with the devil there are—"

"Greg *is* an innocent! He didn't understand."

"He *did* understand. And no. This man's *not* an innocent! Guardians should be preparing for more

336

deadly things! Two on his tail delivers them to Zoltan on a silver platter. It lessens your strength. It invites their deaths."

Shaking her head, she spit out, "You're jealous!"

"Jealous?" He hissed as he closed in, "Of a self-centered *mortal* who knowingly signed his soul away? *Mine* was brutally invaded in the prime of my life! Forget him. This man faces his own short-sightedness. Let it go, Alana." She ignored Michael's warning, and now a breath away, he said stone cold, "I said let it go."

"No. If you won't save him, then I will." She moved away as he snared a wrist. Her mother's face twisted in agony, their treasured baby grand falling apart as Greg played it…Vivid, bizarre scenes raced through her mind. The last thing she wanted to do was beg, but she said, "Please, Michael, *please*."

"Then you must stay here and stay out of it!" His tone was sharp, and when his grip loosened, she rubbed her wrist and turned away. "No Guardians, no interference of any kind and no questions afterward. I do this my way. Agreed?" Hearing the absence of emotion in his tone, she couldn't answer. "Do you agree to the terms, my Guardian?" Huddled to his chest, afraid to close her eyes… The request wasn't negotiable. When he made no attempt to embrace her, she slowly met his barren gaze.

His mood terrified her, and pulling apart from him, she whispered, "I agree."

Not a hint of love or understanding showed as he walked away.

****

Michael entered the hotel's delivery port. On Staircase Four, a thin smile appeared. *How*

337

predictable—a physical fitness nut who didn't trust the elevators in Italy. Gregor's scent ended at Room 405. A shower ran. He forced open the lock on Room 403 and from that room's narrow terrace, took a confident leap into the next balcony into the pianist's bedroom. Ensconced in an upscale chair, he crossed his legs in an arrogant manner, and waited for the mortal to come out of the bathroom.

The naked man's expression was nothing less than terror. With trembling hands, he wrapped the plush hotel towel around his trim waist and breathed out, "What the hell! Y-you're Ally's friend."

"Oh, let me assure you, I'm much more than that."

"I don't under—"

"Don't speak. Get dressed—right now." Michael scanned the shivering human and kept a dangerous smirk.

He looked ready to fade. Struggled with his clothes, finally zippering the expensive trousers and wrestling on a charcoal-colored cashmere sweater. Comically, he fought with the fine-knit socks going on his wet feet, and then slipped into custom-made shoes.

"I-It was just dinner, I—"

"I said don't speak." He added a sinister curl to his lips. "We're not going on a photo shoot with *paparazzi.* Take your passport and wallet. Leave everything else that isn't important to you." The pampered performer looked around as if everything were important. Tailored suits, diamond cufflinks, his watch… Michael stood, purposely playing with him. "Perhaps that came across too harsh. Take the last item you fixated on, nothing else." After a few tries, a diamond encrusted Rolex was secured to Greg's wrist. He added with full disdain as they faced each other, "I wouldn't try anything stupid if I were you. I've got this eternal strength thing going for me. We stroll out of here like long-lost friends. Is that understood?"

The pianist nodded. But at the door, Greg stopped. "The lock—"

"Is as you left it when you entered," he replied in a low, intimidating voice. "I told you not to speak. Did you not understand?" Greg nodded—many times. "Open the door. Walk out. Follow my instructions or your hands will never execute a three-octave chromatic scale again." Heavily insured fingers fumbled with the lock, and Michael's hand slipped over his. To qualify the threat, he applied inhuman pressure. "Now, now, swallow those jittery nerves. If I had wanted to kill you, you'd have already taken your last gasp. Remember. We ride the elevator in silence."

Side by side, they walked through the rear employee-entrance like they belonged there. The backstreet appeared empty, but Michael gave a sharp shove and Greg hit the wall before Zoltan's minion grabbed him. With speed, Michael wrestled it down, pummeled until its face looked like pulp. With a fierce twist, he ripped a strip of thick wood from a vegetable crate and shoved the makeshift stake though its unbeating heart. Before turning to dust and bone, it screeched like a Hell-beast.

Wide-eyed, Greg swayed, and Michael grabbed his arm. "Demons and angels can cross dimensions and vampires are real. Try not to think."

Behind Alana's home, Michael forced the frozen man's long frame into his new car and slammed the door. Greg stared straight ahead, obviously still trying to process what he'd witnessed. Michael felt relieved at the silence as he started the car. But minutes later, the human whispered, "I swear, I just wanted to have dinner with her."

"Don't speak. Don't think about your future. I'm only saving you because *she* wants me to," he mumbled.

Words came in short bursts. "Ally? How? What...are you?"

"That's not important."

"Why kidnap *me*?"

If you only knew, Michael thought. "The last thing I want is chit-chat right now." He followed the directions displayed on a pricey navigational system. "I'm saving your immortal soul, jackass. You know... The thing you signed over to Vashkar Enterprises? Fame can make you its bitch."

The man's shoulders suddenly sagged. "Success came too easy."

"Plus, there's that fine print you conveniently forgot to read. Zoltan is one *very* sadistic vampire. And your career is over." Michael knew how truth could sting. Greg's look of self-loathing was all too familiar. He could relate. At the private airport in La Spezia, they stayed in the car until Cesar's crew secured the doors.

Alana is right. I am jealous. This living, breathing man could grow old with the woman he loves; give her children, a good life.

"Listen to me carefully," he finally said. "Make the best excuse you can to your parents and then drop it. Stay out of Manhattan. And don't ever try to contact Alana again." Greg's heart raced dangerously fast, but Michael had to make a lasting impression. In a murderous tone, he added, "Now get out of my car."

****

Everyone was asleep in the middle of this strange night except Alana who paced his living room. Michael entered. One dim table lamp cast her in shadows. From the side of the couch, he noticed the blank expression.

"As soon as he left Portofino, my...my mind cleared." He could see doubt soar as she walked past to stare out the open window. "Tell me what you did to him." Meeting her there, his hands curled around her waist, and she let out a sharp breath.

So long after midnight, he refused to bicker. They'd wake up everyone if they started. "Part of our agreement is no questions, darlin'." Michael's hands moved to the window frame locking her in as she stared at the dark hills. "He's safe. That's all you need to know." Her shoulders relaxed as a long sigh escaped. He couldn't resist kissing her neck and as she leaned against him, they watched the stars together. Her head rested against his chest.

"Did you put the fear of God into him?"

"That's another question, darlin'. One more and I take matters into my own hands." He cupped her round bottom. As alluring as a temptress, she teased him to a point of passion.

"You didn't do anything like maybe break his left pinky, did you?" Rubbing his thighs, she worked her way toward the zipper of his jeans. "Were you at least civil?"

"You're pushing my buttons...on purpose?"

She turned in his arms to purr, "Every last one, my sweet, sweet love."

The sensual tone caused a fully human reaction,

enough to want immediate release. He'd rip her hot body out of the matronly outfit and take her naked on the dining room table in the moonlight. Their lips slammed together. Like an erotic tango, he steered her through the living room and around the furniture.

"No more questions," he ordered. One hand pushed the bedroom door closed. His jeans unzipped. His shirt slid off. Her temperature would surely rise tonight. Greedy hands boldly released him from his boxers. A throaty moan came from him as her grip slid up his erection. Tugging off the frumpy skirt, her lace bikinis lowered as well. When Alana bent down to slip them off, the image brought such inviting fantasies.

This arousal felt almost unbearable. He ripped every button off the old-maid blouse he hoped to never see again. Sheer fire brimmed in her hazel eyes. Searing kisses covered his chest. Adding madness to desire, both of her hands had him again.

Somehow they turned and his back hit the wall. "Didn't I do this to you earlier tonight?" he managed to say.

Nipping at his shoulder, she grabbed his rear and sighed. "We were so rudely interrupted. But one more question and I take matters into my own hands."

As her hands cupped his ass, he smirked with a devilish twinkle in his eyes. "Oh, darlin', I'd like to see you try."

Chapter 29

Michael's home faced the slope of the north hill, not the sea. Villas wormed up its steep incline, a magnificent sight. Antonio DeMarra lived a short distance away in a small, secluded place at the edge of the seaport. Tonight, besides his wife and children, guests were under the Council member's roof. A Florentine Guardian and his mentor whom Antonio had known for years had gratefully accepted the invitation to sleep there.

This was a blessed home, but that didn't matter to the undead being standing outside in the tranquil hour before dawn. Zoltan's minion loosened a rusted gas pipe at its joint. Fumes saturated the humid air. As ordered, the creature waited six minutes to light the black candle in his hand. The explosion rocked the earth.

****

Their eyes opened a split-second after the deafening sound. Michael pulled on his jeans and ran to the dining room window. Alana grabbed one of his shirts and slipped into a pair of his sweats, rolling the long legs into thick cuffs and tightening the drawstring. She found him and Lukas watching the fireball shoot up to a dark night sky. Hideous flames licked the smoke. "Oh my God, no," she whispered, "It's Antonio's house."

Michael slowly nodded. "Make sure everyone in the building is accounted for. There's nothing we can do. They are gone."

Lukas looked mesmerized by the skyrockets of fire from the earth. "Is it Zoltan?"

Before Michael could answer, a sharp clap of thunder raced through the heavens. Lightning flashed, as if the consecrated building was singled out. Sheets of rain poured down and wind blew it in every direction like the earth had gone off-kilter.

Heavy drops whipped Lukas's face, still awestruck by the hideous sight.

"This is Cyril's work. They're here." His anger deepened. "But so am I." He pulled his son aside to secure their home against the raging storm. Fighting humidity and fast air currents that accompanied this mysterious weather, he locked the flapping shutters.

Alana made it as far as the arch. Lukas sprinted past and into his room as her stomach soured and her fingers dug into the solid wood. Another low rolling cramp began. Her legs wobbled, but she made it to the couch. In total darkness, Michael and Lukas now faced each other. They were both soaked. Michael's hand was still on his son's cheek when everyone at 52 Via Amadeus hurried into the small living room. Each clap of thunder sickened her more. Weird pains jabbed her chest making it difficult to breathe. Her gut lurched again as multiple candles flickered to life. "God, I'm sweating," she moaned. Celia put an arm around her. Never ill, she thought she'd faint.

Heavy raindrops beat at the bricks, drumming sharp staccatos syncopated against frenzied rhythms of turbulent wind. Michael turned to Miles. "Four-thirty in the morning... Mark the hour. Daylight will remain at bay until this is over."

"I'm not about to argue," Miles replied, "But you know this how?"

"This reeks of dark magic. Cyril must be here because Zoltan doesn't pack this kind of power. No electricity, flooding roads, no telephones... Cell towers probably out as well. The seaport's isolated." He caught Thorn's eye. "This is what you saw—days ago."

"It looks like we're all staying for the show," the empath calmly replied.

Running his hands through his hair, Michael cursed under his breath. "Open any window facing in any direction, and we'll have buckets of water on the floor."

The votive candle in Kayla's hand provided enough light to see Alana's drained complexion from across the room. Genuinely concerned, he went over, kneeling in front of the woman he loved. "Do you keep your weapons upstairs?" Alana looked too nauseous for his liking. Each zap of lightning made her wince and moan. When she started to stand, he gently pressed her back into the couch. "Keep her right here, Celia," he whispered. "Just tell me where—oh, right. Thank you, God, for that fully accurate dream of survival. Stay put," he ordered, with a tender hand to her burning cheek. Lukas was already standing by the door. "That goes for you, too," he said in a firm tone.

He ignored his son's, "Come on, Dad, I can—" and flew up the stairs.

Keen eyes swept the third floor. He picked up Gabriella's scent. She had secured every window. Dragging Alana's trunk out of the bedroom closet, he focused his mystical senses. Vampires, undetectable to a human's ear, walked across the flat roof. Opening a living room window, he pushed at a shutter. Two stared up from the street. At the window in the den, two more met his stare.

"Here we fucking go," he hissed.

With the trunk over a shoulder, he raced down the stairs. Kayla and Gabriella were already dressed and waiting in his living room. "Everybody gets a stake," he said to Lukas, who handed them out as he pulled them from the trunk. "Do you keep holy water in the house, *Zia*?" Rosa nodded. "Go, Kayla. Bring it all. You'll drench your necks with it."

Alana's favorite weapon, an ornate silver short-sword came to his hand. Her mystical grip had worn its sturdy leather thin. He thought about his own broadsword—forever lost in a passageway, in Manhattan, the night this whole thing started.

His gaze sank to Alana. "For Lukas," she uttered, and he nodded in tender respect. Her short-sword twisted in his left hand and then sailed though the air, landing in his boy's steady grasp. The way Lukas sliced it through thick air with automatic, decisive strokes, made him uneasy. Reaching back into the trunk, he pulled out delicate blessed beads. A gift from her parents—years before he met her. Battling demons in Manhattan, she was never without them. Tenderly, he slipped the rosary into the shirt pocket over her heart. When he kissed her cheek, her clammy skin brought more fear into his soul.

Miles stood next to the couch. "Why are we doing this? The building's consecrated."

Reaching over to take her father's hand, Celia met

Michael's concerned expression. "We're surrounded by The Summoned Six and then some, Dad. Two vamps on the roof. Feet smoldering even in this deluge. They're aggressive, but not part of the Six."

"No, they're not," Michael confirmed, "Those bastards are on the street waiting for me."

"So we're sitting ducks," Lukas mumbled.

"Do I look like I'm sitting to you? Lose the attitude. Right now! I say move, you move. I say stay put; you stay put. Don't deviate, even an inch. Do you understand?"

Thoughts of Cyril getting to his son had him panicked. His sire had honed, dark magic skills. And he was close, a feral force Lukas couldn't even begin to comprehend.

"Put the sword down," He sternly ordered. When Lukas didn't move fast enough, one swift swipe made the short-sword clang against the wooden patch of floor. He shook his son as a warning. "Tell me you understand!"

"Shit! I hear you," Lukas yelled.

Not satisfied, he hissed, "Try it again."

Lukas swallowed hard. "I-I *totally* understand, Dad."

Once he let go, Lukas literally ran to Miles, a distance away. Edginess churned inside him. His son would remember a harsh, crazed father, not a calm, controlled loving parent. Slowly he crossed the room and kept his tone soft. "I didn't mean to scare you, but once the outside door opens, all hell will break loose. *Everyone* must stay together in the basement." A hand ran down Lukas's face. He pulled him close. "Kayla and Gabby will go with me. You *cannot.* Please do as I ask."

"I-I won't duck out, Dad, I promise," his son whispered.

As Michael kissed his forehead, Alana crept across the living room with Celia. He'd never seen his Guardian as much as sneeze. More panic filled his soul. He pushed it down deep because nothing could cloud his mind right now. "Thorn. Barricade the basement door before we leave."

****

Unsteady over the bathroom sink, Alana groaned again. "God, the taste in my mouth is just awful." Celia had a sopping wet washcloth to her face.

"You're not poisoned, Ally, and I'm not getting this is a stomach bug, either. Come on. I'll walk you back."

"Michael will win." The eternal optimist didn't respond. "Please tell me you see it," she begged.

"I can't, sweetie. A slew of dark seers is purposely mucking my sixth sense."

"Oh God!" She threw up again in the sink.

****

At the hall door, Lukas stayed clipped to his chest. Michael had heard every word spoken between the two women. They came over, and he wanted to swear to Alana that everything would be fine. After a final hug, he watched Celia walk Lukas down the dark stairs. Prepared for this battle with pointed stakes and silver swords, Kayla and Gabriella followed them. Miles had an arm slipped around Alana. She pulled away and clung to Michael's chest biting her lower lip.

"I'm so sorry. I should be at your side. It's in the trunk. Take it," she said.

He wanted to crush her in his arms, bathe himself in her scent. Damp ringlets were brushed from her feverish face, and he kissed her parched lips. In full distress, his Guardian's disappointment had revealed itself. Michael wouldn't let on that he felt blessed relief, too afraid of losing her. After a careful embrace, he peeled her from his chest. She didn't have to say a word. Love radiated from her very soul. In tenderness, he said, "Let your dad take you down, darlin'. I know what I have to do." When Miles had her, a look of mutual respect passed between them.

Now, only Thorn remained.

Reaching into the trunk, the pearl-handled knife slipped into Michael's hand. Entrusted to *his* Guardian not long after he first spoke to her, Michael recalled how Martin Malone presented it to his only son in 1680. It had been tooled by his grandfather, and that life-memory filled his soul.

"That'll do damage, but I doubt it can slice off Zoltan's head…or Cyril's for that matter."

"Don't worry,' Michael replied as Thorn stared at him. "I'll make good use of it."

He thought about the passageway once again. Since 1890, the lost broadsword had been with him. Going into this battle, he felt naked without it. The knife slid into its leather sheath, and he tied its holder to the left loop of his jeans.

Thorn held out the last two containers of Georgian blood. Michael drained one, pushed the other away. "Take it with you. If things don't go my way and you've got to make a run for it, drench the damn things with it." Clasping one massive shoulder he added, "I know you can't fight, but you can defend."

"You know I will. Listen, the mystical mind isn't working right now, so I can't glean an outcome. Just do what you have to."

Thorn walked out first. Michael gripped the knife's pearl hilt, slow to follow his loyal friend down to the first-floor landing—then out the door.

****

Thunder and lightning deafened him. The continuous downpour obscured all vision. Two vampires dropped from the roof to immediately engage Kayla and Gabriella. Their stakes impaled unbeating hearts and both undead things disintegrated swiftly. Behind Michael, both Guardians resumed a ready stance again as he stepped off the curb.

Through sheets of rain, a different class of vampire approached.

"The sun should be shining, but it isn't," Michael stated with contempt. Five more appeared, and with a slow, sarcastic grin, he shouted through the thunder, "The Summoned Six... It will be my pleasure to destroy you. What do you say, guys? Anytime you're ready. What a lousy morning for a rumble, right?" Visibly, the one at the apex had command. "Look at those expensive black suits and shirts, now completely drenched. So you're *really* the superior demons? Where's the enhanced intelligence or did you lose your umbrellas," he arrogantly quipped.

"A filthy nun and a virgin girl." The leader wore a dismissive scowl. "We thought you'd be better prepared."

One vampire shifted, but Michael kept it casual. "Nah, I've been too busy explaining how the world works to my boy, driving a fast car, catching some rays."

"Boring, inconsequential desires of a pathetic mortal. You disgust me."

"You wouldn't remember, would you? Been undead—how many centuries?"

"As long as you, blood-drinker… These pitiful needs revile our kind."

"My, my… Such testiness. Plus, the dreaded *our kind*?" He stared at the silent five. "Come on, guys. Show some back-bone. Get a couple of quality insults in fast because this coward isn't doing it for me." With a smug expression, he took a step closer. "Just as I thought. No balls. Ugly as hell and you smell like stale death." The leader's kick to Michael's stomach sent him into the brick wall, precisely between Gabriella and Kayla. This demon is very juiced, he thought and wincing in pain, he looked behind them and gave an unexpected grin. "We've got back up, ladies."

The leader snickered, baring long fangs. "So have we."

From every doorway, vampires appeared. More jumped from the rooftops. Surrounded by a sea of snarls, when the odd one panicked, Michael lunged, and the battle began.

Gabriella and Kayla as well as an army of Guardians charged. The predetermined formation looked like a macabre ballet. Some attacked the dull-witted minions. More experienced warriors engaged the deadliest creatures. Sure and swift, over a dozen Guardians ensnared the super-charged Summoned Six.

Too fast, for Michael's liking, the twitchy one disintegrated. But sure enough, each nefarious turner methodically met his end with screeches that matched the dark sky's thunder. Alana's perfect strategy continued until the leader managed to maneuver out of the mystical army's web.

Flying at Michael with a pompous snarl, it stopped mere inches away. "You will die, traitor."

Through pounding rain, he hollered, "Where's the sixth?"

"He does the master's bidding."

Renewed terror held him, but he hissed through the mayhem, "Answer my question so I can put you out of your misery."

Vicious and swift, it attacked. He twisted hard and avoided its fangs every time they came too close. Finally, a less speedy lunge, and he hurled the demon into the bricks. Michael's hands fisted its wiry hair and smashed its face into the wall. "*Where* is the sixth!?"

The vampire gave a piercing screech and broke free. Steel-like fists hammered his chest, sending him down and into the center of the flooding street. An icy hand locked his throat. Its foul blood mixed with sheets of rain to drip into his eyes.

"We triumph! Your seed is ours!"

Rage soared as he unsheathed his father's knife. Stunned howls began as he sliced the demon's chest. Its grip loosened, and Michael sprang up, slashing its neck. "Filthy bastard," he screamed. Forcing the undead thing to kneel, one stab severed the spinal cord. He sawed through cartilage until dust and bits of bone floated down the street to the sea.

Every creature that witnessed the destruction of their leader ran. The mystical army changed focus. No vampire would survive.

Lightning flickered in the tar-like sky. Desperate,

he swept the scene. Mind-numbing fear made him sigh his son's name—in defeat.

Slaughtered Guardians. Bloodied warriors. Gabby holding the open door as Kayla dragged a wounded Guardian inside. Bottomless fear consumed him. Gabriella kept shouting, "Champion! Malone! Come on!" Very slowly, her command penetrated his aching soul.

First he staggered, willing his feet to move. Then, he ran to the basement door. Thankfully, it hadn't been touched, and he pounded on thick wood, calling to Thorn.

No response came. So he kicked until the barricade gave way.

****

From the bottom of the stairs, two glassy eyes stared up at him. Michael jumped down, and with a tender hook of Celia's chin, gently begged, "Talk to me, honey." Collapsing in his arms, she shook and cried.

What he saw made him want to scream. The blood came from Rosa and Thorn. In the far corner, Miles slumped against the wall with both legs in an unnatural bend. Alana huddled behind a row of barrels. Dear God, he thought, where is my son?

"I-I d-don't know," Celia stuttered through sobs. "*Zia*, Oh God she's dead and m-my love." She crumbled out of his arms to crawl to Thorn. His attention shifted to a shattered door that led to the adjoining building. "So fast...it took Lukas," Celia muttered.

"Could not stop it," Miles moaned.

Celia cried out, "I can't heal you! I can't even help

you, Daddy."

Each breathless, broken cry cut like a blade.

"Shhh, honey, stay by Thorn. Michael. Go," Miles gasped in uneven breaths.

Watching this tender woman stroke Thorn's broad chest didn't seem real. Michael couldn't accept this tragic scene. Shouting for help as he palmed the rain off his hair and knelt beside her. "I can't stay, Celia. Take good care of my friend. Can you do that for me?" She sobbed, clinging to her soul mate.

Tears clouded his eyes. He made his way around Rosa's lifeless body to Alana. *Unconscious. Unaware.* But her heartbeat was strong, and he moaned a sigh of relief. "You don't even see me, but I thank God you're safe." A shaky knuckle ran down her feverish cheek, and with devotion, he kissed her lips.

In full rage, he willed himself to stand. Fighting the worst fear he'd ever known, he trudged up the basement stairs and into the street.

Water pooled at his feet. Lightning crashed around him. Thunder shook the earth.

****

"Guardians carried Ally away from this horrid scene," Celia whispered to Thorn. "Keep breathing. Please don't leave me, sweetie. I finally found you after so many lifetimes of searching." She kissed his chin, smoothed his curly auburn hair with an unsteady hand. "Dad's pain is enormous, b-but he can't be moved, a-and he'll survive," she added, thinking her soul mate would not. She brought Thorn's massive hand to her heart and through wavering candlelight, allowed herself to look at *Zia* before a Guardian covered her body with a white sheet. Another sob hitched. "Oh, *Zia*... Why did this have to happen to *you*?"

"My dearest friend will rest in the arms of the angels. It was her time, Cecelia." As Mother Anne's hand met her shoulder; a sigh moaned from Celia's soul. "But it is not the Servant's time to pass." Celia sensed the healer's sadness as well as strength. "Let the Guardians bring him up to his bed. Maggie has given your father a sedative."

Softly sobbing, the gentle surgeon's profound grief made Celia shiver. She blinked, ready to cry again as two male Guardians carried Thorn away. With Mother Anne's help, she stood. Together, they ascended the dark stairway. "I can't sense Michael. I can't sense Lukas."

"Cyril has a potent beast-within, cunningly sired by a creature close to Satan himself."

She had to stop. Leaning against the wall in the hall, Maggie passed them and went into *Zia's* home. Mother Anne helped her move again. "It's triage for the wounded. Two Guardians are with your father. Come. I'll take you to Thorn."

Hard, steady rain beat against the shutters as Celia entered Michael's home. Guardians and mentors who had battled an army of vampires made a path for them in reverent silence. Candles blazed everywhere, more than Celia had ever seen. She entered the bedroom with Mother Anne and stared at two healing Sisters. One sat at Thorn's side, her skin as dark as ebony wood. Dwarfed by his enormous frame, she appeared very old. The other healer, tall and stately, had both hands tucked in her habit's long sleeves. *Sister Rosalinda? In Michael's dream he called you the purest of the pure.* Her silent nod was akin to a humble bow. She faced the other healer. *Wisdom radiates from a very old soul. You have tremendous energy in your aura, but I'm sorry. I don't know you, do I?*

The round woman beamed. "I'm Labbiel, Cecelia dear. Annie's told me all about you. Rosalinda and I will care for the brave Servant of Souls," she proclaimed in a voice as righteous as her name. Labbiel had Thorn's massive hand in her thick, wrinkled one. *The lyrical African inflection soothes like a lullaby. What a strange name.* "It means "God has healed" in Ancient Chaldean. The Servant has faced death courageously. But now that Sebastiano is here, his heartbeat will strengthen." As if her words were orders heralded by angels, Monsignor Scarlatti entered with a cooler. "See? Now we have many bottles of consecrated blood." Her determined fists dug deep into the mattress, and Labbiel rose to her full height, a few inches below five feet. "Rosalinda, it is time. Roll up your sleeves and let us begin. Go. Busy yourself, child. He's in healing hands now."

Mother Anne led her to the door, which closed behind her.

****

Useless and drained, lost without Thorn by her side—that's how Celia felt. Gabby grabbed her hand, led her through the wooden arch. Celia sank into a dining room chair. Still soaking wet, Gabby's short blond hair curled at odd angles around her alabaster complexion.

"I know you're worried about your dad. Believe me, the ambulance is almost here. You're staying, and I'll go with him, Celia. Once his legs are set, we'll help knit every bone back together at holy healing speed.

Come on, sister psychic, let's get food into you. I raided Michael's fridge." The ex-Guardian tapped a bowl filled with berries. "There's no electricity yet, but the gas is back. I made some caffeine the old-fashioned way…with *Zia's* two-cup perk pot." Celia looked up, hardly understanding her. "Okay. Fear has put you in, like, ESP shock, kiddo. You need to chill."

She took one blackberry. It tasted sweet and cool. "Lukas must be terrified. You sense Michael, Gabby?"

"Nothing's coming through. All we can do is think a prayer."

"Or ten… Or a thousand—" She ate the next with a little more desire. "Nothing could stop that vamp. It was unreal."

"I can imagine. But this entire event's been way out there, hasn't it?" Celia studied her serious face. "Champion takes out immortal sorcerers and locks down loads of portals. You have every good soul in the world helping to toast those Hell-beasts, and then, said Champion survives with some celestial help, not to mention one fantastic fantasy. Holy healers do one heck of a job getting him on his feet. The mystical being sees his reflection, walks in the sun, and—" Gabriela stopped before the whisper, "experiences total distress."

"What is it?" Celia quickly asked, "Gabby, what are you seeing?"

Chapter 30

A river of mud slid down the sloping hill. Michael fought it. He crawled, covered with rich soil that had nourished beautiful flowers, now drowned and beyond death just like him. His fingers dug into dirt, and he forced himself up, determined to save his child. His bloodline. Steamy rain driven by deadly wind swirled around him. This was the correct path. Halfway up, he pulled off the shredded shirt with screams of frustration. His black jeans soaked through and through like a second skin as he crawled.

Rage filled his soul. Panic filled his mind.

An uprooted tree came directly at him, and he dove to the left. Had he not been faster than a human, it would've crushed him. Erratic lighting bolts seemed to seek him out. The wind like screams from Hell, a warning to give up and give in.

It didn't stop him. Nothing would.

Pelting rain loosened more than earth. Stripped branches, roof tiles, sharp stones, and jagged glass all dislodged by the storm's force. Each one aimed at him as if inanimate objects demanded his defeat. But every obstacle renewed his determination. Focus did not wane. Strength did not give way to exhaustion. The closer he came to the villa, the harder the rain pelted his skin to disguise the scent of a creature that turned an innocent man into a killer over three hundred years ago. Near the circular drive, hail stung his muddy shoulders.

When he grabbed the doorknob, claws clamped his neck and flung him backward.

Before he could break his fall, he tumbled many feet back down the mountain. It stood over him, the last of the Summoned Six with lips drawn back and long fangs bared. Michael struggled up with the hiss, "You're the dead thing that took my son." A backhanded slap sent him facedown again into saturated ground. A thick branch grazed his chest. He waited. The demon leaned in to bite, and with a swift turn, he drove the splintered wood through its unbeating heart before it could screech. Now dust and bone, the final obstacle between him and his son joined debris running toward the seaport. Fatigue hammered his body as he crawled across the driveway screaming, "You cannot stop me, Cyril! I am no longer yours!"

****

Michael scanned the black-marble foyer, the one he had walked in his dream of survival. Dark rooms held the unbearable stench of decomposing animals lining every wall of the place. It sickened him, made him gag. At the foot of the staircase, he spit out the taste of decay. Thin wrought-iron spokes barely held up the railing. Some had separated like twisted spikes.

Nothing. No sound, no sense of Lukas. And he controlled his own desire to rage.

This emptiness wasn't real. His senses had led him here!

"Father wants you back."

The heavy Hungarian accent sounded as clear as if Zoltan stood at his side. He eyed the living room, and in the far dark corner, saw a triumphant smirk. The vampire's polished boots sounded against the marble floor while approaching with a wide grin. "You're a filthy mess."

Michael wiped his mud-stained face. He studied his hands. "That's some fucking nasty weather you brought with you to end the merry month of May. I prefer sunlight now. It suits me. Check out the tan."

"Don't play the casual midnight visitor stopping by for a friendly chat." Zoltan circled slowly. "Fear drips off you like sap from a ripened tree. Father thinks he's highly intelligent. I think the brat's untamable just like you."

"It's genetic—something you'll never understand. Didn't you drain every last family member after Cyril turned you into an undead thing? You could've left one dull, bastard son alive."

"Blood-bonds get in the way. Of that, you are now finally aware."

The sadistic grin, the murderous look in Zoltan's blue eyes... Michael's muddy hands ran down the handmade suit jacket—gave a winning smile. "I guess the European sorcerers don't think you impressive enough to hook you up with a dark seer who has baby-making power. Or maybe they just don't like Hungarians." The biting remark gave enough time to gauge Zoltan's envy. "Or maybe... undead or alive you've always shot blanks. Either way, I did something you can't do. What's the matter, Zoltan? That facial tick shouts jealous bastard in a big way." Dripping dirt from his hair shook free and splattered the vampire's face.

Predictably, Zoltan pulled a silk handkerchief from the suit's breast pocket, carefully daubing the splotches "I thought you'd appreciate my decision to send

Gregor. It confused the object of your eternal obsession. What a quaint, romantic touch, reminiscent of your undead antics. She was tempted, brother. I want my pianist back. His Liszt is exceptional. The performer's passionate interpretation of *The Mephisto Waltz* reminds me of the great composer himself." Replacing the soiled silk, Zoltan smirked, full of conceit. His manicured hands locked behind a straight back. "I'm waiting."

Staring the demon down, he gave a crisp, "No."

"No? But my minions saw the murderous expression on your face in the piazza last night. Did you punish the Guardian for accepting his invitation? Did you make her cry?"

Not about to give the vampire an upper hand, he showed no emotion. "She had nothing to do with what occurred in Manhattan. Where's my boy?"

"Why talk business? Your sinister wit intrigues me. I can see why Father loved you."

"Love? That dead thing doesn't know the meaning of the word. Neither do you."

"Perhaps I should have said his *fixation* with you. You are a magnificent specimen—just as I."

"We're nothing alike. And stop the friggin' storm or this boarded-up shack will take a header down the mountain. Really…don't you think hail at the entrance was overkill? The pounding rain had my attention. Where's my boy?"

"But it didn't keep you from picking up his scent, did it? Oh. It slipped my mind. You're *mystically enhanced*. What exactly does that do to you? Without the beast-within, you appear somewhat scrawny now."

"That's because you're in three-inch heels, and I'm

barefoot."

"You needed *human* minions to destroy vampires. By the way, they were handpicked by the Triumvirate, Michael." Zoltan's head shook in a deliberate fashion. "Your child will not satisfy their losses now. Perhaps the turning of a nosey psychic and a certain ex-Guardian would assuage their agony. I have that authority." One long finger tapped his arrogant smirk. "Here's a thought. You will do the turning after Father brings forth a new beast within you! Demons from every corner of the earth will want to witness the ghoulish side-show of your rebirth—and their undeath."

His face turned smug. So did Michael's as he flung his arms wide. "You want me, you got me. Where's my boy?"

Anger flashed in Zoltan's ice-blue eyes as he lifted one hand, the grandiose move of a gifted showman. "Come, come—one more snide remark before we drain him. I must be truthful. I don't see why our Sire mourned your loss for over a *century*! There is *nothing* charming about you. No finesse. You're still stupidly impetuous! The acquired American accent is harsh on my ears. *And* you're as filthy as fat swine in a trough!"

Michael's hand eased toward the knife. It wasn't there and he couldn't destroy Zoltan with his bare hands. "Cut the shit, Zoltan. Where. Is. My. Son?"

"Tsk, tsk—rudeness... Is it another nasty genetic trait, perhaps? I shall purge the boy of such inherited flaws after he drinks from my swollen vein."

Zoltan's turn-away was a mistake. Michael ripped off a twisted wrought-iron spoke, plunged it through the creature's shoulder. The vampire pulled it out like a mere splinter. He wrenched off another, buried it in

Zoltan's chest. Zoltan's eyes morphed lethal amber. Sharp fangs sprouted. Fingernails turned into black claws. With a deadly growl, Zoltan flew at him.

He sidestepped by less than an inch. "Does the old sire know you'll cut off his head before he drains Lukas? What about your dream to be the biggest *baddest* vampire in the world? You seriously underestimate Cyril. Daddy dearest doesn't know what a narcissistic son of a bitch you are. You *never* share the spotlight!"

Enraged, Zoltan pulled the spoke from his chest— this time with less speed. Blood spilled down the suit. "You will suffer before I destroy you."

Michael's chuckle echoed off the stucco walls. "You're less than me, Zoltan. A miserable wannabe who can't pull off storms and wind. That's why you brought Cyril here, isn't' it? As for the Triumvirate? Don't even *try* to convince me they *really* trust you with all their earthly assets. Like hell they do, bro'!"

The Hungarian lunged, swinging the bloodied spoke. With accuracy, Michael kicked it from his hand. Locked in a savage confrontation, each one was bent on destroying the other. Fangs sank into his shoulder. Michael screamed from the unexpected wound. He wrestled free, keenly aware that *this* vampire survived a taste of consecrated blood. When Zoltan threw him to the foyer floor, he swiped at Zoltan's hand around his neck. Overly confident, Zoltan snickered as his fangs retracted and his amber eyes reappeared ice blue.

Splayed, muddy fingers swept the floor for the spoke. Gripped tight and with speed, Michael drove it through the one place it would do the most damage. Gurgling and skewered through the neck, the sight and sounds of his victim were sickening. Zoltan's blood tricked down Michael's arm as he staggered up, jerking the writhing demon to his feet as well.

Anxious, he growled, "Playtime's over. Take me to my son. I'd rip your head off right now if I didn't *personally* know how vindictive the old sire gets."

Cyril would be below ground. That was a certainty. He dragged Zoltan down rotted basement stairs and eyed two latched doors.

"Which room?" A disgusted glower stayed in Zoltan's bloodshot eyes. Michael had to find something, anything to intimidate him further. He saw a chewed broom pole wedged between staircase and wall and the dream of survival hit him like a heaven-sent jolt. It'd take a miracle for this to puncture Zoltan's useless heart, but he poked at the Hungarian's chest and scowled. "I'm guessing stone room and *not* wine cellar. Cyril likes the ambiance of a dungeon. And if I'm wrong, you can kiss immortality good-bye." The latch splintered off with a sharp kick. Michael strode through the threshold with the writhing vampire impaled on a rusty spoke.

****

Hurricane lamps shed shadowy light in the room's four corners. A child's coffin stood on a stone pedestal in the center, meant for a turning—for his son. Baron Cyril Waczynska, seven centuries old and a creature to be feared, sat motionless in a chair beside it. The only heart beating in this room belonged to a frightened boy.

Wet and shivering, Lukas was very much alive. Chains wrapping his thin wrists looped through a padlocked metal ring ensconced in the far away stone wall. Seeing his son, every bruise and bite he had taken in the last hour throbbed even though they had sealed. Phantom pain, he thought, and I'll never make it to my son with Cyril in the room.

Full of hatred, he yanked the spoke out of Zoltan's neck and kicked him to Cyril's tattered boots. Clutching the bubbling neck wound, the vampire writhed on the floor.

The sire faced him with a hiss. "Michael, my passionate child of the night." Ardent emotion clung to every word. His white as snow, skeletal face had rotten, brown teeth. "How I've missed your ability to kill with a kiss." The raspy voice terrified him as Cyril sucked in noisy breaths to speak. "He is a beautiful boy with blood as addicting as yours." Boney fingers stroked the tattered chair. Cyril's cough and gulps of air filled the stone room.

Fresh punctures on Lukas's wrist renewed his rage. He didn't dare show it. This wasn't the way to handle his sire. As bland as possible, he answered, "He's not yours, Cyril."

"It's Father, my wayward child. How contemptible to overlook etiquette when a turning is imminent!" The demon leaned down with a glare. "Conceal yourself, beast-within! I wish to see only human pain!" Zoltan's demeanor changed, and Cyril eyed Michael again. "What a vicious throat wound you've given him. It will take many minutes to close. It will scar."

"Your vanity is just as I remember it." Michael took a step closer to Lukas, snatching quick glances of him looking down and sobbing louder.

"Now, to the reason for your return—"

"Stop the storm first," he interrupted with a scowl. The chewed broomstick stayed tight in hand; his arms stayed lashed to his muddy chest. Cyril cackled, shook a white finger. With a bored roll of his eyes, Michael muttered, "Stop the storm first *please* I beg this of you, my Sire."

Cyril's wiry arms stretched out. They were still powerful, brutal. Punishing. His feral eyes flashed bright. "Done," he rasped like a king. "But the winds remain until I drain the child. Turning is a savory moment." His gaze narrowed. "How brazen you've become. I see no terror in your stare as I did that December night in 1690. I am disappointed."

"The room is stifling. Chamomile tea settles my stomach. We discuss your immoral soul the night you took my life."

Wonder swept across Cyril's face. "How is this memory possible? Do you also remember your frightened tears, your abysmal pleading?"

In a millisecond, he relived every aspect, but simply stated, "Unchain my son."

Zoltan stood with a sway. Both palms clenched the gaping wound. *"Never!"* he croaked.

Leering at him, Michael waved the broomstick. It focused the vampires on him, not his child. Cyril's jagged claws clicked while staring at Zoltan until he produced the key from his bloodied breast pocket. Full of resentment, the Hungarian strutted to Lukas and removed the padlock.

Chains clattered against stone, and Michael ordered, "Come to me, son." Cowered in the corner, Lukas mopped his swollen eyes and shook his head.

With precise steps to Cyril, Michael bitterly shouted, "Did I forget to mention his *many* problems? The sorcerers did this. Parenting a stubborn kid's a fucking nightmare!"

Zoltan took the bait and turned. His face twisted in an over-dramatic sneer. "His hatred for you allowed me to find him. He rages, vampire, he bleeds—and he hates!"

Lost in fear, his son was easy prey. Something had to shake Lukas out of this nightmare. Then his son would run to freedom while he destroyed both creatures. In a cruel manner, he barked, "Yeah, I'll live with the hate in his heart. Now don't give me a hard time in front of these two morons. Get your ass over here! Wake up, kid! Look at me damn it, *right now*!"

Zoltan strutted two steps forward. The well-built vampire all but blotted out the sight of his crying son. Staring at Michael, he pointed back to Lukas and snickered. "This is what you plead for? A sniveling boy who cringes in mistrust of you? He was born to kill. Emotions confuse his purpose, Michael. This child is—"

Alana's short-sword whooshed. Zoltan's head thumped against the wall before he turned to dust and bits of bone.

"*Mine*, he is mine," Michael whispered, fully amazed. The bloody blade hung mid-air. Immeasurable fear haunted his son's wide eyes. "Give me the sword, son." No response. No movement. And by the time Cyril's howls of anguish subsided, Michael realized it was too late and screamed his son's name.

The sire pulled Lukas tight to his skeletal frame, clutched his son's throat. Cyril gave a breathy laugh. "He'll be a merciless creature. Like his legendary father." One clawed hand squeezed while the other clicked with anticipation. "I could end his life with one thought, but that wouldn't be punishment enough for what you've done."

Gripping the broomstick, Michael lunged. Cyril hissed a caution as an arm tightened across his son's heaving chest. One claw stroked Lukas's jugular, which pulsed at a dangerous speed.

Only three feet away from his petrified child, he stood perfectly still. He knew the mind-game, how a vampire could bend a human's will. A sob stuck in his throat. "I remember the fierceness of your grip on that winter night, my Sire. You held me against the wall." Fresh tears dripping down Lukas's pale cheeks unraveled him as he begged, "Let him live, my Sire."

Cyril simply smiled at his once-favorite son.

He had to gamble. Had to trigger a response without suspicion. "Keep looking at me, little boy. Don't move. Just listen." A loving gaze and calm words hadn't stopped his son's heart from pounding or his teeth from chattering. Cyril scraped a claw against his neck. Lukas turned his face away. He had to think quick, hoped with all his soul that Lukas would understand. "No. Please. Just look at me. Don't move. Don't bolt. Stay put."

Guarded eyes met his, and clenching the broomstick in a death grip, Michael's mind raced. "Show me you understand and do exactly as I say."

A forced whimper…a hesitant nod made him crazy. Lukas's teary eyes bore right through his. Very hushed, his son replied, "Yes, Father. I promise, I won't duck out. I won't move."

His son's shoulders relaxed, drifted into Cyril's chest. Another strangled sob escaped, but Lukas went limp in the sire's arms. His son's pulsing jugular teased a deep grunt from Cyril's throat as the beast-within readied itself to drink.

Dear God. I am out of time. "Father, I beg you do not do this! Turning a child is not your way! Take me back instead. I do not fight. Please... I will never stray again—always to kill as you have taught me!"

The crook of his sire's head reeked of self-centered hunger. Blood dripped from the jagged claw that raked his son's neck for a taste. For a thrill. Cyril's senses would soon heighten, just as they had that long ago night in 1690 when the sire appeared drugged by the draw of his bloodline.

Full of despair he whispered, "A tiny bead of scarlet on an Englishman's lip," He stepped closer. "Take me back, Sire. Take all human desires away as you did so long ago."

Lukas showed full submission. Cyril had always preferred the absence of a struggle, and then Michael watched his arm ease off his son's chest. The hand at his son's neck slid down to a sagging shoulder. But the demon's rotted fangs bared, ready to assuage an ancient hunger.

"No, Father! Create a beast to swallow *my* soul! It is my choice! Please, Sire!" Each plea pierced the silence. In true panic, staring at the child he so deeply loved, he screamed, "Let him go *now!*"

As if practiced hundreds of times for this moment, father and son reacted as one. With swift precision, Lukas ducked and twisted hard. Michael rammed the broomstick through Cyril's chest. Pinned to the stone wall, the demon's screech, a deafening roar from Hell began. One gnarled hand wrapped the chewed pole. Michael held firm as his left hand shot out. Lukas placed Alana's shortsword in it, and then backed away. With calculated cruelty, Michael hissed, "You took my life. You made me a monster." His tone sank to merciless hate. "Go back to Hell."

The blade sailed through Cyril's neck. Thick black dust and chunks of brittle bone rained down. The broomstick landed on the filthy mound with a soft thud.

Michael let go of the sword and staggered back. His knees hit the stone floor. The vampire legacy, that part of his long, undead existence, had come to an end. The twisted night of turning, terror that defined two centuries of killing now avenged. His eyes clouded and closed. Muffled sobs wrenched from the depths of his soul.

It was finished. Final.

His son's trembling hands eased down his face. His thin arms came around his shoulders. Weary beyond belief, his head rested against the strong heart drumming inside Lukas's chest. It brought blessed relief. And he clung to his son, his brave child. Finally, he whispered, "Let's go home." Squaring his shoulders, he stood to study the cold, cold room. In his fantasy, he had carried his dying child up to safety. But it had been just that. A fantasy. Not reality.

Pulling Lukas close, he added, "Thank God you don't *always* listen to me." Hand in hand, they left the destitute villa. He didn't look back. Neither did Lukas.

****

Saturated earth remained slippery, but the unnatural weather had stopped as soon as Cyril met oblivion. A clear, cloudless sky turned this nightmare into a perfect morning. Side by side, they walked down the mountain. Near the bottom, the red-brick building came into view.

Lukas abruptly stopped, sank to the wet ground and pulled both knees to his chest. Hiding his face, he mumbled, "I won't go back there. Don't make me."

Even soothing words wouldn't help right now. Guilt often becomes a familiar companion, and he knew his son's world was shattered yet again. Although Lukas resisted, Michael lifted him into his arms and held him tight the rest of the way down the mountain.

At the building's door, he put him down, but Lukas refused to enter. Tears shimmered on his lashes, ready to spill again. "Everyone here knows I wanted to do that to you."

Michael held his chin, captured his swollen eyes. "But you didn't, and you never would."

"I killed *Zia* and Thorn ...Just like I killed Helena."

"No, you didn't kill anyone. You're a very courageous young man who has faced terror, lived through it, and survived." Not knowing what to expect himself, he held his son's hand as they went up the stairs. They entered their cozy home in a village known for its tranquil beauty. Sunlight streamed through the open windows. Welcoming aromas of coffee and fresh-baked cinnamon toast wafted through clean, spring air.

With a warm smile and open arms, Mother Anne took Lukas into her embrace. Her light-gray eyes held full understanding while saying, "You're exhausted, Champion. Everything you need is upstairs. I'll take very good care of him."

****

Heavy, slow steps brought him to the third floor. Sorrow engulfed the quiet building. He heard every beating heart, aware that each mourned loss in its own way. After draining two glass containers of blessed blood, he moved through Alana's bedroom where shutters stood open, inviting gentle breezes from the Mediterranean Sea.

He stripped off his clothes and stood under the trickle of a hot shower. Mud washed off as well as the stench of death. With his head hung low, his fists met the wet tiles. *More lives lost. More innocents caught in the middle of an ungodly war…more horrific memories for my son.*

To feel it all meant more guilt upon his conscience. Unrelenting tears blended with soapy, lavender-scented water, blood, and dirt before disappearing down the drain.

Afterward, he took a careful look at the cloudy image in the bathroom mirror. *Is this evidence of my soul, and what I choose to take upon it? Only the man who lost his life in 1690 had a crystal-clear reflection. Days ago, his confession had been made with a contrite mind to find peace.* But everything since the night he was sired belonged to *this* Michael Malone.

Clean clothes waited on Alana's bed. *Black shirt, black jeans—casual clothes for a not-so-casual day.* He dressed and then slipped into the soft Italian loafers. Less than confident strides took him through Alana's home. Silence… Deafening silence surrounded him.

He made his way down to his home—down to her.

Chapter 31

"Tell me she's okay," he said.

"Alana's perfectly fine," Mother Anne confirmed in a calm voice. "She's taken accurate accounts for Miles—from everyone involved. Your room has become an office."

"And Miles...Thorn?"

"Miles is in a local hospital. Gabriella's with him. You should know Cesar had the flight switched to tomorrow morning because of the weather. And Thorn's resting comfortably. All wounds have closed, but I've ordered bed rest. Labbiel and Rosalinda tended to him."

In disbelief, he stared at her. "*Sister* Rosalinda?"

"Yes. She's an exceptional healer, Michael. So is Labbiel. Two powerful souls tended our brave empath. Rosalinda sends warm regards. She wants you to know she prefers folk ballads." He had to grin at the comment. "To address your questions, Celia and Lukas are with Thorn. Magdalena's making arrangements for her mother's funeral." Guilt filled him, and the healer chided, "No. You will not take ownership of *anything* that happened today. To quote your dream—there *are* casualties in war. My dearest friend was prepared. Her mission was completed. It all comes down to one's own destiny."

He looked away. "I can't help feeling more than responsible. Two Council members, Antonio's entire

373

family, many Guardians—the list goes on and on."

"None of this is on your soul, and I had better not see culpability in your mind. Is that clear, young man?" He gave a shrug. "I expect an out-loud answer."

Awkwardly he replied, "I hear you, Mother, but—"

"Do this with a discerning mind. Explain what you know to be truly fact and after you see it on paper, bury it in your soul. Should you require a serious reality check, be confident that I will find you." He couldn't stop a sheepish grin. With a morsel of humor, she added, "And if you step out of line, I know what makes you tremble."

"You and everyone else," he mumbled.

"I've sent Rosa's recipe to Brother Thomas to supplement your sustenance. I sense your worry, but Lukas will be fine. He's had a shower and some breakfast. Leave him to his new best friends and go to Alana." She paused before saying, "To assist you through this incredible journey fills my soul with joy. We do rather exceptional work, do we not?"

"Yes, you do, Mother." His charming smile faded as he walked away. Because many items needed attention before leaving Alana and his son.

****

Alana threw the pen on the bed and ran to his open arms. He slid her up his body, covered her with kisses. "You smell good, and you look even better, and you feel—" He cut her off with another kiss.

When her feet met the carpet, he searched her face. "How are *you* feeling?"

"Sadder than sad... *Zia* was many things to me, all of them precious. I'm blessed that I had a chance to know her. She visited us once. I was only five, but she stayed very vivid in my mind. My parents said a particular place in Heaven was reserved for her. Now I know why. She filled a void that's been in me since they died."

"I'm so very sorry, my love. I'm truly at a loss—"

Her finger came to his lips. "This wasn't your fault. Evil led those vampires here. I've talked to dozens of Guardians from all over Europe. Gabby said there were many, many more. And the actual count of vamps no longer walking this earth keeps growing. News reports blame the freaky weather on an atmospheric disturbance. I guess it's what innocents can accept."

When he settled into the upholstered chair, she curled onto his lap. He kissed her again. "So how are you *feeling*? I didn't think a person could be that pale and still be alive. You scared me, darlin'."

She smiled. "Oh, that… Yeah, I *know*. Gabby calls it Divine Intervention. Celia insists I wasn't supposed to be at your side. God knows, it's where I wanted to be, where I thought I should be."

"I commend such meticulous strategy, my Guardian. You are a gifted warrior. But please, don't *ever* get so sick again."

"As soon as the storm ended, the dizziness did too. God, I hate dry heaves," she said with a sour expression. His arms felt like heaven around her. "Enough about me. I hear you really kicked evil's ass again."

"Yep. Lukas and I kicked it back to Hell where it belongs." He told Alana everything. Starting with the confrontation in the street; ending with Lukas's guilt. "Mother Anne says he'll be able to deal with this. I'm not about to doubt her. But you should've seen him, darlin'. Absolute focus and deadly accurate—I am amazed!"

"You're bursting with pride, Daddy. He'll be the fiercest Guardian ever called."

Michael sighed. "*Another* decade of worry?"

"Lukas has incredible form. I saw the way he caught my short-sword. Only fifteen and he takes out a powerful demon like Zoltan? He's already a legend. With all of us loving him, he'll be strong and super-smart as well as totally handsome with that intense appeal and arrogant manner—just like you." She narrowed her eyes. "Are you blushing?"

A steamy kiss was her answer. It filled her soul. When he pulled away, she sensed a grimness begin.

"Tomorrow, after Lukas leaves... I sign the document. I'll be away a long, long time."

Her heart was already breaking, her body already missing him. *Think positive; be confident*, she told herself. She kissed the palm of his hand, pressed it possessively to her breast.

"I'll be waiting, and I don't care how long it takes."

"You'll be alone."

"Like that could ever happen? Our home will be full of good people—all sending you our strength." The subject had to change, and she kissed his cheek. "Can I reopen Portofino's best bookstore?"

"That's fine." He gave a thin smile, touched the locket around her neck as if lost in memories of a life long gone. "Love truly has many meanings, doesn't it? I will miss you, my Guardian. You are my world. One more night with you in my arms... Is it too much to ask?"

"I wouldn't have it any other way."

"I have many things to do, and I want to spend some time alone with Lukas. Any suggestion on how that can happen? He seems to be in demand right now."

They both stood as she said, "You'll love my plan."

"I hope you have a good one." Michael leaned down as she whispered in his ear. A smirk began. "What do you say to a quiet family dinner on the piazza, just the three of us tonight?"

"How early can I make the reservation for?" Her hands ran down his chest. His expression turned sensual. She watched him leave, and even when she closed her eyes, she could still see the commanding Champion who owned her heart. *Intense masculine features, his loving soul—any woman would long for these—in any century. He is perfection.*

****

Michael entered the bookshop through the back-office's hall door. With a slow stroll through polished shelves, he sensed Antonio's meticulous management. A soft knock sounded, and as Patrick Christenson followed him into the small office, he asked, "Think you can spend the rest of your life here?"

The wiry accountant in his forties leaned back in a chair with a loose frown. "I don't think I'll miss Manhattan too much. I can grow your portfolio from anywhere, Michael. But this is one beautiful place. Monica and the girls love it already. So what do you have in mind?"

He gave specific instructions, leaving the best for last. "There are two villas for sale, midway up the mountain. Buy them both. One has a wrought-iron staircase with missing spokes. I want it demolished. The other's in good shape. Authorize repairs for you, Monica and the girls." Christenson began to object, and Michael added, "I insist. You cannot go back to Manhattan. Does your wife understand?"

"Yes, but I'll need a reason why we're choosing Portofino."

"As CEO of The Malone Corporation you can tell your wife anything you want. Name your salary, as long as it's more than double your current one. Is that a good enough reason?"

"Of course, but—"

"Good. In a few days, introduce yourself to Alana. Provide her with all she asks for. Make sure everyone on the list I gave you is taken care of while I'm gone." His tone turned ice cold. "Your first assignment is to take apart Vashkar Enterprises. The owner isn't around anymore. Don't ask, and I won't tell. If it has subsidiaries we can clean up, make an offer. Those that smell dirty, ruin them fast. Am I clear?"

"Give me a year and you'll be the most admired entrepreneur in Europe."

"I honestly don't care about that type of prestige. No articles, publicity, pictures of Lukas or Alana...or anything," he firmly added.

"Consider it done. I owe you, Michael."

"No, you don't. Some day I'll tell you how saving your soul almost sixteen years ago led to me saving mine." They shook hands, ended the meeting. After Christenson left, he locked the door. One item off his list, five more innocents safe, he thought, now ready to face the empath.

****

An animated discussion between Celia and Lukas put him at ease for the moment. They continued to laugh, and Michael zeroed in on her holding his son's hand. "Alana wants you."

Lukas gave a casual "Yeah, sure," before leaving.

Michael's smile disappeared when Celia's hand came to his cheek. "You're okay. I prayed you would be," she whispered.

He hugged her, rested his chin on the top of her short, red hair. "Ah, Celia B... You're so very special to me—but you already know that. Can I be alone with your boyfriend for a while?"

Thorn started to get out of bed. "You don't need Celia's permission. I'm right as rain and raring to go."

Celia glared at his loyal friend before closing the door. He pulled the chair away from the bed to accommodate his long legs and propped both feet on the bed, facing Thorn.

"Lay back down right now. I know you did your best. Don't look away, Empath, and no tears, apologies, or guilt."

"It burst through that bolted door and immediately snapped both of Miles's legs. I swear I'll never forget the sound. Then it ripped off his cross, which didn't even burn its hand. One of the Summoned Six, I'm guessing, made all the more diabolical with Cyril's dark magic."

Michael had never heard such anger, and flatly replied, "It turned into dust and bone just like any other vampire. Keep going."

"I threw consecrated blood at it! *Zia* doused it with holy water as Celia shoved Alana behind some barrels. Nothing stopped it. The vicious thing put a fist right through *Zia's* chest. I kept the terrified kid behind me. Celia sensed his mind go blank, but Lukas held on to Alana's short-sword. I grabbed him back, and then the damn thing shredded me with its claws, bit me too! Then I went down bleeding like a…well, just bleeding."

"It didn't go for Alana and Celia. Why?"

"I have no idea. I'm thinking we had Heavenly help."

"In more ways than one."

"Or maybe my Cecelia is much more gifted than she realizes. The kid told us what happened with Zoltan and Cyril. You both did good, Champ." He paused as Michael let out a weary groan. "Ah… Mother Annie's right. This isn't yours. She had a scolding heart-to-heart with you, didn't she?"

He shifted with a bristle. "And too many people know how my father kept me in line."

"Everyone just finds your reaction amusing. Good parenting leaves a lasting impression. And that part of your dream of survival? It stood out. And you know—"

"An empath can't lie. I remember. Listen, about tomorrow."

"It's taken care of."

"Can I at least finish? He may get upset. She may get upset. Can you help or not?"

Grinning after a ripe pause, Thorn asked, "Do you need to hear it out loud?"

"No, but thanks—and I'll say it again. I *never* liked this non-verbal thing you do. It's creepy." He stood ready to steal his son. A humorous glare came at him. "Talk fast, Empath."

"Forget about standing on some rocky coast trying to catch a few fish. Too cliché for such a spunky kid.

Alana's suggestion is good. Or try Miniature golf. It's relaxing."

"I hate golf," Michael said with a look of disgust. "How about—"

"Miniature golf—you won't regret it."

"There's no way in Hell," he mumbled, leaving Thorn alone and laughing.

****

Miles knew why they had come. Alana had already called. Sitting on the edge of the bed, Lukas stared at the twin casts. "We'd have been here sooner, Mister B. Dad doesn't believe in asking for directions. He got really lost."

"It's a guy thing. You'll grow into it," Michael assured. "How are you, Miles?"

"Been better, but the legs will heal." He studied the quiet teen. "So, young Lukas Malone, I hear you're a marvel with the short-sword. Excellent! I want to hear it all."

As Lukas shrugged, Michael asked, "Can I leave for a while? I have a thing about hospitals. There's a café across the street. I'll work on my tan if that's okay with you?"

"Sure," Lukas answered, still staring at the casts.

Miles gave the worried father a parent-to-parent look of approval. "Will you bring back a decaf? What this hospital passes off as coffee is positively horrid."

****

Sitting at an outdoor table, Michael focused on Miles's window. The conversation made him smile. The fact that Lukas actually believed a mystical being with total recall had gotten lost on the way here amused him. Alana's brilliant idea had allowed them a chance to talk.

Looking up at a cloudless sky, he sensed the exact hour and minute. There will be just enough time to get home, get ready for dinner with my family, he thought in awe of the word, of the feeling it gave. Their easy banter in the hospital room proved Lukas would indeed move past this latest horror. A special bond solidified between his son and the researcher—a healthy one. He'd seen it in the dream of survival, and it showed days ago when Miles brought Lukas to him on the night of his awakening. The topic switched to school, and with a cold decaf in hand, Michael headed back to Miles's room, relieved to cross another very worrisome issue off his list.

****

Speeding down the coastal highway, he caught his son's frown. "Why so quiet?"

Lukas blew out a long breath. "Is tonight a special occasion?"

"What?"

"Alana said she's wearing a special dress. Are you wearing that new suit?"

"Why?"

"I don't own one. Don't want one either," he grumbled.

"You have a blue, button-down shirt and a clean pair of khakis." He waited for the battle of wits to begin.

"Shit," Lukas mumbled.

"Learn another expression, little boy." His son closed his eyes, and by the time Michael pulled up to Alana's garage, he saw a full-blown pout. "What's this about?"

"Maybe it's everything. Maybe I'm gonna miss you." Lukas stared straight ahead. "I'm gonna miss you like hell." Lukas jumped out and slammed the car door.

Heaviness claimed Michael's soul as he followed his son around to the front entrance.

****

Thorn's snores sounded like a truck grinding its gears. Celia sat beside him reading a book. Michael gave her a helpless look, and she narrowed a green-eyed glare. With a jolt, he caught the suggestion. Watching Lukas pull off his sneakers, he leaned down and whispered, "Come with me."

In the master bedroom, he handed Lukas something very sacred to him..

"What *is* this?" Lukas turned it over, undid the clasp, and sat on the sleigh bed as Michael sank into the upholstered chair. "There's like, a *really* old scent in here...ink and weird paper."

"Boy, you really *are* good. I can't believe you caught that through glass. Open it."

"Witnessed by— from 1690? Wait, Dad." His eyes widened as he read.

"This is from my sisters. Anne was the oldest," he said as his son read.

"Wow. It's like they knew. And way cool writing...loopy and flowing like yours."

"Take it with you to England. Keep it safe while I'm away. Your aunts would have adored you. Spoiled you the way they spoiled me." He rubbed his chin, not able to take his eyes off this brave child. "Look, I'm sorry if what I agreed to do for the Georgians makes you angry."

"I'm not angry. Well, maybe a little. What if

something goes wrong while you're gone?"

Relieved to hear the truth, he answered, "Nothing will go wrong."

"But there are three wizards on every continent. What if—"

"They can't have you, little boy. You're mine. You always were and ever shall be."

When they stood, his son accepted another crushing hug. His precious child stayed tight in his arms. "I gave my word."

"Yeah, I know."

In a very parental voice, he said, "So, go get ready and—"

Like a typical teen, Lukas rolled his eyes. "Yeah, yeah… wear the blue shirt and khakis."

Alone and lost in his own anxiousness, Michael stood looking out the window.

"Giving him the letter," Thorn said from the doorway, "Letting the kid talk out his feelings, visiting Miles. Those were 'good parent' things you did."

"You're supposed to be in bed."

"Nah—I'm fine, but you're not. A solid family. That's what we are to him. So relax and enjoy tonight. Oh, and in case you're interested, Celia and I are having a movie marathon in Alana's den after we have dinner with Gabby and Maggie, *after* we visit Miles."

He turned with a smirk. "I get the picture. Then it's one-on-one time for you and Celia."

"Oh no! Is it even possible? Did my *mystical* ability to read heart and head rub off on you when I saved your sanity?"

Michael closed the door, blocked out Thorn's comical grin.

Chapter 32

Alana awoke curled alone in the sleigh bed. A pink sky hinted the early hour. Fresh coffee's rich aroma wafted through the half-open door of Michael's bedroom. After stretching her arms across the bed, she brought his pillow to her breasts. The mattress on his side was already cold. *I won't cry...at least not in front of him. Stay still and breathe in Michael's scent. So earthy...it's always been the same since that night in the park, the first time he came close enough to kiss.* Her naked body pressed into the spot where he had slept. The dark, cotton bedding didn't feel soft and silky like hers, one floor above. It was masculine and strong, solid and protective, just like her soulmate.

****

Turning onto his side, Lukas's eyes fluttered opened. He awoke earlier than usual, the room quiet...his home quiet. He pulled the pillow close, hugged it to his heart. *Today's the day. A new part of my life begins...new school, new friends, new country. I had happy years with Helena.* The angel's love had been palpable—sturdy yet tender. *Then years of terror and torture, lies and loneliness. They don't seem real anymore.* Revenge had sustained him. But now, when he thought about the father who truly loved him, that pain dissolved and pride in being Michael Malone's son took hold. *I'm going to miss him like hell.* His eyes filled and the pillow absorbed his sobs.

****

At a dining room window, Michael scanned the hill. In the hour before sunrise, he had walked its steep slope to search for the object he now held. Reverently, he wiped it clean.

For more than three centuries, the only hands that have held it are mine and hers. Our individual scents have merged into one. The pearl-handled blade is no longer the singular link to a human life. His sister's letter was real. And in *this* existence, what he now had was invaluable. A woman loved him. A child needed him. Closing his eyes, he reveled in the sound of two heartbeats. *It is sobering, this ability to love. I'd walk through the fires of Hell for either of them...both of them. They are my family, my entire world.*

****

As morning dawned, Monsignor Scarlatti knelt at the altar feeling the weight of his years, the weight of his earthly mission. *There is still much work to be done. Good and evil will forever challenge one another.* The event taking place at sunset held his focus. Certain words penetrated his morning meditation—impossible, unprecedented, and extraordinary. None captured the true essence of what had happened to Michael Malone. In previous hours of humble reflection, he had asked for guidance to author The Document of Atonement. This would be Michael's final assignment. *It will tear his brave soul apart and bring him to the depths of misery. The Champion's destiny is once again cloaked in mystery. So it shall remain throughout his solitary penance.* With sadness in his heart, the priest bowed his head in compassionate prayer.

****

Brother Thomas, once called Philip, studied a small, dark room with furniture stark and old. This part of the abbey, rarely used, didn't have electricity. Three oil lamps were placed strategic—one on a small armoire, one on a desk, and one on the nightstand next to a bed. The launch that arrived this morning brought a few items San Marco's guest would need.

When the ex-Guardian finished placing Michael's clothes in the armoire, he went over to the desk to check every item sent by the Sovereign Council. Twenty thick black journals, leather-bound and lined, filled the drawers. An assortment of ink pens, all indigo blue, all snug in a silver box, awaited Michael's hand. He straightened the journal lying on top of the desk. It, like the others, was embossed with silver Roman Numerals to chronicle specific years. Each had Michael Malone's name—specific volumes to describe a decade of death. *I'm prepared to watch over this important visitor. I know Michael well enough. He'll spend hours looking out at the night sky thinking about Ally and Lukas.* The Queen Anne chair was the only luxury requested. With each item in its proper place, Philip fixed the chair so it faced the solitary window.

****

"Twelve noon has come and gone," Michael barked into Alana's cell phone. Not able to remain calm any longer, he paced the hangar's cement floor. "Where are you? It's precisely 2:39 pm."

Thorn's steady voice replied, "Celia had a difficult time convincing the country doctor that her father's well enough to fly. Then she asked Doc Chamberlain to step in and mounds of paperwork got quickly processed. We're almost there, but there's another reason we're delayed. I think you should know."

"What. Say it fast."

"They brought in a teenage girl's body. Fishermen found it while checking the coast after Cyril's storm. It was the closest hospital…uh, morgue…I'm not sure."

Michael stared at Lukas talking to Alana a distance away. "Do I need to hear this?"

"Yes, you do. The hospital couldn't handle the press…the craziness. Serafina Ravento was wanted for questioning because her grandmother was murdered days ago. No TV reporter even mentioned the pentagram they found her in. On the beach by some rocks with a trace of human blood on them." More anxious, Michael turned away, half listening as Thorn added, "I sense how she died, Michael. We're just pulling in now. I can see the hangar."

The line went dead.

Dark magic, dark seers… Michael froze. *Through a misguided child Zoltan found my son. And one more lost soul to atone for.*

****

Lukas hung back watching two medics role the stretcher with Miles into the plane. Even at such a distance, he heard his father's clipped comments. He sensed his father's tension, really hoping his father would stop this from happening and they'd stay together.

"You'll call as soon as you land, right?" Alana suddenly asked.

"Yeah, sure." Lukas was convinced it would happen and it eased his mind that Alana cared. They had common ground. He liked her a lot. But then everyone boarded—except for him.

He edged away, stood with both his hands crammed into his back pockets. He couldn't hide the pout as his father's long, sure strides brought him closer. Full of bitterness, he realized this really was going to happen and blurted out, "The Council could give you a laptop, you know. It's quicker than writing everything out. This really sucks."

"I don't care if it's a computer or a steno pad. I don't like to write the way you do. You have to board." His father's tense fingers brushed through his short brown hair. "The next time I see you this will be history. It'll grow out…soon enough."

He stared at the ground, not wanting to cry.

After a long sigh, his father had him in a secure hug. Furiously, his eyes fluttered against the dark shirt. He couldn't let go. Such comfort found only in his arms. "I don't understand… This is totally lame."

Prying open his son's strong arms, Michael kissed his forehead. He could stay like this forever. "We've gone over this one too many times, and you *do* understand. Quit stalling and no tears." He didn't know if he was talking to his son or himself. "Be good or else—" sounded more parental than he expected it would.

His son's deep-blue eyes were swimming in tears. "Yeah… I know. I love you, Dad."

He swallowed hard, barely got out, "I love you, too." He had to let go. When he did, he watched his son climb the portable ramp.

Alana slipped her hand into his. Engines roared, and his son turned in the open door.

"I really love you, Dad," came from his son's lips,

inaudible over the deafening sound.

"I really love you, my precious son," was his soft reply.

Alana had to pull him back to the car. Michael palmed his eyes and handed her the car key. "You're *actually* letting me drive this?"

He gave a nod and sat in the passenger's seat, for once. She drove off the airfield, parked a safe distance away to watch take-off. And once on the two-lane road her typical, less-than-safe maneuvers were replaced with cautious ones.

Neither spoke. They knew how each other felt.

Last midnight's unrestrained passion had been equally urgent in both of them. He proved his devotion with every touch, every taste, every kiss. Her inner strength buoyed the courage he so desperately needed to walk away from her and Lukas.

She parked the car behind their home. They strolled, hand in hand, through the piazza and walked the tranquil shoreline. The conversation had been open and honest. As the sun began to fade, knowing what had to be done, they arrived at San Giorgio's.

Michael faced her at the door to the small white church. "I have to go the rest of the way alone. I—" Her kiss wouldn't allow him to finish the statement. Locked in each other's arms, he found love in her eyes, not the pain of separation.

"I'd walk through the fires of Hell for you, my Guardian."

One delicate finger touched his lips. "Forever and always, my love," she softly replied.

He left her on the worn steps and entered the church.

****

With pen in hand, Monsignor Scarlatti stood at the altar. Michael walked the center aisle with a slow, determined gait. The priest motioned him to the most sacred space, and he hesitated, never imagining he'd be able to touch the blessed table in his undeath.

"Do you come here of your own free will?"

"Yes," answered a mystical being.

"Do you accept the terms presented in this agreement?"

"Yes," replied a Champion.

Monsignor Scarlatti blessed the document, handed him the pen. Michael took it in his left hand to write his full, christened name.

With genuine warmth, the priest stated, "It is witnessed. Go with God, my son." Firmly, he clasped Michael's shoulder as if to strengthen him for the uncomfortable task that waited at San Marco's Abbey.

Part Three - Home

Chapter 33

The flawless February sky dims as sun begins to set. It fills with hues of pink and gray. No sound comes from empty paths below my window, which would've been unusual at dusk if I were in a major city. This is an island, secluded and ancient—a place of prayer, reflection. No cars, no buses carrying people to and from important places and events.

There has never been anything like that here.

The sounds of birds gently singing evening songs on the breeze can be heard if one sits very still, listens with respect. Waves lap slowly on the shore, a lullaby to a trained ear. Time and tide pass. Day becomes night.

Above all, there is simply the silence.

My eyes have grown sensitive to daylight. When the last trace of sun disappears and the dark-blue blanket over the earth fades to blackness, I lift the cloudy glass and open the shutters to breathe in the sea air, crisp and cool in my lungs. Speckled birds with wings of brown take nightly refuge in the trees. Another day ends.

There is simply the silence.

Michael lit the oil lamp on a desk of sturdy oak. He sat back and put down the pen. Soft light cast dull shadows across the small room leaving corners dark and mysterious.

There was nothing much to see, anyway. The Queen Anne chair by the window felt deep and comfortable, very much out of character for this hidden place of refuge. Still pensive, he settled in it. The chair's floral pattern was in stark contrast to the otherwise-understated décor. It had a high back and two strong arms, which he often wrapped his cool fingers around. Gripping tight while searching for peace. Alana insisted it come with him—her scent an eternal reminder of the woman he would always love.

The room had no mirrors. He didn't need one. Guilt had swallowed his soul, had taken away his reflection. Most of the armoire was empty. A few changes of jeans and shirts, all monotone black, six pairs of socks and one pair of shoes required very little room. He never worried about matching, and there was no need to be fashion-conscious in this sacred place. All living inhabitants wore robes of coarse brown wool.

He did his best to stay out of their way.

Sleep for one such as he was induced somnolence. No dreams. No tossing or turning. No movement. When his astute senses heralded another sunset, he prepared to face a night of loneliness and solitude—self-imposed and necessary. His long, lean frame stretched to the bed's full length, standard issue for the Abbey, narrow and firm. Uncomfortable wooden slats and a rutted headboard added nothing to the room's décor.

It didn't matter.

Daily sustenance, carefully placed outside the locked door in a discrete, dull-ceramic container, stood waiting. It was brought at the same time after Evening Vespers by Brother Thomas. Carefully measured and always fresh, he drank the blood of animals, never the sweet nectar of a human that creatures like him craved.

No excesses. No excuses. He took only enough to continue this existence. He might still be technically classified as an immortal creature of the night, but by no means could he be considered a typical one.

There is no more to write. The thought made him reflect on what had brought him to this state of mind. *Last May, I accomplished something thought impossible, and had been rescued from a fate worse than undeath with help from more than a few. Nine months have passed.*

The official report stated how his body had been incinerated on the ninth night of captivity. The liaison's unwise decision to leave him poisoned, bled out in a chamber on Sub-Level Five, caused upheaval with the sorcerers who controlled six other continents. Michael imagined the look of infinite agony on Clayton's face when Zoltan turned the power-crazed liaison into a living torch.

Crammed shivering and naked into the wooden cage soaked with oil… I'd liked to have heard the bastard scratch and scream like a trapped rat. I'd have tossed the burning black candle in with melodramatic flair myself. Justice came slow and much deserved. But North American portals, demonic dimensional hubs swirled to a screaming close the night he did battle with Hell-beasts. They had never reopened.

Michael lifted an ancient latch-handle, opened the thick, wooden door. With ceramic pitcher in hand, he sank back into the chair. Filling a familiar crystal cup, he drank slowly, thirst minimal tonight. No urgent task needed his attention. The last volume had been sent to Monsignor Scarlatti twelve hours ago at sunrise. The

Georgian Council would read every word before he'd be summoned, released from this tiny island. What was asked had been accomplished. Every detail recorded as accurately as if it occurred yesterday and not centuries ago.

The face of every victim was now branded on his brain—painted portraits on a canvas of death. Like Shakespearean soliloquies, their pleas for mercy memorized. He had journaled every nuance, a painful undertaking that filled twenty leather-bound books. Staring out into the quiet night he tasted the last of thick scarlet liquid poured into the cup he'd fed from since the first day of his awakening.

My love for Alana and Lukas is all that sustains this weary soul. Very soon, I'll wrap her in my arms; hold her tight to this unbeating heart. I'll prove to my son that I didn't abandon him.

His eyes closed. Alana's scent washed over him. After nine months it still filtered through the chair's material. From deep within his soul, he called to her. Their bond was eternal. *Alana, my beacon of hope... Lukas, my purpose...* Only this consumed him.

When his eyes opened, stars had appeared in a dark-velvet sky. Finding the brightest one, he whispered with devotion, "My Guardian...my love."

Chapter 34

The last day of March was slow to fade away as Michael Malone sat in front of The Georgian Sovereign Council. Two new members now replaced Rosa Bellini and Antonio DeMarra. One had healed Thorn and the other, who knew more about Michael than anyone else, acknowledged him with a respectful nod.

Michael crossed his long legs and folded his unsteady hands. More than a month ago he had completed the proscribed task. The unexplained, additional wait had taken its toll on his soul. On his mind. Wondering whether or not what he'd written would be deemed acceptable he had gotten restless.

Then, this sunset, his suit and a starched white shirt arrived. Now here he sat, full of doubt and less than patient.

Monsignor Scarlatti had introduced the Georgian Council. A detailed history of the events had opened this marathon of a meeting. The lively discussion of his journal entries dragged on.

But now, Margaret Smirkovska's ice-blue eyes penetrated his very soul. "We highly commend your thoroughness—*and* candor," she finally said in an open fashion.

"Thank you," he replied, unable to break from her intense gaze.

"Before the Council makes its determination, some members have additional questions," Monsignor Scarlatti informed.

Mother Anne quickly asked, "Are you anxious to get home, Champion?" Her warm tone should've filled him with blessed peace, but one word brought troubling emotions to the surface.

"No, Mother. I am not." *It's true. Revisiting my deadly past shatters all confidence after ten solid months of nothing else.*

"Your journals are very disturbing," Joseph Atherton said. "Each volume reads like a novel. But we've seen this evil. We know it exists. I'm intrigued, Mister Malone. How did you feel when writing all of this?"

"The faces, the murders, the ones I left barely alive... Each is as real to me today as they were centuries ago."

Some nights I couldn't continue. Some days I stared at the blank page. Anguish knotted my soul. This pain never goes away. Michael looked down.

"Yet he forced himself to do this," Cesar Gonzales stated. "After all he's been through, this merciless undertaking comes to us complete."

Brother Giovanni motioned to speak. "Hundreds of souls now have peace. *Signore* Malone accepted his penance with quiet reverence for each victim of the beast within him. I had not been convinced last May that he'd accomplish our request, but I've come to respect this Champion. Brother Thomas verifies his diligence never wavered, nor did the immortal being request latitude."

With a clearing of his throat, Monsignor Scarlatti nodded. "Eugenia, state your question please."

A blond woman in her late fifties smiled tightly. "I still take issue with one statement." Her Dutch accent was hard to understand. "Shortly after awakened, you stated: "I will not accept the vampire's sins as my own." I ask, Sir, do you still feel this way?"

The question hung in the air for a full minute.

"No. My mouth drank their blood; my body violated their innocence. The beast- within invaded me, and I invaded them. I accept full responsibility, Madam."

How poignantly she reveals a most private fear…that my soul cannot be cleansed.

Once more, he felt drawn to Margaret's piercing gaze as she shook her head. "But you didn't commit these murders as a living man and as a demon, you couldn't access free will."

He glanced at Mother Anne for support or comfort—he didn't know which. "The memories are mine, Madam. I live with them."

Firmly, Mother responded, "We've already determined that his body became an instrument for the destruction of innocents. Keep in mind, this man did not *author* any of it. Are you satisfied, Eugenia?"

The woman's study of him continued. "Yes, my concern is satisfied."

Hiro Kuma kept his gaze on a thick notebook. "Did you sire, vampire?"

"Excuse me?" Michael asked, respectful.

Kuma wrote as he spoke. "The question's simple. Have you turned anyone?"

"No."

"Why is that? You were most vicious, certainly capable of it."

Never expecting *this* question, twelve curious faces now stared at him. "I-I… It wasn't what I chose to do."

"Hiro makes a valid point," Atherton said. "You had the ability. You must've had the desire."

After an uncomfortable shift, he leaned forward. "I never killed a child or a Guardian. I had that capability as well." A frustrated pause followed. "I didn't need vacant, undead minions following me around. I honestly don't know what you're looking for."

Still writing, Kuma stated in clipped words, "It is a necessary inquiry. From your text, it is obvious you created parameters as a vampire. Did you also set parameters as a Champion?"

"*Parameters*? Look, you're the ones who call me a Champion. I'm not a hero. I do what has to be done. I sent three immortal, evil things into oblivion, which shut down an entire continent's portals. I've destroyed *many* evil things since 1890—including my sire. I don't like where this is going. I did what this Council asked me to do. Is it enough or is there something I overlooked that's bothering all of you?" Annoyed, he leaned back. Measured arrogance surfaced, and a warning glance came from Mother Anne. He sighed, shut his eyes. "I apologize for my rudeness. Did I answer your question?"

Over the rims of thick glasses, Kuma gave a cold, "Yes."

Michael found his focus drawn to a small, rotund nun next to Mother Anne. Looking a century old, her eyes glimmered with the vivacity of a young woman. *Absolute goodness, the same purity in Sister Rosalinda during the dream of survival...* A grave expression appeared on her wrinkled face.

"You are unsettled, Champion. Many good souls miss you."

He inclined his head in respect. "I miss them too, Sister."

"Describe the taming of the beast-within, which ended the existence of the killer who committed these horrendous acts."

Completely astonished, he stared at her. *After ten months of revisiting my actions without a conscience, I have no courage left! No. No more of this.*

Quickly, Mother Anne glared his way. "You stood in the chapel of the cloistered motherhouse. Death surrounded you." *This must be done, young soul.*

He absolutely froze. *I cannot face what I am again. No, Mother, please, let this end.* Staring into her resolute eyes, he struggled against her iron will and shook his head. "No. I-I cannot."

The other new Council member had not asked one question, but he had witnessed many events that had led Michael here. Without hesitation, Miles stated, "I believe it occurred the night of December fourteen, 1890. Georgian research suggests right after midnight. You stood in the Order's newly built chapel. Thirty-six innocent souls lay dead around you." Like a caring parent, Miles gave an encouraging nod.

Utter helplessness filled him. Both hands locked to the chair's wooden arms. He straightened his shoulders. With uneven whispers, he described his most despicable act. "I... I drained the last novice. Heard her heart stop. It had been in my mind for weeks...a killing spree like none before. But this rampage was different. After... instead of euphoria I wallowed in self-loathing. Emptiness... So many bodies like a feast of death. The beast-within went wild, ecstatic over such a unique slaughter. It shouldn't have mattered to me. Virginal blood glutted my swollen veins. Yet there I stood, drenched with their life-force. I was demon, and for the first time horrified at what I'd done." His dry throat constricted, making the ability to speak more difficult. "I don't know if somehow I managed to think an apology or what. I held the gilded rail as the air around the altar started to shimmer. An opening appeared. I heard my name and the altar gate opened. I approached curious, intrigued." He didn't want to continue. *Mother Anne knows the real reason, the truth which I cannot...* "No. I sought my own death," he said.

"What did the voice say?" the ancient healer asked.

"Your sisters are not here," he barely whispered. "Yet I had singled out these holy women to drink and drain. My fist punctured the swirling air. I deserved a merciless death. I hoped it would burn me, destroy me, but—" Nervous. Unsteady. He wanted to beg the Council for the stake and end this.

"The angel pulled you into another dimension," Mother Anne stated.

Helena... With eyes cast down, he gave a slow nod. "The Old One's world was different. I knew I stood before an angel. I expected Hell, but it seemed like...Heaven. Bright with sunshine—something I hadn't seen since 1690. I filled my rotted lungs with sweet air. I felt warm again. Helena embraced me, held me tight. Others appeared. I couldn't see faces, just forms." Full of fear, he wanted to stop, but couldn't. "The beast- within howled, ordered me to run. My feet were like lead, and I sank to my knees begging for death. Helena's touch drove the beast-within wild, snarling and snapping. She didn't let go of my shoulders for a very long time—until I felt courage clear a spot in my conscience." His words came with hesitance. "I screamed for destruction. Her demand, however, did not waver, and I cowered. I wailed."

These are private words, Mother, private memories painted with deep remorse.

But you must continue, Michael, and put aside your despair.

He cleared his throat. "Helena presented the choice: Accept eternal damnation or make amends. She said I could control the beast-within. Then she allowed me to see what lived in my soul. With rage I cannot describe, I wanted it gone. I wrestled the demon inside of it, fully determined to win. When I overpowered it, the angel let go. I tumbled through space, through time until there I lay on snow-covered ground in the passageway. The date was still December Fourteenth, 1890, but I was now a *very* different creature of the night. You know the rest." Another word would break him apart. It was as if he were on a rocky precipice… ready to fall.

Many Council members had compassion in their eyes. And after poignant silence, the small nun rapped on the conference table. "One last matter, Champion. One unspoken desire still hides in your soul. So that all on this Council may truly understand you, reveal it please."

Her request sounded like an edict. Trembling, he folded his hand on his lap, unable to look up. *This is the ultimate punishment. My unfinished human life will haunt me throughout eternity. I have fallen off the cliff's edge forever aware of this one, unattainable goal.* In a hushed tone, with every ounce of self-control he could find within, he replied, "With respect, Sister, I will not.

I apologize from the depths of my soul."

"This inquisition is over. *Signore*, please wait in the church," the monsignor stated.

****

Michael didn't know whether he had passed or had failed. Wrapped once more in uneasy solitude, he stared at the altar. He had been summoned at sundown. Midnight now approached. If he had learned anything during this self-imposed seclusion, it was patience. Yet he remained very bothered and full of defeat.

In the last pew, darkness gave him blessed comfort. Even without light, he clearly saw the sacred table. He pushed sentiment away from thought.

My act of confession, twenty volumes of painstaking accuracy, might not fulfill their mandate. It might not be enough. I am freshly repulsed. Every action still hammers my conscience. How had the Council even agreed to my rescue last May? It's a total mystery. Pristine souls, mystical healers, had shown a vampire tender mercy. They never once judged—nor would they ever.

Now, twelve individuals discussed his fate. He studied the crucifix. *Time doesn't matter. I have perpetuity. Eternal damnation, not eternal rest is my true destiny. How did I let this happen? How could something like me expect love or ask commitment from a woman so full of life? Why lead my son to believe that something like me could teach him right from wrong?*

Uneasiness brought a different conclusion—one he didn't expect to feel.

Dim lights flickered on, offering just enough brightness for the Council to see their way to the altar. The knot in his gut tightened.

Oh dear God, how do I face this?

Monsignor Scarlatti called him forward. Somehow, he made the walk. Mother Anne and the other healer guided him to the altar itself. The rest of the Council closed in around him. Monsignor Scarlatti placed the decree on the altar saying, "We, The Sovereign Council of The Georgian Circle, do hereby accept The Document of Atonement as written by an immortal being with conscience and soul. Our request is satisfied. Do you come here of your own free will?"

Unsteady, he whispered, "Yes."

"Did you complete this task fully aware that absolution cannot be given?'

Sorrow filled his soul. "Yes."

Eleven important signatures filled eleven empty lines. Monsignor Scarlatti was the last to sign. Then, he handed Michael the pen. "With your mark, this agreement shall be bound."

On the last line of the last page, he signed. No sound was heard, but a sense of finality was felt as Monsignor announced, "So it is recorded. Michael Martin Malone is considered by all Georgians, by all Guardians of Souls, a unique being. This mystical existence is accepted. Placed above the Law of the Kill, he is relied upon as a Champion for the innocent in this world."

One by one, Council members began to leave.

He said nothing. Did nothing. With hands at his side, he simply stood in front of the altar. Four hearts still beat around him. A firm hand clasped his shoulder.

"Now it is finished, my son," the monsignor said before he walked away.

Three beating hearts remained.

The ancient healer approached and shook his hand, pumping briskly with a tremendous grip. The top of her head didn't quite reach the middle of his chest.

"We haven't been properly introduced. I'm Labbiel."

"You healed my friend. I'm eternally grateful."

"You saved thousands of innocents from torture and death. *I* am eternally grateful. Shall we go one for one, child?" The straightforward response caught him off guard. He was mesmerized by her blazing ebony eyes, the melodic African accent. "All this pomp and circumstance... I've seen too much of it in ninety-six years. My question is the only important one, which goes directly to the heart of who *you* really are." After a gentle pat of his hand, she walked slowly out of the church.

"I read your reaction," Mother Anne quickly said. "Rosalinda balances her nature. That's why both of them healed Thorn—as if I'm telling you something you can't see for yourself."

He allowed a small smile, but Miles appeared full of pride, his handshake genuine and firm. "Welcome back, Michael. You've been very missed by many."

"Congratulations, Researcher. The Council couldn't have chosen a better man. How's my boy?"

"He's exceptionally well and anxious to see you. What a joy to have around, especially with—" Miles stopped, said with curiosity, "Are you all right? Come. Alana's waiting with Lukas, so we'll talk as we walk."

"No. I'm not... I can't... Please tell them I have always loved them so very much. Thanks, Miles." He slipped out of the handshake and turned away.

"Yes, of course. We'll see you shortly, then,"

Miles replied in a subtle tone.

****

Miles saw the serious expression on Mother Anne's face before he left to assist Sister Labbiel back to the red-brick building. They walked slowly on the quiet street.

"I am upset, Researcher. But the answer is in God's hands now. I thought something like this might happen."

"When Michael Malone is concerned, things don't always go as planned, Sister."

"I sensed it even before I touched his hand. Everything's bombarding his conscience. I told Sebastiano it would. Told Annie, too. And Margaret sees his soul." She shook her head. "The destinies he has saved number in the millions, not the thousands— the millions. He should have told them. Everyone would have witnessed Divine Grace as well as the depths of his soul's lament. I will not rest until he sees with new eyes."

Miles didn't understand her cryptic words as every unhurried step brought more exhaustion. But his concern soared for Lukas and Alana. As soon as they stepped off the elevator and into Alana's living room, the elderly healer gave Gabriella and Magdalena a quick glance. They automatically excused themselves and went down to Rosa's life-long home on the second floor. *No doubt they will meditate*, he assumed, *perhaps send Mother Anne their strength of mind as she talks to him.*

Thorn settled Sister Labbiel between him and Celia on Alana's couch. Lukas didn't look up from his book, and after trying to calm his daughter's fears, Miles went down to his wife's waiting arms.

"I can't do anything more about tonight," he told Laura Bookman. Thoroughly worn out, as his head hit the pillow, he fell asleep.

****

Alana wanted to run to the church as the healing sister announced, "That will not help him. It won't be much longer."

"The hour is late for you, Sister," Thorn said again, but she didn't respond.

Staring out the window and praying for the incredible being she loved, she thought about Lukas, who still appeared relaxed in an armchair. *How can he read a book tonight? I was so excited when the Queen Anne chair arrived at sunset. The first thing I did was sit in it to totally drink in his father's scent. This ordeal is over. We'll move on together—as a family. Everything looks different now—everything is different..*

The wide sleigh bed fit her bedroom in a stately way. Lukas had turned the guestroom into a typical teenager's room. She had let him pick out a desk unit for doing schoolwork on the weekends when he visited with Celia and Thorn.

There's so much to tell you...ten months worth!

Mentoring Kayla, running the bookstore... Gabby decided to teach first grade in a nearby town, and everyone congregated in her home for dinner. Maggie shared *Zia's* love for fine Italian cuisine, had taught her how to cook. Maggie moved her surgical practice to the small hospital that had cared for Miles and stayed downstairs with Gabby during the week. *Wait till you see the frantic Friday nights, my love... Daddy B now boards Cesar's private plane like a pro. The flight from*

Gatwick also includes…

"Oh God, Celia, he doesn't know about the baby!" Alana suddenly said. "Remember how you told me? That was just a few days after Michael left."

Celia nodded, still holding Labbiel's hand—and very reserved, replied, "That good news can wait, Ally."

Alana recalled Lukas's day-by-day description of her sister's changing body, and he still doted on her. Then a month ago, Cesar flew Alana to Hampton Hill a day before the joyous event. Their tiny, red-haired baby boy had arrived two weeks early.

"Your dad's going to be so proud of you, Lu," she said, but Lukas didn't look up. *Is he nervous? I know I am. He so reminds me of…* "Michael," Alana whispered. *But those sandy-blond curls are, once again, unruly, and too many girls suddenly have to buy a book on the Saturdays he works in the shop.* "I know he misses you, Lu."

That didn't get him to look up, either.

On the same day Celia gave birth, the last of Michael's journals had arrived. Her father had hurried back to Portofino, and Alana's anticipation shot through the roof. Two weeks later, she returned to find more tension carved on his face. A week ago, the rest of her family arrived, and now, Lukas flatly refused to return for school.

Leaning out the window to stare down the deserted street, she began to worry. Celia had given her a psychic play-by-play…up until an hour ago.

What's taking so long, my love? It's past midnight.

Chapter 35

They stood silent in the small church. A being beyond death and a wise, elderly nun. Slowly, painfully, the penitent's vision blurred. Completely humbled, Michael's hand traced the starched warps and woof of the purple Lenten linen on a marble altar. Just like the ache in his soul, pure love and deep regret were tightly interwoven.

"Caught between Heaven and Hell, I planned my death. With all ties to those I love severed, neither would incur the wrath of evil's retribution nor suffer the repercussion of my actions. It didn't go as planned." He was shaken to the very core of his guilty soul.

Mother Anne came to his side. "You must not despair."

"Helena used the very same words."

"My heart was opened by the angel the moment I eased a young man's fear— when he awakened in an unfamiliar world."

He heard more than the elderly healer's compassion. He sensed Helena's presence through her. And when Mother Anne took his hand, he heard the angel say, *"Champion, you have journeyed through the depths of forgotten emotions to find understanding."*

Tears overtook his vision as he sank to his knees. His shoulders folded inward, and he buried his face in the hem of Mother Anne's habit.

"Angel, you should have let me die."

Mother Anne knelt beside him, smoothed his hair.

"Anne has given you courage. Labbiel has voiced my request."

Wretchedness made him tremble. Breathless hitches began as he replied, "What I've done never leaves me. What I desire can never be. Thank you for allowing this soul to experience what I never felt as a living man." Swiping his eyes, he straightened his shoulders. The request would bring true finality. "I beg you... Dear God, let this existence end. I am ready to enter Hell."

Excruciating pain knifed through him. His screams filled the church before collapsing in Mother Anne's arms. Every vein constricted as if one by one they could be ripped out of his skin. Choking and wild, he clutched his burning chest.

She held him tight, brushed his brow and brought her hand to his heart. Then Helena's voice resounded through his fading brain. *"You chose the righteous path. Every step brought you towards redemption. You are the son of my bloodline ...More than a man, less than an angel."*

He saw himself falling though the portal and floundering for over a century until the love of a child forced him to walk a courageous path, until the love of a woman reawakened his moral conscience.

And this existence slipped away.

A slight throb and then another. Then his heart assumed a natural tempo of its own. The first breath came shallow, the second a powerful gasp. Blood raced through his veins as his eyes opened on an unfinished life.

Mother Anne calmly stroked his cheek. "Breathe in

and out, young man."

"My God," he whispered. "This… is not… possible."

"All things are possible, Champion. Haven't you learned that particular lesson already?"

Chapter 36

Alana turned from the window as Gabby ran in and bent over Sister Labbiel with a serious expression. Thorn helped Gabby get her up. "Ah, it is time," the elderly healer stated, "Have patience, *cara*, soon he will come to you."

As they left, she thought she had heard *Zia* Rosa's voice. And then Lukas suddenly threw down his book.

"What's the matter, Lu. Are you okay?" she asked, hoping he'd say something...anything! He gave a blank nod, disappeared into his room and closed the door.

Celia suddenly gasped. Her eyes went wide, and Alana stiffened as they hugged.

"Oh, God... What's wrong?"

"Ally, we'll talk tomorrow, okay?" Then *she* left without saying anything else!

Trying to not panic, Alana stared at Thorn. "Tell me. Tell me now. What's going on?" She couldn't read his expression, but his eyes glazed over very fast. When Thorn hugged her, every anxious question left her mind, and then *he* walked out the door.

Very much like a troubling night last May, Alana stood in an empty living room. But this time, a sense of calm washed over her. *Whatever it is, I will handle it. I just want him home...* She walked into her bedroom, closed the door. Settling into the upholstered chair, she drank in Michael's scent and waited.

****

His mystical senses picked up an unfamiliar heartbeat as soon as he and Mother Anne entered the red-brick building. He waited for her to go inside the second-floor apartment that used to be Rosa's home. When the lock twisted, he turned to focus on the apartment directly across. A new life was safely cradled in a wicker bassinet next to his parents.

Grinning easy, he said in a soft voice, "Welcome to the world, little one."

Slowly he climbed the next flight of stairs, hesitated briefly before walking inside. This was his family's home. Without a sound, he went directly to the guestroom and when he entered, Lukas turned from the window. Those deep-blue eyes could've drilled a hole clear through his chest, his son's expression unreadable. He memorized every aspect of his growing boy. Approaching with confident, long strides, he held his son in a powerful hug, kissing the mop of sandy hair, very unwilling to let go.

Lukas stared at his chest. "Wait... I can't believe... Like, no *way*, Dad."

"You're four inches taller, and I've missed you, too. It's late. Go to bed and we'll talk in the morning." Michael couldn't resist another fierce hug before he left the room.

****

His fingers ran down her bedroom's polished door. After a deep, even breath, he sighed, "Oh God, how I've missed you," and when he walked in, the woman he loved sat up straighter in the chair.

He gave a thin smile. She smiled back.

Alana had a thought—something she had never dared to dream.

Walking to the bedroom window, bathed in moonlight, she knew he wanted her to come to him. As if her mind couldn't accept what her soul already knew, her walk to him was slow and steady. Then her hand came to rest on the center of his chest.

Full of wonder and barely able to speak, she whispered, "Michael, my love."

"My Guardian…my love," he replied, barely able to contain what he felt—in his now beating heart.

A word about the author...

Always an avid reader, the realm of paranormal fiction continues to be the perfect landing point for M. Flagg. After a successful career as a music teacher and an urban school administrator, she continues to spin stories of passion, love and redemption. Besides being published in the genre of paranormal fiction, she has been a contributor in a book on urban music education and has also authored an article for Still Standing, a web-magazine about loss and healing. Her Action Research Project was recognized for Outstanding Writing in 2006 and she was named a Distinguished Music Educator at the Yale Music Symposium in 2010. A life-long New Jersey resident, M. Flagg is a member of Liberty States Fiction Writers and serves as a Professor in Residence at a local university.